CONTAINMENT FAILURE

A Special Agent Dylan Kane Thriller

By
J. Robert Kennedy

James Acton Thrillers
The Protocol
Brass Monkey
Broken Dove
The Templar's Relic
Flags of Sin
The Arab Fall

Detective Shakespeare Mysteries
Depraved Difference
Tick Tock
The Redeemer

Special Agent Dylan Kane Thrillers
Rogue Operator
Containment Failure

Zander Varga, Vampire Detective
The Turned

CONTAINMENT FAILURE

A Special Agent Dylan Kane Thriller

J. ROBERT KENNEDY

ISBN-10: 1491246316

ISBN-13: 978-1491246313

First Edition

10 9 8 7 6 5 4 3 2 1

For Gary and Daryl.

Friends gone, but not forgotten.

CONTAINMENT FAILURE

A Special Agent Dylan Kane Thriller

"The idea of infection began to be taken far more seriously than it ever had before. Hospitals transformed themselves in response to the new plague - sometimes for the better, but often for the worse, as when, in fear, they cast their ulcerated patients out into the streets."

Peter Lewis Allen

"There is a sufficiency in the world for man's need but not for man's greed."

Mahatma Gandhi

PREFACE

The Black Death is the most devastating plague in recorded history. At its peak during 1348-1350 AD, it reduced the population of Europe by anywhere from 30 to 60 percent. Europe took 150 years to recover its lost population, and centuries to recover from the religious, political and social chaos that resulted.

Imagine where America would be tomorrow, if today, one hundred fifty million of its citizens were to die, along with half the populations of its trading partners.

The science described in what follows has been simplified for dramatic purposes, however the concepts described are real, and are cutting edge techniques that *will* be available in the near future. What is described can happen, what motivates it has happened. The horror that unfolds may very well be a scenario that if not we, then our children, will soon face. To dismiss the possibility is to ignore history.

J. ROBERT KENNEDY

Inside the Quarantine Zone
Outbreak Day #11

Kyle Patrick motioned for everyone to get down as a troop transport rolled by, its rear filled with people just like him, desperate to escape the plague ravaging this once proud city. He looked back and gave his parents a slight smile. He could tell his mother was tired. They had been dodging patrols and overhead drones for hours as they made their way through the nearly deserted streets from his parents' house to the border of the quarantine.

He looked up for a drone or helicopter, and seeing none, moved from around the concrete barrier and inched forward, watching for any additional patrols. Clear, he darted across the road and into an alley, double-checking for any more troops, then motioned the others forward.

His father helped his mother across the road, followed by two more families they had found, both with little children, all equally scared. None of them were displaying symptoms, and none of them wanted that to change. They weren't infected, but if they stayed within the city limits, they knew they might eventually catch it. When the President had ordered the total containment of the city, they had been shocked, and as the footage continued to play out on television showing tens of thousands of troops surrounding the city, of the airport being shutdown, all outbound flights still in the air being forced to return, train and boat traffic stopped, freeways being shut down, and people being forced back into the city limits at gunpoint by soldiers in hazmat suits, they knew they had to get out of here, and their time was running out.

Within hours the cordon would be complete, and there'd be no means of escape. It had been a family conference like no other. His mother had wanted to stay put and take their chances. Kyle knew she was as scared as they were, but he figured she didn't feel she could make the journey. Luckily they lived in the outskirts, so the quarantine zone wasn't that far, and he and his dad had convinced her she could make it. She had proven a trooper, but the exhausted look on her face as his parents cleared the street had him very concerned.

"You guys rest, I'm going to scout ahead." He pulled out his cellphone and brought up a map of their GPS location. "According to this in less than a quarter mile we'll hit farmland. We just need to get there, and we're out of the quarantine zone." He put a hand on his mother's shoulder and gave it a squeeze. "I'll be back in half an hour. You guys keep out of sight and rest."

Kyle then turned and ran down the alleyway, coming to a halt at the end then quickly looking left and right then up. Clear. He darted across the street, past several more houses, over a fence, through a ditch, then as he crested the top of the ditch and pushed through some tall grass along its edge he suddenly emerged in pristine farmland.

And nearly cried in happiness. Carefully scanning the area, he saw no one, civilian or military. Overhead a drone circled and he scurried back to the ditch, rolling down the side and into the cold mud and water at the bottom. He flipped over on his back, staring up to see if he could spot the drone, but it was out of sight. He pushed himself to his knees, then a crouch, and spotted it leaving to the west.

Climbing up the other side of the ditch, he pulled a pair of cutters from his backpack and cut a hole in the fence so it wouldn't slow them up when making their escape. He took a swig of water from a bottle, then making sure the coast was clear, quickly returned to where he had left the others.

And they weren't there.

"Mom! Dad!" he called in a hoarse whisper.

Nothing.

The gnashing of gears and roar of an accelerating engine had him jumping for cover. There was a mandatory stay-at-home order for all non-essential personnel, and he and his parents were definitely non-essential. He didn't know about the others. He didn't care. He just needed to get his folks to the other side of the quarantine zone, then to their family in Lafitte who would hide them. A call had already been placed and his uncle would be waiting for them not five miles from here.

Another transport went by, the rear loaded with more people, but from his vantage point, he couldn't tell if any of them were his parents.

He was starting to get worried.

He scanned the ground for any evidence of a scuffle, but could see nothing. *If you had to hide, where would you hide?* He spotted a side door to the building he was hugging, and approached. He tapped three times, gingerly.

Nothing.

"It's me, Kyle!" he said, only as loud as he thought he needed to be heard through the door.

The knob turned and the door opened an inch, then pushed open all the way as he was hauled inside. At first he was shocked, but as soon as the door closed a light flicked on and he was surrounded by his parents and the two other families.

They were all eating food from what looked like a storeroom, filling up on water and apparently using the services of a toilet in the back, the wife of one of the men just exiting, jumping slightly at the sight of him. He looked at himself, realizing he must look a mess from the ditch.

"Oh thank God!" exclaimed his mother, hugging him. "We were so worried!"

"What is this place?"

"Mom and pop store," said his father. "I tried the door and it was unlocked. We called but there doesn't seem to be anybody home."

"They probably buggered out of here when the trouble first hit. They're so close to the edge of the zone," said one of the men named Dan, his wife Sophie the one who had just left the bathroom.

"I found a way through. It's pretty easy, seems clear. We should go now before that changes." Kyle gripped the doorknob, then looked back. "Is everybody ready?"

Nods from everyone, and a weak smile from his mother, replied.

"I'm going to check to make sure it's clear, then I'll give you the signal. Go to the left, to the end of the alley. Hold up there so we can make sure the coast is clear."

Kyle pushed the door open an inch and looked, then listened. Nothing. He exited quickly, closing the door behind him, then darted to the alley to make sure their rear was covered, then confirming it was clear, returned to the door and knocked. The door opened, and they all filed out as he sprinted ahead to the other end of the alley. Finding it clear, he raced to the other side of the road, took cover, then holding his breath, listened. He could hear almost nothing over the hammering of his own heart. He tried to calm himself as he looked again.

It looked clear.

He held up two fingers, then motioned for them to join him. This was the signal for his parents. They rushed across the street and joined him.

"Go to the end of this street. You'll see a fence. Just stay out of sight until we join you." He looked at his mom. "Take your time. I have to wait for the others so there's no rush."

His parents continued on at a less hurried pace, and he checked to see if everything was still clear. As he poked his head out, he saw a head in the window of the house the other families were hidden beside. The person was pointing to the right. Kyle looked but didn't see anything, then leaned out a little farther and gasped. There was a Humvee two blocks down, parked between two buildings, four soldiers in hazmat suits looking at something.

He gave the thumbs up to the person in the house, who quickly disappeared behind their curtain. He peeked back at the Humvee and the team. They still weren't looking this way.

He motioned for both families to come, rapidly motioning for them to hurry. Dan and Sophie, carrying their kids burst from the alleyway, rushing across the road, as the second family, Frank and Christa, with their one kid in Frank's arms, followed suit.

Kyle kept urging them on as he watched the soldiers. One began to turn, his arm extending behind him, indicating Kyle's direction. As all four soldiers began to turn, Frank cleared the road and Kyle ducked out of sight.

"Keep going, all the way to the fence!" he ordered, and without looking back to see if they had been spotted, he raced after them, quickly overtaking them. He reached the last house and joined his parents who appeared to have just arrived. A quick glance showed everything still clear, and no signs of pursuit behind them. He darted across the final road, pushing through the opening he had cut in the fence, then motioning for the others to join him.

His parents came first. His dad pushed through the fence, then they both helped his mother. Kyle pointed ahead. "Down into the ditch, then up the other side. Through some grass and there's a farmer's field. We'll join you there."

His dad nodded, then gripped Kyle's shoulder.

"I'm proud of you, son."

Kyle felt himself choke up. He managed a nod and a smile.

"Go!" he urged.

His dad squeezed his shoulder again, then helped his wife toward the ditch. Kyle checked if everything was clear, then motioned for the other families to come. In less than a minute they were all through the fence and heading for the ditch. Kyle jumped into the mud and saw his parents just clearing the other side. He helped the others down then scrambled up the edge. He took the baby Dan was carrying and placed him on the grass. He reached down and pulled Dan up, who then took care of Sophie and their second child. Kyle helped Frank and Christa with their child, and when they were all successfully out of the ditch, they pushed through the grass to the field and freedom.

He pointed to the other side of the field.

"We just need to get there, across one road, then we can make our way through the fields, keeping out of sight until the next road. We can call my Uncle Charlie to pick us up there."

A noise above them caused Kyle's head to pivot up.

"Shit!"

It was a drone, approaching from the south. Kyle looked for cover and saw a hedgerow just ahead. "Hide in the hedge!" he yelled, grabbing the other side of his mother and helping his dad nearly carry her the fifty feet to the tall, thick hedge that most likely acted as some sort of windbreak for the farm. They reached it and he pressed his body into the thick cedar, his arms and legs getting scratched up badly.

He felt the hedge shaking as the others did the same, then they all remained quiet as the drone passed overhead. As the drone's engine slowly faded, he began to breathe a sigh of relief when a thumping sound in the distance rapidly got louder.

"It's a helicopter!" exclaimed Dan.

"Stay hidden, maybe they can't see us!" yelled Frank.

A military chopper roared overhead, then banked to face the hedge. It was obvious it knew exactly where they were. Kyle stepped back slightly and looked at his father. It was pretty clear the situation was helpless.

18

"They won't shoot us, will they?" he asked.

His father shook his head. "I don't know."

"We're Americans. They're Americans. They wouldn't, would they?"

His father looked uncertain. "I would hope not."

"There's an opening here," said his mother, almost matter-of-factly. Kyle and his father joined her, noting the two foot gap.

"There's one down here too!" called Dan. "There's no way they'll shoot us. We're citizens. Let's just—"

He was cut off by a loudspeaker on the helicopter.

"This is Colonel Jackson of the National Guard. You are in violation of a Federally mandated quarantine. You are ordered to turn around and return to your homes. If you do not turn around, we will be forced to open fire. Lethal force has been authorized."

"Lethal force?" repeated Frank. "They're going to kill us!"

Suddenly the most terrifying noise Kyle had ever heard erupted from the front of the helicopter, fire breathing from the guns mounted on it. They all ducked and it took a few moments for Kyle to realize they weren't being shot at. He tentatively looked and saw the ground being torn apart.

"It's just a warning shot!" yelled Kyle. "They're not shooting at us!"

"To hell with this!" yelled Frank, grabbing his wife and bolting back toward the ditch, his child clutched in his arms.

"I've got kids, I can't risk it!" yelled Dan, pushing through the opening, one arm raised in the air, the other clutching his baby, his wife doing the same.

The voice roared through the speaker again.

"Return to your homes and you won't be harmed." There was a pause then the voice sounded raised. *"Now!"*

Dan suddenly erupted from the hole in the hedge, his wife following, and they raced after Frank and Christa leaving only Kyle and his parents.

19

"Let's go under the chopper, then to that farmhouse on the right. We might get lucky. There's no way they'll shoot us!"

Kyle's dad nodded, then they pushed through the opening, rushing under the chopper, his mother seeming to have found her wings, adrenaline doing amazing things. They turned toward the farmhouse, pushing themselves as hard as they could toward the safety of the old but well maintained building. Kyle heard the chopper bank behind them in pursuit.

"They're coming!" he yelled.

"Halt immediately! You are in violation of a mandatory quarantine. We are authorized to use deadly force. I say again, halt immediately, or we will open fire."

They continued forward, then the terrifying roar of the guns erupted behind them. Kyle ducked, but didn't stop running, instead helping his mother forward as the ground in front of them was shredded. His father slowed down, turning back to look at them.

"Keep going!" yelled his dad. "They won't shoot us!"

The guns erupted again, this time ripping apart the field even closer to their position. Kyle wondered how close they might get before there was a risk of actually getting hit. The chopper was so close now that the wind from the blades thumping at the air was tossing the crops about, his hair whipping into his eyes, stinging his face.

"You have five seconds to comply, otherwise lethal force is authorized." The voice lowered, finally sounding almost human. *"Please stop. We have no choice but to fire. Don't make me do it."*

Kyle's dad slowed down, turning back to them, shaking his head. The farmhouse was tantalizingly close. If they could just make it there, there's no way they'd be fired at. The chopper wouldn't risk there being other innocent people inside.

And it was that thought that caused Kyle to almost stop in his tracks.

What are we doing?

A wave of nausea swept over him as he realized their selfishness. *What if one of us is infected?* They could infect those in the farmhouse, who had done nothing wrong. If they made it to his Uncle's, they could infect them all.

This is wrong!

"Dad, stop!" he yelled just as what sounded almost like a whisper came from the speaker hovering behind them.

"I'm sorry."

Kyle could hear the chopper repositioning as he called again for his father to stop, but either he couldn't hear him or he wasn't listening. Then suddenly from the corner of his eye Kyle saw two army vehicles racing down the road and he almost breathed a sigh of relief knowing they were about to be captured. The first vehicle pulled into the lane leading to the farmhouse then rounded the property, coming to a halt less than fifty feet from his father, soldiers jumping from the rear, surrounding them, their hazmat suits making them anonymous, terrifying.

Kyle's dad fell to his knees, his hands clasped on top of his head as his mother dropped beside him, exhausted. Kyle saw one of the troops wave off the chopper, then he heard the helicopter bank and the thumping of the blades rapidly disappear into the distance.

Kyle dropped to his knees as two soldiers approached him. Conflicting emotions filled his heart, part of him disappointed they had been caught, the other relieved they had been, a growing part of his mind realizing what they were doing was wrong.

He just couldn't believe this was happening in New Orleans.

Saints vs. Raiders, Mercedes-Benz Superdome, New Orleans, Louisiana
Outbreak Day #1 – Zero Hour

"Hey, what the hell are you doing back here?"

The voice, raised, echoed through the narrow utility room housing feeds into the cooling system for this portion of the massive Superdome. Mike Milner didn't flinch, but his heart did skip a beat as he continued rotating the wrench. He was so close to completing his task, so close to his pay day, that there was no way he was going to allow some rent-a-cop to ruin his day.

"Look at my binder over there," he said, jerking his head toward a scuffed black binder sitting atop an electrical cabinet. He heard the feet shuffle toward the binder as he twisted one last time, the connection sealed, his job almost done.

"What's this shit?" asked the guard.

Apparently my paperwork isn't in order.

"You need to come with me, buddy, until we get this sorted out."

"No problem, officer."

Milner reached into his pocket, gripping the small Walther PPKE he had hidden there. As he turned, a smile plastered on his face to set the poor bastard at ease, his hand came up in his pocket, and he squeezed the trigger.

The report was loud in the confined space, but as fortune would have it, something had the seventy-three thousand gathered on their feet, screaming at the night air.

It went unnoticed to all.

All except the poor sonofabitch who had walked in on him, as he gripped his chest, surprise scrawled across his face as he slowly sank to his knees.

"I'm really sorry about this," said Milner. "But you shouldn't have been so good at your job."

Milner turned around and spun the valve on the canister he had just hooked into the cooling system, opening it wide. Within minutes the gas would be spread throughout the complex, and his job done. What he had actually hooked into the cooling system he had no clue. That was above his pay grade. He'd been hired to do a job, and that's what he was doing. In his trade you didn't ask questions because answers got you killed. So did curiosity.

Milner stuffed the body of the unfortunate guard behind the cooling unit and out of sight, leaving a small pool of blood on the floor. Removing a plastic bottle from his kit, he poured the contents out onto the blood stain, immediately turning the crimson puddle black, thickening it within moments. Now the blood looked like an oil stain, something that wouldn't be unexpected in a utility closet.

Approaching the door, he fished his cellphone from his pocket and dialed the number to activate his diversion. Pressing *Send*, he counted to ten, then smiled as the commotion outside grew in intensity as his remote trigger fried a relay device at the Entergy New Orleans "vault" just outside the stadium, recreating the Super Bowl blackout.

I guess they never did fix the problem!

He smiled to himself as he turned the knob, stepping out into the darkness, the only light now from the emergency lighting system as the Superdome lost partial power. By the sounds of things, the game was delayed, and Milner could imagine the panic that must be setting in amongst some of the tens of thousands of fans in attendance, and if he knew the media, they'd be making a field day out of the situation, spreading the panic to the audience watching on television at homes and bars across the city.

But Milner didn't really care. He was here for a payday. A *big* payday. This little job was netting him six figures. Half was already sitting in his Cayman account less a significant cash withdrawal now hidden in his apartment; the other half would be deposited tonight by his contact after a meet. Then he'd be out of New Orleans and off to the Dominican until the money ran out, then back for another gig.

It was a great life.

Milner strolled past the staff rushing by, wondering if they'd be able to get the power restored in time so the game could resume. He hoped so. After all, he had put a fin down on the Raiders to win.

He strolled by the guards, nodding to them as he passed, his tool kit swinging as he whistled a tune inspired by the concern surrounding him.

It's the end of the world as we know it.

And I feel fine.

New Orleans, Louisiana
Outbreak Day #10

Tammy looked in the mirror at the face staring back at her. Gray, ashen, pale. *Shit.* And she felt like shit too. In fact, she felt worse than she could ever remember. The whites of her eyes were red with fatigue, her brow was covered in sweat, and there were deep black circles under her eyes.

And she was due at work in forty minutes.

She splashed some water on her face, the effort exhausting, but willed her way through it. Missing work wasn't an option. She knew her boss was looking for an excuse to fire her after she had spurned the creep's advances, and in today's economy, a job was a job, whether it was good or not, and with a six year old son and a deadbeat father, she needed every penny she could scrape together just to keep them fed with a roof over their head, even if it meant working at a coffee shop fulltime and the Superdome whenever there was an event.

Maybe I'll take Mom up on her offer and move in with her.

She knew her mother could use the help. She had just finished a battle with breast cancer, apparently successfully, and had a double-mastectomy to prevent any further threat. Tammy thought it was giving up on life, her mother still fairly young and attractive. Tammy's dad had died in Afghanistan ten years ago, and her mom had mourned long and hard.

And it had been especially hard battling the cancer without him at her side. It had almost killed her, like it had grandma, but modern medicine and a will to see her grandson grow up had got her through it, and now she was cancer free.

But in the mirror, she reminded herself of how her mother looked on the bad days.

It's not cancer, you idiot. Stop worrying!

She stumbled into the hallway, her son Jeffrey waiting at the door, and stuffed her feet in her shoes. Heading out the door, she hurried to the bus stop. The roar of the diesel engine behind her prompted her to raise her hand weakly, but not to turn and look, too exhausted to put the necessary effort into the muscles.

Thankfully her neighbor Grace held the bus, urging her on with one foot through the doors, the other on the ground. It took every ounce of her strength to cover the distance, Jeffrey pulling her most of the way, but she finally did, pulling herself up the steps and onto the bus. As she reached for her bus pass she felt the world spin, then go black as she collapsed onto the floor, Jeffrey crying by her side.

Isolation Ward, Interim Louisiana State University (LSU) Public Hospital, New Orleans, Louisiana

It was a gray fog, terrifying. Tammy could see nothing but the gray, hear nothing but the void around her. And she couldn't move. She could feel her heart slamming in her chest, the roar of her pulse filling her ears, drilling through the void, pushing her toward some new destination, a destination she didn't know, a destination she feared as much as she did her current situation.

Murmurs.

And beeping sounds.

She focused, cut through the fog, calmed the pounding of her heart, and with a jolt, the world flooded back, filling the void with the reality it had been protecting her from. She sat up with a gasp, something choking her. Her instinct was to cough, to rid herself of whatever was in her throat, and as she did so, she felt something attached to her face. She grabbed at it, trying to yank it away, but she felt hands seizing her, pushing her back down, and repositioning whatever she had pulled over her mouth.

"It's okay, you're safe," said a soothing voice, a woman's, a voice that reminded her of her grandmother when she was younger. "You're in a hospital. What you're feeling are breathing tubes. Just breathe normally, and you'll get used to it very quickly, okay?"

Tammy opened her eyes, not realizing they had been squeezed shut. Her vision was blurred, and she blinked several times to try and clear it. She could see a form hovering over her, but the image didn't clear.

"I can't—" she began, but stopped, unable to talk with the tubes in her mouth.

"Don't try to speak. I'll get the doctor and he'll explain the situation to you, okay?"

She nodded, the nurse slowly coming into focus, and as she stepped away, the room she was in snapped into clarity and she gasped, causing another bout of coughing. Recovered, she looked around. She was in a large ward, dozens of beds separated by maybe five feet, filled with women of varying ages, all looking like hell.

All looking exactly as she felt.

What's going on here?

She felt her heart begin to slam in her chest as panic began to set in. A shadow leaned across her, blocking the overhead lighting, and she yelped as her eyes shifted from the misery surrounding her to the mask covered face of a doctor not much older than her if the lack of lines around his eyes were any indication.

This kid is going to take care of me?

She stifled her complaint, not that she could have vocalized it, and instead turned it inward to add to her misery.

Maybe if you had done something with your life, you too could have been a doctor.

"My name is Dr. Corkery. Don't try to talk. You collapsed on the bus and were brought here earlier this morning. It looks like you have some sort of virus. Nothing to worry about, we're treating you with antivirals." He motioned to the rest of the room. "As you can see, there's a bug going around. As a precaution we're isolating everybody so it doesn't spread."

Suddenly she remembered what had happened. Leaving the house, getting on the bus, then blacking out.

Jeffrey!

Her eyes shot open and she tried to talk but the doctor held up his hand.

"Your son is alright. Your mother is here with him. I'll try to arrange for you to talk to them in a little while, okay?"

She nodded in relief as Dr. Corkery was handed something that took his attention away from her. His eyes narrowed as he looked at what appeared to be an iPad or some sort of tablet computer. She desperately wanted to know what had him so concerned, but with these damned tubes down her throat, she couldn't say a word.

"Is this correct?" he asked the nurse quietly.

Tammy couldn't see the nurse, but apparently whatever he was looking at was confirmed.

"Okay. I'm calling it. Tell Dr. Newton to issue a Code Seven. We need all hands on deck. And we'll need to notify the CDC, we might need some help on this one."

"Yes, Doctor."

Dr. Corkery turned back to Tammy, his eyes smiling.

"Looks like we have quite the flu outbreak going on! But don't you worry, these things usually run their course within a week."

A week!

The concern in her eyes wasn't lost on the doctor.

"Don't worry, it will fly by before you know it."

He patted her shoulder and moved on to the next bed, leaving her fears unaddressed.

What about my job? I can't afford to miss a week!

Dr. Fred Newton's Office, Acting Administrator

Interim LSU Public Hospital, New Orleans, Louisiana

"Are you sure?"

Dr. Fred Newton screwed up his face, unconvinced. Corkery was young, and the young were prone to panic. *It's a flu outbreak for Christ's sake!* Every year it was the same thing. A bug would make its rounds, people would get sick, and the beds would fill with the elderly and asthmatics and others with preexisting conditions.

Nurse Ogawa nodded.

"That's what he said."

Newton frowned.

"You don't call in the CDC for a flu outbreak." He sighed. "But you do report the numbers." He looked at the screen and his budget numbers which were looking so good. If the Code Seven state lasted more than a few days, that budget would be blown, and he'd be going cap in hand to the board for more. He chewed on his cheek for a moment, then turned back to his head nurse. "Fine. There's no arguing with the volume. Code Seven it is, have the calls go out. Anyone in town and sober is to report to work. Set up the rotating schedule as per the plan."

"And the CDC?"

"Send them their data *as per protocol*. Each morning."

"Yes, Doctor."

Ogawa left his office leaving Newton to stare at his spreadsheet, the smile that had been there gone. He positioned his cursor and began to update the spreadsheet for a one week outbreak of the flu.

Isolation Ward, Interim LSU Public Hospital, New Orleans, Louisiana

Tammy's bed had been pushed near the window of the isolation ward, her breathing tubes removed now that she was conscious and rehydrated. On the other side of the glass stood her mother, her son Jeffrey standing on a chair so he could see inside. Tammy had a smile etched on her face, determined to look strong for her little man, but each time she made eye contact with her mother she knew she wasn't fooling her.

If this is a flu, it's the worst flu I've ever had.

Or even heard about.

A flurry of nurses and the doctor she had seen earlier rushed by outside as she heard a commotion behind her. She tried to push herself up to look, but was too weak, instead all she could do was listen.

And it terrified her.

In amongst the cacophony of beeping machines, she could hear one with a steady tone, a tone she had heard enough on TV to know it meant someone's heart had stopped. She could hear shouts but make no sense of them, the "visiting area" as she had come to think of this place isolated from the rest of the ward, separated enough to not be able to see anything back in the ward.

She looked at her mother and saw a tear escape her left eye, racing down her cheek toward her neck.

If this is just a flu, why are you crying?

"Why don't you say goodbye to mommy, then go get yourself a candy bar and eat it over there, okay?" her mom said to Jeffrey, whose bored expression spread into a smile.

"Bye Mommy!" he said, hastily kissing the glass, then disappearing as he jumped off the chair.

"Bye dear!" said Tammy, knowing her precious son was probably out of earshot already. She looked at her mother. "What's wrong? What aren't you telling me?"

Her mother shook her head, closing her eyes and looking away.

"Tell me."

Her mother looked back at her, her eyes now filled with tears, sending Tammy's heart racing in fear. Her mother was a strong woman, the toughest she knew. She had been through the death of a husband and breast cancer. She was a survivor, and Tammy couldn't recall the woman crying in all her years.

But today, she couldn't hide it.

"What's wrong?" demanded Tammy, the fear in her voice palpable, enough that she was glad Jeffrey was being spoiled with his favorite treat.

She could hear a deep breath through the speaker as her mother wiped her eyes with a tissue.

"I heard on the radio on the way here that there's some sort of virus hitting the city."

"Yeah, a flu. I'll be fine in a few days."

"Is that what they told you?"

Tammy's eyebrows shot up at the question, then she had to admit she couldn't remember. She rewound the events of the past few hours, but couldn't be sure.

"I think so."

Her mother turned away again, but spoke.

"On the radio they said people are dying." Her voice cracked on the last word, and her shoulders heaved as a huge weight suddenly pressed on

Tammy's chest, the gravity of the situation hitting her as she noticed the panic that had been occurring in the ward had ceased.

And so had the steady tone from the heart monitor.

Did they save her, or did they turn it off because she died?

As her question echoed in her head, her heart stopped with a sudden realization as she replayed her journey to the visiting area.

She turned to mother.

"Mom?"

Her mother turned to face her, eyes red, cheeks flushed.

"Yes, Dear?"

"Did they say whether or not it was only affecting women?"

World Health Organization Conference on H5N1, Marseilles, France

"…and the results were remarkable. Our testing has shown no sign of the virus in eighty-three percent of our test subjects not receiving the placebo, and a massive reduction in the viral count in the remaining subjects. We have extended the study on these remaining subjects to see if we can further reduce their blood counts, and results are promising. In fact, if I may be so bold at a conference such as this, the results are stunning."

Dr. Hermann Kapp paused to take a sip of water as the delegates he was addressing absorbed the bombshell he had just dropped on them. An antiviral that actually worked, worked quickly, and worked on nearly 100% of the patients. It was still probably a decade away from production, and would need to go through extensive testing, but their approach was unique, and impossible only a few years ago, the technology and knowhow simply nonexistent.

The patents had been applied for, but not yet awarded, therefore the details on how they had accomplished their miraculous feat wouldn't be revealed today, but the generalities should be enough to have the medical community abuzz for years.

And our competitors hell-bent on stealing the secret.

He returned the glass to the podium, and noticed his smartphone sitting on the dais vibrate with a message. He chose to ignore it.

"How we were able to accomplish this I cannot get into, obviously, however I can say this. We have developed a process that allows us to target specific gene sequences, and annihilate the cells displaying these sequences. So when we have a viral outbreak, we simply—and it is by no means simple"—chuckles filled the room—"we simply need to decode the virus, program our antiviral to target the specific gene sequence, then begin mass production and distribution. We estimate our turnaround time would be less than one week from identification to start of production."

His phone vibrated again and he took a sip of water as he swiped his finger across the display, then brought up the message.

TO ALL: Another outbreak has occurred. This one much more serious. Must discuss immediately.

Kapp's heart leapt, but he kept his cool as he finished his drink, placing the cup down and looking back at the audience. Perhaps years from now, when historians examined the footage of this moment, they might see the slight surprise registered on his face, the change in pallor, the quickening of his breathing, but that assumed the secret got out, and assumed they had been unable to stop it.

Then again, if they were unable to stop this madness, there might very well be nobody left to care about this moment in history.

Conference Room C, Interim LSU Public Hospital, New Orleans, Louisiana

Dr. Douglas Corkery massaged his temples, his elbows resting on the arms of his chair as he listened to the hospital administrator, Dr. Fred Newton, drone on about the budget and how we risked going over it should the infection continue.

I hate bureaucrats!

He let out a loud sigh, pushing himself up straight as the room turned to the source of the exasperation.

"Do you have something to add, Doug?"

Corkery nodded as he took a deep breath, trying to control his frustration.

"Yes, I do." He pointed at the display showing budget projections. "Why are we in here, wasting time, hearing about budgets, when we have patients down the hall dying? Forgive my language, but who gives a damn about budget numbers? Deal with those after the fact. We are doctors! It is our job to take care of these people, whatever the cost." He pushed a stack of folders toward the center of the table. "I've got thirty-eight patients in isolation already, with more coming in every hour, and a second one just died, with over two dozen looking like they won't last the day. We have an outbreak of something we haven't seen before, and we need help!" He looked around the table in earnest, the doctors assembled nodding their heads in agreement, the bean counters avoiding his stare. His head whipped back to Newton. "When can we expect the CDC to arrive?"

Newton cleared his throat, the uncomfortable expression on his face raising alarm bells.

"*Please* tell me you contacted the CDC."

All eyes were now on Newton.

"They'll get our daily stats sent to them in the morning as per protocol."

"What?" exclaimed Corkery. "We have people dying, of what we don't know, and you haven't elevated our status? Protocol clearly dictates you contact the CDC of any outbreak! What the hell were you thinking? You used to be a doctor once, remember your goddamned oath!" Corkery could feel his face burn with rage, a rage he couldn't recall ever feeling before. This was insanity, bureaucratic insanity that would cost lives.

There was an uncomfortable pause after his outburst, which was finally ended by Newton standing up, leaning forward on his knuckles.

"I don't need to defend myself to you," he growled. "I've been a doctor for over thirty years, and you haven't even seen your first decade. Contacting the CDC is my call, and I'll do it when I feel it's necessary."

Corkery's mind was reeling. *Why won't he contact the CDC? Is it ego? Is it that he can't admit a mistake?* That had to be it. He had known Newton to dig in his heels from time to time, even if it was obvious he was wrong, but never on a medical matter so serious. For a doctor to put ego ahead of the wellbeing of his patients was inexcusable. Career ending if word got out.

And if this outbreak was as bad as he thought it was, Newton would be answerable to authorities far higher than anyone in this room.

And with this virus appearing to target only women, which was unheard of in his experience, they could be dealing with something far worse, which would have Newton answerable to the ultimate authority should not calling in the CDC cause this to spread even farther.

He'd be answerable to God himself.

Corkery's pager buzzed on his hip, as did every other doctor's in the room. He grabbed it.

Code Blue, ICU 2.

He jumped from the table and headed out the door, followed by all of the on-duty doctors, leaving Newton and his bean counters to stare after them.

Sofitel Marseille Vieux Port Hotel, Marseilles, France

Dr. Hermann Kapp closed the door, locking it securely, then did a quick survey of the room to make certain he was alone. Satisfied, he closed the drapes, turned on the lights, then powered on his laptop, facing the screen away from the window, its casing designed to block anything from being able to read the screen through the cover, and generating enough interference to prevent any other type of electronic eavesdropping.

It was the latest Dell Latitude E6540 laptop, state of the art, secure, rugged, impervious to tampering and monitoring if used properly, with a layer of customization not available to the general public.

And the amount of training he had received on its security features had seemed ridiculous at first, but with what had been happening over the past year, they had been able to keep the secret from getting out, despite operatives spread around the planet searching for the culprit. Unfortunately he must be using similar equipment, as they had no trace of him, and he seemed to be able to operate with impunity.

But eventually he would slip up, Kapp and his associates just prayed it wouldn't be too late, the man's demands, and demonstrations, continually more outlandish, and more severe, each time.

Kapp expertly operated the laptop and soon had a grid of faces, several still blank and logging in as he had just done. Nothing was said until the final board member had connected to the secure server.

The chairman spoke first, his image expanding to fill a quarter of the screen as his microphone activated, *Hans Schreiber, Chairman* displayed under the image, the *BioDyne Pharma* logo prominently displayed behind him. Kapp had known Chairman Schreiber for over a decade, before he had been elected Chairman, and before Kapp had even been on the board. It was Kapp's work on the genetically targeted antiviral serum that had earned him his position. It had made Kapp a rich man, the stock options and bonuses staggering.

But this was big pharma. Mega billion dollar deals, mega billion dollar drug sales, and this particular drug would revolutionize the world—making them all ridiculously rich.

"Ladies and gentlemen, I'll keep this brief as information is just beginning to come in. But is appears as if Dr. Urban has released another variation of the antiviral, this one on a scale far higher than we expected."

Murmuring filled Kapp's headset, his own mouth remaining clamped shut as his heart raced with the implications. *What genetic sequence has he targeted this time?* Dr. Victor Urban had been a brilliant scientist. *Was still* a brilliant scientist. It was his idea they had been working on for the past decade. It was he who had figured out how to design the drug to target specific genetic sequences, then destroy the cells with that sequence.

It was brilliant, outside of the box research that would change the world. And like most out of the box thinking, it was devised by a man who was borderline insane. At least it was a running joke in the lab that he was mad until that fateful day when he didn't show up for work eighteen months ago.

It was six months later that the first terrifying message had arrived, and when they had all discovered it wasn't just madness that consumed Dr. Urban, but greed as well.

"What kind of scale are we talking?" asked Kapp, the first to recover from the shock, but like the rest, equally scared to hear the answer.

"We don't know yet, however he's promised a target of half a percent."

"Half a percent!" exclaimed one of the others.

"Where?" asked Kapp.

"We haven't got that information yet, but based upon previous releases, I think we have to take him at his word."

Nods filled the screen as Kapp leaned back in his chair, massaging his temples with one hand, his eyes closed. There had been two previous attacks, or "releases" of the antiviral. The first had been in a theatre in Los Angeles, which was when they had discovered he had been able to aerosolize it, an incredible achievement.

The man is *a genius.*

The entire theatre had been exposed to the antiviral, which when inhaled, immediately went to work, seeking out the genetic sequence it had been programmed for. In the first case, he had targeted natural redheads, which was only about two percent of the California population, and with the antiviral designed to break down within an hour when exposed to the air, and non-transmissible once inside the body, it hadn't spread beyond those watching the 7pm showing of Red Tails.

Fortunately only three had been exposed, and all died within ten days, in separate hospitals, with symptoms suggesting pneumonia.

No one noticed the pattern except the board, and only because Urban had notified them of what to look for after they had fulfilled his first demand for payment in exchange for information. It was only one million dollars, paid to a bank in the Cayman Islands, and came with the promise he would do nothing for six months. Then six months had passed, and another message.

LaGuardia Airport in New York City. This time he targeted Marfan Syndrome, a rare disorder of the connective tissues that affects about one in five thousand people. A few had died, spread across the world, with no one except BioDyne Pharma noticing. But it had been the largest scale attack yet.

And there had been a mutation.

The virus had been transmitted beyond the initial carriers.

This wasn't supposed to happen, and BioDyne's scientists theorized—since they didn't have a sample—it was due to the alterations made in aerosolizing the compound. It had mutated and found a way to transmit beyond the host, which was terrifying. The antiviral was specifically designed to not be transmittable. After all, a cure that could spread would reduce their profits.

And this was what was driving the panic now. The authorities hadn't been called in, but millions were being spent to try and track Urban down. All in the name of profits. If it were revealed a madman was loose with a BioDyne drug capable of killing anyone with a specific gene sequence, their stock would plummet, and the company would probably never survive.

And it had to, for it was the only hope to stop Urban, especially after this apparent mutation.

The next six months of peace were bought with ten million dollars of blood money, and that six months ended ten days ago.

"Has there been any word from the CDC?" asked Harris, one of the oldest members of the board.

"Nothing. Which is odd if Urban is telling us the truth."

"Unless it's mutated again and taking longer than usual," replied Harris.

"Let's hope that hasn't happened." Chairman Schreiber sighed, taking off his glasses and pinching the bridge of his nose. "I don't know what to do, people. This time he wants one hundred million. We can afford it of course, but next time can we expect one billion? And where does paying him get us? It buys us six more months to do what? We've had no success in finding him. We're no closer today than we were a year ago when this started."

Hyatt, their most senior researcher, cleared his throat and his image expanded on the screen. He scratched his nose, then leaned into the camera, the effect disconcerting, his geek visage, pimply and unkempt, taking on a fishbowl appearance that belied his genius. He had been Urban's protégé, and would probably equal or surpass him someday.

When Hyatt spoke, people listened.

"I wouldn't quite say that."

Isolation Ward, Interim LSU Public Hospital, New Orleans, Louisiana

Dr. Douglas Corkery drew the sheet up over yet another woman, dead in her prime as several of his colleagues did the same with their patients. They were at seven dead now, with no signs of recovery in anyone. This was getting ridiculous. *Scratch that. It* is *ridiculous!* People were dying. More were arriving every hour, and the idiot in charge was too pigheaded to ask for help, more concerned about being right, and being in line with his budget expectations.

He fished his cellphone out of his pocket and dialed a colleague at Tulane Hospital. It rang three times before his squash buddy and med school pal Jack Kilborn answered.

"Hey Doug, pretty busy right now."

"No problem, Jack. It'll only take a minute. Have you guys got a major viral outbreak there?"

There was a pause. "Well, I wouldn't call it major, only a few people—" Kilborn paused. "Hey, how'd you know about that?"

"We've got a major outbreak here. Over fifty people, seven dead already."

"Jesus!"

"Please tell me you've sent this into the CDC."

"No, it's only a few people. It will go in with tomorrow's numbers. Why? Surely you guys already have!"

"Our moron *acting* administrator Dr. Fred Newton won't contact them."

"That guy's a stubborn asshole!"

"No shit." Corkery lowered his voice. "Can you hear me?"

"Yes."

44

"Can you get your guys to send in the numbers, and make a mention that you've heard LSU is far worse?"

"I'll see what I can do. I'll call you back in a few."

Corkery returned the phone to his pocket then continued his rounds, praying the CDC would be notified shortly. If they weren't, he vowed to call them himself within an hour.

Even if it meant ending his career at LSU.

Office of Public Health Preparedness and Response
Centers for Disease Control and Prevention (CDC), Atlanta, Georgia

Dr. Katherine Best took a too large bite of her six inch Subway ham sandwich—not toasted. She didn't understand the appeal. Subway should be a nice, cool, refreshing sandwich. Lots of lettuce, tomatoes, cucumbers and olives, with lite mayo. And American cheese if she were feeling indulgent, the firmer texture of the cheese more to her liking than the other choices.

To die for.

Healthy, tasty, filling, and cool.

Born and raised in Fargo, North Dakota, this time of year was supposed to be cold. When she had left, she never thought she would miss it, but the past five years in Atlanta had cured her of that, and now she found every day at least warm, which meant a lot of cooler meals, especially lunches. Salads and cold subs.

And nothing was worse than greasy fingers with ketchup and mustard surging outside the bun while eating a hamburger when you were trying to read email at your desk. An email caught her attention and she opened it immediately, her mouth, at first rapidly chewing her latest bite, slowed until it reached a full stop, still full.

She grabbed the phone and quickly dialed an extension rarely used before she remembered her full mouth. Quickly chewing, she managed to swallow just in time.

"Rapid Response Team."

"This is Dr. Best. We have a possible outbreak in New Orleans. Unknown viral agent, at least seven dead in less than twenty-four hours."

"Seven in twenty four hours? Why haven't we heard of it?"

She could understand the shock at the other end of the line. It matched her own, but the email was from a med school friend who she trusted. These weren't official channels, but according to the email, those channels wouldn't be informed until tomorrow morning.

When it could very well be too late.

Sofitel Marseille Vieux Port Hotel, Marseilles, France

Dr. Hermann Kapp reached forward to kill the feed from the now adjourned virtual meeting when the Chairman suddenly spoke.

"Wait a minute!"

Kapp's finger remained suspended in midair, then he slowly eased back in his chair as he saw Chairman Schreiber read a piece of paper he had just been handed. He shook his head, removing his glasses, and stared at the camera.

"The CDC has been made aware of an outbreak in New Orleans. Viral, at least seven dead, dozens infected. This could be our outbreak."

"When are we supposed to hear from him?"

Schreiber looked at his watch.

"Not for another twenty one hours."

"What do we do?" asked Kapp. "Nobody has ever known about the outbreaks before. There's no hiding it now that the CDC is involved." Kapp's eyes flicked over to the icon with their brilliant researcher. "Dr. Hyatt, is it possible for them to trace this back to us?"

Hyatt nodded. "We've applied for patents on our methods. If they really wanted to, they could put two and two together."

"How likely do you think that is?"

"Very. These are smart people, and if there are over fifty people infected already, and previous experience suggest they will all die, there is no way the CDC will let this go."

Everyone was silent as this sank in.

"I think we need to get ahead of it," said Kapp. "Go to the CDC, come clean, and maybe with their resources we can find him. We've got six months before the next attack and we shouldn't waste a minute of it."

There were a few nods, but most heads remained still.

Schreiber finally sighed and nodded.

"Kapp, I want you to run with this."

Kapp felt his heart leap into his throat.

"Me?"

"Yes. You're our best speaker, best public relations guy. I want you to be the face of the company if and when this hits the news. Use whoever you need, but try to minimize the damage to the company. We'll cooperate fully. I don't want the next outbreak on my conscience—I already can't sleep at night, and this is only getting worse."

Kapp felt the tightness in his chest, the sweat above his lip, the moisture oozing from his palms, for he knew what this meant.

As the public face of the company on this matter, if things went awry, he'd be the first to go down.

And the first to go to prison.

Cafeteria, Interim LSU Public Hospital, New Orleans, Louisiana

Dr. Douglas Corkery sat in the cafeteria, his head on the table, his coffee and lunch forgotten. He was exhausted and was due to leave, but couldn't bring himself to do it. He had patients. Scared patients, sick patients. Dying patients.

And so far he had been powerless to stop anything.

Fifteen dead already. He had just ordered all female nurses and doctors out of the Isolation Ward, since it seemed to only be targeting women, and had ordered triage to deal with women first, immediately isolating any with cold or flu symptoms.

The only good news was that the arrivals seemed to be slowing down; only one in the last hour.

Whatever they were dealing with seemed to have hit everyone at nearly the same time, with most of the patients arriving within the past twelve hours. He had called colleagues at several other hospitals in the area and they all had cases, but those were few. It seemed the epicenter was here, and it had him wondering.

What was unique about this part of the city?

The Superdome!

His eyes shot open and he sat up as his mind raced, his hands shoveling food into his mouth, the fries and club sandwich going unnoticed, their purpose merely fuel for the fire he would need if he were to last the night. As he swallowed each bite, his theory continued to expand. There were events at the Superdome all the time. Football games, concerts, celebrations.

Could they have all been exposed at the Superdome?

But if something this serious had been going around at the Superdome, there should be hundreds if not thousands of victims.

And why only women?

And some of the women he had to admit didn't strike him as football fans. But it could have been a concert. He'd have to check what events there had been then begin to question the patients.

Shoving the last wedge of sandwich into his mouth, he wiped his face and headed back to the Isolation Ward to try and find that missing link between them all.

Outside the Interim LSU Public Hospital, New Orleans, Louisiana

Dr. Katherine Best barely waited for the skids to hit the ground before she jumped out of the chopper that had brought her from the airport. The scene presented to her was one of near panic. Police were everywhere, and as per protocol, all patients not exhibiting symptoms of the outbreak were being redirected to other hospitals in the city, and those already at other hospitals were being transported here if they were healthy enough.

Most weren't.

All new patients in the city would arrive here, which would help contain the research and treatment, the numbers of new patients dwindling rapidly as the day went by.

It makes no sense!

For the numbers to occur like they did, it implied a near simultaneous infection. It was as if there was no Patient Zero, which to her meant several terrifying things. One, there was a Patient Zero out there, who infected the rest somehow, and was most likely now dead, his, or more likely her, death chalked up to pneumonia and buried somewhere, their secrets probably locked in a grave or cremated, never to be discovered.

If that were the case, it indicated an incredibly virulent virus to infect so many so quickly, which was terrifying. Could this be just the first wave? Patient Zero infects them at a movie theatre or some other public venue, then after an incubation period, those infected begin to exhibit symptoms, and begin arriving at the hospital today?

And how long was that period?

And worse, how many others did they infect while going about their daily lives in the city?

The first wave was around one hundred people. The second wave could be massive, easily in the thousands or tens of thousands.

Then there was the other possibility that had occurred to her.

Terrorism.

A virus that acted like no other, nearly 100% fatal, with a sudden mass infection.

She prayed that wasn't the case. If it were, they likely had no chance of preventing it from being used all over the country.

She saw the CDC vehicles parked to the left, near a side entrance, an isolation tube already set up leading from a large temporary sealed tent where the doctors would suit up and decontaminate themselves when leaving. If her instructions had been followed, which she was certain they were, that isolation tube would lead all the way to the Isolation Unit of the hospital, and join another temporary working area that would isolate that entire ward from the rest of the hospital. Those inside would not leave until they had been screened and cleared, and as of yet, they didn't even know what to look for.

One of her colleagues based in New Orleans waved and ran toward her. As was her habit, she made certain her right hand was occupied to prevent the natural instinct of shaking hands, and her colleague, equally well briefed on protocols, smiled as he approached, his own right hand occupied by a tablet computer.

"Good to see you, Doctor. Pleasant flight?"

Katherine nodded at Dr. Barry Johnston, an experienced infectious diseases specialist who had been with the CDC when she was just a teenager, his own upward mobility halted by his desire to remain on the front lines and not push paper. "Good to see you too, Doctor." She glanced over her shoulder at the departing chopper. "I guess you get used to it," she replied as she began to walk toward the decontamination area, Johnston at her side. "Sit rep?"

"One hundred and four are now in isolation. Thirty eight are dead and isolated in a special area we've set up in the morgue. Toxicology has already begun. We should have the first results coming back within the hour."

"Any idea of what they all have in common besides being women?"

"As a matter of fact, yes. Oh, and it's no longer just women."

Katherine's heart almost stopped as quickly as her feet brought her to a halt. She looked at Johnston, certain the fear she felt was written all over her face.

"What?"

"We have one man, brought in thirty minutes ago from another hospital. He has all the same symptoms, but at this point we don't know if it's the same strain, so we have him isolated from the others."

"Could it be a mutation?"

Johnston shrugged his shoulders. "We won't know until we can isolate the virus and begin analyzing it, but…" His voice trailed off, and she knew why. Neither of them wanted to state the obvious.

If this virus can mutate this quickly, it might already be too late to prevent its spread.

"Any signs of improvements in the patients?" she asked instead.

"None. From what we can tell, from initial symptoms to death is anywhere from twenty four to forty eight hours."

"That could be what saves us."

Johnston nodded his understanding. "Assuming the incubation period is short."

"And we have no idea on that?"

"Actually, we might. Let's get you suited up and inside so you can talk to the doctor himself who might have figured it out."

She nodded as she stepped inside the plastic bubble meant to protect them all from the spread of the disease. On autopilot, she suited up as her mind raced. If the disease killed its victims within forty-eight hours, and the incubation period was short enough, it could flame out before it spread too far. There might just be hope to stop this, but it was going to be nasty, and time was of the essence.

Suited up, she stepped through into the decontamination area, received a blast of air to loosen any foreign substances that might be on the suit so as to prevent any new toxins from entering, then stepped into the long tube after checking that her independent oxygen supply was functioning.

She followed Johnston and within minutes was in the isolation ward being introduced to an exhausted young doctor named Corkery.

"Dr. Katherine Best, pleased to meet you. I understand you may have figured out the common link?"

Corkery nodded his head, his eyes drooping, black circles threatening to bore into his skull as he sat back down, Katherine and Johnston pulling chairs out to face him.

"We interviewed everyone we could, and after a couple of dozen I realized that several worked at the Superdome, then it all clicked."

"What?" asked Katherine, her heart already racing as she realized how large the exposure might be.

"Almost every single person here was at the Saints game ten days ago."

"Oh no!" she whispered, her head spinning toward Johnston. "That means it could be across the country already!"

Johnston shook his head, his frown deep. "Forget the country. NFL games are tourist destinations. They attract visitors from around the entire world. This thing could already be global."

Isolation Ward, Interim LSU Public Hospital, New Orleans, Louisiana

Tammy could barely feel the hand holding hers, her body so weak she had no idea how long she had been here, and could hardly remember where she was. Like the others around her, she had taken to muttering, with occasional bouts of lucidity that could last mere seconds, or minutes. But never long.

"I have to get to work tomorrow otherwise I'll be fired."

She could see the doctor's eyes smiling down at her as his face mask crinkled from the grin underneath.

"Don't you worry about that. I'll personally talk to your boss."

She forced a smile which immediately collapsed back into a frown.

"I'm not going to make it, am I?"

The doctor squeezed her hand a little tighter.

"The CDC is here now. We've got the best doctors in the world looking into this. They'll have a cure before you know it."

"You're lying. We're all dying. Fast. I figured I'd die young from breast cancer like my grandmothers. My mother beat it, but she's stronger than I am."

The doctor's eyes narrowed slightly.

"You have a lot of breast cancer in the family?"

She nodded.

"Mother, grandmothers, a few aunts. It's like both sides of our family are cursed."

The doctor nodded slowly, then she felt a stabbing pain in her chest. She gasped, her back arching, then she collapsed into the bed, unable to see or say anything, her world rapidly dimming, her mind presenting her with one last image, that of her son, sitting beside her happily as they watched Monsters Inc. 3D at the theatre just a few weeks before, sharing popcorn and a large Diet Coke.

Her last thoughts brought a smile to her face, as she could hear shouts in the far distance on the other side of the darkness, then a steady tone as her body finally gave up, leaving a six year old son alone, with no parents to love and care for him.

Isolation Ward, Interim LSU Public Hospital, New Orleans, Louisiana

Dr. Corkery watched as the mother and son of his latest patient to succumb to the virus were escorted out. They would have to remain in isolation until they knew how to test for the virus, but his mind was already somewhere else.

Breast cancer.

These were all women save one, and men could get breast cancer, it just wasn't common. His patient's dying words had struck him because he had noted that several of those sick had been former breast cancer patients, and one had mentioned she had just received her biopsy results, positive for cancer just two days before.

That was just too big a coincidence.

He turned to look for Dr. Best, it a little difficult to spot her since everyone was in green hazmat suits. The hospital staff working in the ward were allowed to continue using their basic procedures, the thinking that they were already exposed, so there was no point in taking any further precautions than having them isolated within the ward and the expanded zone set up by the CDC.

"Dr. Best?" he called out to the room, and a figure turned and waved. He smiled and approached.

"Dr. Corkery. When's the last time you had some sleep? I want you to go get a minimum three hours sleep. Just go and don't set an alarm. You'll be far more valuable to us if you're well rested than you are now."

Corkery knew she was right, and he would follow her orders after he had delivered his message, a message which was already becoming foggy with the mere thought of sleep already overwhelming him.

He yawned and felt his chin drop as sleep took over.

His head popped up, a slight surge of adrenaline giving him just enough.

"I think these women all have or have had breast cancer."

"What?"

"You heard me. Screen them. Check their histories. I think they all have breast cancer."

And finally he could stand no longer, dropping into Dr. Best's arms as she called for help. He could feel hands on him, holding him up, and he had little flashes of being carried to a ward with beds.

Then nothing, sleep completely taking over.

Isolation Ward, Interim LSU Public Hospital, New Orleans, Louisiana
Outbreak Day #11

The idea was crazy. *Breast cancer!* How would a virus target only patients who had experienced breast cancer? But this Dr. Corkery was smart. Very smart, and she decided it was best not to ignore him. The canvassing had gone quickly, patients asked directly, families consulted, medical records scanned. And in the end the results had proven shocking.

Over one third of the women had fought breast cancer at some point in their life, and over ninety percent had a history of breast cancer in the family. The chance of that being a coincidence was statistically impossible.

But how was the virus targeting them?

It had already been confirmed the virus was new, something they'd never seen before, and it was being mapped now with the most advanced machines available anywhere. But she knew there wasn't much they could do to save these people before that was complete. They were dying so quickly now, she feared there'd be none left by tomorrow.

She looked at a nearby wall clock.

My God! It's tomorrow already!

With the quarantine in place, and there nothing beyond their existing protocols to follow, she proceeded toward the exit. The decontamination completed, she stepped out into the fresh air for the first time in hours, sucking in the cool night air.

"Dr. Best!"

She turned and saw Dr. Barry Johnston sitting on a nearby bench, waving her over.

The bench looked inviting.

She joined him, plunking herself down beside him and leaning back, her head dangling over the back of the bench, her hair hanging freely as it strained for the grass below.

She sighed.

"What do you think?" he asked.

"I think we might get lucky."

"How's that?"

"It's killing people so quickly, they don't have a lot of time to infect others. Assuming that's even possible. We still don't know how it spreads, or how these people were infected. Christ, for all we know they ate infected nachos at the game."

"It's the cheese sauce that'll kill ya."

She smiled, managing a chuckle.

"Can you call that stuff cheese?"

"No idea. But you and I both know it's not contaminated nachos, tacos, or buttered popcorn. Unless only women were eating them. And very few at that."

She sucked in a long breath threw her nose, then pushed it out quickly.

"I know." She paused as she tried to put everything together, but her mind was a fog, it desperate for sleep. She sat up and leaned forward, her elbows on her knees, and yawned.

"I need some rack time."

Johnston jerked his head, indicating the road behind them. "They've got us booked at the Holiday Inn. There's special shuttles for us, or you can walk it in about fifteen minutes. Front desk has your name and your luggage has already been put in your room."

"Thanks." Katherine rose and stretched, the walk to the hotel suddenly seeming long. She looked for the shuttle and spotted it on the main road. She turned to Johnston.

"You get some rest as well, otherwise we'll both be useless tomorrow."

He smiled and nodded. "I'll be along shortly."

Katherine wished him a goodnight and began the quick march toward the shuttle, her mind already creating a checklist of things she'd need to do first thing in the morning, should she be fortunate enough to get a full night's sleep. But if history taught her anything, she'd be lucky to get a couple of hours, the chances of her phone ringing with some urgent news nearly 100%.

She tried to clear her mind, pushing the sights and sounds from today's events out of her mind, slowly preparing herself for bed, her ritual while on one of these outbreaks to be nearly zoned out by the time her keycard hit the door. As she stepped inside, she'd peel out of her clothes and accoutrements, tossing them strategically into two piles, one for laundry like undergarments, the other for use the next morning like shoes and ID.

And by the time she'd be naked, she'd have her nightgown pulled from her "go" bag, it tossed over her shoulders and covering her body as she dropped into the bed, and if all went according to plan, she'd be asleep within moments.

As she crossed the security lines, she was suddenly bombarded with camera bulbs flashing, the bright lights of television cameras shining in her eyes, and microphones filling her face. She continued her practiced march, merely repeating "no comment" to any and all questions, dealing with the press not her job. Her job was identification, classification, and containment of the virus. The press was only used to transmit information they needed the public to know, and for now all that had been communicated, as per protocol, were what symptoms to look for, and if you had them, to isolate yourself and call 9-1-1, and for those not infected to practice proper hygiene.

She continued past the throng and toward the shuttle, no one apparently willing to follow the anonymous woman at the risk of missing someone truly important. Little did they know she was probably the most important person on site, and would be the one to determine what course of action to take.

She climbed into the shuttle and without a word the driver started the engine, having them at the hotel in minutes. When she arrived a doorman opened the door for her and gave her a tip of the hat.

"Good evening, miss."

She smiled and stepped through, the "miss" not going unnoticed. The day it was "ma'am" she'd have to reexamine her life if she weren't married with at least one child occupying her time. Though she was a career oriented woman now, she didn't intend it to be her entire life. She was a firm believer that women could be both mother and professional, and besides, the type of work she did would protect her future children, and millions of others.

She walked up to the front desk, the lone attendant looking impossibly awake.

"Good evening. How can I help you?"

"Dr. Katherine Best, CDC. I believe you have a reservation for me?"

The man nodded, tapping away at a keyboard then programming a keycard, thankfully keeping the chitchat to a minimum as she continued her unwinding. He handed her the card.

"Your luggage is already in your room. I've taken the liberty of already having our turndown service visit as I suspected most of you would be coming in very late. Did you want a wakeup call?"

"Six a.m."

He nodded, entering it into the computer.

"Done."

"Dr. Best?"

She turned to see a business suit approaching her, mid-forties, good looking, very formal. And familiar looking.

"Do I know you?"

"Dr. Hermann Kapp. BioDyne Pharma."

"Ahh, I thought I recognized you." She eyed the elevators so invitingly close. "Look Doctor, I'm exhausted. Can we do this in the morning?" she asked as she started for the elevators.

"I think you'll want to hear what I have to say?"

"Unless it's how you've got a new drug that crams eight hours of sleep into two, I'm not interested. In case you haven't noticed, we've got a major outbreak here."

He nodded, a concerned look on his face.

"That's why I'm here."

Katherine halted her march to the elevators. "Do you know something?"

"Doctor, I know everything."

Oval Office, White House, Washington, DC

Katherine's heart pounded in her chest. She had provided many reports in the past that she knew made it up to the President's staff, but never before had she briefed any of his staff in person, let alone the man himself. It was exciting. Thrilling. Exhilarating.

And she wanted to throw up.

She and Dr. Kapp were led through the curved door by the Secretary of the Department of Health and Human Services, Dick Barry. As she cleared the threshold, she sucked in a breath when she saw how many were gathered, most standing, the President perched on the edge of his desk.

"Mr. President, may I present Dr. Katherine Best of the CDC and Dr. Hermann Kapp from BioDyne Pharma."

The President stepped forward, his trademark smile spreading across his face as he extended a hand. Katherine accepted it, as did Kapp, before they were directed to chairs by the Commander in Chief. She rarely shook hands in her business, but you don't leave the President of the United States hanging.

God he looks old!

She remembered the young, vibrant man she had watched in his first term campaign, and to compare that to the graying, weathered man now, she wondered if the job were worth it. She made a mental note to Google before and after images of former presidents to see if they all aged as quickly.

The President sat across from her, leaning forward, his elbows on his knees, hands clasped loosely together.

"I've assembled everyone I could think of here this morning so no time is wasted. What's the situation?"

Katherine took a breath, her eyes making the rounds of the rooms. Most of the faces she recognized from the news. Secretaries of State, Defense and Homeland Security, along with the Chairman of the Joint Chiefs of Staff among others she didn't recognize, all stared at her, awaiting her words.

"Mr. President. We have a viral outbreak in New Orleans. Until several hours ago we had no idea of its origins, or its virology. Dr. Kapp here was able to provide us with a wealth of information, and it is, needless to say, terrifying." She turned to Dr. Kapp. "If you would, Doctor?" she said, motioning toward the President.

"Mr. President. It is good to see you again. We met once in Geneva, about six years ago."

"I remember, Doctor. It's unfortunate we meet again under such circumstances."

Kapp bowed his head in agreement.

"Sir, several years ago a brilliant scientist working for our company made an astounding breakthrough that will ultimately revolutionize medicine as we know it. He invented an antiviral that was able to target specific genetic patterns. To put it in easier terms for all of us to understand, imagine a bullet able to be fired into a crowd of people, but it would only target the one person it was programmed for, and if it didn't find that person, it would self-destruct, leaving no one harmed. But if it did find that person, it would kill them, and only them."

Katherine noticed the Chairman of the JCS's eyebrows shoot up as he no doubt wished the military analog was available.

"Now, imagine we took that a step further. Imagine we were able to program that bullet to only target those with brown eyes and fire that bullet, or an entire clip of bullets into a crowd, and only those with brown eyes would be killed.

"Well, this is what Dr. Victor Urban did. He invented an antiviral that could be programmed to target a specific genetic sequence, then destroy it. This means if there was a virus outbreak, we could decode its genome, then program the antiviral to target only cells infected with the virus. You'd inject the patient, and it would target only the infected cells, destroying them, and moving on. Imagine the applications? HIV, malaria, hepatitis and more. All wiped out by a genetically targeted drug."

"Very impressive. Now how is it connected to New Orleans?"

Dr. Kapp shifted in his seat, exchanging a quick glance with Katherine, who gave him a reassuring smile, tilting her head slightly toward the President. His lips turned to mere lines as they pressed together tightly, then he finally let out the breath he apparently had been holding.

"Mr. President, Dr. Urban disappeared eighteen months ago, and hasn't been seen since." It seemed the entire room leaned toward the good doctor. "But we have heard from him. On three occasions."

Katherine reached into her briefcase, removing a sheaf of file folders containing supporting data for what was about to be said. She handed the first to the President, who handed it without looking to his Chief of Staff. She passed the rest to the person beside her to hand out. That happened to be the Secretary of Defense.

"The first time we heard from him was twelve months ago. He took credit for releasing the antiviral into a movie theatre in Los Angeles."

"Why haven't I heard of this before?" asked the President, sitting up and looking around the room.

"Because, sir, we didn't know about it until a few hours ago," answered Katherine. "I've got our people looking into it right now, but it will take time."

"Why?"

"The bodies will need to be exhumed, that's assuming they weren't cremated."

"How many?" asked the President, his voice subdued.

"In this first incident, he targeted those with red hair. Genetic redheads obviously, not bottled. Since this is less than five percent of the American population, and it was a small theatre, only three died."

"*Only* three."

Kapp dipped his head in acknowledgement. "I understand, sir. Three too many."

"And why did you keep this quiet?" asked the Secretary of Defense sitting beside her.

Kapp turned to face him. "He demanded one million dollars and promised he would do nothing for six months, but if we were to notify the authorities, he would unleash a massive, broad attack on a major city. The board felt we had to go along with his demands."

"Just a second," interrupted the Secretary of Defense. "I thought you injected this antiviral. How did he infect an entire theatre?"

"That's what we asked, and the only way we can figure he could is that he has aerosolized it somehow. His threat certainly implied this."

"So he can spray this thing anywhere he wants?"

Kapp nodded.

"You people are insane!" exclaimed the Chairman. "Didn't you think of the harm this thing could do?"

"Of course we did, sir, which is why we designed it as an injectable, and gave it a very short half-life of less than a day. This way it was non-transmittable except by blood, and if used in a controlled way, should be perfectly safe. And besides, it was genetically targeted so it would only affect those who possessed the gene it was designed to destroy."

The Chairman was about to say something when Katherine interrupted.

"Let me just say one thing. At this juncture time is of the essence. Dr. Kapp has come forward at the behest of BioDyne Pharma to help us, and has assured me that their entire company is at our disposal to help stop this. After we have, and after we have Dr. Urban in custody, I'm certain there will be plenty of time for the blame game. For now I suggest we limit ourselves to the facts, and what we're going to do about the current situation."

The President saved the Chairman from having to respond.

"You said that was the first time. Tell us about the second."

Kapp returned his attention to the Commander in Chief.

"Sir, six months after the first incident we were contacted by Dr. Urban."

"How?" asked a man standing in the back of the room. If the Oval Office had a dark corner, he seemed to have found it. Katherine recognized the man from somewhere, but didn't know who he was.

"Sir?" asked Kapp.

"How has he been communicating with you?"

"Secure email. We've been trying to trace him, but we've never had much success. Anytime our people get there, he's long gone."

"You'll provide us with all of this data."

It was a statement, but Kapp apparently decided to deal with it as a question.

"Of course." He turned back to the President. "This time he wanted ten million dollars, and informed us the outbreak was at LaGuardia Airport, and that he had targeted a rare genetic disorder called Marfan Syndrome. It affects about one in ten to twenty thousand births. We were able to find a handful of people around the world who had been at LaGuardia that day, who had the disorder, and died. But there was something else."

"What?" asked the President, again leaning forward.

"One of those who died, who had the disorder, had never been in LaGuardia, but died with the same symptoms as did the others, within ten days of the infection."

"And your theory?"

"Our theory is that in aerosolizing the antiviral, Dr. Urban has unintentionally allowed it to mutate. It can now transmit beyond the initial host. At least that's our theory."

"What do you need to prove your theory?"

"A sample of the altered antiviral. We've never seen it, we've only seen its affects."

Katherine leaned forward.

"Now that we know about this, we've got teams heading for LaGuardia and the theatre now, but we're not hopeful. This latest outbreak however we've narrowed down to the Superdome. We're searching it now to see if we can find out how he infected those in attendance."

"This latest outbreak, what's different?"

"The disorder he targeted is far more common than the second attack. The first attack we theorize the antiviral hadn't mutated. We're assuming he continued to work on it after this first outbreak and the mutation took place in the LaGuardia attack with a genetic sequence that only targeted a very rare subset of people. Those carrying it would have to transmit it somehow within a day before it would be dormant. Right now we don't know how it is retransmitted. We should hopefully know more in a couple of days."

Kapp cleared his throat. "Our theory is that the mutation only occurs in those who have the targeted gene. This narrows down the transmission pool considerably, making the transmission in the second attack a near fluke, it turning out that one of the LaGuardia victims was a friend of someone else with the disorder, and she infected him. He died at nearly the same time, because he picked her up at the airport. Once those with the virus *and* the gene it was targeting died, the virus flamed out, the other carriers who didn't have the gene merely ridding their bodies of the antiviral, the bulk of it after a day."

"And in this latest case?"

"Dr. Urban contacted us, wanted one hundred million this time—"

"Increasing tenfold each time," muttered the JCDS.

"—and we've already paid it."

"And the same six month reprieve?"

"Yes. Along with the data on what the antiviral is targeting this time."

The President leaned back in his chair, rubbing his chin.

"It sounds to me like we have six months to catch a madman before he unleashes something even worse than what we have now."

"Agreed," said Katherine. "However we have an immediate problem now."

"I realize that, however you have it contained, do you not?"

Katherine shook her head. "Not in any way, sir."

"Explain."

"Sir, almost seventy-five thousand people were at the Saints game. That's ticket holders, press, staff and athletes. According to Dr. Urban's communique, this particular antiviral is targeting women who carry the breast cancer gene—"

"Like Angelina?" piped in the Secretary of Defense.

"Yes, exactly like her," replied Katherine. "This affects less than one percent of all women, however if it were to continue to spread, unchecked, we are looking at potentially one in every two hundred women on the planet dying over the next six months. And as long as the antiviral is out there, it has more chances to mutate into something worse."

"But you said this is only transmittable by someone who has the gene *and* the antiviral."

Katherine nodded. "That's what BioDyne thought after the LaGuardia attack. But things may have changed."

"*May?*"

"We have had two cases arrive with all the symptoms just a few hours ago, but who have had no known exposure to anyone involved."

"Couldn't they have been exposed on a bus or in a mall?"

"Yes, sir. But these two people were on a fishing trip for a week in the middle of nowhere. They didn't return until the day of the game. They presented twenty four hours after the first of our patients began arriving. This means they were exposed most likely within one day of the initial release of the antiviral."

"So there was time."

"Yes, sir, there was. The only problem is this: one of them swears he was dropped off at home by his buddy, who is also infected, and saw no one since except his friend for the next three days."

"How's that possible?"

"He's some sort of Internet worker. Works from home, and has minimal contact with the outside world. The only person that visited him was his buddy, who returned a few hours later to drop off something left in the trunk. Then nothing for two days."

"Then he picked up the virus later," said the Secretary of Defense.

"If it was later, he wouldn't be presenting now. He'd be presenting several days from now." Katherine shook her head. "No, this man was infected within hours of his friend. Their arrival in New Orleans was just before the game ended, and they claimed they made no stops for the last few hours of travel. That means the most likely explanation is his friend, who visited a restaurant after the game was over, then visited him on the way home to drop off a bag, was exposed at the restaurant, then unintentionally infected him."

"And I'm assuming this first man does not have the gene?"

Katherine shook his head. "Dr. Urban says it is targeting *women* with the gene, not men with the gene. We're confirming it now, and should know shortly."

"And if it comes back negative?"

"Then we have person to person transmission, without blood, and without the targeted gene." Katherine looked around the room, then back at the President. "It means that we may have already lost control of this."

Katherine could have sworn the President aged in front of her eyes.

"God help us all," he muttered. "What do you recommend?"

"The full quarantine of New Orleans to start, and if this continues to spread, a full shutdown of all air, land and sea travel."

"That's madness!" exclaimed the Secretary of State. "You'll destroy the nation's economy. We're talking about a flu outbreak here that can target only one in two hundred women!"

"No, sir, we are not. We are talking about an antiviral that kills one hundred percent of its victims, and we have two people, who we presume do not have the targeted gene, sick, transmitted presumably through the air. This is a worst case scenario we are looking at here. If this thing has mutated to target anything it comes in contact with, and it is airborne, and it maintains its mortality rate, we are looking at an extinction level event here."

The room fell silent, no one knowing what to say to her sobering words. Finally the President rose, causing everyone else to follow suit.

"I hear a lot of *if*'s in your scenario. What we do know for now seems to merit a quarantine of New Orleans. I'll grant you that. As well, I want any and all assets of this country devoted to tracking down Dr. Urban. Our goals are twofold. One, to prevent the spread of the current virus, and two, to prevent the release of the next virus in six months. I will let you know my decision shortly." He turned to Katherine and Dr. Kapp. "Thank you both for coming in." He turned toward his desk and the meeting broke, everyone shuffling out the door. As Katherine was about to leave, she felt a hand on her shoulder. She turned to look, and it was the man who had been lurking in "the corner".

"Come with me, would you?"

The way he said it wasn't a request, and it sent a shiver down her spine. She looked back at the President, who was pulling at his graying hair, his face another ten years older.

White House, Washington, DC

Leif Morrison examined the surroundings out of habit as Dr. Katherine Best climbed into his limousine. He joined her inside and the chauffeur closed the door, moments later climbing in the front. Morrison pressed the button for the intercom.

"Take us around the block, Jerry."

"Yes, sir."

The car slowly began to move, and Morrison turned to his passenger.

"Do you know who I am?"

She shook her head. "You look familiar, but I'm sorry, I don't know."

"I'm Leif Morrison, National Clandestine Services Chief, CIA."

"CIA?"

He nodded and smiled, trying to impair the natural instinct she must be fighting to become incommunicado.

"What do you want with me?"

He chuckled.

"Nothing with you, don't worry. I find that when outsiders give briefings to the President, they don't always say everything they want to say, because they're too afraid of what he may do, and if they're wrong, they'll wear it."

Dr. Best remained silent, but at least looked him in the eye.

"What I want to know from you, is how close are we to this doomsday scenario?"

Her lips pursed and she looked away.

"Nothing you say will go beyond this car. I just need to know what level of threat I'm dealing with."

She looked back at him and sighed.

"Sir, if the latest information concerning the two men I mentioned is accurate, and they don't have the gene, we could be looking at a worldwide pandemic that could kill billions."

"If not everyone?"

"There's always a small segment of the population that is immune, so one percent might survive. The question is whether or not the virus continues to mutate. If it does, even those who survive the initial wave could be taken by the second or third. Those that survive would have to isolate themselves completely until they could be assured the virus had run its course. And unfortunately we don't know whether the mutated virus could be carried by animals or lay dormant in our soil." She shook her head. "Sir, that's the worst case scenario. How close are we to that? Too close as far as I'm concerned."

Morrison frowned.

"That was my assessment of what you and Dr. Kapp presented." He shifted in his seat, presenting his front to her. "What is your impression of Kapp?"

"Seems genuine. Straight shooter. He came to me, told me everything he knew, answered all my questions."

"You assume he told you everything."

She dipped her head.

"Granted." She turned to face him. "Why don't you ask him yourself?"

He smiled.

"Oh, we will."

His phone vibrated in his pocket and a moment later so did his guest's. He pulled out his phone and looked at the message.

New Orleans quarantine approved.

Hotel Tambor, Tambor Bay, Costa Rica

Special Agent Dylan Kane groaned with pleasure as he lay on the private beach, the breeze steady but gentle off the ocean cooling his skin, the flapping of the cloth umbrella jammed into the pristine sand providing protection from the oils being massaged into his skin.

Massaged by two of the loveliest pairs of hands he had yet to encounter.

Catalina and Jazmin may not have been masseuses by trade, but they were experts at providing pleasure, and right now he was in heaven, their tiny hands working opposite ends of his body as he relaxed on his beach towel, drifting in and out of sleep.

His mind began to slip and memories of last night with Jazmin, and the night before with Catalina, brought a smile to his face. They were local girls, beautiful, looking for fun with a rich tourist and perhaps a bobble or two they could pawn to help their families after he had departed. There was no money exchanged here, just good times.

Very good times.

He felt Little Dylan stir, and the more he tried to not concentrate on it, the more it became a problem.

I hope they don't ask me to turn over.

His watch suddenly gave him a slight electrical shock indicating he had an urgent message. The shock method was far more discrete than a visual, auditory or vibrating signal. Only he knew it happened, it was strong enough to get your attention, even when asleep, and would be noticed by no one. And if the watch had been removed for some reason, the signal was only sent if it was on an arm, and the owner of that arm would have had to enter a coded sequence after fastening the clasp to activate the messaging system, so even if stolen or confiscated, no messages would come through.

But now one had.

I'm on vacation!

After finishing up in Syria then Egypt, he had taken a break, his old archeology professor, James Acton, actually seeing him at the airport in Cairo just before catching the first of several flights that would take him where he was now.

Costa Rica.

Professor Acton had almost blown it, jumping from his seat, then realizing he couldn't be seen talking to his old student, he had dropped back down without blowing Kane's cover, and he hoped next time Acton would do better, if there ever was a next time.

But here, in Costa Rica, a place he absolutely loved for its near perfect weather, amazing beaches and stunning women, nobody knew him except the staff at the hotel, and a few locals he'd befriended over the years.

The worst part of being a spy—okay, perhaps not *the* worst—is running into someone from your past who has no idea what you do. A high school sweetheart, an old army buddy, a friend of your mother's. Hell, even your mother! The last thing you wanted was to be on an op and have someone call out, "Hey, Dylan, it's me Jim!" when you're tailing someone.

Which was why they trained you to ignore your name being called so you didn't react, and if you were pursued and confronted, you would answer them in a foreign language if you could, looking confused and moving on.

But the best way was to just have a different hair style.

In high school he had kept his hair short for football, ditto for college. When he left college to join the army and fight terrorism he was nearly shaved bald. Now he had a healthy mane that he had never sported in his previous life. His friends now were few, and his family didn't travel, so the risk of being spotted and recognized were slim.

It was a lonely life, but a life he loved.

When he had been recruited out of the Delta Force and into the Special Operations Group of the CIA it had been one of the most exciting and thrilling days of his life.

Then he had gone through the training.

If he had thought Delta was tough, he didn't after. CIA training was completely solo. You weren't trained to work with others, you were trained to work alone. Sure some ops had him working with others, hell, a few weeks ago he had worked with some of his old Delta buddies, but more often than not he was holed up somewhere uncomfortable and lonely.

Lucky for him he was a loner. Always had been. Though popular in high school, his best times were in his room, alone, playing his video games, watching movies, reading. He was rarely on the phone, rarely went out during the week, and used the excuse his folks were strict. His mother had always been encouraging him to go out, so as a compromise he had hooked up with Chris Leroux, a younger, geekier schoolmate who was waaay smarter than him. Leroux would tutor him for hours, and they had formed a bond that had lasted into adulthood, Leroux independently pursuing a similar career—CIA research analyst.

"I've gotta get up, ladies," he said, pushing himself to his feet. There were giggles as the bulge in his shorts was prominently revealed. He winked at them as he adjusted himself. "How about we take care of that in about ten minutes?"

More giggles.

And nods.

He went to his cabin on the beach and entered the coded sequence into his watch, the message scrolling by raising his eyebrows.

You've been activated. Standby for orders.

He logged into his laptop and connected to Langley via satellite, but no orders had arrived yet. There was a tap at the door and he smiled as Catalina and Jazmin stepped inside, peeling off their bikinis.

He was still covered head to toe in oil, and as the two willing partners smeared themselves against him, he felt Dylan Jr. cast an eye on the situation, as its master hoped those impending orders would take their sweet time in arriving.

CIA Headquarters, Langley, Virginia

National Clandestine Service Chief for the CIA, Leif Morrison, sat at his desk, scanning the highlights of the intel as it was gleaned from the material provided by Dr. Kapp and BioDyne. The best analysts in the world at every agency at the US government's disposal were poring over the data in a race to be first to find the madman behind these attacks.

Why would someone do this? What possible motivation?

According to the medical files Dr. Urban was healthy, by all accounts happily married with two kids, and rich from stock options. His IQ was through the roof, and he was considered eccentric to a point, suffering from a little Obsessive Compulsive Disorder, but that meant he flicked a light switch a few too many times, not killed people for kicks.

Morrison's gut was telling him something else was going on here. Something more than a megalomaniac after money.

But what, he didn't know.

He had agents spread across the world being notified to stand by for orders, but at this point he had none to give them. A dossier was being assembled rapidly with their preliminary information, and it would be transmitted throughout the world to their operators, who would then use their own contacts in the underworld to try and find the man who might just end mankind's reign on Earth.

He looked at the picture of his wife Cheryl on the corner of his desk. She was smiling—laughing actually—her arms spread out across the railing of a friend's yacht, by all appearances having the time of her life. But she was three month's into chemo at that point, good days mixed with bad days.

And that was a good day.

She had pulled through, and the doctors said she was cancer free after five years of follow-ups.

For now.

He remembered how she had been so embarrassed by her body after the double-mastectomy, and how he had tried to assure her it was okay, that he still found her attractive. When the implants had been done, she felt better about herself and she had even upped the ante so to speak to his surprise.

He picked up the phone, speed dialing her number.

It rang several times then she picked up, out of breath.

"Hi, darling, sorry, I was in the shower."

"Hi, hon, sorry for interrupting, but I need you to do something for me."

"What's that?"

"Pack a bag and go to the cottage."

"Why?"

"Just pack for two weeks. When you get into town, buy as much food as you can fit in the trunk, gas it up, then go to the cottage. Don't tell anyone where you're going. Just get there, then call me."

"You're scaring me."

"I'm sorry, hon, but I need you to do this for me."

"Why?"

"Once you're in the car, turn the radio on, and you'll know why. Call the kids and get them to join you there."

"But—"

"Just do it, honey! I've got to go. I love you."

He hung up before she could ask any further questions. He knew what he had just done was wrong, against every principle he had been taught, but he didn't care. If this virus got out, he wanted his family safe. He realized that everyone should have the same opportunity, but he knew damned well it wasn't practical. Not everyone had a cottage, and not everyone had some place to go.

And if everyone was told the same thing, there'd be mass panic.

The chaos about to happen in New Orleans would cause panic enough.

Superdome, New Orleans, Louisiana

Sergeant Greg Michael stood facing two dozen young officers, the massive Superdome behind him. To his left and right were hundreds of additional officers, all getting briefed. It reminded him of Hurricane Katrina, though this time the tension seemed even higher. They all knew there was some sort of deadly virus outbreak but as it stood right now, only women seemed to need to worry.

But despite that, every female officer had reported for duty.

"We're searching this building from top to bottom. We're not sure what we're looking for, except that it should be something that can spray a gas into the air. Our job will be to escort these HVAC guys"—he jerked a thumb over his shoulder at a group of heating, ventilation, and air conditioning specialists—"to wherever they need to go. Two of us per team. If they find anything, secure the area and report back." He pointed into his group at the greenest rookie of them all, Jackie Macleod. "Macleod, you're with me." He clapped his hands together. "Let's go people. The sooner we find what we're looking for, the sooner we can stop this outbreak."

The group broke up immediately into their traditional pairings and joined the dozen pairs of specialists. Sergeant Michael stepped up to one of the pairs. "I'm Sergeant Michael. This"—he motioned over his shoulder at the approaching Macleod—"is Officer Macleod. You lead, we'll follow."

The elder of the two men stepped forward, extending his hand. "Good to meet you. I'm Neil, this is Lee," he said, motioning at his younger partner.

Michael waved off the handshake. "We've got a virus going around, so let's minimize physical contact, okay?" He noted Lee's and Macleod's hands dart away from each other moments before connecting. He raised his voice to those still within earshot. "That goes for everyone! Minimize physical contact! We don't know how this thing is spread, and those with a set of swingers don't get cocky, you may just bring it home and infect your wife, daughter or mother."

He made a show of removing a pair of latex gloves and snapping them on, prompting the rest to do the same. He motioned for Neil and Lee to lead the way. "After you, gentlemen."

Neil nodded, eyeing the gloves and looking slightly uncomfortable. Michael smiled and pulled another pair from his belt. "Like a pair?"

Neil smiled, taking them and snapping them on as Macleod offered a pair to Lee. The two men took a few moments to get the gloves on, it taking a practiced hand to do it efficiently. Finally gloved, they made their way into the massive structure, the men obviously having been here before as they navigated the maintenance tunnels with confidence.

"What the hell?"

It was the older specialist Neil who first came to a halt. Sergeant Michael rounded the duo and his eyebrows shot up in surprise. Police tape crisscrossed the door along with a seal across the lock warning anyone who broke it that they may be subject to arrest.

Michael held his mike to his mouth.

"This is ten-william-fifteen, we've got a crime scene marked off at our location. Request permission to breach the seal, over."

"Roger that, ten-william-fifteen, hold for instructions, over."

"What do you think happened here, Sergeant?"

Michael looked at Macleod and shrugged his shoulders. "Maybe it's related to the power failure during the game?"

"I thought they traced that to be something outside. A transformer or something? Like at the Super Bowl."

"Then you know more than me."

"Could be the murder?"

"Huh?" echoed Michael and Macleod.

Lee looked at them. "You mean you didn't hear about the murder?"

Michael shook his head. "No, spill."

"Yeah, they found a security guard shot to death a few days after the game. It was one of our guys who actually found him, stuffed behind an air exchanger."

Michael looked at the door, the bright yellow tape a stark contrast to the black painted door.

"Could be—"

His radio interrupted him.

"Ten-william-fifteen, you're a go for breach. Homicide Detective assigned to the case is on route to your position, over."

Homicide? Then it must be the murder.

"Roger that dispatch, breaching now. Over and out."

He clipped his mike to his vest and nodded for Officer Macleod to cut the seal. She stepped forward, tore the tape down, sliced the seal along the door frame, then ripped the portion covering the keyhole away. She stepped back and Neil was about to step forward with the key when Michael held out his hand.

"Better let me."

He took the key, pushed it into the lock and turned. There was a click and he turned the knob, pushing the door open.

The stench was overwhelming.

"My God! Haven't they cleaned this crime scene yet?"

They all stepped back, the smell overwhelming as three days of human decay, followed by a week of confinement oozed out the door and into the corridor. Neil and Lee put on facemasks from their kits, offering a pair to Michael and Macleod, all continuing to wait for the air to clear a bit. Michael stepped inside, looking for something to prop the door open with. Finding nothing, he reached up and unscrewed the bolt to the pneumatic door closer. He swung the door all the way open, and it stayed. He and Macleod then advanced into the cramped utility room, making certain it was clear, then stepped back out.

Michael's eyes were watering from the stench as he stepped back into the corridor, Macleod looking a little gray at his side.

"All yours gentlemen," said Michael through his mask, motioning them inside with an outstretched arm.

Neil stepped inside, his younger partner, Lee, hesitating then finally following. Michael chuckled as he heard Lee gag, then the thought of the kid yacking caused his own stomach to flip and he stepped farther from the door.

A quick glance at Macleod and he was surprised to see she seemed unaffected.

"This doesn't bother you?"

"Four baby brothers. I've been changing diapers for most of my life. Some of the stuff that came out of those little bastards would make grown men weep. Out here it's not too bad." She nodded toward the two men inside the cramped room. "Those guys I feel sorry for. That's like putting your head in the diaper."

Michael chuckled, finding the conversation was distracting him from the thick air.

"Found something!" called Neil. Michael looked to see him beckoning them inside.

Christ, it had to be us.

He stepped inside and saw Neil pointing at a canister sitting on the floor behind the exchanger, a long black hose attaching it to a series of other hoses. It all meant nothing to him, but from the looks of the shiny new fitting on the hose, he would guess it was a recent addition.

"What is it?"

"Somebody's added something to the ventilation. This canister is cranked fully open," said Neil, pointing at the unmarked canister. "This hose feeds it directly into the system, so when the system fires up, it pumps it into the air exchanger, and throughout the building, or at least throughout the area that this unit services."

"Which is?"

"Pretty much half the complex."

Lee reached forward with a wrench, quickly fitting it over the collar holding the hose in place when everyone shouted, "No!"

The young man froze. "What?"

"What the hell are you doing?" asked Michael.

"Removing it so you can have your guys examine it."

"Gently remove the wrench," said the more experienced Neil, reaching out to steady the now shaking hands of the young man. "We don't want to mess with their evidence now, do we?"

Lee shook his head, removing the wrench, and pocketing it. He stepped back, a little paler than when he arrived.

Michael breathed a sigh of relief. He, probably like the others with the obvious exception of Lee, was pretty sure the canister was empty and no longer a danger, but there was no point in risking it. This was the CDC's job now.

"Everybody out," ordered Michael. Macleod exited first, followed by Neil and Lee. Michael exited and closed the door tight, grabbing his mike.

"Dispatch, this is ten-william-fifteen. I think we found what you're looking for, over."

Michael gripped the mask over his face a little tighter, wondering what the hell he had just gotten himself into, and if it was related to the homicide that had obviously taken place here.

Leroux Residence, Fairfax Towers, Falls Church, Virginia

Chris Leroux stretched, one leg extending out, the opposite arm reaching over his head, and with a groan, he reversed the stretch, his head turning to the other side, a smile of contentment smeared across his face that quickly disappeared when he saw the empty bed beside him.

He immediately awoke, pushing himself up on his elbows.

"Honey?"

There was no answer, but the sound of the shower running quickly put that question to rest. The shower shut off, and Sherrie's happy humming became audible and Chris frowned.

She's only that happy right after we've shivered the timbers, or when she's going out on an op.

Chris swung himself out of bed, knowing full well which one it was, and grabbed his phone, suddenly remembering that was what had awoken him.

Report to office immediately.

"Argh!" This was supposed to be a day off for both of them. A lazy day in bed, a nice afternoon playing tourist, a quiet romantic dinner, a movie on the couch with some ice cream and hot raspberry sauce, and a whole lotta lovin'.

But instead, all they'd get now is a few extra hours sleep.

He stood up, pulled down then kicked off his boxers, and opened the door to the bathroom. Steam rolled out into the bedroom and he smiled at the spectacular love of his life that stood in front of the fogged up mirror, humming while drying her hair. He stepped up behind her and reached around, cupping her breasts. She yelped then smiled, leaning into him and give her bum a wiggle to get things stirring, but he was way ahead of her. He gently kissed her shoulder.

"Going somewhere?" he asked.

She moaned, turning around and embracing him, her naked body pressed against his, as he pulled her in tightly, the grinding sending Little Chris into a frenzy.

She pushed him away.

"Sorry, Dear, but I've got to report in for an op."

Chris groaned, looking down at his wagging member then at the object of his desire as she left the bathroom. He waddled out after her, wagging his pride back and forth like a dog's tail. "Aww, hon!"

Sherrie looked and burst out laughing at the sight.

"Put that thing away, we've got to get to work."

Chris looked down then back at Sherrie, a pout on his face.

Sherrie looked at him then let out a burst of false exasperation.

"Fine, a quickie. And I do mean quick!" She marched over to him and shoved him backward, onto the bed. Straddling him, she dropped down, mashing her breasts against his bare chest, her mouth at his ear, whispering words that made his heart skip a beat, the shy man he was only months before now full of confidence, thanks to a woman out of his league, that had given him a chance. "You're lucky I find you so irresistible," she whispered, her breath hot against his neck. I can never say no to you."

He flipped her over, kissing her hard as she wrapped her legs around his waist, pulling him inside. She pulled his hair, separating their lips.

"Remember, I said quick."

Chris smiled, and proceeded to follow his orders.

I-10 Northbound, New Orleans Louisiana

Kyle Patrick rolled the window of his Ford F-150 down and leaned out the window, looking up while trying to keep one eye on the road. Dozens of helicopters, scratch that, hundreds, all military, flew by overhead, the sky full. He heard a horn honk and he looked ahead then slammed on his brakes as the traffic had come to a halt.

What the hell is going on?

He turned the radio on, and his jaw dropped.

"—complete quarantine. I repeat, authorities have informed us that the President has ordered a complete quarantine of New Orleans due to the recent virus outbreak that began yesterday. All air traffic has been halted. No civilian air traffic will be permitted to enter or leave airspace surrounding the city, and shockingly, we have just discovered that the Air Force is operating under shoot-down orders. Any air traffic disobeying the quarantine will be shot down."

"My God!"

Kyle couldn't believe his ears. The shutdown extended to rail and shipping, and as traffic began to move again, slowly, the reporter described the shutdown of all roads leading into and out of the city. As the traffic inched forward he saw several National Guard vehicles ahead, camouflaged men with automatic weapons directing the traffic down the off ramp and back into the city.

And they were all wearing what looked to him like hazmat suits.

Jesus, this is serious!

He felt his chest tighten as his heart began to pound. His hands shook as he reached for the dial to turn up the volume, real palpable fear gripping him as he listened to the report, wondering what he should do next, for now his movements dictated by the soldiers manning the blockade.

"—*CDC spokesperson Anthony Wade said the situation was serious, but there was no need to panic. The CDC advises all residents remain in their homes and not attempt to leave the city. Should anyone display flu like symptoms, it is essential that you call 9-1-1. Do not leave your home. If someone has symptoms in your home, isolate them, call 9-1-1, and an ambulance will pick them up. At this time it is not known how the disease is transmitted, however good hygiene and isolation is the best way we know how to prevent the spread. Wash your hands, wash down all surfaces with a mild bleach solution, and minimize contact with your neighbors. The next update from the CDC—*"

Kyle blindly followed the car in front of him, debating where to go. He could go back to his apartment. At least there he'd be alone. But did he really want to be alone? He could go to his folks place, but what if he were infected? He could infect them. If they were to die because of him, he'd never forgive himself.

His phone rang. It took several rings for him to realize what was happening. He grabbed it and took the call.

"Hello?"

"Kyle, it's Mom. Are you okay?"

"Yeah, I-I'm fine. Christ, Mom, have you heard the news?"

"Yes. I want you to come here right away."

"Really? What if I'm infected?"

"Then we get sick together. Come home. Your father and I have lots of food and water here unlike your empty fridge. We'll ride this thing out together, as a family."

Kyle's shoulders sank in relief, the decision made for him.

"I'm on my way," he choked out, ending the call as he was turned back onto the freeway, heading back the way he had just come.

God, please help us!

En route to CIA Headquarters, Langley, Virginia

Chris Leroux couldn't believe what he had just heard, even turning up the radio and switching to several different stations. Every station that had a human being at the other end seemed to be talking about nothing but. Even the music stations were dedicating songs to the people of New Orleans, their DJs giving sound bites in between tracks. There was no escaping the story, and he had no doubt it was why they were being called into work.

"What do you think is going on?" asked Sherrie, sitting in the passenger seat, leaning forward as she looked in the side mirror, probably checking to make sure their escort was in tow. They had been assigned an escort since the incident several months ago with The Assembly, a secret organization that seemed to have its fingers into the worlds' finances and governments to a degree so terrifying it kept Chris up at night sometimes. The team of four now watched Leroux's back as he was now tasked to investigate the organization. Sherrie was an active operator so wasn't their responsibility. In fact, Leroux knew the agency probably considered her additional security for him since that was her original assignment until they had developed feelings for each other.

He stole a quick glance at her and smiled at the memories from this morning, then frowned at another report about people trying to escape the quarantine zone.

"I think we're being called in because of this, and since this is domestic, and we're technically foreign, I'm guessing this isn't some natural occurrence."

"Terrorism?"

He shrugged as he turned.

"Could be. We'll probably be briefed as soon as we get in."

Sherrie looked at him, her hand squeezing his thigh. "I'm scared."

"Me too. For them to quarantine a city…" His voice trailed off as he shook his head. "I just can't believe it. It's like something out of a horror movie."

"You don't think—" Sherrie cut herself off. "Forget it."

"What, that it's zombies?"

She smacked his shoulder and laughed. "No! That's not what I was going to say!"

Leroux rubbed his shoulder. "Ow! Don't forget you're a trained agent, licensed to kill, hands are a registered weapon, and all that stuff."

"Ohhh, I'm sorry, baby!" she cooed as she leaned over and kissed where she had hit. "Is that better?"

"Yes. And you *were* thinking zombies."

This time he was ready and when the blow came he jerked toward the window, avoiding it. She shook her head, trying to hide her smile.

"Next week let's go see something nice and tame instead of World War Z, okay?"

She laughed, then pointed ahead. "Slow down. That light's going to change before our escort can reach it."

Leroux lifted his foot slightly off the gas as the flashing red crossing signal turned solid, and the traffic light went amber then red. He was still getting used to essentially driving in a convoy, but with Sherrie along, she always seemed to know when he was forgetting.

"I wonder if you're going out of country again."

Sherrie put her arm over his shoulders, massaging his neck. "No idea. If this is related to New Orleans, and it's terrorist related, then probably. Hopefully not too long."

"It'll take as long as it takes. Don't worry, I'm used to being alone."

She squeezed a little tighter and extended her fingers up the back of his head, gently massaging his scalp. "I'll miss you."

"You better."

"Christ, will you look at that!"

They had exited the highway for the south-east entrance to CIA Headquarters when Leroux was forced to come to a stop far from the gate, a large lineup of vehicles waiting to clear security.

"They must have called *every*one in," commented Sherrie as they inched forward.

One of the guards was walking up the line of vehicles, checking ID, directing visitors to the visitor area, trying to speed things along so staff could get through quicker. As he approached, Leroux rolled his window down and presented both their IDs. The guard scanned both passes then handed them back.

"Please proceed up the left and directly inside, then report to your supervisor immediately."

Sherrie leaned toward the driver's side window.

"We have an escort vehicle behind us. They *will* be accompanying us."

"Understood." The man stepped back and waved Leroux into the left lane. He cranked the wheel and headed the wrong way down the road, their tail waved by after them, and stopped at what would normally be the exit gate. Again their IDs were checked as dogs sniffed the vehicle and men circled it with mirrors held on long poles, looking for bombs or other foreign devices. Leroux didn't bother mentioning that the escort did that several times a day regardless. The first time he had mentioned it had prompted an entire teardown of the vehicle.

Never again.

Finished, they were cleared and they rushed to the parking lot then inside, only to find another line up, this time people being sent through some sort of scanner manned by people in biohazard suits. When Leroux passed through, he looked back and realized it was an infrared scanner measuring their body temperatures. There was a trickle of people being turned around and sent for what he assumed was further testing.

He breathed a sigh of relief when Sherrie was cleared.

"See you soon," he said, giving her a kiss.

"Unless I'm tasked elsewhere." She winked. "Don't wait up."

Sherrie headed for the clandestine section of Langley, Leroux following her with his eyes, hoping for a look back. She was almost out of sight when she spun and blew him a kiss. A smile was permanently plastered on his face as he headed for the analysis section. When he arrived in his office area, the place was filled, day shifts and night shifts mingling, competing for desk space. Fortunately for Leroux, he was senior enough to merit his own dedicated terminal in his own open office cubicle.

The smile gone, he hung his jacket on a hanger then immediately headed for the Director's office. As he approached, Morrison's secretary smiled at him.

"Conference Room B. Briefing starts in five."

Leroux nodded and began to trot toward the room, joined by other late arrivals.

I guess there wasn't time for that nookie.

He crammed himself into the back of the room and the doors were closed as the Director stood at the front. The nearly one hundred senior analysts fell quiet instantly.

"Good afternoon everyone. I won't waste any time as there's none to waste. This morning the President authorized the complete quarantine of New Orleans, with shoot to kill orders if anyone attempts to break the quarantine. This is the largest quarantine in the history of our country, and potentially the greatest threat we have ever faced. Indeed, it may be the greatest threat mankind has ever faced."

Leroux gulped, exchanging glances with those around him.

Please don't let it be zombies.

"This is what we know." And for the next ten minutes the Director related how BioDyne had been covering up one of their researchers having gone nutbar, the attacks in LA and LaGuardia, and now the New Orleans Saints game, how the antiviral he had invented had been modified by this Dr. Urban, and how it had mutated, spreading beyond its original intended targets. Leroux's mind wandered for a moment when the antiviral was first explained.

Incredible!

It was revolutionary, world altering, and now, potentially world ending.

"Bottom line, people, is this thing has mutated, has a one hundred percent fatality rate, and just may be spreading through the general populace, depending upon when the mutation took place.

"But that's not *our* concern. CDC will track this thing, and try to stop the spread. Our job is to find this Dr. Urban, at all costs. We cannot let a fourth event occur, and to be honest, if we can't get containment, or find a cure, CDC's projections are that there might not be enough people left alive on the planet to care.

"This is it people, this is the end game. If we fail, it's all over. So we won't fail. The President has suspended all laws that have restricted us in the past. What that means for those in this room, is that you can look at anything, foreign or domestic. No wiretap authorization, no court orders, no nothing. You need something, you get it. You want something, you take it. Don't wait on anyone for permission, just do it. Your individual supervisors will have instructions as to your assignments.

"We are now working on alternating shifts. Eight hours on, eight hours off. Don't tell your loved ones, otherwise we could create even more panic than will already be happening beyond these doors. Call whoever you need to call to tell them you'll be working and sleeping here. Cover story is a major terrorist threat geared around taking advantage of our being distracted by the New Orleans situation." Morrison paused, staring out at the crowd, the next words from his mouth stressed with a tone Leroux had never heard from the Director.

"We are not working on New Orleans, clear? If the public thought we were, then the current cover of this being a naturally occurring, limited risk virus, would blow up in our faces. As it stands, we'll be lucky if that cover lasts for more than a day. Dismissed."

He immediately left the room, leaving everyone staring at each other, then someone yelled, "Let's get to work!", and the room emptied in a hurry, Leroux rushing for his desk, thanking God it wasn't zombies, but even more terrified of what they truly were dealing with, a madman with a virus that could be genetically targeted to kill any group of people. It was sickening, and he found his mind being consumed by the horror of it all as he dropped into his seat, not sure where to begin.

As he was logging in, his Blackberry vibrated with a secure message.

Report to Director Morrison's office immediately.

He jumped up, wondering what the Director wanted from him now. He had been exclusively tasked with pursuing The Assembly, and they were so well buried, he had had almost no success yet.

In fact, he had had none.

Arriving at Director Morrison's office, he was waved directly in, and found Morrison sitting at a side table in a comfortable leather chair, another occupied by a man Leroux didn't recognize. Leroux closed the door and sat in the chair pointed to by Morrison.

"This is Dr. Hermann Kapp from BioDyne Pharma," said Morrison, motioning toward the man occupying the other chair. Leroux leaned forward to shake the man's hand, who left them clasped across his stomach.

"You'll forgive me for not shaking hands. I think with this pandemic, we should all minimize personal contact."

Leroux nodded as he made a quick mental tally of all the people and things he had touched since yesterday.

His skin crawled.

"Mr. Leroux is one of our top analysts. He has a knack for tracking communications back to their source. I'm assigning him to try and find your Dr. Urban."

"Just Mr. Leroux?"

Kapp seemed surprised and disappointed.

Morrison chuckled.

"No, of course not. We've got teams being assigned right now, as do other agencies. I wanted you to meet Mr. Leroux however, as, like I said, he's one of our best, and has a habit of being able to take two apparently completely unrelated pieces of information and join them together, revealing new truths that ultimately lead to our target. You will each have the other's personal phone number. Chris, if you have a question, you call Dr. Kapp, day or night. Dr. Kapp, should you think there is something Chris should know that you've forgotten, you call him. Day or night. Time is of the essence."

"Of course, of course," agreed Kapp as he removed a card from his pocket, then thought better of it. "Cards can transmit germs. How about I text you my number?" Moments later the numbers were exchanged electronically, and Morrison turned to Leroux.

"Anything you want to ask to get started?"

Leroux nodded, his mind having been racing from the moment the briefing had begun.

"Does Dr. Urban have a family?"

Kapp nodded. "A wife and two daughters. By all accounts they were very close, but he appears to have left them behind."

Leroux nodded. "I'll start there. If they were close, then they're most likely communicating. I'll need everything you have on them, lists of employees going back to the time he joined the company, any friends you know of, where he travelled on company and personal business. Everything. The more you give me, the more chances I have of connecting the dots." He turned to Morrison. "I'd also suggest we have the FBI pick up his family for questioning."

Morrison smiled slightly.

"Already being taken care of. They should be here before the end of the day."

"Here?"

"They're in Canada. Mrs. Urban is Canadian. She apparently moved back after her husband disappeared."

"Are the Canadians cooperating?"

"I'm sure they would eventually, but we haven't told them of our interest. We have no time for bureaucracy getting in the way."

"Are there plans to inform foreign governments of what we know?" Leroux waved his hand. "Sorry, sir, I shouldn't have asked that."

Morrison bobbed his head in agreement.

"A little above your pay grade. Focus on your job. Find Urban. That bastard might have a cure for all we know."

"Yes, sir," said Leroux, standing up, clasping his hands behind his back as a reminder to avoid shaking hands. "Doctor, if you could have everything emailed to my account as soon as possible, I'll get to work."

Kapp nodded, his fingers flying on his Blackberry Q10 keyboard. "Everything has naturally already been compiled by our people as we tried to find him ourselves. It should be in your email within the next few minutes."

Leroux nodded, and left the room, excited about the new hunt he was about to begin.

And scared at the implications of failure.

Decontamination Zone, Interim LSU Public Hospital, New Orleans, Louisiana

Dr. Katherine Best stared at the reports as they rolled across the screen. The quarantine was quickly coming into place, but not quick enough for her liking. As soon as word had come out that the airports, railways and shipping were all being shutdown, some segments of the population had panicked as was expected. The freeways had jammed within the first hour, and an unknown number of residents had managed to escape before the roadblocks were in place.

Damn the press!

The shutdown had been a secret. They wanted the roadblocks in place, the quarantine complete, before they went public with the news, but instead, the local press had caught wind of massive cancellations at the airport, then somebody had leaked why, and then the cat was out of the bag, scurrying around the airwaves, destroying any hope of a complete quarantine.

The roads were now closed, traffic cameras being examined to identify the cars that had left the city over the past ten days in the desperate hope of tracking down all those who might be infected.

It was hopeless.

National Guard units from the surrounding states were deploying to block all traffic going into or coming out of Louisiana, but with there being so many roads, at best they might just stem the flow. Cordons were being set up to try and turn around traffic and all airports and trains were being shutdown throughout the state, the President ordering the expanded quarantine. Refugee camps were just starting to be set up for those trapped with nowhere to go and the conspiracy theory mill was going at full tilt.

Unfortunately this time it was more accurate than the crazies even knew.

"Dr. Best!"

She turned to see a beaming Dr. Johnston.

"What is it?"

"We found it?"

"What?"

"The canister used to infect the Superdome!"

Katherine smiled, this the first piece of good news she had had all day.

"When will it be here?"

"Chopper is on its way to pick it up right now."

"Where was it?"

"Apparently tied into the ventilation system. And there's something else."

"What?"

"There was a body discovered in the same room about a week ago. We might actually finally have a lead!"

Katherine nodded. A murder meant a murderer, and that murderer might very well be Dr. Urban himself.

"Do the police have any leads?"

"I'm checking now. Hopefully I'll have something for you soon."

She nodded, returning to the reports streaming in. The good news was that the flood of people at hospitals across the city were proving to be mostly false alarms. Possible new cases were a trickle an hour, and she was assured by Atlanta that they'd have a blood test before the end of the day to identify those truly infected thanks to the cooperation of BioDyne Pharma.

Thank God they came forward!

She'd hate to think where'd they'd be in this without them. Now at least they weren't working blind. They had scientists who could answer questions, who knew exactly what they were dealing with, and could speed up their regular processes dramatically.

It was hope.

Now all we need is a cure.

Outside the Superdome, New Orleans, Louisiana

Detective Isabelle Laprise pulled her car up to a throng of emergency personnel, flicking off the integrated emergency lights, their flashing blue proving to be not much of an advantage in the traffic chaos that was forming on the roads as the citizenry of the city discovered the quarantine, then decided to promptly get in their cars to test it.

Maybe tomorrow things will be better.

She could understand the panic, but what the hell was the point in leaving your house? The authorities were saying stay put, so stay put. Why would you want to risk spreading an infectious disease to the friends or family you were trying to escape the city to stay with?

A report on her car radio as she had pulled in had said the water supply was perfectly safe, and that door to door food delivery would be starting tomorrow. Part of her wondered how they could know the water supply was safe. It didn't matter. If they were all going to die a horrible death from some unknown disease, then so be it. She wasn't afraid to die, she had no husband or boyfriend, no kids she knew of, and no family to speak of, her parents dead when she was in college.

She did have her grandparents though, but they were old, and she knew her granddaddy would probably welcome death considering he had said as much at Thanksgiving.

"I can't wait ta die!" he had said. "I can't walk right no more, I can't sit right no more, I can't shit right no more. Why the *hell* would I wanna keep livin', with all these damned things wrong with me. I take twenty different pills, four times a day, just to keep me going, and the side effects half the time are worse than the damned thing they're supposed to treat! This ain't life, this is existin'!"

Her grandmother had tut-tutted him in a way that made Isabelle think this was an old rant, so decided to pay it no mind. But knowing her granddaddy, if he had the energy he'd be at the mall with his tongue glued to the top of the handrail of the escalator, just hoping he'd catch something that could kill him.

Too bad you don't have boobs, granddaddy.

From what she had heard, almost all the victims so far were women. Which meant she herself was probably at more risk than her aging grandfather.

I hope grandma will be okay.

She climbed out of the car as the thumping of a chopper overhead grabbed everyone's attention. Instead of watching the chopper however, she rushed to the entrance she had been told to report to when she saw a cylinder being wheeled out by a group of hazmat suits.

That's from my damned crime scene!

"Wait a minute!" she yelled, running toward them, her badge held high in the air. She was ignored at first until she finally was close enough for them to hear her. One looked at her and stopped the procession as the chopper landed a couple of hundred feet away, whipping the dust and litter of the massive stadium about until the blades finally slowed down. "Is that from my crime scene?" she demanded.

The one apparently in charge looked at her.

"This cylinder has been taken into the custody of the CDC under author—"

"I don't give a shit under what authority you've taken it. I damned well know that your authority trumps mine. I just want to know if anybody had the presence of mind to check for prints or any other trace evidence before pulling it out of there? A good young man died, and it's probably because of this."

"Ma'am—"

"Detective."

"Detective, we could be looking at billions dead." The man turned to the others. "Let's go."

Billions?

Isabelle stood there dumbfounded at the statement.

Was it really that bad?

She suddenly felt naked as she watched the group in hazmat suits rush to the chopper with their prize. Several of the others who were within earshot were exchanging the same shocked look she was probably displaying.

Billions?

"Excuse me, Detective?"

She turned toward the voice, snapping her shocked jaw shut.

"Yes?"

"Sergeant Greg Michael, Detective. There were some crime scene techs here. I saw them in the parking lot when we arrived. I guess it was sort of an all hands on deck type thing—"

"You're rambling, Sergeant."

The Sergeant's partner, a much younger female officer, stifled a grin.

"Sorry, Detective. Not every day you hear the world's ending."

Isabelle frowned.

Billions?

"Anyway, I had Officer Macleod here"—he jerked a thumb at the smile beside him—"go get them, and they checked out the cylinder before those CDC people got here. No fibers, no prints. I'm afraid it's a dead end." He held up his phone. "I did get photos of it before they took it out, and close ups of some numbers that were etched on the bottom. Probably from the factory."

"Good work, Sergeant," said Isabelle as the chopper powered up, halting the conversation, her mind already awhirl at the possibilities of this new piece of evidence. Obviously her murder was connected to this virus. They might be able to trace the cylinder back to whoever manufactured it, then eventually to whoever bought it. It was a long shot. She had no idea if these sort of things were actually traceable.

So far the case was pretty much a bust. She had an unauthorized person entering the room ten minutes before the power failure, pulling some sort of kit on a trolley, then the murdered guard about five minutes later, and then just after the power failure, one person left, again pulling the kit. It was too much of a coincidence, and her theory that the two were connected was laughed out of the Captain's office. There was no electrical in that room, it was heating and cooling only. And besides, less than a week later they had traced the problem to some damned vault nowhere near the room, the same problem that Entergy had claimed was fixed after the Super Bowl.

But it was just too damned big of a coincidence for her to buy that the two things weren't connected. And now with that room almost definitely linked to the virus, she was sure of it. The kit he was carrying on the dolly must have had the cylinder inside. The power failure was obviously some sort of diversion, either triggered remotely or by an accomplice.

If only I had the resources the Feds have!

"Look!"

The chopper had finally left, and she saw Officer Macleod pointing up at the sky. Isabelle turned to look and gasped.

What the hell?

Five thousand feet over the Superdome, New Orleans, Louisiana

Special Agent Dylan Kane gripped the netting at the rear of the C-130J "Super" Hercules aircraft as the rear ramp descended, the air whipping about the cabin. The pilot had offered to land at Louis Armstrong airport, but there was no time. Kane had been sent instructions within thirty minutes of being activated—thirty fantastic minutes. He had hightailed it to the airport, chartered a jet on the Company credit card, landed at Naval Air Station Joint Reserve Base New Orleans, then onto this Herc, all within eight hours.

Uncle Sam spares no expense when needed.

When he had left all he knew was he was needed in country. During the flight he had received the briefing notes on what was going on, and it had shocked him. His first instinct was to call his parents and tell them to get supplies and button up the house, but that would have been illegal, and unfair.

And hopefully unnecessary.

But as word of the containment failure reached him, he began to regret his earlier decision to not reach out. It wasn't until he was on the ground at the Naval Air Station that he had received his final orders. The source of the virus had been found and he was to go into New Orleans itself to try and trace the origin of that canister.

At all costs.

There was a private communique from the National Clandestine Services Chief himself, Director Morrison, attached to the file.

Consider yourself unleashed.

His heart had skipped a beat at that. It was essentially code telling him that there were no rules. Any and all laws could be violated in carrying out his mission, including breaking and entering, assault, torture, even murder. Whatever it took.

And that was when he realized how serious the situation truly was.

They're scared. Damned scared.

He stepped off the back of the ramp, hurtling through the air, his eyes quickly scanning the ground below. It only took a few moments to find the massive Superdome below him, and he aimed himself for the impressive structure while monitoring his altitude. At two thousand feet he pulled his cord, opening the chute above him, then gently coasted the rest of the way, looking for a good spot to land.

That'll do.

A chopper had just taken off, leaving a clear area close to the building. Minutes later he was on the ground, hauling in his chute as dozens of police rushed him, their weapons drawn. His chute secure from dragging him away, he turned to the gathered throng.

"Is there a Detective Isabelle Laprise here?"

Sherbrooke, Québec, Canada

Agent Sherrie White sat parked in her black SUV, Québec plates, waiting for her targets to arrive home. A private plane had brought her from Langley to Montreal, Québec, Canada and her fake Canadian passport had her through customs in minutes. Her SUV had been prepositioned for her, and now she waited for Dr. Urban's family to arrive home, it already confirmed they had left the school seven minutes ago.

This would be one of her more difficult assignments. She was a relatively junior agent. This was her first assignment out of country, and even though it was only Canada, hardly a country filled with people who wanted to kill American spies, it was still exciting. The clandestine feeling of sneaking across a border with false ID was exhilarating, but she had prepared herself for this particular assignment to be difficult.

After all, she was picking up a woman and her two kids, and taking them across the border back to the United States. If they were willing to cooperate, and they had passports, she'd simply drive them all across the border and she'd be done with it.

But if they didn't have passports, she'd have to smuggle them across, and that most likely meant they wouldn't cooperate.

She was prepared for that, but it wouldn't be pleasant.

A silver Mercedes ML350 SUV rounded a corner and approached, pulling into the driveway of her target and entering the garage. She waited for the garage door to close, then backed herself in the driveway, right up to the garage door. She took one last look at the photos on her phone to confirm her targets, then exited her vehicle and approached the front door, her heart pounding in anticipation of what to expect. She rang the doorbell, and a few moments later the door opened, leaving Sherrie confused.

"Mrs. Urban?" she said in English, not bothering with the pretense of speaking French, knowing full well that the Urbans were native English speakers.

"Yes."

"Mrs. Melissa Urban, wife of Dr. Victor Urban?"

The woman's smile seemed to crack slightly. "Yes."

"I'm Detective Sergeant Sherrie Waterford, Sûreté du Québec," said Sherrie, pulling out her wallet and flipping it open to reveal Québec police identification. "May I come in?"

The woman nodded, stepping aside. Sherrie entered the home, quickly sweeping the area with her eyes, keeping her back directed at the wall so she could see the woman who had answered at all times.

Because the woman who claimed to be Melissa Urban, wife of Dr. Victor Urban, other than being blonde and petite, didn't at all resemble the file photos she had been provided with.

"Is this about my husband?"

Sherrie slowly stepped farther into the house, listening for any hints of others. She could hear kids upstairs, but no evidence of any other adults.

Which meant nothing if they were hiding.

"Yes it is," replied Sherrie.

"Have you found him?"

The woman's expression looked hopeful, if not genuine. Sherrie felt like she was seeing a bad play, the woman pretending to be Melissa Urban the understudy for the real thing. Sherrie casually reached for her weapon tucked into her back belt.

"No, we were hoping you might know where he was."

The woman shrugged her shoulders. "He went to work almost two years ago and never came home. I haven't heard from him since."

"Yet you moved."

Again the woman shrugged. "I had a job offer, I took it. I need to move on with my life."

Sherrie's hand was now gripping the gun. She whipped it around and to her surprise the woman knocked it out of her hand with a round house kick, then followed that up with a jab to the nose that had Sherrie seeing stars. She stumbled backward, dropping her clutch to the ground and raising her hands in defense as she blinked to clear her vision.

A blur came at her, fast, and she struck out at the center of it with a quick snap kick. She was rewarded with a grunt, then a backhand to the side of her head that sent her to the floor and into a table with a crash. Cries from upstairs were answered with a curt reply.

"Stay up stairs, kids, Mommy's busy."

Busy kicking my ass!

Sherrie sucked in a deep breath, holding it for a five count as she tried to calm herself. She had never been in this situation before. In training she always knew she would walk away in the end, perhaps bruised and humiliated, but not dead.

And today could be her last day. She backed away from the rapidly clearing blur, fists raised, and found herself in the kitchen. Her eyes darted around, looking for a weapon, and spotted the knife block to her right. She grabbed the biggest blade and whipped it overhand at the imposter. The women grabbed the door of the fridge, yanking it open, the blade embedding itself in the stainless steel.

Sherrie stepped forward, kicking back the door. It slammed into the woman, sending her back several feet as Sherrie ripped the knife free and pressed her first advantage, snap kicking the woman in the left breast, the pain obvious on her face, and with her vision finally cleared, Sherrie could see the fear in her opponent's eyes for the first time.

She's just as scared as I am!

She hacked at the air with the knife, forcing the woman back into the living room, her eyes scanning the floor for her weapon. Spotting the grip just under the nearby loveseat, she swung at the air again, rounding toward the weapon, then kicked the loveseat aside, exposing the gun. In a desperation move her opponent leapt for the gun and Sherrie plunged the knife down, catching the woman in the shoulder, embedding the blade a good two to three inches. She screamed out in pain as she collapsed to the floor, blood staining her white blouse as Sherrie stepped on the shoulder, pulling the knife out and grabbing her gun off the floor.

She backed away, leaving the bleeding woman on the floor, whimpering as Sherrie whipped the knife at the far wall, it embedding itself far out of reach. With her weapon trained on her now downed opponent, she returned to the hallway and retrieved her clutch. Reaching in, she pulled out a hypodermic and tossed it to the woman. It clattered on the hardwood and rolled to a stop near her right hand.

"Inject yourself."

"Fuck you."

"Inject yourself or I kill your kids."

"You wouldn't."

"Do you have any idea what's going on here?"

The woman just glared at her.

"People are dying, and if we can't stop it, it could be the end of everything."

"What the hell are you talking about?"

"Haven't you been watching the news? New Orleans?"

"What about it? Some sort of flu outbreak."

"Do you seriously think the President would quarantine a city of half a million people with shoot to kill orders for a flu?"

The woman blanched, looking upstairs, the stifled sobs of the children echoing down the stairs. "Listen, I was just hired to do a job, that's it. They're paying me two hundred grand a year to just pretend I'm this guy's wife. I don't know anything beyond that."

"And the kids?"

"They're hers. But, please don't hurt them."

"I won't if you inject yourself."

"Why?"

"Because you're coming back with me."

"What about my shoulder?"

"I'll dress it as soon as you inject yourself."

"And the kids?"

"As soon as we're across the border, I'll have the authorities contacted." Sherrie flicked the gun at her. "Now pick up the damned needle and jam it in your thigh."

The woman picked up the needle, hesitating for a moment, then did as she was told, wincing as the needle pierced her skin. She pushed the plunger, and within seconds collapsed to the ground, out cold.

Now the hard part.

Superdome, New Orleans, Louisiana

Detective Isabelle Laprise couldn't believe her eyes. Some jackhole was skydiving into the Superdome parking lot. She looked up and it appeared to be some sort of military transport that had dropped the fool into the city despite the quarantine.

What kind of moron would want to enter New Orleans now?

She moved along with the crowd of officers surrounding what appeared would be the person's landing zone, the area recently left clear by the helicopter that had picked up the canister. All eyes were on the sky as the person expertly guided their chute then executed an easy two foot landing with a final flare of his chute. Spinning around, the man grabbed his chute, pulling it in and folding it up as half the police force aimed their weapons at him.

He turned to face the front of the Superdome and said the one set of words that couldn't stun her more.

"Is there a Detective Isabelle Laprise here?"

Her eyes shot wide open and her heart pounded a little harder in her chest. She pushed through the crowd and out into the open, her hand on her pistol grip, still holstered.

"Right here. Who the hell are you?"

The man removed his helmet revealing a stunningly attractive face framed with a matted down mane of hair. His well-tanned face put him in his late twenties, his chiseled features she imagined extended to his entire body, and she felt herself tingle at the thought of this hero dropping from the sky, despite the chaos surrounding them, and asking for her specifically.

If this isn't the start of some over the top romance novel, then I don't know what is.

His smile of greeting nearly took out her knees as he walked toward her, the swagger reminiscent of something from Top Gun. But this guy's features were all Iceman. Tanned and light.

And about ten years too young for her fantasies.

Okay, five.

She laughed to herself as a chant of *Cougar! Cougar!* erupted in her head.

"I'm Special Agent Dylan Black, FBI." He held out his credentials and she glanced at them, figuring there was no way he was bullshitting her. He extended a hand and gave her a firm handshake, his warm but dry skin setting her palm on fire.

"Detective Laprise. Just what the hell are you doing here, Special Agent Black?"

"Call me Dylan. You should be hearing from your supervisor any second now."

As if the man had sent the message himself, her phone buzzed on her hip. She took the call, holding the phone to her ear.

"Laprise here."

"This is Captain Enright. Has he arrived?"

"If you're talking about our FBI parachutist, then yes."

"Good. You're to cooperate with him fully. He's taking over your case—"

"But, Captain!"

"No buts, you know what's going on. He's got access to resources we can only dream of. Take advantage of him"—her mind darted to a shower scene as their new arrival stripped out of his jumpsuit—"in any way you can. This murder is the only lead we have."

"Fine."

"Good luck."

118

The call ended and she clipped her phone back on her hip, waving off the crowd surrounding them. "He's okay," she said, the officers holstering their weapons and returning to what they had been doing, which was milling around since the canister had been found so quickly. She turned to her guest.

"So, you're in charge, what do you want to do?"

"Let's backtrack our killer."

"Just like that?" She felt her blood boil a bit at the arrogance of the man's statement. "What the hell do you think we've been trying to do for the past week?"

He smiled, the flash of his teeth completely disarming.

"You don't have access to the cool toys I do." He pointed at a massive mobile command center with FBI emblazoned across the side as it pulled up not a hundred feet away.

Very cool toys!

Approaching Stanstead, Québec, Canada

Sherrie White's heart was slamming in her chest. She knew they were on to her, one of the damned kids having called 9-1-1 just as she had been taught. She had barely left the house before the police arrived, their flashing cherries in her rear view mirror as she had turned off the street. Her imposter wife was in the back, covered in a blanket, her wrists and ankles zip tied, her mouth taped over with duct tape.

But none of that would matter if she were caught. She knew she was essentially unleashed on this mission, but she still couldn't see herself crossing certain lines. She was allowed to kill the kids, but she'd never do that. Never. And she was allowed to kill anybody who got in her way, including Canadian police. But she couldn't see herself doing that either.

And the tail she had picked up ten minutes ago told her they were on to her, and most likely setting up a road block to catch her. Which is why she was patched into Langley right now on the car's Bluetooth.

"You've got my position?"

"Affirmative."

"I've picked up a tail I need to know what's ahead."

"Roger that," came the disembodied voice of a satellite surveillance specialist in some secret bunker somewhere in the continental US. "I'm showing a police roadblock two miles from your position."

"Recommended alternate routes."

"Take your next left now."

The voice was calm on the other end, but Sherrie was forced to slam her brakes on then crank her wheel as she released them halfway, sending her SUV careening around the turn and down what appeared to be a farmer's road, crops high on either side of the dirt lane. Regaining her speed, she glanced in her rearview mirror and saw her tail turn in.

She pressed a little harder, the vehicle threatening to fishtail her into the ditch lining either side of the road. "Tail still in pursuit."

"Take the next right. If you step on it you'll get ahead of them setting up a new roadblock."

"Roger that." She gripped the steering wheel hard, and as soon as pavement came into sight she cranked the wheel to the right, skidding onto the road, nearly taking it on two wheels as horns honked at her. She immediately floored it, manually shifting the large vehicle to make up precious seconds as she blasted down the two lane highway, traffic fortunately light.

A traffic light ahead was red. One car was stopped, blocking her lane.

"Traffic check at next light. Am I clear to go through?"

"One vehicle approaching from your right, none from your left. Vehicle appears to be slowing down for approaching police vehicles. You have approximately ten seconds before police vehicles reach the intersection."

Sherrie pushed the accelerator even harder into the floor, it already at its design limit. As the intersection rapidly approached, a quick look to her right showed a stream of police cars racing toward her, and one in her rearview mirror still some distance back.

"Report!"

"Still clear."

Here goes nothing!

She was tempted to close her eyes, but instead moved over into the opposing lane, honking her horn just in case her eyes in the sky were wrong, or had missed pedestrians. The SUV blasted past the stopped car and into the intersection just as the Sûreté du Québec police cars were slowing to block the intersection. She whipped through, narrowly missing the first cop car, and continued on, the units now turning to follow her.

"Report!"

"Less than three miles to the border. Turn left at the stop sign coming up in a quarter mile, then go straight all the way to the border, two miles. A chopper is waiting for you."

She spotted the octagonal stop sign ahead, but with the tall crops it was hard to see if there was any traffic.

"Report on approaching traffic."

"You've got a rig coming from your right, slowing for a stop, nothing else. Note behind you, you've got a cruiser approaching rapidly."

Sherrie checked her rearview mirror, then positioned herself in the center of the two lanes. There was nothing she could do about them now. She had to brake to make the turn, and she could only hope her pursuer would be hesitant to smash his cruiser into her. The stop sign was rapidly approaching and at one hundred feet she locked her brakes up, the ABS kicking in to allow her to control the skid, then just as she was nearing the stop sign, she cranked the wheel hard to the left, the eighteen wheeler to her right laying on its horn as she blasted past the stop sign and into the intersection, the SUV skidding at a ninety degree angle.

She felt a jolt as the closest cruiser following her slammed into her driver's side rear end, but she was already accelerating away from the intersection, her heart hammering in her chest as adrenaline fueled her escape. She was flying past houses now, in a residential area of the tiny town that straddled the border.

"Report on border."

"It's unguarded with a gate blocking the street. We will transmit a signal to open the gate on your mark."

"Roger that, go ahead and open the gate."

As her SUV raced toward the metal barrier a vehicle crested the hill, heading toward the gate, lights on top marking it as some sort of official vehicle. As the gate finished opening she blasted past, leaving a line of Canadian police vehicles screeching to a halt in puffs of smoke as the SUV in front of her turned its lights on and blocked the road.

"Somebody didn't get the memo!" yelled Sherrie as she continued toward the vehicle now blocking her way without slowing down. There was no room to go around him. She cranked the wheel to the right, hammering on her brakes, rushing onto the grass, taking out several street signs and sideswiping a dark green building as she sailed past the US border patrol unit.

As she struggled to regain control of the vehicle, she blew through a stop sign and checked her rearview mirror to see the border patrol turning to pursue.

"Where's that chopper?"

"Field on your left," replied her eye in the sky as she hammered on the brakes, the field with the chopper idling suddenly appearing. With her speed killed, she turned off the road and gunned it through the field toward the chopper, then skidded to a halt.

Jumping out, two personnel rushed toward her as she opened the rear doors. Her imposter was grabbed by the two men and carried toward the chopper as the border patrol vehicle jumped the road and entered the field, closing the distance rapidly. Sherrie pulled herself up and onto the chopper as the skids lifted off the ground, the border agent jumping from his SUV, his weapon aimed at them, but holding his fire as he apparently saw the US government markings on the tail.

She put a headset on and adjusted the mike. "Tell Langley we have the package, and it's not Dr. Urban's wife, it's an imposter."

"Roger that."

"Also, tell them to notify the Canadian authorities that there are two children alone at the Urban residence that need to be picked up."

She listened as the pilot relayed the information and her eyes closed, her tactical breathing taking over to lower her heart rate and reduce the impact of all the adrenaline running through her veins. It had been terrifying, and had certainly not gone to plan, but no one had suspected that it wouldn't be Urban's wife.

It was the unplanned for things that caused missions to go awry.

But it was the unplanned for things that also made them exciting.

And she wouldn't change a thing.

Superdome, New Orleans, Louisiana

Special Agent Dylan Kane opened the side door of the massive FBI mobile command unit, holding it aside for Detective Isabelle Laprise. She put one foot up on the step then turned toward the two officers she had been with.

"You two stick around, we may need some extra hands."

The sergeant nodded, the young officer flashed an excited smile, apparently not realizing what the sergeant did: by sticking with the detective, they'd most likely be traveling into the belly of the beast, with a more likely chance of catching whatever it was they were trying to contain.

But that was their job.

Public safety.

Isabelle stepped inside, Kane following, shutting the door behind them. Only one of the half dozen inside bothered to even look at the new arrivals. The agent stepped forward, her eyes elevatoring him then her competition. Her frown suggested she found herself beaten by Isabelle who though may be around forty appeared quite fit and attractive.

In Kane's initial assessment of Isabelle, which he did to everyone, he noted no wedding ring, in fact no rings of any kind, and no telltale marks or tan lines to suggest she just removed them for the job.

And the dossier he had read on her when he was in the air confirmed it.

"I'm Special Agent in Charge Hewett. Forgive me if I don't shake your hand," she added with a deepening frown when Isabelle reached out.

"Of course," mumbled Isabelle, apparently slightly embarrassed. But she didn't have the benefit of the sign hanging behind the two new arrivals that Kane had noticed when he first stepped inside.

Shaking hands spreads germs!

Hewett pointed at the screens.

"We've been tracking your boy."

Isabelle looked at the screen. "How far did you get? We lost him within five minutes of leaving, and could only trace him three minutes prior to his arrival."

Hewett smiled, pleased apparently that they had done better.

"We've identified him—"

"You identified him!"

Hewett's smile broadened even more at her rival's shock.

"His name is Mike Milner." She pointed at one of the screens displaying a summary of his FBI record. "Thirty-eight years old, five foot eleven, hundred seventy five pounds, has a string of arrests around the country, mostly B and E. A few years ago we lost track of him. He was suspected in a few more major heists, one where a security guard was shot. He was good and getting better."

Isabelle leaned in, staring at the monitor with her killer's picture.

"How do you know it's him? We couldn't get any photos of his face."

"We were able to piece together partials, then found a great shot from an ATM camera as he was driving by near his apartment."

"Where's that?"

"Gravier Street."

"That's fantastic!" smiled Isabelle, turning to Kane. "You weren't kidding about the toys!" She turned back to Hewett. "Do we have any idea if he's still there?"

Hewett shook her head.

"Lobby camera footage we've managed to access shows him entering, but not leaving. Unfortunately there are other exits that aren't monitored, so we don't know. We'll leave that to local PD." Hewett turned to Kane. "We're backtracking his movements. We have him meeting with someone

126

at Saint Louis Cemetery." She motioned for some footage to be brought up and one of those manning the stations complied. "It's fuzzy because of the distance," explained Hewett, pointing at the pixelated image. "But we're almost certain this is Milner meeting with someone. There's an exchange here"—she pointed at what appeared to be something being handed from one man to the other—"and then they go their separate ways." In the image Milner walked toward the camera, still too fuzzy for Kane to be certain it was him, then climbed into a car and drove off. The other man went deeper into the cemetery and out of sight.

"Any luck picking the other subject up?"

"Negative," said Hewett, shaking her head. "We're still searching though. We just found this meeting about fifteen minutes ago."

"Excellent work," said Kane, his head bobbing his pleasure. "By the way, how'd you know what apartment was Milner's? Surely he didn't use his real name."

"He checked his mail on the way in so we got his unit number off the box. He's renting under Mike Smith."

"And you've pulled all bookings?"

"Of course. He was booked for one week ago on a Delta flight to the Dominican Republic."

"And let me guess, he missed his flight."

"How'd you guess?"

"This thing is too big to leave loose ends."

"You're expecting a corpse?"

Kane frowned, nodding his head.

"Dead men tell no tales." He sucked in a breath. "Anything else?"

"Not yet," replied Hewett.

"Okay, you've got my number and the Detective's?"

"Yes."

"Then send everything you've got as it comes in to both of us. Send us his photo and particulars now, along with the address. We're going over there now, see if we get lucky. Focus on the meeting at the cemetery. We need to know who hired him. Back track Milner's financials as well. We need to know where he shopped, who he ate with, anything. He may have had an accomplice, or he may have mentioned something to a friend. Does he have family?"

"Oklahoma."

"Send agents there now, interrogate them. If they won't cooperate, arrest them as suspected terrorists—"

"Are you kidding?"

Kane shook his head.

"This is end of the world shit, the President has essentially suspended the constitution."

"Can he do that?"

"I don't think he cares right now. If this thing gets away from us, there'll be nobody left to impeach him. If he prevents Armageddon, he'll be a hero."

Hewett paled slightly. "I knew it was bad, but hearing someone actually put it that way…" Her voice drifted as her eyes glassed over. "I have a son." Isabelle reached out and squeezed her arm. Hewett eyed the hand, but instead of shaking it away, put her own hand on top and squeezed for a moment, giving Isabelle a smile.

"Let's focus on the job, and catch these people. CDC is working on a cure, I'm sure, and we still don't know how infectious it is, everyone is just playing it safe." Kane pointed at Hewett. "I'll contact you when we check out Milner's apartment."

Hewett nodded, blinking her eyes clear.

"Good luck."

"Thanks," said Isabelle as they exited the command center. Kane motioned to the two cops. "We're heading to Gravier Street. Know where it is?"

"Of course."

"Okay, get your cruiser, we'll follow. Lights and sirens all the way, we don't have any time to waste."

"I'll get it!" The sergeant tossed the keys to the young officer who sprinted toward a dwindling gaggle of vehicles as the police assigned to the search were reassigned.

Kane turned to Isabelle.

"I guess we'll use your car since I dropped in without one."

She gave him a bit of a grin, shaking her head.

"We need to work on your sense of humor."

Kane placed his hand over his heart.

"Hey, easy. I could be dying."

Isabelle dropped her chin toward her chest, looking up at him with a cocked eyebrow.

"Gallows humor now?"

"Not funny?"

"Not funny."

"Let's get your car. I'll think of better jokes on the way."

"I hope you're a better agent than comedian."

Kane laughed as he followed her to an unmarked vehicle parked nearby.

"Don't worry. Even if I'm no good, my team is."

His mind flashed to Leroux, wondering what he was doing during this crisis. If he knew the Director, he probably had him on something critical.

You don't waste talent like that tracking down quarantine escapees.

Patrick Residence, New Orleans, Louisiana

The Patrick family sat glued to the television, the radio also set to a news channel, and Kyle with his iPad on his lap as he pulled up feeds from the Internet. Each thing he read had him shaking his head. Finally he had enough.

"They're not giving us the full story!"

His mom turned to him.

"What do you mean?"

"I mean the mainstream media is just spewing the government propaganda. The web is telling a different story. They're saying that the virus is pretty much contained to one hospital, and it's only affecting women who have a history of breast cancer in their family."

"What? That doesn't make any sense at all," said his father, skepticism dripping from his tongue. "I've never heard of a virus that only targets women let alone those with breast cancer."

"But what if it's true? They're saying the real risk is if this thing mutates beyond the initial group. They're shutting down the city. We'll be trapped here with a virus that is out of control."

"We'll just sit here and mind our own business. We've got plenty of food and water. We'll just ride it out like we did Katrina."

"Dad, we got so damned lucky with that hurricane, we shouldn't tempt fate twice. We need to get out of here now while we still have the chance."

His father watched footage of helicopters flying overhead, troops in hazmat suits being deployed, blocking roads and the port, his hands gripping the arms of his chair tighter and tighter, his knuckles white.

"Kyle's right. We have to get out of here now. I'll call my brother, he'll pick us up outside of the city."

Kyle jumped up, thanking God they had seen the light.

"I'll go pack a couple of bags with food and water," he said, heading for the kitchen.

"I'm not going."

He spun around to look at his mother, firmly planted in her chair, her shoulders sagging. He was about to say something when a chopper thundered overhead, vibrating the entire house.

He pointed to his dad. "You convince her. I'm packing."

And with that he headed into the kitchen and began loading the table with things for their journey as his father began to calmly reason with his wife.

I hope he's quick about it. In another hour it will be too late.

Stanardsville, Virginia

Cheryl Morrison eyed her gas tank. The needle had just crossed a quarter tank, and she hated ever driving with it under half. The radio had made it obvious why her husband had told her to go to the cottage. The virus hitting New Orleans must not only be dangerous, but must have escaped the quarantine zone.

But it couldn't have made it this far yet. Could it?

A gas station, the last one before the cottage, came into sight.

We need gas.

She pulled in, thanking God that the pumps had been upgraded to self-serve with a pay-at-the-pump service. She grabbed some wipes from the glove compartment and climbed out. Inserting her card, she wrapped a wipe around her hand, entered her PIN then selected regular, her daughter explaining to her one day how premium was a scam since almost all cars today were designed to work anywhere in the world, and 87 octane in some countries *was* premium. At worst you lost a few horsepower, and the way she drove, she'd never notice as she saved hundreds of dollars a year.

With the fuel pumping, she turned to survey the scene. The small corner store attached to the garage seemed to be busier than usual, the parking lot fuller than she had ever seen it on their weekend jaunts to the country. Some shouting from inside had her gripping the handle on the hose even harder, willing the fuel to pump faster. She watched the counter spinning higher and higher, but it seemed impossibly slow as a scream broke out, then a gunshot.

She ducked, but kept her grip on the hose as she peeked around the fuel pump. People were running from the store and scattering in every direction, screams of terror erupting from their lips. Another shot then the jerking of the hose as the tank was finally full nearly had her peeing her pants. She released the trigger and slowly pulled the nozzle from the tank. She reached up blindly, screwing the cap in place and flipping the cover closed, trying not to make any noise.

She nearly yelped when a man burst from the store, pushing a small cart loaded with supplies, one hand on the cart, the other brandishing a handgun. His wild eyed expression was one of panic and fear, a man out of touch with reality, and a man representative of what was to come as the panic of New Orleans spread.

Soon it would be every man for himself.

"Fuck! Fuck! Fuck! Fuck!" he screamed at the top of his lungs as he stared at a car that she assumed was his. A car that was blocked in by a late arrival who had simply parked perpendicular to three cars, blocking them all. His head spun around, then his eyes came to rest on her. He began to push the cart toward her, his gun extended in front of him, aimed at her. She ducked behind the pump, slowly rising in case she had to run, still gripping the hose.

He rounded the pump, aiming the weapon directly at her. She stood up, her hands shaking as she slowly raised them, now wishing she had made a pit stop before she had left the house.

"Give me the fucking keys."

She nodded, her head vibrating in fear as she searched her body for the keys, her mind a blank slate as to where they might be. The man extended his arm even farther, uselessly cocking the weapon, he having seen too many Hollywood movies.

"Now!"

"I-I'm trying," cried Cheryl. "I-I can't f-find them."

The man raised his arm and fired in the air. Cheryl screamed, her body tensing, her hand squeezing the trigger on the hose. Gasoline spurted from the nozzle, arcing through the air and splattering all over the crazed man.

He squeezed his eyes shut, cursing as he tried to wipe the toxic fluid off his face with his sleeves, the gun still waving dangerously around. Cheryl threw the hose on the ground then rounded the car, finally remembering where the keys were. She jumped inside, closed the door and turned the keys.

Nothing.

Shit!

She pressed her foot on the brake and was about to try again when she saw something from the corner of her eye. It was the barrel of a gun, pointed at her window, her attacker still squinting in agony, but his eyes cleared enough for him to see her trying to make his escape.

"I gave you a chance, lady!"

She watched the trigger finger slowly begin to squeeze, and she said a silent prayer.

Suddenly the man's body jerked, the bullet fired, shattering the driver side window, as his body flew past the front of her car, followed by the SUV that had just mowed him down. She jerked forward, her head hitting the steering wheel as she tried to avoid a bullet that had long since hit its mark, only its mark had been lost due to the sudden impact of the SUV's bumper.

It had blown a hole in her headrest.

She sat for a moment, her hands gripping the steering wheel, her entire body shaking as she cried, then she heard someone yelling through the fog as her left ear, numbed from the blast only two feet from her head, slowly recovered.

"Mom!"

Her head jerked toward the sound, then through the blur of tear filled eyes she saw her door open and a pair of hands reach in. She fought them off, screaming, "No! No! No!" as she did so, then finally she felt the arms envelope her, holding her tight.

"Mom, it's me, Charlie!"

And she recognized the voice, her shoulders sagging in relief as she felt her adult son embrace her, his arms the very protection she needed from a world going mad.

Mike Milner Residence, Gravier Street, New Orleans, Louisiana

Special Agent Dylan Kane knocked on the door. He knew it was useless, but he took a chance. As expected, they were greeted by silence. At least silence from the apartment in question. Up and down the hallway of the shithole they stood in were screaming matches, crying, music pumping from under doors, and television sets all turned up, probably to drown out the misery escaping the other doors.

He wondered if anyone in the building even knew what was going on outside, every television station he could make out playing some garbage reality show, a true sign of the decay of Western civilization if there ever was one.

He hammered on the door again.

"FBI! Open up! We have a warrant to search these premises!"

He grinned at Detective Laprise's questioning look and shrugged his shoulders.

"He's dead already, what's he going to do? Sue me in the afterlife?"

Isabelle shook her head, drawing her weapon and before he could stop her, had kicked open the door. He pushed her back and to the side of the door as he rolled his back against the wall.

"Bombs people! Bombs!" he tutted. "Always be prepared for booby traps when dealing with people like this."

"People like what?"

"International terrorists."

Isabelle didn't seem convinced.

"You're not FBI are you?"

Kane raised his eyebrows, then poked his head inside the apartment.

"Did I ever say I was?"

Isabelle seemed to be searching her memory, then glanced at the officers, who both shrugged.

Kane stepped inside, checking the door to make sure there wasn't a failed mechanism, then continued inside. The apartment was surprisingly clean. In fact, it was too clean. Either their suspect Milner was meticulous in keeping the place prepared for a quick exit that wouldn't require much of a wiping down, or it had been wiped down by professionals after doing him in.

Either way Kane was still convinced Milner was dead.

But if he was, he wasn't here. There was no hint of decay, nothing to suggest that a body had ever been here for a long time, rotting away as bodies do. He quickly cleared the open concept living area, then the bathroom including shower, then the one bedroom.

Nothing.

"Clear!" he called, the others doing the same.

"Found something!"

It was the young female officer Macleod.

Kane stepped around Isabelle who had entered the bedroom, and looked to see Macleod staring at a chest freezer that was in the entry closet. She lifted the lid as Kane yelled, "No!"

The eruption was enormous. Macleod was blasted backward, into her partner, who absorbed much of the initial impact, their two bodies then being shoved into the kitchen, the old sergeant slamming into the fridge. Kane whipped around and dove away from the doorway, clotheslining Isabelle, pulling her with him as they both hit the double bed. He wrapped his arms around her shoulders and waist, spinning them both across the bed and down onto the floor, coming to rest with his back to the door, shielding the detective.

All around them drywall dust and smoke filled the air, debris rained down on them, a blast of heat cascading over their bodies as Isabelle screamed into his shoulder. He continued to grip her tight, his eyes squeezed shut, his mouth sealed as he held his breath.

Then the wind rushed back over them as air rushed in to fill the void left behind by the explosion chewing through the oxygen. Kane opened his eyes slightly, revealing smoldering wreckage all around them, but no fire. He eased his grip on the detective then lay her gently on her back as she gasped for breath. He pulled a handkerchief from his pocket and placed it over her mouth, he covering his with his shirt sleeve.

"Breathe through this until the dust settles." He stood up and examined himself quickly for any injuries. "Are you okay?"

She nodded, holding up a hand which he took and pulled her to her feet.

"Thanks to you." She shook herself off, as did he as he threw open the windows in the bedroom. The wall between the living area and the bedroom was all but gone, only studwork remaining, even some of those blasted apart. The living area was unrecognizable as Kane led the way from the bedroom. The freezer that had been booby-trapped was blown open from within, and judging by the gooey mass inside, it had contained a body.

Isabelle groaned when she saw it, even Kane having a hard time taking it all in. A grunt from behind had both of them spinning around. Against the fridge were the bodies of the two officers. Young Officer Macleod was obviously dead, her body scorched and impaled with a piece of the freezer.

"Help."

It was faint and they both rushed forward, pulling the body of Macleod free. Behind her was the sergeant, pressed against the dented fridge door. His hands were burnt, his scalp and forehead singed, but the bulk of his body had been protected by his young partner.

Kane immediately dropped beside him and began to check him over as Isabelle called for an ambulance and backup. Sergeant Michael was breathing, wincing with each breath, but seemed to be alive, saved by his partner who was most likely dead the instant of the blast.

"How do you feel?" asked Isabelle as she took a knee.

"Like a freight train hit me."

"You're not that far off," smiled Kane, trying to distract the man from the pain.

"Macleod?"

Isabelle shook her head.

"She didn't make it."

"Fuck."

"It wasn't her fault. These were pros," said Kane. "Anybody could have opened something, touched something."

Michael reached up and grabbed Kane by the shoulder, his dark black hands belching an eye watering stench.

"If I don't make it, don't tell her parents she fucked up. Tell them she was following orders."

Kane nodded, patting the man on the shoulder.

"She died a hero, doing her job, and saved your life in doing it. That's the story they'll hear. From you."

Michael's hand dropped to the floor, and his eyes closed. Kane reached forward, feeling the man's neck.

"Is he—?"

"No. He's just passed out from the pain."

Kane stood up and surveyed the damage. If there was any evidence in here, they weren't going to find it now, at least not in time. He pulled out his phone and hit the speed dial for the FBI Command Center.

"Special Agent Hewlett here."

"This is Special Agent Black. There's been an explosion at the apartment. Some sort of booby trap set up on a freezer. Looks like there was a body inside. Not much left now. Get a team down here to see if they can identify the body, and find out what they can about the device. It might lead us somewhere. Also, start running all the faces you can find through our databases of known bomb makers, mercenaries, the usual non-Islamists. This has nothing to do with religion."

"Will do. Are you okay?"

"We've got one officer dead, one severely wounded. Paramedics are on the way along with local LEO's. Get your team out here ASAP."

"Will do."

Kane ended the call as the local Law Enforcement Officers began to respond, their sirens heard through the open window. Sergeant Michael continued to slip in and out of consciousness as Isabelle comforted him. Kane grabbed a knife from the counter and a set of tongs from the drawer, then stepped over to the freezer. An arm was still obvious from the mess, and he used the tongs to lift it apart from the rest of the body, revealing a hand.

The fingers were still intact, as was a large ring on the pinky, and a watch, nothing special, on the wrist. He took photos of each, then emailed them to Hewlett along with a text message.

See if these match the video.

Kane began to scan the apartment to see if he could find anything of use, but his hopes were low. He turned as several officers rushed into the apartment, followed by an EMT crew. He and Isabelle showed their ID as Isabelle got out of the way, taking command of the situation.

"Two men on the door, the rest I want canvassing the adjoining apartments, plus two floors up and down, check for other casualties."

The officers ran off to their assignments as the paramedics worked. Kane stepped into the bathroom and found it in shambles, the tile work all shattered, the mirror sitting in the sink, broken into several large pieces, leaving a large white square on the wall where the bathroom had once been painted around it.

And a small hole, about the size of several bricks, cut into the drywall.

With a small box sitting inside.

He examined the box and alcove before touching it, then gently extracted it, all the while watching for any type of pressure switch or wire. He was pretty certain it wouldn't be wired, the previous explosive obviously set up by Milner's killer, not Milner himself. This box was clearly Milner's, the hiding place having fooled anyone who may have searched the apartment prior to the explosion.

Kane opened the small box. Inside was a large stack of cash. Very large. Some false IDs, a passport, plane ticket, and a set of numbers that he recognized as a bank account, the letterhead it was written on from a bank in the Caymans.

Bingo!

CIA Headquarters, Langley, Virginia

Chris Leroux heard the coded chime as the priority message arrived. Only specially encoded messages had this sound, regular emails an entirely different one, indicating he could ignore them if needed. He Alt-Tabbed to his email and saw the message among dozens of others unread. He double-clicked, entered his password, and a message from Dylan Kane was displayed.

He hadn't seen Kane since the night Sherrie moved in, and had only received one message in the entire time since, and it was just a 'Happy Birthday' message he wasn't able to reply to.

It had been delivered under his door by someone other than Kane, he was sure. And whoever they were had skills, as they had managed to do it despite a team of agents assigned to protect him 24/7. Then again, knowing Kane, he might have used an operative with clearance to do it.

He didn't care. It was just a thrill to hear from him when he did, but today it was all business. A quick greeting then a bank name and account number.

I've sent it through channels, but thought you might want it a little quicker. Good hunting. DK.

Leroux had dozens of searches running through their databases, and as results came in, they would appear in his Inbox and he'd review them, launching more searches, dismissing some tangents, and generally drilling down as far as he could, looking for some connection somewhere that would lead to Dr. Urban.

And he had had limited success. The imposter that Sherrie had captured had come onto the scene eighteen months ago when she up and moved to

Sherbrooke, Québec to be a teacher. The "real" Melissa Urban was originally from Québec and had met her future husband in Florida on vacation. They had kept in touch, eventually marrying two years later. She moved to Florida where his job was, became a housewife once the first child was born, and led a quiet life raising them.

Agents canvassing the old neighborhood reported most people could barely even describe her, she and her husband leading quiet lives, not socializing much. There were no reports of domestic problems, no money problems, no health problems. The neighbors hadn't even noticed that the husband had disappeared.

Financial records showed the company continued to pay the man's salary for a few months, then stopped, then started again after the first attack. Dr. Kapp from BioDyne had said it was in hopes of placating Urban, the thinking that if the man knew his family was being taken care of, he might be less hostile toward humanity in general.

If it worked, all it did was delay things, as the attacks continued.

After the paychecks had stopped, their spending pattern changed almost immediately, according to bank records. This made sense to Leroux, and he didn't pay it much mind. It was the change in the locations of the essentials that triggered alarm bells. On Friday they were getting their gas at Texaco, on Monday Shell, their groceries at Ralph's, then at Wal-Mart. Hair at Louise's then at the Mod Shoppe. Then less than a month later they were in Québec, and with checks from her teaching job, then from BioDyne being deposited, their spending patterns had changed even more dramatically.

While the real Melissa Urban was an avid and apparently talented cook, the "new" Mrs. Urban ordered out and ate out frequently, whereas this pattern of spending was almost nonexistent in Florida. As well, her hair appointments increased in cost and frequency, which suggested to Leroux dye jobs, as the real Mrs. Urban was a natural blonde.

Leroux was convinced the weekend the spending patterns changed was when the switch was made. He had already passed the information along and agents were looking into it now to see if they could find anything on camera footage but it was a long shot, most footage backups long since destroyed and overwritten.

He had searches running for any reports of a woman with two children missing. It was assumed these were the Urban children, but they couldn't be sure. The Urban children were young enough that they now could conceivably believe that this woman was their mother and not say anything to anyone. Leroux secretly hoped that they were the Urban children, at least that way they knew they were alive, and now safely in the hands of Canadian authorities. Blood typing and DNA testing being performed now would give them more information shortly.

The Canadians were pissed at the abduction, and apparently an apology had been issued claiming an operative had overstepped her bounds, and that the subject would be released back to the Canadians shortly. That was just a BS cover story of course. She'd be handed back when they were finished with her. And if that took days or weeks, then so be it. By then the secret would be out, and the Canadians would be too busy closing their borders and would be happy to have one less person to worry about.

Leroux launched another search, supplying the bank account information. Shortly he would have a transaction report on the account, then would begin to backtrack any and all deposits and withdrawals done electronically. That would be the challenge. Each search of a non-US bank required hacks, and his requests would go out to their teams around the world, with a priority tag, to do their magic and gain entry into some of the most secure servers in the world.

It could be done, but it could be time consuming. Quite a few of the mob type banks had been infiltrated with software installed on the machines to allow them backdoor access, but most banks hadn't received that treatment, and those that had quite often found the illicit software and removed it.

Leroux mentally crossed his fingers as he hoped for the best.

His query running, he took a moment to flip over to CNN to see the latest public perception of the problems, and gasped at a live report leading the page.

This isn't right!

North of New Orleans, 1.2 miles outside the quarantine zone

Colonel Jeremiah Jackson, J.J. to his friends and family, pointed to a hedge a quarter of a mile to their right. The Black Hawk helicopter banked, closing the distance in seconds, then hovered in front of the bushes, the group of escapees huddling behind the eight foot high row of cedars now obvious. He activated the external speaker.

"This is Colonel Jackson of the National Guard. You are in violation of a Federally mandated quarantine. You are ordered to turn around and return to your homes. If you do not turn around, we will be forced to open fire. Lethal force has been authorized."

He never thought he'd say those words, not to American citizens. There were almost a dozen people down there, and from what he could see, they were families. Three perhaps four, that had found a way out before the cordon around the city could be completed. This was happening all around the city, and teams were being dispatched as UAV's patrolling the skies found them, their infrared sensors picking them out easily.

So far nobody had challenged the teams, all returning peacefully, but this time he had no boots on the ground to stop them. They were at least ten minutes away, and the only thing that stood between this disease possibly spreading and containment, was him and his helicopter.

The group in the hedge however didn't appear ready to cooperate.

"Let's throw a little dirt in their faces. Put a few rounds between us and the hedge."

"Roger that."

The pilot opened fire with the .50 caliber, tearing apart the farmer's field along a thirty foot swath in front of the hedge hiding the escapees. When the chatter of the cannon stopped, several people tentatively stepped forward, their hands raised. They appeared to be a family, a man and woman with two small children. Another family with a small child bolted back toward the city.

"Let them go," said Colonel Jackson. "They won't be trying that again." He activated the external speaker. "Return to your homes and you won't be harmed." He paused, and when they didn't move, he raised his voice. "Now!"

The man pushed through an opening in the hedge and raced after the other family, his wife close behind, their children held close. Jackson was about to activate his mike when a third group suddenly emerged from the hedge, racing right toward them then under the chopper. The pilot banked, reacquiring the targets, Jackson on the mike.

"Halt immediately! You are in violation of a mandatory quarantine. We are authorized to use deadly force. I say again, halt immediately, or we will open fire."

The family, a husband in the lead, urging his wife and what appeared to be a teenaged son forward, showed no signs of slowing down.

"Fire some warning shots in front of them."

"Roger that."

The cannons rumbled, flame bursting from the barrels as the ground was torn apart in their escapees' path. He could see the father turn back, the words he yelled obvious even at this distance.

"Keep going! They won't shoot us!"

Colonel Jackson felt his chest tighten. They weren't going to cooperate, and they were under a false assumption that he wouldn't eliminate them. When he had been briefed about the quarantine, and told of the shoot to kill orders, even he had questioned them. But when it was explained what they might be dealing with, and how just one infected person could lead to its worldwide spread, he had understood.

It was shitty, but they had no choice.

"Fire again."

"Roger that."

Again the bullets tore into the ground, this time closer, and again the family showed no signs of stopping.

He activated the speaker.

"You have five seconds to comply, otherwise lethal force is authorized." He lowered his voice slightly, relaxing the mechanical nature he had been trained to use in military communications. "Please stop. We have no choice but to fire. Don't make me do it."

The father slowed down, looking back at the helicopter hovering in front of them, the pilot having repositioned. The man looked back at his wife, then shook his head, running toward a farmhouse nearby. A farmhouse that probably had people in it, people outside the quarantine zone, who had done nothing wrong but be in the path of these frightened people.

"I'm sorry," he said, turning off the speaker.

"Eliminate the targets."

"But, sir, they're just scared parents with their kid!"

"You have your orders."

"Sir…" The pilot's voice drifted off, then a burst of static indicating a deep breath filled the headset, then a monotone voice. "Understood."

He banked toward the fleeing family when Colonel Jackson saw something from the corner of his eye. His head spun and he saw two troop transport vehicles racing down the road, the first vehicle turning onto the road leading to the farmhouse.

"Hold your fire!"

"Roger that, holding fire."

Troops in NBC "bunny" suits jumped from the back of the truck and raced toward the family, quickly surrounding them, the commander on the scene waving at the chopper, indicating the situation was under control.

"Return to base," ordered Jackson, releasing a breath he hadn't realized he had been holding. He knew this was something being repeated all around the city, and he knew these poor helicopter crews were going to face the same decision they had. Kill innocent Americans, or let them go. He didn't know if he could count on his men to follow their orders, it going completely against their training.

And right now, at this moment, he didn't know if he could punish them for disobeying, his own emotions so conflicted.

God help us.

Interrogation Room B, CIA Headquarters, Langley, Virginia

"Why don't you give up the act, and begin cooperating?"

"I want a lawyer."

Agent Sherrie White smiled, shaking her head. She had been trained to not let her frustration show, but she was getting tired of the stonewalling already. Her witness had been allowed to stew for about an hour, provided nothing but water and a television tuned to CNN—her suggestion to let the woman know what was going on. But it wasn't working.

"You're not entitled." She leaned on the table, her knuckles pressed hard against the pressboard. "Do you have any idea what the hell is going on?"

"I want a lawyer."

"You do realize that you are in it up to here"—she motioned with her hand at her throat—"with this virus mess?"

The woman's eyes narrowed almost imperceptibly, then returned to normal.

"I want a lawyer."

But it was too late. Sherrie knew she had caught her.

"So you have no idea what's actually going on here."

"I want—"

"—a lawyer. I know you want a lawyer, and you're not entitled." Sherrie sat down across from her, leaning in, looking directly at the woman. "Do you want to know why you're not entitled?"

No answer other than the woman looking away.

"Because the situation with this virus is so dangerous, the President has essentially suspended all the rules. I can do anything I want to you. I can torture you, I can kill your kids, hell, I can even torture your kids. I can kill you. It doesn't matter. I won't get in trouble."

The woman said nothing, but her eyes flared slightly again at the mention of her kids. Sherrie didn't know if that meant they were her own kids, or if she had just grown attached to them after so much time living together.

"Do you want to know why I can do this? Why the President felt he should give this power to agents like me?"

Again no answer, but the woman's eyes had drifted to the television still playing in the background.

"Because what the public doesn't know, is that this virus has mutated, and can now be spread person to person with ease, and has a near one hundred percent fatality rate." Another flare of the eyes, this time not hidden as she focused more on the screen. "Do you understand what that means?"

Again no response, but there was a slight shift of the body toward Sherrie, suggesting she wanted to know the answer.

"It's judgment day. The end of days. A plague that will wipe out ninety-nine percent of the population, and right now there's nothing we can do about it."

The woman was definitely a little paler, her mouth open slightly as she watched the CNN feed, her eyes darting back and forth as she read the ticker.

"Now I'm sure you're wondering what this has to do with you. But I think you've already guessed. You're impersonating the wife of Dr. Victor Urban. Dr. Urban is, or was, a renowned viral researcher with BioDyne Pharma. *He* is responsible for the current situation. *He* released the virus, demanding payment or he'll do something even worse next time. This is his third attack in a year, each one separated by six months. The problem is, next time, there won't be anyone around to care. We need to find him before it's too late. We need to prevent any future attacks, but also see if he can help us find a cure for this existing virus." Sherrie leaned to the side to catch the woman's eyes. "Help us."

A tear rolled down the woman's cheek, and in the corner of Sherrie's eye she could see body bags being loaded in the back of an army vehicle. Finally the woman turned to Sherrie.

"I had no idea. I was paid fifty grand for every month I had to take care of these two kids. I had to pretend I was this guy's wife, live her life, and I'd get the cash deposited into an account each month. All I knew was he was some doctor, some researcher. They got me a job in Canada, moved us there almost immediately after I replaced the mother, and it didn't take long for the kids to start calling me Mommy." She sniffed. "I don't think they even realize I'm not her anymore, they're so young."

"What's your name?"

"Jessica Flowers."

"When were you born?"

"August fourth, seventy-seven."

That should be enough for the guys on the other side of the window.

"What happened to the real Melissa Urban?"

She shrugged.

"No idea. I received a package in the mail. Inside was a set of keys, a license plate number and two addresses; one for where the car was, the other for the house. There were detailed files on the wife and kids, her habits, list of places to avoid, everything, and a date and time. I got my ass there, found the car in a mall parking lot, drove to the house, the kids came home from school, and I took over her life."

"Do you still have this envelope?"

"It's taped under the drawer of the nightstand in the master bedroom, right hand side of the bed."

"And the bank account number you've been getting your deposits sent to?"

She nodded toward the envelope of personal effects.

"In my wallet."

Sherrie emptied the envelope's contents onto the table. Grabbing the wallet and opening it up, she looked at Flowers. "Where?"

"Let me," said Flowers, reaching forward.

Sherrie leaned back, distancing herself.

"No, tell me where it is."

She had been trained to not let the suspect touch anything that might be concealing something, such as a cyanide pill, and wasn't about to lose their only potential lead.

"First section, folded up piece of yellow paper at the bottom."

Sherrie flipped open the front section and immediately spotted the small paper. Reaching in, she pulled it out and carefully unfolded it, revealing a bank account number. She put the folded open paper flat on the desk so the overhead camera could pull the number and send it to whatever analyst was available.

"So in all of this you never saw anyone."

An emphatic headshake. "No."

"No further correspondence?"

"Just the initial instructions."

"How did you know to move to Canada?"

"It was in the original instructions."

"And how long were you supposed to do this?"

"Two years."

"Exactly?"

153

"Exactly."

"How were you originally contacted? You said all the instructions were in the envelope, but how did you find the job?"

Flowers suddenly looked uncomfortable, and Sherrie knew she was about to get some other tidbit out of her. But Flowers said nothing, instead looked at the television, then at her fingernails.

"You can tell me now, or we can toss you in a cell and beat it out of you. Like I said, no rules."

"My brother."

"Explain."

"My brother is sick, terminal. He had less than six months to live, nothing had worked, so we started making plans. Then some guy shows up in his hospital room and says he can cure him, but I have to do something in return."

"Pretend to be someone's wife."

Flowers nodded.

"And what happened."

"My brother was given some sort of treatment. A doctor came once a week to his room and gave him injections, then he started to get better. Within weeks he was perfectly healthy. That's when I received the envelope with the instructions on my end of the bargain."

"And nothing seemed odd about this?"

"Of course! I'm not an idiot. But these people had saved my brother, and I had agreed to do whatever they wanted. It wasn't like they were asking me to kill someone, and they were even offering to pay me, despite what they had already done." She looked at Sherrie then shrugged her shoulders. "I couldn't see a downside."

"Except that it was illegal."

"Well, yeah, I guess. But maybe the mother had agreed."

"You don't actually believe that, do you?"

Flowers eyes and voice dropped.

"No."

"So there were two men? The first who came to you with the offer, the second a doctor?"

Flowers nodded.

"Would you recognize them again if you saw them?"

"I think so."

Sherrie brought up a grid of random mug shots that generally matched Dr. Urban's description, including one of the man himself. She pushed the tablet toward Flowers.

"Recognize anyone?"

Her finger immediately went to the photo of Urban.

"That's the doctor!"

"Did he ever say anything?"

"No. Well, that is except to say the first time he entered our room that he was here to administer the injections, and he wasn't to be spoken to."

"Did he seem comfortable? Angry? Agitated? Scared?"

Flowers' eyes took on a distant look as they reached back in time.

"He seemed in a hurry, that's for sure. Maybe a little scared? I don't know. We were just so excited that somebody was helping us, especially after the first treatment showed improvement."

"And they never told you what this treatment was?"

"No."

"And what did your brother have?"

"HIV. AIDS. Full blown, final stages. The drugs weren't working anymore. Not that they ever really did with him."

"And what did the doctor's say?"

"They still don't believe the tests. They're claiming it's in remission, but they can't find the virus in his blood anymore. I think the treatments cured him, killed the virus, and now he's got a second chance at life."

Sherrie had almost stopped listening. Clearly the antiviral had been used on Flowers' brother, and he had been cured. The antiviral was obviously fantastic, but none of this was making sense. Why would Urban arrange the replacement of his own wife but not take the kids?

He wouldn't.

Which meant he was being coerced.

Which changes everything!

Mike Milner Residence, 837 Gravier Street, New Orleans, Louisiana

Special Agent Dylan Kane watched as the ambulance carrying the crispy but alive Sergeant Michael pulled away. Isabelle was still shaken, but seemed to have her wits about her. Officer Macleod's body hadn't been removed yet as the crime scene team was still photographing everything, and at the moment, her body was evidence.

His stomach rumbled and he gave it a pat, glancing around to see if there was any place to eat where they were, but there was nothing save apartments.

And one corner store tucked in the bottom of the building they were standing in front of. He strode toward the entrance and looked over at Isabelle.

"You want something?"

She shook her head.

"You can eat after that?"

He shrugged his shoulders.

"A man's gotta eat. I don't know when I'm going to get another chance."

"You go ahead," she said as a body bag was carried from the front entrance. Kane paused, turning to face the young officer and pay his respects, his eyes closed momentarily in silent prayer. When the coroner pulled away, Kane resumed his hunt for food, quickly closing the distance between him and the entrance to the corner store.

As he opened the door he heard the clicking of sensible shoes running up behind him. He turned and smiled at the detective as she came to a stop beside him.

"Got your appetite back?"

"Nope."

She pointed at a camera in the front corner of the store meant to cover the entrance. It also had a full, unhindered view of the front entrance of the apartment.

Kane's eyebrows climbed his forehead in appreciation.

"I'd have caught that if I wasn't so damned hungry," he said with a smile, his stomach growling in evidence.

"Riiight," said Isabelle, drawing out the word.

"I'm hurt you don't believe me."

"A guy parachutes into the center of a quarantine zone is surprised I don't believe much of what comes out of his mouth?"

"Ouch," said Kane, following her into the brightly lit store. "I'm a very honest guy once you get to know me."

"Oh, I have no doubt. And there's no way you're FBI. Those moves you put on me back there were Special Forces of some type."

Kane momentarily tried to think of when he had put the moves on her, then realized she was talking about saving her life. He gave her another once over and decided that if he were given the opportunity, he would indeed put the moves on her. Though older, her body was terrific.

And she could probably deliver a good ass kicking if he didn't watch himself.

"Saw it in a movie," he replied.

"Seeing is one thing. Executing it is another." She flashed her badge at the bored clerk as Kane went deeper into the store to forage. A bag of Frito Lay's Ruffles sour cream and onion flavored chips, a Snickers bar (plus one for the road) and a can of Diet Coke, along with a bag of beef jerky constituted one hell of a great dinner as he approached the counter. He placed his haul on the Plexiglas countertop, then grinned at Isabelle's expression.

"How the hell do you keep that figure eating like that?" she asked.

"Practicing rolling people away from explosions?"

"Is that second Snickers for me?"

"Yes, yes it is."

"Good. Suddenly I'm hungry."

"Just a second, I forgot something." Kane returned to the candy bar aisle and grabbed another Snickers as the clerk returned. Kane tossed the bar on the counter and Isabelle chuckled.

"So, what do you have?"

"It's all digital. My boss say's we keep every camera feed for a month in case there's a serious discrepancy on the inventory."

"When was your last inventory?"

The kid shrugged. "Not sure, but next Tuesday we're closed overnight for inventory, so I guess about three weeks."

Isabelle shot a smile at Kane.

"We'll need that footage."

Holiday Inn – Downtown Superdome, New Orleans, Louisiana

Dr. Katherine Best stretched like a cat. She looked at her watch. Three hours. Three hours of precious time, but three hours of even more precious sleep that would have her productive for the next twelve. And those missed three hours were mostly waiting around for others to do their jobs.

She swung herself from her bed and rubbed her eyes. Another knock at her door reminded her of what had woken her. She threw on a robe then went to the door and opened it, smiling at the young man bringing her the room service she had ordered for exactly this minute. As he did his routine of prepping everything, she glanced at her phone and saw a mess of emails and text messages to go through. She had left specific instructions with Dr. Johnston to not call her unless there was something important. He had kept his word apparently. When she got back to the staging area, it would be his turn to catch some sleep.

She signed the bill, adding the government allowable tip amount, then attacked her meal, shoveling it into her face in a very unladylike fashion as she quickly read her text messages and emails. As she swallowed a mouthful of orange juice she smiled.

Screening test ready.

That was huge news. Not worth waking her up for, she agreed, the others onsite perfectly capable of putting it into action. A follow up email from Johnston proved her faith. Everyone in the hospital was being screened, their samples being sent to Atlanta and various other facilities for testing. It would take hours to start getting the first results back, the BioDyne Pharma antiviral detection procedure being very quick as it didn't need to find an immune response to a virus growing in a blood sample. It

160

wasn't the speed of the test that would be the problem, it would be the volume. Thousands needed to be screened, and eventually perhaps millions.

What they needed was a cure. They needed something that would allow them to bypass the screening, and just inject everyone with a cure. But that would take more time. Assuming there even was a cure.

At least now though they would be able to tell if their outlier cases did indeed have the virus. One man who had shown up with the initial cases, but it turned out he had been born a woman. Something he had neglected to mention on his admission forms. It was the two fishing buddies that concerned her now. She prayed they were just sick with some flu, but she already knew the answer scrolling through her emails.

The first cases were beginning to present all over the country.

And with the virus, came the panic.

CIA Headquarters, Langley, Virginia

Chris Leroux squeezed the trigger on the shotgun, blasting another one of the bastards away as dozens more closed in. His heart slammed in his chest as the hordes rushed toward him, but he was out of ammo. This was it. The end. He had sworn he'd keep one last bullet for himself. There was no way he wanted to die like these other poor freaks.

He kicked the first one to reach him in the chest, sending the man flying back into a compatriot, then he felt something grab his hair. They were behind him now. He tore his head away, feeling the hair rip, his elbows flying, his feet kicking, but it was no use, there were just too many.

Teeth sank into his arm, then his shoulder, and he cried out in agony.

"Honey, are you okay?"

Oh my God! Sherrie's here!

He looked over his shoulder and saw her decaying face, the bloodlust in her eyes as she reached for his face, mouthing the words again.

"Honey, wake up!"

She grabbed his shoulder and with the horror of knowing his beloved had been taken by the plague setting in, he knew all hope was now lost.

She shook his shoulder.

"Chris! Wake up!"

He nearly jumped a foot from his chair, then jerked away from the hand on his shoulder.

"Bad dream?"

He looked up at Sherrie who had a grin on her face. He quickly wiped his mouth in case there was any drool, then breathed a sigh of relief that the game of Resident Evil he had been dreaming about was only that. A dream.

"Zombies."

She laughed then dropped into the spare seat, pulling it closer to him, placing one hand on his thigh, the other on the back of his head, drawing him in closer.

"Was I in it?"

"Umm, yeah, but—"

"But I was a zombie?"

He nodded.

"Well then, you know it's only a dream. I'm too kick-ass to be turned."

She planted a kiss on him that had the already fading zombies running for the darkest reaches of his mind as libido raised its head.

"You've been on a mission," he mumbled when she finally came up for air.

"Mmmmm," she said, going in for a second attack.

It was always the same. Whenever she got back from a mission, they had wild sex, her adrenaline always pumped. Needless to say he always looked forward to it. But they were at the office, in the middle of a crisis, and nothing was going to get done about that here.

She planted another kiss on him, one that began to get a little inappropriate for the office as her right hand climbed up his thigh, beginning to squeeze something that had no mind to protest, then broke away, flushed.

"Not here," she said, looking around. "Argh, I wish we could go somewhere."

Gawd do I wish we could go somewhere!

"Me too, hon. This entire end of the world thing is killing sex lives everywhere."

She burst out laughing, pushing away from him.

"So, can you talk about it?" he asked.

"Yeah. Picked up Dr. Urban's wife. Turned out to be an imposter."

She quickly related the day's events and the highlights of the interrogation, Leroux switching from gaga boyfriend to CIA analyst mode.

His Blackberry began beeping an alarm, and Leroux quickly grabbed it, shutting it off.

"Nap's over."

Sherrie smiled, then suddenly looked tired.

"What's wrong?"

"Nothing. I guess the adrenaline is wearing off. I'm going to be crashing soon."

"Funny, you never seem tired when you get home after a mission."

She winked at him and leaned forward, grabbing both his thighs.

"That's because I usually have something to keep the adrenaline pumping for a few more hours."

Leroux felt himself blush with a rush of blood midpoint between the hands. He put his hands on hers then slowly pushed them away.

"I need to go to the Director's office in ten minutes, and right now I'm a friggin' tripod."

Sherrie dropped her head and raised her eyebrows.

"Now, honey, I wouldn't go that far."

Leroux flushed some more, but played along at the insult of his manhood.

"Ouch. That hurt."

"I think it would hurt more if you tried to walk on the little guy."

Leroux moaned. "Never *ever* say the word 'little' when talking about a man's, you know, thing."

Sherrie laughed, patting him on the leg again, Little Chris already racing for cover.

"Don't worry, dear, you might not hit bottom but you scrape the hell out of the sides, which I think you can tell is more than enough for me."

He wasn't sure if he had just been insulted or complimented, but he decided to go with the latter since he had never had any complaints from her. He opened up his Inbox and began to quickly scan the results.

He smiled.

"Progress!" He pointed at one of the results showing bank account tracing. "Man, if we could do our jobs like this all the time, we'd save so much time!"

"And we'd live in a police state."

Leroux frowned.

"Yeah, you're right of course." He actually felt kind of ashamed at his excitement. Sherrie was right, and he had to remember that. In fact, over the years he'd been an analyst in the CIA the things they were allowed to get away with continued to grow, the powers they had continually creeping toward that very police state. It was a slippery slope, and if the people didn't wake up soon, America might as well be China.

He was reminded of what a friend had once called it. *Frog water.* If you put a frog in a pot of boiling water, it jumps out, because it knows it's hot. But if you put the frog in cool water, then slowly boil the water, the frog will stay put, eventually dying, because it didn't notice the increase in temperature.

It was the same with the American public. If after 9/11 they had known right away of all the changes that would occur over the next ten years to their rights and freedoms, to the powers granted their security apparatus, they would have said no. But introduce it a little at a time, distract them with other things, and ten years later they don't even realize they're not living in the same country.

But for people like Leroux, it did make it much easier to spy on American and foreign citizens, and now with all controls lifted, things were flying in.

"While you were gone we caught a lead in New Orleans. Kane found the guy who planted a cylinder of the aerosolized antiviral at the Superdome. He was dead, but he found a bank account number in the Caymans. Your imposter Mrs. Urban's bank account number was just linked to it."

"How?"

"Both accounts received payments from another account."

"And who owns the other account?"

"Some bullshit Cayman Islands corporation. The system's trying to trace that down. Shouldn't be too long. My guess though is that there will be a series of blinds set up before we can trace them. But we'll do it. We'll find him."

"Him?"

"Urban."

"Do you really think he's the guy?"

"What do you mean?"

"I mean, it seems to me that he's being coerced. His wife's been kidnapped, a stranger is taking care of his kids, and he apparently appeared frightened when treating the brother. I think there's a lot more going on here than we were led to believe."

Leroux paused for a minute, then his Blackberry demanded his attention again.

"I've got to meet with the Director. I think you should come."

"Love to."

Morrison Cottage, Dyke, Virginia

Cheryl Morrison sat on the front porch of the family cottage, the magnificent view of the Blue Ridge Mountains lost on her. It was peaceful. Incredibly peaceful. It was almost enough to forget the chaos that was beginning to spread across the country. Incidents like what had happened back at the gas station were repeating themselves everywhere as people panicked and began to hoard. National Guards nationwide were beginning to deploy to maintain calm.

It was terrifying. Terrifying to the point she had to get out of the cottage and into the fresh air where she couldn't hear the television Charlie had blaring. And what was even more terrifying to her now was that the cellular network seemed to be jammed. She couldn't reach her husband nor her daughter. Dozens of attempts at Leif's cellphone and office number finally got his voicemail, where she left him a garbled message she was sure, trying to make it sound like he didn't need to worry about her or the kids, but the fact she could barely remember the message left her thinking it might have been panicked.

Because dozens and dozens of attempts to reach their daughter Alexis had failed. When she had called Alexis earlier, she had been reluctant to agree to come to the cottage, but after Cheryl had practically begged her, finally telling her to 'turn on the damned TV and wake up!', she changed her mind. She'd be coming in from DC, so it would take a little longer, but she hadn't thought it would be this long, and like any mother's mind, it was inventing dozens of scenarios where her baby was dead.

Footsteps behind her startled her, but it was only Charlie.

"Cases are showing up everywhere now."

"Uh huh."

"Nobody's dying yet, at least not outside of New Orleans. But the Internet says anytime now."

"The Internet."

She didn't have much respect for it. It was filled with half-truths and lies, that kids and the naïve took at face value. She knew her husband even used the Internet to place cover stories and discredit true stories. It was war in the information age, and whoever had the best hackers and bullshit artists would win.

"Yeah, the conspiracy sites are going nuts. Who knows what to believe, but even CNN is starting to report that the virus has killed nearly one hundred percent of the first wave of infected people."

"Uh huh."

Where's Alexis?

The phone rang, causing Cheryl to jump, Charlie rushing in to grab it.

"Hello?"

There was a pause, then Charlie's footfalls, heavy, hammered toward the porch.

"Mom! It's Alexis! She's in trouble!"

Cheryl grabbed the phone as she stood up.

"Mom! You gotta help me! I'm being chased by some guys in a truck!"

"What?"

"They rammed me twice! I'm a bit ahead of them now, but I don't know how much longer I can hang on!"

Cheryl's heart slammed into her chest with each word erupting from her terrified daughter's mouth.

"Where are you?"

"I'm only a couple of miles from the cottage! Oh God no!"

There was a terrific banging sound, then static. Her daughter was crying and screaming on the other end, and Cheryl felt like she was going to throw up, her daughter's desperate pleas going unanswered, Cheryl powerless to help her.

"Mom! Are you still there?"

"Yes, are you okay?"

"Yes, they lost control when they hit me, I'm getting ahead. What do I do?"

"Come here. Your brother and I are here. It will be safe."

"But then they'll just hurt all of us, maybe kill us."

"Don't worry about that. Hang up the phone, concentrate on your driving. Get here as fast as you can."

"Okay, Mom. I love you."

"I love you too, dear."

The call ended and Cheryl rushed into the cottage, turning to Charlie.

"Enable the defenses."

Charlie's eyebrows shot up.

"I thought we weren't supposed to touch that, it was CIA only."

"To hell with the rules. Activate it. The code is Alpha-Delta-Tango-Enter-nine-six-four-four-two-seven-Enter. Got it?"

Charlie shook his head, racing for the control panel near the wall by the fireplace. Cheryl saw him begin to enter the code as she ran into the games room, entering a six digit code on the wall panel that she never thought she'd have to use.

The pool table began to flip, a cover sliding into place to secure anything on top. Flipped completely over, the cover that was once the bottom slid open, and a series of drawers ejected around the entire table, revealing weapons of all sizes, ammunition, grenades, knives and more.

"After Alpha-Delta-Tango, what is it?"

She repeated the seven digits.

"Got it!" yelled Charlie. Cheryl heard the mechanisms in the house kick in as armor plating dropped over the windows and doors, the walls themselves already reinforced to be able to take a hit from anything handheld including RPGs. Leif had trained her in everything over the years, and stressed the importance as to why. He never spoke of his work, but he never shied away from the dangers of it. He had a detail always assigned to him, and his family did at certain times, but usually they were on their own to live their lives, which was what she preferred.

But today, being the wife of the Director of National Clandestine Services, she would use the tools made available to her to save her daughter. She stuffed a knife and a Glock 22 in her back belt, grabbed an MP5A2 submachine gun, and a Mossberg 500 Homeland Defender shotgun for Charlie. She was about to walk away from the table when she stuffed a couple of grenades in each pocket.

"She's here!" yelled Charlie from the front of the cottage.

Cheryl rushed toward his voice, tossing the shotgun and several boxes of shells at a nearby chair.

"Get ready," she said, checking her own weapon and loading it.

"Holy shit!" exclaimed Charlie, who quickly began to load the shotgun.

Screaming from outside, though muffled, was none the less heartbreaking. Cheryl entered the code to open the front door, then stepped onto the porch. Alexis's SUV sliding to a halt in the gravel only feet from the porch. The door flew open and Alexis rounded it, her face red and tear streaked as she rushed toward her mother. Throwing her arms around her, she screamed at the sound of a pickup truck pulling into the circular driveway, the sounds of several men hooting and hollering in a frenzy.

Cheryl pushed her daughter inside as Charlie stepped out with the shotgun, raising it at the truck. Cheryl stepped down from the porch and around Alexis's SUV, firing several rounds into the ground in front of the now stopped vehicle, its occupants freezing at the sound of the bullets tearing into the gravel. Cheryl aimed the weapon at the windshield.

"I suggest you all turn around and leave now!"

She was running on adrenaline now, her hands beginning to shake as she tried to steady her breathing. She knew it would take several minutes to get control of her shakes, but she didn't think she had that kind of time. This was going to end one way or another in the next sixty seconds. She flicked the weapon to fully automatic.

The driver stepped out, his hands up, a smile on his face.

"Now, you're not going to shoot us, are you? A little old lady like yourself?"

Old my ass. I oughta shoot you just for that.

The man, maybe thirty, if that, began to approach, his hands still raised.

"Now all we want is what's in the back of her truck. Things are going to hell, and we just want our share."

Cheryl pointed the weapon directly at the man's chest. This caused him to pause, then he continued forward, motioning for the other three to join him. The passenger door opened then the two doors of the rear cab as his friends joined him. They were all approaching her now, and she stepped back, trying to keep some distance.

They're not going to stop. They're going to kill you, then your son, then rape and murder your daughter.

"This is your final warning."

The driver stopped, his smile disappearing.

"Fuck you, lady. Your time is over."

He rushed at her and she squeezed the trigger, a burst of lead erupting from the barrel, leaving a row of holes from the man's stomach up to his left shoulder as the other three scattered.

A shot roared from the other side of the SUV and a body flew back into view as Charlie took out one of the men. Cheryl swung her weapon at a third man who seemed to be reaching for something in his pocket that she had to assume was a weapon.

She squeezed the trigger again, hitting him in the back then the head, the body dropping in a quivering heap. The final man dove into the front seat of their truck from the passenger side. Charlie emptied a barrel into the windshield as the engine roared to life. He advanced quickly, the shotgun held high against his shoulder as he chambered another round.

"Wait!" yelled Cheryl but it was too late. The muzzle flashed as the round was fired through the hole already made in the windshield. The final survivor ducked in time, the back of the seat and headrest riddled with holes. The rear tires spun and the front tires turned as the man drove blind, tearing out of their gravel driveway, his head finally making an appearance when the back of the truck was between him and their weapons.

"Why did you let him get away?" demanded Charlie, clearly exasperated.

"He was leaving. You don't shoot someone when they're clearly running away."

"Running away, yeah, probably to get more of his friends!"

Cheryl nodded, realizing he was probably right.

"Nevertheless, I don't want us being accused of murder."

"Are you guys okay?"

It was Alexis, standing in the doorway brandishing a handgun.

"We're fine!" called Cheryl, looking at the three bodies.

"What are we going to do with them?" asked Charlie.

"We can't move them. This is a crime scene. I guess we'll call the sheriff."

"Let's just hope one of these guys isn't a friend of his."

Cheryl frowned, holding out her arm as Alexis joined them, putting her head on her mother's shoulder.

"Maybe we should just call Dad."

CIA Headquarters, Langley, Virginia

Morrison sat behind his desk, his fingers steepled in front of his face, his lips pursed as he stared into space. Leroux wasn't sure if he should say something and exchanged a quick glance with Sherrie. Both had been talking for almost the past ten minutes, with Morrison saying little if anything, the Director's side of the conversation more often than not some sort of guttural sound.

Something's bothering him.

Leroux wondered if it was appropriate to ask your boss, a man so high up on the ladder he could probably order you killed without question, if he was feeling alright. Leroux decided against it.

Morrison's phone rang and he jumped at it, seeming to forget he wasn't alone.

"Are you okay?"—"What?"—"How many?"—"Is she okay?"—"Did you arm the system?"—"One got away?"—"Who have you called?"—"Good, just stay inside, I'll take care of things."—"Love you too."

Leroux had tried not to eavesdrop, but it was impossible. The office was large, but not that large, and his boss had been so agitated, he had made no attempt to lower his voice. The receiver hit the cradle and Morrison sighed, then seemed to remember they were in the room.

"Sorry for that, personal call. Family."

"Are they okay?" asked Sherrie.

Glad she had the balls to ask!

"My wife and kids are at our cottage. They were attacked by four men. Three are dead, but one got away."

Leroux's heart was pounding in his chest just thinking of it. His mind immediately filled with images of his own family, and how scared they must be, and how he had no power to help them.

"Do you want me to go get them?"

It was Sherrie who asked, and the Director's eyebrows shot up at the suggestion.

"That wouldn't be appropriate. Our families shouldn't get any special treatment because we work at the CIA."

"Sir, the Director of National Clandestine Services' secondary residence was attacked by unknown hostiles with unknown intent. At least one is still alive, with possibly more accomplices on the way. Security of the Director's family, so they cannot be used in an attempt at extortion against him is in the best interest of the nation, especially in a time of crisis."

God I love that woman!

Morrison's head was bobbing slightly as he listened.

"I hadn't thought of it that way, and as selfish as it sounds, you're right. Go get them, take whatever resources you need. My assistant has the address. Full biohazard protocols are now in effect, so make sure you follow them and put my family into quarantine when they get here. CDC apparently has a blood test now. Screening has already begun in New Orleans and all major Federal facilities. We'll at least start to be able to know who's infected and who isn't."

"But how many do we test? All seven billion?"

"If we have to. The protocols for the test are being sent to every government in the world. Quarantines are already being set up at airports, and the EU, Canada and China have already shutdown all international air travel. We expect full shutdown within the next few hours."

"Jesus," muttered Leroux. "I never thought I'd see the day."

Morrison nodded. "Neither did I." He turned to Sherrie. "You're dismissed, good luck."

Sherrie got up from her chair, gave Leroux a wink, then as she was about to open the door, Morrison spoke up.

"And Agent White?"

"Yes, sir?"

"Thank you."

She smiled then left the office, closing the door behind her. Leroux was about to stand up when Morrison waved him back into his chair. "Don't worry, you'll get a chance to say goodbye." Morrison leaned back in his chair. "This theory of Agent White's about Dr. Urban being coerced. What do you think?"

Leroux leaned forward.

"I think she's right. Stand in for the wife, leaving the kids in place, means this wasn't a getaway to a new life with his family. Unless the guy really hates his kids!" Leroux's mind spun for a moment at the thought. "After all, he seems to have no qualms about killing people, so maybe he doesn't care about them."

"Then he probably wouldn't care about his wife either. Let's assume he does love his kids."

"Then leaving the kids behind with a stranger has to have him worrying constantly. Who knows if the wife is even alive? Maybe they killed her, or are holding her as another way of getting him to cooperate. The children being with the stranger is the key. He has to assume the imposter has orders to kill the kids if necessary."

"Sounds solid. What else?"

"Well, we know he's not working alone. There's the man who planted the canister at the Superdome, there's the man who hired that man, there's whoever killed him. Also, we have the person who recruited the wife stand-in. He could be the same person who hired the guy in New Orleans, who knows, but when there's more than one person, it's a conspiracy."

"I agree. I think Agent White's theory is correct. Now we have to hope that if Urban is an unwilling partner in all this, that if we are able to somehow find him, we'll be able to get him to cooperate. He just may have a cure for what we're now facing."

"What are the latest projections?"

"If the mutated strain were to get into the general population, with a one-hundred percent kill rate, we're looking at total annihilation within less than a year. Some will survive of course, the President has already given orders to start prepping certain offshore facilities, and other countries will be doing the same. The human race will survive, but in isolated pockets until we can figure out how to reclaim the mainland."

"I try not to think about it, otherwise I can't concentrate on my work."

"Me as well," said Morrison, nodding. He sat up in his chair, moving his mouse to clear the screensaver. "And speaking of work, we both better get back at it."

"Thank you, sir," said Leroux as he stood up then left the office, sending Sherrie a text. Within a few seconds she replied.

Meet me where we first made love in five minutes.

Little Chris jumped at the message as Leroux raced for his desk. He quickly checked the status of his searches, initiated his follow ups, then raced toward the temporary quarters where they had been housed after the attack on his apartment several months ago. Memories of that experience flashed through his mind, and he was thankful he wasn't wearing track pants.

He reached the door and opened it, holding his breath in anticipation. It was dark inside, the only sound his own heart slamming in his chest.

"Hello?"

Nothing.

Suddenly the door was pushed shut behind him followed by a click of the lock. He was shoved against the wall, hard, then he felt a pair of lips pressed on his, hands ripping off his clothes as he remained still, momentarily stunned.

"We've got *maybe* fifteen minutes!" said Sherrie breathlessly.

Leroux's body flew into motion, not willing to waste a second of their precious time, the troubles of the outside world momentarily forgotten.

Isolation Ward, Interim LSU Public Hospital, New Orleans, Louisiana

Dr. Katherine Best winced as the obviously tired nurse took her blood sample. She like the rest were being screened for the antiviral using the new test developed by the CDC and BioDyne Pharma. The first results were starting to come in, and wisely Dr. Johnston had ordered the outlier cases, the two men infected in their isolation ward, be screened first, the third man who had been brought in with the initial wave of women actually born a woman and being treated as such from a medical standpoint.

And both men were positive.

Genetic tests ordered by Dr. Corkery, the young doctor who had notified them of the outbreak, were also starting to arrive, showing all of the women whose results had come back did indeed have the same genetic mutation, along with the first "male" who had arrived with the initial batch. The genetic defect which affected less than half a percent of the population, led to a highly increased risk of breast cancer in women, which essentially proved Corkery's theory, and corroborated what Dr. Kapp from BioDyne Pharma had said their message from Dr. Urban had claimed about the antiviral.

This antiviral was designed to target specific genetic sequences. The problem in this case was that a genetic deformity you were born with was in *all* of your DNA, therefore the antiviral was targeting the victim's entire body, eventually killing them. An actual virus like HIV or the flu would only infect some of the body, and the antiviral would kill only those bad cells. If the antiviral were used as designed, it would do wonders. But programming it to target genetic birth defects was just madness.

A hazmat suit rounded the corner, its orange color indicating their exposure classification. Dr. Corkery's face was revealed through the window, a smile on it that widened when he saw Best.

"I take it your blood test cleared you?"

He nodded.

"Now it's round two. I have to stay isolated in this suit for the next few hours until the second test is negative, then I can join you guys in those lovely green suits."

Best laughed. "I guess you haven't seen daylight or smelt fresh air in quite a while."

Corkery nodded.

"Reminds me of med school." His face became all business. "I understand we have mixed news back."

She nodded.

"Looks like you were right on what the original antiviral was designed to target. But the two outliers both have the virus, obviously aren't women, and don't have the mutation, so they shouldn't have been targeted."

"How are they progressing?"

"Similar to the others, however a little slower. There's definitely something different here, but we don't know what yet."

"I assume you're having the antiviral in their blood compared to the original?"

"Of course, but it will take time. The initial analysis says it's essentially the same. They're trying to identify the differences now, and then determine exactly what those differences mean. We've sent samples of both to BioDyne Pharma to see if their scientists can make head or tail of it since it was originally their creation."

"Anything further on transmission?"

"It's airborne, we know that for sure. We're doing testing to see how long it survives outside the host and under what conditions. We've got teams growing it like crazy so we can start to try figuring out how to destroy it. It's going to take time, which is the one thing we don't have."

Corkery frowned just as another Code Blue blared over the PA.

"I'll take this," he said, "these are my patients."

Best nodded and Corkery rushed into the isolation unit as one of the final remaining patients passed.

And Best kept wondering if a second wave of infections was about to start arriving.

Gravier Street, New Orleans, Louisiana

Dylan Kane leaned back, stretching the kinks out of his back. He leaned forward and took a swig of his Diet Coke, all the while keeping his eyes glued to the screen. It hadn't taken too long to get the digital footage from the owner of the corner store embedded in the apartment where Milner had lived, but there was no rhyme or reason to the hard drive he had provided.

And he hadn't stuck around to explain it, his drop off more resembling a drive-by than anything else. So he and Isabelle had commandeered a terminal in the FBI mobile HQ, now located out front of the apartment building, uploaded the footage to Langley, and waited for the first results to begin coming in. It hadn't taken long, and they had now spent almost two hours staring at digitally enhanced faces with date and time stamps to see if anyone jumped out at them. After the first half hour, some of the faces began to come in again with identities attached to them and their FBI files.

The unfortunate part about dealing with a dump apartment building like the one Milner had lived in was that almost everyone had a file, making their job even more difficult. The original lobby footage hadn't proved useful, the angle actually away from the entrance, only showing the mailboxes they had identified Milner's apartment number from. This new storefront camera though could prove a goldmine.

"That's Milner there," said Isabelle, pointing at the screen. Kane had to admit he had almost missed it. She clicked on the photo, then activated the link back to the original footage. "That's the night before he installed the canister."

"Looks like he's alone," said Kane as he fired the image number back to Langley over his phone, telling them that this was their high priority target and that they needed his comings and goings identified, along with anybody who might be with him or anybody entering the building after him that didn't live there.

On the terminal a database was building as the faces came in. Many were duplicates as residents came and went, and the computer, using facial recognition software, was able to catch the duplicates and combine them into single files, then when their identities came in from one of the many government databases they were tapped into, classify them as resident, non-resident, or unknown. The database was quickly filling in, the amount of computer power being dedicated by Langley massive, as this was their best lead for the moment.

FBI Special Agent Hewlett cleared her throat, handing over a tablet computer. "We've got footage of our cemetery guy. Pulled it from a security camera."

Kane took the tablet and held it out so both he and Isabelle could see it.

"You're sure it's him?" asked Isabelle. "He was barely pixels in the other shot."

"He's coming out of the same cemetery at the same time in the same direction as the other man, dressed in the same color clothes. This is the guy all right."

"I agree," said Kane, nodding, as he quickly read the summary. "So we don't know who he is?"

"No. We've uploaded it to our people and sent it to Langley. Hopefully we'll have something shortly."

Kane pursed his lips.

"Got somewhere to sleep around here?"

"We've got rooms reserved at the Holiday Inn near the Superdome. Just show them your ID and they'll give you a room."

"Sounds good." Kane turned to Isabelle. "How about we both get some rest until something solid shows up. I have a feeling once it does, we'll have no time for sleep until this thing is over."

Isabelle stood up.

"Agreed. But come stay at my place. It's only ten minutes from here, and with a virus going around, staying at a public place probably isn't a great idea."

Kane rose from his seat and turned to Hewlett. "You know how to reach us. Call me if anything actionable comes in."

"Will do," said Hewlett, stifling a yawn.

"And you better get some sleep too," said Kane with a smile.

Hewlett nodded, returning the smile as she checked her watch.

"My replacement is here in ten minutes then I'm getting eight sweet hours."

Kane chuckled as Isabelle opened the door. He looked at Hewlett. "If you get eight hours, I'm buying the beer when this is all over."

Hewlett closed her eyes for a moment, sighing.

"I'll be happy with three. Just three uninterrupted hours in a comfortable bed."

"Sweet dreams," said Kane with a laugh as he stepped outside and closed the door. Isabelle was already climbing into her car, yawning in anticipation of their purpose. Kane strode over to the car and climbed in the passenger side. He put his seatbelt on and closed his eyes as Isabelle pulled out and into the non-existent traffic.

"This city's becoming a ghost town."

Kane opened his eyes. There were police and military vehicles moving, ambulances and fire, but almost no civilian traffic, the few civilian cars to be seen most likely unmarked cars, or emergency workers on their way to or from their shifts. There were however a few cars here and there that seemed to be driven by terrified people, most likely out on some emergency errand for water or food, their cupboards woefully unprepared for an emergency like this.

Always be prepared for two weeks of no government services!

With the crap he had seen around the world, with the number of fanatics inside and outside of the US that he knew about, whenever he made it home to visit his folks he always made sure they were well supplied. He had set up four large storage bins in their basement now containing enough emergency rations, medical supplies and tools, along with cash, silver and gold, batteries, solar and crank chargers, and much more in the event things truly went to shit.

It was something he felt every American should do. Not just in case some wacko did something, but other things such as power blackouts, hurricanes, viruses, riots. There was no shortage of things that could go wrong that you couldn't predict or outrun. Sometimes your only choice is to hunker down and wait it out. And being well supplied makes it much more likely you'll survive doing so.

They rounded a corner, Kane's eyes closed again as he prepared himself for the coming sleep, when he felt the car begin to slow.

"What's this?" he heard Isabelle mutter.

Kane opened his eyes and looked. A group of men, it looked like six, were beating on a lone man, his car, a Jaguar, sitting nearby, its driver side door open. Isabelle was about to reach for her radio when Kane stopped her.

"No point wasting police resources on something like this. Wait here, I'll take care of it."

"What? I'm coming with you."

"If things go wrong, come in shooting, but there's no point in both of us possibly being exposed to the virus."

"Fine. I hope you know what you're doing."

"Me too!" grinned Kane as he climbed out of the now stopped car. He approached the group, the victim now curled up in a ball on the ground as he protected his stomach and head from further blows.

"Hey!" yelled Kane as he approached, halting the attack as the group of punks turned to see who had the gall to interrupt their fun.

"Walk on cracker or you'll get some of this too," yelled one of them, apparently the leader, the rest appearing to be at least a few years younger than this one's twenty years at best. These were street kids taking advantage of the situation.

"I'm afraid I can't do that," said Kane, circling to the right so the group would turn away from the victim's car. He knew if he could draw them away the man might be able to make it into his car and get away. Kane pointed at the car. "Don't you know what kind of car that is? It's a Jaguar. Don't you think this poor bastard has enough problems in his life driving that thing? He doesn't need to get beat up on by you guys to be in misery, he's a Jag owner!"

One of the kids laughed, then looked at the glare from the alpha male of the group.

"You weren't thinking of stealing his car, were you?" asked Kane, continuing to round the group. "You have to know that the damned thing would break down on you if you got into a chase. Hell, this guy was probably on his way back from the garage getting something fixed when you guys stopped him."

Another giggle, another glare.

"I've just about heard enough from you," said the alpha male. "Get him!" he bravely ordered his young cohorts.

They rushed forward, giggles and grins gone, gangster sneers carefully painted on their faces. Kane snap kicked the first arrival in the stomach, doubling him over. Kane stepped back, grabbing the second one by the shirt, pulling him with his left hand toward his right, which he used to crush the boy's windpipe enough to take him out of the game, but not permanently. A roundhouse dropped the third to the pavement, rolling him onto the road, moaning in pain as his two buddies sought their revenge.

Kane smacked the next one, open palmed on the face, dropping him in a stinging mess of watering eyes as the victim scrambled away to his car.

Good! Get out of here before they realize what's happening.

Kane grabbed the final boy from the initial rush and squeezed him by the throat, lifting him into the air several inches as he applied pressure to the arteries supplying oxygen to the brain. The boy's eyes began to droop and Kane tossed him to the side.

The leader stepped forward.

"Enough's enough!" he yelled as he reached for something behind him. Kane grabbed his gun tucked into his belt when he noticed the victim hadn't fled at all, but had instead opened his trunk and retrieved a golf club. He swung at the alpha dog's legs, nailing him in the side of the knee, sending him screaming to the pavement, his gun clattering to the ground.

The man then raised his club high in the air, double fisted over the head, then dropped the titanium head hard and fast on the guys back. Kane could have sworn he heard vertebrae shatter as the punk cried out in pain. The others were now starting to get up and Kane pulled his weapon, pointing it at them.

"Get your asses home. If I see any of you out again, I'll shoot you first and won't even bother asking questions." Nobody moved. "Get!" They scattered, leaving their leader on the ground, crying in pain as the jag owner landed another blow.

"I think he's had enough," said Kane, approaching. The man stopped and looked up at Kane, his face covered in blood and sweat, several prominent cuts on his face, but nothing he wouldn't survive. "I'd say you should go to a hospital, but with what's happening, I'd say get your ass home, clean up your wounds, and consider yourself lucky."

The man nodded, extending his hand.

"Fred Newton."

Kane holstered his gun.

"Sorry if I don't shake hands, what with the virus and you being covered in blood."

Newton stood up and laughed, then winced.

"You're right, of course." He stepped over to his trunk and tossed the club inside, closing the lid. "Thanks for stopping, you didn't have to do that."

"No problem. Now I'll say to you like I said to them. Get home and stay home. Things are going to shit fast."

Newton nodded as he climbed into his car, closing the door. He leaned out the window.

"And by the way. Jags are fantastic cars. I'll let you get away with it this time since you saved my life, but next time, I'll force you to drive one!"

Kane laughed and motioned with his hand for Newton to leave.

"Get out of here before that thing breaks down and I have to call you a tow."

Newton laughed, revving the engine.

"Thanks again," he said with a serious expression, then turned and gunned the vehicle into the city streets, hopefully heading home if he knew what was good for him.

Kane looked at the mess that was the alpha leader lying on the sidewalk, groaning. There was nothing he could do to help him, his spine was most likely shattered. He returned to the car with Isabelle and climbed in.

"Better call for an ambulance for him."

"What should I report? You let the victim go."

"Just say we found him like that."

Isabelle shrugged her shoulders.

"Fine by me. It would have been easier if you had let the guy kill him though."

Kane nodded his head, but having inflicted enough death in his lifetime, he knew that one Mr. Fred Newton, Jaguar lover, might have felt better for the moment in killing his assailant, but in the long run, would be haunted by it. Instead, he now would go on with his life knowing he had fought his assailant and won, and he most likely would never know what condition he had left the piece of garbage in, other than the fact he was alive.

Which was far easier to sleep with.

Kane yawned as the adrenaline rush he was on crashed.

"Let's get to your place. I need to sleep, stat."

Isabelle echoed the yawn, pulling the car back onto the road.

"We'll be there in five minutes."

Kane was asleep before the next turn.

Morrison Cottage, Dyke, Virginia

Cheryl Morrison's head drooped then popped back up, looking around to see if anything had changed, how long she had been asleep unknown. Nothing had. Alexis had cried herself to sleep on the loveseat almost an hour ago, and Charlie stood vigil watching the outdoor cameras in his dad's office.

Cheryl had tried to stay awake, but she had to get some rest, even if only for a quick power nap. She pushed herself up from the couch to make sure Charlie was awake. She found him cradling the shotgun in his lap, his eyes glued to the cameras, leaving them only when his hand darted to the large bowl of chips he had poured himself, or the large glass of pop he was nursing.

"How are you doing?" she asked, walking over and squeezing his shoulders.

"Good. No action outside." He looked up over his shoulder at her. "Maybe they won't come back."

"Maybe." She sighed. "I'm going to get some sleep. Use the alarm to wake me if something happens, or if you get tired, come get me and I'll take over."

"Sure, Mom."

She gave his shoulders another squeeze then went to the master bedroom, the usual spectacular view blocked by metal screens. It was depressing, but she didn't have the energy to care. Her head hit the pillow and she was out like a light within seconds.

The phone rang.

She woke up, spinning herself so her feet were on the floor almost on instinct. The phone rang again. She reached for it and hit the *Talk* button.

"Hello?"

"Hello. Mrs. Morrison?"

"Who is this?"

"This is Deputy Wright from the Greene County Sheriff's Office. We've had a report of shots fired in your area. Are you okay?"

"Yes, I'm fine."

Her heart was pounding. Their cottage was fairly remote, however it was definitely conceivable that someone heard the shots, especially with the number of shots that were fired.

"What about the other two with you? Are they okay?"

"Everyone is fine here, Deputy."

Cheryl heard Charlie's feet pounding on the hardwood floors and he burst into the bedroom as she put a finger to her lips, then covered the mouthpiece.

"They're here!" he whispered. "A cop car and two more trucks. At least ten people. Only one cop though."

"And what about the people who came to your cottage earlier?"

Cheryl's heart slammed into her chest as she stood up, grabbing her weapon and following Charlie back to Leif's office. Alexis was already there, pointing at the camera angle they needed to see.

"You mean the ones who tried to kill my daughter, and then us?"

"I mean the unarmed men you shot and killed in cold blood."

"My daughter was attacked by four men in a pickup truck, pursued to our cottage, then they refused to stand down when ordered to. They rushed my position, and I was forced to defend myself. Three were shot, we let one leave."

"Mrs. Morrison, I'm well aware of who your husband is, but if you think you can get away with shooting three unarmed people, including my brother, you're sadly mistaken."

"I'd like to talk to the Sheriff please."

"You can talk to him when you surrender yourselves."

Cheryl decided to play dumb.

"You're here?"

"You know very well we're here, Mrs. Morrison. You've got cameras all over the place. I'm asking that you come out now, peacefully, or you will force us to come in and get you."

"Deputy Wright, was it? If you can show me a warrant, we'll come out."

Cheryl had no intention of stepping one foot outside these walls, warrant or not, but she needed to get a sense of the situation. A lone cop, brother to one of the dead apparently, with ten of his friends, didn't sound like any police operation she had ever heard of.

"I don't need a warrant, Mrs. Robinson. I'm arresting you on suspicion of murder. The bodies are outside and I have a witness. There's no need for a warrant."

He was right of course, but it also meant that no one in town probably officially knew what he was doing. At least if a judge had signed off on something, they might expect "justice" of some sort. Instead, this had all the appearances of a lynch mob.

"They're surrounding us," whispered Charlie, pointing at various cameras showing the men spreading out.

"If you're here officially, Deputy, then why are you the only police officer here? Who are the other men with you?"

"They have all been deputized for this one arrest as we are shorthanded due to the virus scare."

Cheryl covered the mouth piece, turning to Charlie.

"Call your Dad on the other line."

"Speed dial one?"

Cheryl shook her head. "That's his regular number. Speed dial seven is the emergency number."

"I think we're done talking, Deputy. Have someone from the FBI come here, with credentials I can have verified by my husband, and we'll surrender. Not before."

She ended the call, handing the phone to Alexis, then took the other phone from Charlie.

"Director Morrison's office. How can I help you?"

"This is Cheryl. I need to speak with him immediately."

"I'm sorry, ma'am, he's with the President. May I assist you?"

"We are about to be attacked by ten armed men in our cottage. We need help."

"One moment please, let me connect you to the extraction team."

Extraction team?

Gunshots suddenly began to ping off the armored windows, echoing throughout the house from all sides. Cheryl instinctively ducked as Alexis yelped and climbed under the desk. Charlie rounded the desk, eyeing the cameras.

"They're attacking from all sides!" He pointed at a camera showing the front of the house. "It looks like they're going to try and pull open the door!"

Cheryl looked and saw two men pulling a chain from the back of a truck that had pulled within ten feet of their porch.

If they get inside, we're dead!

She grabbed her Glock off the desk and raced for the front of the house, the phone still pressed to her ear. Pulling open the front door, she slid aside the Judas hole at chest height just as she heard something on the other end of the line.

"This is Agent White. What is your status?"

"We're under attack by at least ten people. We're surrounded, and they are attempting to pull off the front door."

Cheryl looked through the hole and saw the two men climbing the steps, the chain draped across the hood of Alexis's SUV.

"Back off!" she yelled through the hole. The two men stopped, then one reached for a gun holstered on his hip. She pointed the weapon through the hole, took aim and fired, dropping the man as the phone clattered to the floor. She got a bead on the second one and decided if she didn't do it now, she'd be forced to deal with him later, and she might not have the advantage.

She squeezed the trigger and he dropped.

Suddenly a hand grabbed the barrel of the gun from outside, somebody having snuck up the front of the house from the side. She cried out and squeezed the trigger. The man yelped in pain and footfalls could be heard retreating along the porch.

Cheryl closed the Judas hole, then the door, and picked up the phone.

"Mrs. Morrison, are you there!"

"Yes, yes, I'm here."

"We're coming to get you. ETA—"

The phone went dead at the same time as the lights, the generator taking a few seconds to kick in. As the lights came back on, the dull drone of the generator, secured in a concrete bunker with the only entrance from within the cottage, was the only sound she could hear. She held the phone to her ear.

It was still dead.

And she had no idea when help would arrive.

Approaching Morrison Cottage, Dyke, Virginia

Command Sergeant Major Burt "Big Dog" Dawson, BD for short, eyed the incredibly young CIA agent leading the mission. Several Delta Force teams, including his Bravo Team, had been seconded to the CIA for domestic missions during the crisis. Rarely did he have to go on a mission on domestic soil, even though Delta were the only branch of the United States military exempt from Posse Comitatus if ordered by the President, and from what Dawson could tell, every branch of the government was operating with no holds barred.

The country was going to hell, and this time he had no one to fight.

The young agent turned to him, her conversation with one of their subjects having been cut off. "We're going into a hot LZ. It looks like they're under attack by approximately ten armed men."

Dawson frowned as he shrugged his shoulders, shifting the weight of his gear slightly, the Nuclear-Biological-Chemical NBC hazmat gear they were forced to wear making fighting a little more difficult. Now they were going into a hot LZ.

This just keeps getting better.

"I recommend we find another place to land then double-time it in. Put the bird back in the air, it can be our eyes and provide cover. Once we've secured the area, we'll extract at the originally planned LZ."

"Agreed," replied Agent White as she relayed new orders to the pilot. He wondered if that were her name, or code, his alias usually Mr. White. He turned to his team, a team much smaller than he would have liked with perhaps a dozen opponents facing them, but right now they were working in groups of four to maximize their ability to supplement the CIA operations. His second most senior man, Mike "Red" Belme was leading team two, and Leon "Atlas" James was leading team three. In the chopper with him he had Will "Spock" Lightman, Carl "Niner" Sung and Gerry "Jimmy Olson" Hudson with him. All experienced operators, men he wouldn't hesitate to trust with his life.

"You all heard that?" There were nods. "Spock, you're with me and Agent White. Jimmy and Niner, take our flank, eliminate anything that isn't us. Our subjects are holed up in a reinforced cottage. It's the National Clandestine Service Chief's family we're going after, so let's try not to shoot them."

Everyone looked at Niner for some flippant comment but got nothing except him turning his entire upper body to face each of them for a moment. Finally he said something.

"What? You expect me to be funny in this damned bunny suit? You know me, it's all in the delivery. My facial expressions, my posture, my—"

"I think we got it," interrupted Spock, his trademark eyebrow not visible to the team either.

Jimmy looked at Agent White. "Sorry, Agent. Our humor is handicapped by our equipment today."

White looked at Jimmy. "I'm sure they weren't thinking of that when they designed it." She shrugged her shoulders. "But don't worry, Sergeant. From what I can see, you look plenty funny to me."

Niner roared, punching Jimmy's shoulder.

"She *owned* you, bra!"

Jimmy rubbed his shoulder, wagging his finger at the young agent.

"You're on my list now!" he scolded as he laughed. "You're fair game now!"

"Bring it on!" urged White.

"ETA sixty seconds," said the pilot over the comm. The side door was slid open by a crewmember and Dawson looked out to see they were being dropped on a dirt road. A quick scan of the area and he knew right where they were from his briefing. This would be the road leading up to the cottage.

The wheels touched down and Dawson jumped out, followed by the rest of his team and the young agent. The chopper was airborne again within seconds, now their eye in the sky. Dawson checked the tactical computer zipped into his arm and selected a view of the area provided by the chopper, infrared images beginning to glow as it gained altitude. He pointed at the display.

"There's the cottage. Looks like eight hostiles surrounding it, two recently dead near the front. Probably the gunfire you heard when talking to the subject."

Agent White nodded, then pointed up the road. "Let's move. We don't know how long they can hold out. Once we get near the cottage, we'll split up into two teams, and eliminate the targets."

"Agreed." Dawson turned to his men. "Let's go gentlemen. Niner, you take point."

"Is this because I'm Asian?"

"Of course."

Niner trotted out ahead, then the rest followed, Niner quickly putting some distance between them. Jimmy came next, about twenty feet ahead of Dawson and White, with Spock taking up the rear. It didn't take long for the sound of gunfire to be heard through the thick trees, and according to the GPS on his tactical computer, they were nearly at the cottage when they found Niner taking a knee in the brush to the side of the road, his fist held up indicating they should stop.

They all moved to the side, taking a knee and cover. Dawson activated his comm.

"Report."

"Two hostiles hiding behind a truck, twenty meters head of me. On the number two side of the structure there are three more, and I can see muzzle flashes on the number four side. Tac computer shows two there, plus two more at the rear on the number three side."

"Roger that. Jimmy, you and Niner take out the two nearest us quietly."

Jimmy rushed forward to join Niner as the rest of the team advanced to Niner's former position where they had a clear view of Niner and Jimmy. Both had their knives out and within seconds had pounced on their targets, hands cupped over the enemy mouths, knives slitting their throats. After gently lowering the bodies to the ground, they took up positions behind the wheels of the truck.

"Niner, Jimmy, break left, take out the targets on the number two side on my mark. We'll go right, take out the number four side."

"Roger that," said Niner as he and Jimmy retreated into the trees on the left side of the road. Dawson moved forward to get a visual on the three north side targets and cursed.

"What is it?" asked White.

"They're up to something."

One of the men ran from his position, carrying what looked like a chain, dragging it from the front of a police SUV, lights still flashing, to the front porch. He crawled the rest of the way, then when he reached the door, Dawson saw a Judas hole slide open and a gun appear. The man though seemed prepared for this, his angle making it almost impossible to get a shot off at him.

Instead he held his position, tight and low against the wall, then when the person inside stopped to reload, he jumped up, shoved the hook into the Judas hole, then pulled the chain tight as he retreated. Dawson could see hands desperately trying to dislodge the hook from the hole, to no avail.

"Now! Now! Now!" yelled the man. Dawson saw the SUV's tires spin as the man let go of the chain, diving to the ground. The SUV struggled for a moment then the front door came flying off. There was a scream of a woman from inside and suddenly two men came running around the corner from the one-two corner to the left of the porch, two men racing to join them from the one-four corner to the right, as what looked like a sheriff's deputy jumped out of the SUV to join them.

"Situation's changed. Advance now!"

"Roger that!"

Dawson jumped up, rushing forward, his MP5K aiming at the first man about to enter. He fired, dropping the man. The second tripped over the first, but managed to roll inside the door. Flashes of weapons fire could be seen through the gaping door as Dawson pressed his advance. Gunfire from the left took out two of the attackers advancing from the right, and White's gun belched out several shots, removing the deputy from the equation.

"Niner, Jimmy, take the rear, eliminate that target. We're going in."

"Roger that."

Out of the corner of his eye he saw Niner and Jimmy dart across the cleared area in front of the cottage and toward the rear as Dawson's boots hit the porch. Screams from inside, along with gunfire, had him rush through the door, Spock on his heels, White covering their rear. He crossed the threshold, indicating Spock take the right, and he turned left, toward the screams.

He advanced quickly, weapon high, slightly hunched over and rounded a corner, entering what appeared to be an office, the one target that had managed to get inside firing shotgun blast after shotgun blast at a desk, behind which there were screams and cries in response. Dawson put his weapon against the back of the man's head and squeezed the trigger, spraying his brain matter across the room.

The corpse dropped to the floor with a thud.

"United States Military. Is Mrs. Morrison in here?"

There was no reply, simply more crying, then suddenly a voice cut through it.

"Y-yes, I'm here."

Agent White appeared to Dawson's left, and he waved her forward.

"Mrs. Morrison? I'm Agent White. Your husband sent us to extract you. Can you please lower any weapons you might have, and come out from behind the desk?"

A burst of gunfire could be heard from outside which was met with more cries from behind the desk.

"Final target eliminated. All clear," came Niner's voice.

"The last hostile has been eliminated," said Dawson. "You're safe now." He activated the comm. "Niner, call in the chopper."

"Roger that."

Within seconds he could hear the thumping of the massive blades as they sliced through the air, preparing to land in front of the cottage. A head poked out from behind the desk, revealing an exhausted woman, her face red and streaked with tears, her hands held up, shaking, as she emerged from their hiding place. Two more heads joined her as the adult children crawled out from under the desk.

Agent White stepped forward, extending her gloved hand to Mrs. Morrison.

"You're safe now. Let's get you to Langley."

Mrs. Morrison fell forward into White's arms, hugging her as she sobbed "Thank you!" over and over, the two kids hugging them both.

Dawson smiled, stepping forward to help move the huddle toward the chopper.

"The sooner we're out of here, the sooner you can all be reunited."

The mass broke apart, and he led them to the chopper, the rest of his team holding covering positions until the family was onboard. As they lifted into the air, Dawson couldn't help but wonder if things like this were playing out all over the country, the victims not lucky enough to have a family member high enough in the government to warrant a CIA/Delta intervention.

Things are going to get worse before they get better.

CIA Headquarters, Langley, Virginia

Chris Leroux's computer beeped an alert that had him flipping over to his inbox. His heart raced in excitement as he scanned the contents of the message just received, his jaw dropping with each new revelation. The deposits into the imposter Jessica "Mrs. Urban" Flowers and Mike "The Canister Planter" Milner had been traced back after several bounces to the same account. That account had backtracked through several more dummy corporations to a standard front corporation in the Cayman Islands. These were companies that acted as middlemen between the banks and other foreign individuals or companies. Their names would be on the bank files, but the funds, less a generous fee for the middlemen, would still be owned by the foreign entity.

These were designed to try and stop computer traces in their tracks. With the digital trail dead, all transactions at this point in cash and in person, it was next to impossible to trace the money beyond the fronts. The fronts were doing nothing illegal according to Cayman Islands law, and the government was reluctant to change the rules, lest they lose the billions sheltered in their banks.

But with the gloves off, according to the report, a two man team kidnapped the owner of the middleman company, forced him to open his paper files, and the hunt was back on. Several more bounces and they had their man.

Scott Fowler.

The name meant nothing to Leroux until he began to read the CIA and FBI files on the man, and his jaw hit the floor.

"Holy shit!"

He fired the name into his search algorithms to begin tracking down every financial transaction, sighting, phone conversation, email—anything that could be used to locate the man. This Fowler had to be found—fast. It would be difficult, but Leroux relished the thought of catching this bastard. He activated his final tracking routine, then grabbed the phone and dialed the Director's office.

"This is Leroux. I need to see him right away."

"He's not available right now, can I take a message."

"It's urgent; I've identified the guy behind this."

"He's at the isolation ward, his family has just arrived. Do you—"

"Tell him I'll meet him there!"

Leroux hung up the phone, printed off the file on Scott Fowler on his secure printer in his cubicle, then rushed toward isolation.

I wonder if Sherrie is there?

Quarantine Zone, CIA Headquarters, Langley, Virginia

Leroux watched as two workers sprayed the hallway, starting at the ceiling and working their way down, then repeating the process, moving along about ten feet at a time.

"What is that?" he asked the guard accompanying them.

"Some sort of bleach solution. It's supposed to pretty much kill anything. We're going into a phased lockdown. Everyone gets tested. Once tested, you're restricted to your zone and floor until the test results for your entire area come through. If you're entire area is clear, then you're allowed to move into adjacent cleared areas. If someone is infected, they are taken to quarantine, the area is cleaned again, and you're all tested again in twenty four hours."

"Jesus."

"I hope He's got nothing to do with this. If He does, I'm sensing some biblical wrath of God stuff coming on."

Leroux nodded, his eyes glued to the practiced technique of the men spraying the bleach.

A knock at the glass had his head spinning. He smiled as he saw Sherrie waving to him. He opened the door and entered the room next to her isolation chamber, sitting down and grabbing the phone on the table.

"How are you?" he asked, placing his bare hand on the glass.

"I'm fine." She pressed her hand against the glass as well. "It was pretty exciting if you know what I mean." Her eyebrows bobbed up and down suggestively.

Little Chris twitched.

"Well, nothing we can do about that now." He lowered his voice. "Did you see what it's like on the outside?"

She shook her head. "Not much. Where we were was pretty isolated, but from what I was seeing, law and order is starting to break down. We had to take out about ten guys trying to kill the Morrisons. It was crazy. One of them was a sheriff's deputy!"

"Man, I hope my parents are okay."

"You haven't been able to reach them?"

"We're in a communications lockdown right now."

Sherrie fished something out of her pocket, then placed it against the glass. It was her personal cellphone; not company issue. She hit redial on the phone and he immediately recognized the number before she put the phone back in sleep mode.

Mom and dad!

She gave him a wink and he sighed in relief. At least now he knew they would know what was going on, that he was safe, and what they should do to be safe themselves. They had a chance.

God I love her!

"I'm stuck in here until I'm cleared. I guess they're starting some isolation grid. They hope to have the entire building cleared within twenty-four hours."

"Yeah, I just heard. We might not see each other for a while."

A pout spread across her face.

"I'm going to miss you."

"Me too, hon."

She sucked in a breath then nodded at the folder he had brought with him.

"Any luck with that intel I got you?"

A smile beamed from Leroux's face.

"Absolutely! Thanks in no small part to you I found out who might be behind this. He pulled out the photo and held it up so she could see. "Meet Scott Fowler, the guy at the end of the trail."

Sherrie leaned forward. "Have you shown that to our imposter yet? He matches the description of the guy who recruited her."

"Not yet. I'll do that as soon as I brief the Director." He returned the photo to the file. "Oh, and you'll never guess who Fowler used to work for."

The door behind Leroux opened as he asked the question.

"Who?" asked the Director as he stepped inside.

Leroux jumped up, bowing his head slightly.

"Hello, sir. Sorry, I was waiting for you to finish with your family."

Morrison waved him off.

"Don't worry about it." He approached the mirror and held his hand out for the phone Leroux still gripped. Leroux handed it to him. "Agent White, I just wanted to thank you for a job very well done. I just heard from my wife about the situation you faced, and it sounds like you not only arrived in the nick of time, but conducted yourselves bravely and effectively."

Sherrie was standing as well, almost at attention.

"Thank you, sir. I had a good team, sir."

"Yes you did. One of the best. But it was your mission, and it was a success. I and my family thank you." He handed the phone back to Leroux, then pointed at him. "You're with me." Morrison strode from the room, leaving Leroux torn between love and duty.

"Go!" yelled Sherrie at his indecision.

"Bye, sorry!" he said to the receiver, slamming it in its cradle as he blew her a kiss then raced after the Director who by now was at the elevators.

206

"What have you found?" asked Morrison as they both entered the elevator.

"I've traced the accounts back to a Scott Fowler," said Leroux, handing the file to Morrison. "He's a former Senior Vice President at BioDyne Pharma."

Morrison's eyebrows shot up.

"You've got to be kidding me!" he exclaimed, jabbing his finger at the photo. "This is the same guy the FBI and Kane just identified as our cemetery man in New Orleans." The doors opened not on the floor Leroux had expected. He followed Morrison, almost at a trot. "I need to see her," he said to a pair of guards at the far end of a hall. He was buzzed through and a guard manning a desk was just getting up. "Never mind," said Morrison, marching down to the only cell occupied today.

He held up the photo of Scott Fowler to their prisoner.

"Can you identify this man?"

Flowers rose from her cot and stepped toward the photo.

She nodded. "Yup. That's the guy who promised to cure my brother."

Morrison spun on his heel, heading for the door.

"Finally! Some progress!"

Detective Laprise's Apartment, New Orleans, Louisiana

Detective Isabelle Laprise woke with a start. She quickly glanced around the room to confirm she was alone, then checked her watch. She had been asleep almost three hours, but something had woken her. A quick check of her cellphone showed no missed calls or messages.

A moan from the living room had her out of bed, reaching for her weapon, her holster draped across the back of a chair sitting in front of her dresser. Silently she removed it as another moan drifted into her bedroom, then a whisper.

Kane was asleep on the pullout couch, or at least he should be, but these sounds she was hearing as she approached the door sounded like pain.

Maybe he's sick?

The thought froze her in her tracks.

Then you are too.

She realized it was true. They had spent so much time together in a cramped FBI mobile HQ, her car, the apartment. If he was sick, so was she.

She opened the door to her bedroom and the moans and whispers were louder. With her weapon extended in front of her, she rounded the couch and cleared the room, finding only Kane, lying far more naked than she had left him, on the couch, moaning and muttering to himself. She lowered her weapon, and knelt down beside him, unsure of what to do.

He's having a nightmare.

"Abort! Abort! Abort!" he muttered as he writhed under the sheet that now barely covered him, his body covered in sweat from head to toe, his chest heaving with each agitated breath. "Oh God no! Oh God please no!"

The agony in his voice tore at her heart as she leaned in to touch him, to comfort him, the anguish unlike anything she had ever heard. She felt her eyes begin to tear up, her chest tighten as he repeated his plea.

Then suddenly he bolted upright, his eyes wide open, tears flowing freely down his cheeks as he caught his breath. His eyes squeezed shut, blocking the tears, then suddenly they were open again, staring at her as she knelt beside him.

"Are you okay?" he asked. "Has there been news?"

"Yes, I'm okay, no there's been no news. You were having a nightmare."

He wiped the tears from his eyes and cheeks, then sat up.

"Anything you want to talk about?"

He shook his head.

"Classified."

"You'd have to kill me?"

He chuckled, but there was no heart in it, so she decided to drop it.

"Do you think you'll be able to get back to sleep?"

He nodded.

"Don't worry about me, I'll be okay."

He didn't sound convincing.

"Would you—" She stopped, stunned she was about to suggest this, but now with the words almost out, she couldn't exactly not complete the sentence. She looked at the floor instead. "Would you like to sleep in my bed?"

"No, you keep that. I'm comfortable here."

Argh! He's going to make me say it, isn't he!

"I meant with me. Maybe you'll sleep better if you're not alone." She wagged a finger at him with half a smile. "No funny business."

He laughed.

"I don't know if that's a good idea."

"Hey, it's the end of the world. Who's gonna know." She stood up and extended her hand. "Come on, let's get some sleep."

He smiled and took her hand, standing up. She led him to the bedroom, having to remind herself to let go of his hand, he being the most stunning creature to have ever crossed the threshold of her bedroom in far too many years.

Ever!

She pointed at the usually empty side. "Get in bed, I'm going to powder my nose."

"Thanks," said Kane, giving her a genuine smile of gratitude then dropping onto the bed with a bounce, his rippling muscles sending tingling sensations up and down her core.

She had a quick tinkle, washed her hands, checked her teeth, swished some mouthwash, then returned to the dark bedroom, her eyes adjusting from the light in the bathroom. She rounded the bed and climbed in, facing him, but not touching him, her pulse racing as she tried to control her breathing, unsure of whether or not she should say something.

Fortunately Kane took care of that for her.

With steady, deep breaths, the object of her fantasy already asleep.

Decontamination Zone, Interim LSU Public Hospital, New Orleans, Louisiana
Outbreak Day #12

Dr. Katherine Best stripped out of her hazmat suit then stepped into the decontamination chamber, closing her eyes. As she was hit with bursts of air and various other chemicals, she held her breath then heard the all clear. Stepping out, she dried off and got into a jumpsuit, finally stepping out into a much larger isolation tent that had been set up over the past day. It was massive and multi chambered, an inflatable research lab. Dozens of technicians and scientists filled the area as fans roared in the distance keeping the pressure inside higher than that outside so no virus could enter.

Dr. Barry Johnston waved her over.

"Just in time, we're about to start the briefing," he said as she dropped into a small metal chair. She nodded to those around her, most of the faces familiar including Dr. Corkery, now sporting a green jumpsuit indicating he was clear of the virus, and an Army officer and several of his aides she hadn't met yet.

"This is Colonel Jeremiah Jackson from the Louisiana National Guard," said Johnston, sensing the question in her mind. "He's in charge of enforcing the quarantine. Colonel, this is Dr. Katherine Best, she's in charge of our operation here."

Pleasantries were exchanged without handshakes, and Johnston gave the rundown of the latest news that had an emergency page go out to all department heads.

"Here's the latest we know, and it's a stunner." He paused for a moment, but nobody asked the question, so he continued. "We just heard back from the BioDyne Pharma people." He clicked a button on a handheld pointer and the large screen displayed a split screen of the two antivirals she recognized by now as the original, and the mutated that the two friends had brought in after their fishing trip. "On your left is our original antiviral, genetically encoded to target women with the BRCA1 genetic defect that less than one percent of the population carries— commonly known as the breast cancer gene." He pointed to the image on the right. "Here, we have the second antiviral, confirmed to be a derivative of the original antiviral developed by BioDyne, but!"—he said the last word louder, pausing to get everyone's attention—"this one was never designed to target the BRCA1 genetic defect."

He paused triumphantly.

The Colonel cleared his throat.

"Forgive me, Doctor, but let's pretend I have no clue what conclusion you just made. Let's have it in English."

Johnston turned a few shades paler and flushed at the same time, his cheeks now a rosy red.

"I'm so sorry, Colonel. What it means is BioDyne has essentially told us this second antiviral is *not* a mutation, but a completely separate creation of its own. It means that the first virus didn't mutate. We are dealing with a separate outbreak, of a separate antiviral."

"So a second attack?"

Johnston nodded as Katherine's mind reeled with the implications. This had the potential to be good news, or bad news. Or both.

"So what does this mean?" asked Colonel Jackson. "This quarantine was put in place because we thought a virus with a one hundred percent kill rate was concentrated here, and had mutated and was spreading outside of the city. How does this new information change that reasoning?"

Katherine leaned forward. "Let's look at this from two perspectives. First is the original antiviral. It showed itself ten days after the initial exposure. The only people confirmed to have the antiviral are women who all have this rare genetic defect. According to BioDyne, the only way it can be transmitted from person to person is if that second person also has the same targeted gene sequence. If they don't, it's harmless and can't be passed on. Our testing at the Superdome has shown no active antiviral anywhere in the structure, which tells us it can't last airborne for too long. We still don't know how long, our tests are still ongoing. So far it seems at least twenty four hours, but much longer than that is rare.

"Bottom line, Colonel, is that I think we will see the end of the first outbreak in the next twenty-four to forty-eight hours."

The Colonel smiled, slapping his knees. "That's fantastic. And from what I'm hearing, the risk of this spreading is next to nothing. Perhaps we can lift the quarantine?"

"We're forgetting the second outbreak. This seems to be presenting itself in the same way, on the same cycle, with an unknown release point. We don't know where this came from, and we can only assume when. We also don't know who it's targeting yet, or how widespread it is."

Colonel Jackson's smile disappeared. "Out of the frying pan and into the fire," he muttered.

"Perhaps. We need to trace these men's steps. Every single thing they did from the moment they stepped off that boat. They did something that got them exposed."

"Do we know about the outbreaks in the other cities yet? Which antiviral they are?"

Katherine shook her head.

"Somewhat. We know we have had a few women test positive for the initial antiviral. All were at the Saints game, and all have the gene sequence in question. All of the others so far are either just regular flus, or the testing hasn't come back yet."

"So we could still have a global pandemic on our hands targeting an unknown group of people with a one hundred percent kill rate," summarized the Colonel.

Katherine sighed.

"Yes. We'll know better once we see how our two patients here respond over the coming hours and hopefully days. It may just be a bad flu reaction, or it may be deadly like the others. Time will give us those answers. In the meantime, I need to put together a timeline."

"I'll take care of that, Doctor," said Dr. Corkery, raising his hand. "I'm from the area, so anything they say will make more sense to me. I also have some experience in this."

Katherine turned to the Colonel. "It was Dr. Corkery who discovered much of what we now know."

"Fine. I think we'll have to brief the President as soon as possible with this new information."

"Agreed," said Johnston. "I'll set up a video conference shortly. If there aren't any additional questions, I'll let everyone get back to their duties." Silence. "Very well, next briefing in eight hours."

The meeting broke, with Katherine approaching Dr. Corkery.

"Want some help?"

"Absolutely!" he said with a smile. "We don't have any time to waste if these two are on the same track as our previous patients."

The two went through decon then donned their suits, and fifteen minutes later were at the side of the first patient, Stanley Lafayette, who was in worse condition than his friend, Richard Cross who lay in the next bed. Katherine sat at Stanley's side, Corkery standing beside her, with Richard's bed close enough to hear the conversation.

The two men had agreed that they never left the boat, it having sleeping quarters for two, and hadn't encountered anyone beyond a wave and a 'hello' from the deck. After docking at the end of their trip, they dropped off the rental keys in a lockbox, climbed in Richard's car, then returned home. Richard dropped Stanley off, then went home, grabbed some dinner at a restaurant, then stopped back at Stanley's house to drop off something left in the trunk. Stanley didn't encounter anybody else until calling 9-1-1.

Dr. Corkery had been taking notes throughout, as had Katherine. His pen tapped the notepad.

"If we assume you didn't get infected along the way, then Richard, you must have contracted it after Stanley was dropped off, then infected Stanley when you returned to pick up your bag."

"Bastard," moaned Stanley, who then laughed once, triggering a coughing fit.

"Sorry, buddy," said Richard, who truly did sound mortified. "Then why is he so much sicker than me? Shouldn't I have gotten sick first?"

Katherine shook her head. "No. The progression of the disease is pretty consistent between patients, but not exact. The unusual nature of the first group is that we know when they were infected. They were all infected at the Saints game, and we know it was initiated during the power outage. This means people were exposed within perhaps a two hour period. We've seen people coming in from nine to eleven days after. The variation between yourselves is probably the same thing."

"So you're sure there's no other way you could have come in contact with someone?" asked Corkery, looking at Stanley. "No pizza delivery, mail man, meter reader, canvasser, anything?"

Stanley shook his head.

"I almost never answer the door unless I'm expecting someone," he whispered.

Richard agreed. "I had to ring three times to get him to answer. He's notorious for that."

"And nothing along the way. No other boater that you walked by on the pier. You mentioned you put keys in a drop box? Did you touch it?"

"I did that," said Richard, "and no, I didn't touch it, you just dropped them in a pretty wide slot on the top. No lid to open or anything."

"Gate?"

"It was open."

Corkery frowned, exchanging a glance with Katherine. She knew what he was going after. If Richard was the source, they had an entire bar full of patrons who could be the source. If it were Stanley, the source pool was far lower.

They had to know.

"The truck stop!" exclaimed Richard.

Stanley's eyes shot open as he stifled another cough.

"Yes, I forgot about that," he said, hacking through the sentence.

"What truck stop?"

"Off the I-10 in Slidell, I can't remember what it's called, but it's huge. We stopped because micro-bladder here had to use the bathroom," said Richard, jerking a thumb at Stanley.

"Piss off."

"We stopped, he went to the bathroom, I stayed in the car."

"What did you do inside?" asked Katherine.

"Pissed."

"Anything else?"

"Umm, washed my hands."

"Did you encounter anyone?"

"Probably dozens. I just walked to the bathroom, did my business, washed my hands, dried them, then returned to the car."

"Okay, we'll check it out."

"Do you think that's the source?" asked Richard.

216

Katherine shrugged.

"Perhaps. We haven't had big reports of your variation of the antiviral reported within the city. This makes me think the source is from outside. Someone at the bar would have had to be infected for you to catch it there. If that were the case, we should have a cluster of infections around that area, instead we only have you two, plus reports around the country of similar symptoms."

"But couldn't I have infected the bar if we picked it up at the truck stop?"

"Yes, but it's unlikely you would have infected everyone. Remember, you weren't showing symptoms so you would have just been breathing, not coughing or sneezing, which is what would propel something like that throughout the restaurant. No, I think we might find our source is the truck stop, or someone that Stanley walked by who was infected." Katherine rose. "Thank you for your time, gentlemen. We'll let you know if we find anything."

Katherine walked out of the isolation chamber, followed by Corkery.

"What do you think?" he asked.

"I'm leaning toward the truck stop. Either way we're screwed. If this more general variation has been floating out there for over ten days, it will have gone worldwide no matter where it originated from."

"Then what will we do."

"Pray."

Detective Laprise's Apartment, New Orleans, Louisiana

Detective Isabelle Laprise woke to the smell of something wonderful. She groaned in pleasure at having what felt like a full six or better hours of sleep, and a quick peek at the alarm clock confirmed it. She rolled over and saw the other side of the bed empty, to which she had to admit a twinge of regret.

Get over it! He's just a kid!

She rolled out of bed and checked herself out in the mirror.

Damned fine for forty. He should be so lucky to tap this!

She did a sexy pose and laughed to herself, heading for the bathroom.

"Is that you? Breakfast in five!" yelled Kane's voice from the other room.

"Okay!"

"How do you like your eggs?"

"Over easy!"

"Roger that!"

She quickly straightened herself out, gave her teeth the once over with a toothbrush and swooshed some mouthwash. Brushing her hair then pulling it back into a no-fuss ponytail, she looked at herself then immediately let her hair down.

Much better.

She shook her head at herself.

You're hopeless!

She returned to her bedroom, pulled a pair of yoga pants on that made her ass look like you could bounce quarters off it, and a loose sweater to make her look modest, then moseyed out into the kitchen.

218

"What's all this?" she asked, stunned. Not only were there bacon, sausage, eggs and toast, along with a fresh pot of coffee, you would have never known that the act of cooking had taken place, the kitchen nearly spotless.

All those muscles and he cooks and cleans too!

"Mmmm, nummers!"

"Huh?"

"This looks delicious!"

Kane smiled. "Perfect timing. Let's eat, get ready, and hit the streets. Apparently we've got some info on the bomb fragment they want to show us but not send out over the airwaves."

"Really? That was quick."

"I guess the end of the world means the end of red tape."

Kane placed the two plates at the dinner table, pulled out Isabelle's chair, pushing it in for her as she sat down, then poured her coffee.

"How do you take it?"

"Black. You?"

"Never touch the stuff unless I'm undercover." He pointed at the glass of water by his plate. "That or Diet Coke for me."

"Really? Haven't met many law enforcement or military types that didn't devour the stuff."

Kane sat down across from her, dipping a wedge of toast in his egg yolk, then taking a bite. Isabelle had to admit she didn't normally partake in breakfast beyond coffee, but she was famished, and after all his hard work, she wanted to make him feel like it was appreciated. She aped him, dipping her toast in the perfectly made to order egg.

"I've never been into hot drinks. Tea, coffee, hot chocolate. Nada. The colder the better. I don't even like red wine—"

"Get out!" she said, pointing at the door.

"But I do like white, if it's cold."

"Okay, you can stay." She sipped her coffee. "Must be tough on missions."

"Can be, but you learn to tolerate it."

Isabelle found herself devouring the meal, her stomach overcoming its lack of experience in eating this type of food. She knew her thighs might regret it later, but her lips were loving it. She glanced at Kane's plate and made a conscious effort to slow down.

"I wonder what they found?" she said as she sipped her coffee. "I've never had to deal with a bomb before. What *could* they find?"

"Well, they'll probably know what type of explosive, what form it was in before detonation, where it was located, how it was triggered, and what type of trigger it was. All these combined can sometimes narrow it down to a particular bomb maker. If we're really lucky we may get something identifying, but that's highly unlikely unless the guy is so cocky he doesn't care. There's some like that; they figure either they won't live long enough for it to matter, or they think they're untouchable. Those are usually government sponsored or former government."

"Let's hope we get lucky. Maybe we can find the bomber and who hired him. Then maybe they've got a cure for this damned thing."

"From your lips to God's ears."

VoyageCenters of America, Gause Blvd, Slidell, Louisiana

Dr. Katherine Best jumped down from the truck she was in, the white paint and bright blue lettering setting it apart from most of the vehicles in the massive parking lot. That and the fact it was accompanied by half a dozen similarly painted vehicles.

She must have made quite the sight for those milling about the parking lot. She found the best way to deal with these situations was to walk with purpose to wherever she needed to go, but in this case, it was right into the thick of the restaurant which if the number of rigs were any indication, was jam packed, probably with truckers stranded due to the quarantine of their destination.

Several squad cars from the local police stood nearby, they having been notified in case there might be trouble. And sitting out of sight down the road were three transports full of National Guard troops in hazmat suits if needed.

She hoped it wouldn't get ugly, but scared people tended to panic, and this crowd had access to big, heavy, nearly unstoppable vehicles.

That have been crisscrossing this country for possibly ten days, carrying a deadly pandemic.

She waved to what appeared to be the senior officer on the scene as he sauntered over, bold as brass.

"Who's in charge here?" he asked.

"I am, Dr. Katherine Best, CDC."

"Wrong. I'm in charge. This is my jurisdiction, and I'll say what does and doesn't go on around here. Clear?"

"Very." She pulled her phone from one of the many pockets in her hazmat suit, the portable air unit on her back cramping her style slightly. She selected a number from her contacts list and dialed, waiting a moment.

"This is Dr. Katherine Best, CDC. I need some red tape cut. Is he available?"

"One moment, Doctor."

"Hello?"

"Hello, Mr. Secretary. I have an officer"—she leaned over to him—"I didn't get your name?"

"Umm, Deputy Bryant."

"A Deputy Bryant who doesn't seem to understand the situation."

"Put him on."

She handed the phone to the now nervous Deputy. A short conversation, mostly one sided, the side she could hear merely a string of 'yes, sir's and 'I understand, sir's, then finally a much paler Deputy Bryant handed the phone back.

She placed it to her ear, the sound slightly muffled through the material.

"Sir?"

"Everything should be good now."

"Thank you, sir."

"Anytime."

The call ended, the Secretary of Homeland Security she was sure having a full plate on a day like today. She turned to Deputy Bryant.

"Now that we understand the pecking order, I'll need your men to block the roads and stay outside in case we need crowd control. No one enters or leaves this parking lot. You can accompany me inside."

"Inside?"

"Inside."

He eyeballed her suit.

"Can I get one of those?"

She shook her head.

"Sorry, probably already too late."

She waved as if tossing a line, indicating the gathered mass of CDC personnel should move forward. As they approached the building, the civilians parted way, some scurrying toward their vehicles. She glanced over her shoulders and saw the squad cars being positioned to block anybody from leaving, but just seeing some of the people running toward their vehicles told her this was going to hell quickly.

They entered the building, Deputy Bryant opening the door for her. She stepped inside and a silence swept the room, the entire packed restaurant turning toward her and her team, frozen in time.

No avoiding this.

She stepped forward, holding her hands up in front of her to calm them.

"My name is Dr. Katherine Best from the Centers for Disease Control and Prevention. There is no need to panic; we're just here on a routine inspection. Don't let our outfits scare you, they're for your protection as much as ours. We're just going to take some samples, inspect your bathrooms, then leave. Continue enjoying your meals, we aren't the food inspectors!"

She tried to insert as much of a jovial tone as she could, but she wasn't sure it was working. Now the best thing to do would be to ignore them, and move on with their business. She pointed to two techs, lowering her voice.

"You two take samples from the front door all the way to the bathroom. Quickly, quietly, then return to the vehicles. The sooner these people aren't looking at hazmat suits, the better."

The two techs nodded.

"Bathrooms?" she asked the Deputy.

"This way, Doctor."

Deputy Bryant led them down a short hall where it split in two. To the left was the women's bathroom, the right men's.

"I'll get you to empty it out, Deputy."

"Yes, Doctor."

He disappeared for a few minutes and several confused souls exited, and were even more confused when greeted by a bunch of hazmat suit wearing scientists. The deputy reappeared.

"One guy refuses to leave. Says he won't until he's done."

"Fine." Katherine pushed the door open, waving her team in with her. She pushed each of the stall doors until she found the locked one. She turned to her team. "Start taking samples of everything. We're pretty sure this flesh eating disease will be on a toilet seat, so start with those. I can't believe how quickly it ate through the last guy's testicles. I've never seen that before."

There was a yelp on the other side of the door, the sound of toilet paper being put to use and a flush as the man burst out the door, pulling up his jeans. The look on his face was priceless—sheer terror. She was certain if she had said something about it eating an arm or leg off, it wouldn't have got a reaction. But mention the boys, and men immediately panic. Even on the battlefield, when she had done a stint in Iraq on an exchange program, the first question out of most of the guys who had wounds "down there" was about the wellbeing of their most favorite body part.

"What should I do? What's this testicle eating disease?"

"Don't worry about it. If you feel any itchiness, see your doctor. Now please leave us to do our job."

The man rushed out, hands unwashed, but with the antiviral possibly spreading from this room, it was probably better. Her team was quick and efficient. There was no time to waste, surfaces quickly swabbed and vacuumed to her satisfaction. She exited the bathroom, and found Deputy Bryant with a large man in a wife beater t-shirt.

"Doctor, this is the day manager, Jimmy Dupuis."

"Mr. Dupuis. Can you tell me if anything unusual has happened around here in the past few weeks? Anybody here that shouldn't have been? Any unexplained occurrences? Equipment show up unexpectedly? Anything?"

Dupuis shook his head.

"Nothing that I can think of. We have our share of fights and whatnot, but it's a truck stop, so that's to be expected, especially after the quarantine. People are sleeping in their trucks, getting on each other's nerves. We don't even bother calling the cops, we just send them outside until they tire themselves out."

"Any repairs lately? Any servicing?"

"We had an appliance guy in a week ago to fix the fryer, but that's it."

"Nothing else. Nothing in the bathroom area? Nothing dealing with air conditioning, heating, cooling?"

"Oh shit, that's right! We had an HVAC guy come in about two weeks ago, can't remember which day. Said he was doing some warranty repair. I didn't pay much attention after he said that there was no charge, the manufacturer was paying for it."

"Where did he go?"

"The roof I think, then the utility closet."

"Where's that?"

Dupuis jerked his thumb at a door beside the men's bathroom.

"Right there."

"Can you let us in?"

"Sure." Dupuis fished a bunch of keys from his pocket, flipped through until he found the right one, then unlocked the door. Reaching in he turned on the light, then stepped back. "Help yourselves."

"Thanks."

Katherine entered the dark and dank room. It was mostly concrete, loaded with piping along the wall adjacent to the men's washroom, and along the ceiling. On the opposite side were electrical panels, but no signs of any heating and cooling equipment.

"And he came in here?" she asked as she walked in deeper.

"Yes."

"Any idea why?"

But as she asked her question she came to a stop, it answered. Sitting tucked in between two large pipes was a cylinder exactly like that found at the Superdome. Her heart pounded in excitement at having found the source, and terror at what it meant.

"Doctor!"

She spun toward the door to see one of her techs pushing his way through.

"There's a problem outside! You better come! Quick!"

She pointed at the cylinder and looked at her team.

"This is it. Find out what it's connected to, quarantine it, then we'll have to quarantine the entire restaurant," she said as she pushed her way through the throng. Shouting from within the restaurant and from outside greeted her as she made her way to the door. The customers seemed to be surging toward the windows to see whatever it was that was happening outside.

She pushed through the doors to the parking lot and stopped in her tracks.

Oh shit!

An eighteen wheeler fuel truck was roaring toward the two cop cars blocking one of the exits. The officers were waving desperately for him to stop, but the crazed expression Katherine caught through his side view mirror told her everything she needed to know.

He was *not* going to stop.

She grabbed her cellphone from her pocket and dialed Colonel Jackson's number.

"This is Dr. Best, we've found the source of the second antiviral, it's the truck stop. I'm ordering this place quarantined, but we've got a semi running the blockade."

"We're on our way."

Gunshots rang out but it was too late, the officers at the blockade too busy running for their lives to hit the broadside of a barn, diving into the ditch on either side of the exit as the rig smashed into the two patrol cars, sending them spinning out of the way to either side. Katherine's hand darted up, covering her mouth through her hazmat suit in shock as she saw one of the cars roll into the ditch where two of the officers had jumped to get clear.

She began to run toward the ditch as the semi, seemingly undeterred by the two vehicles it had just shoved away, continued forward, crossing a strip of grass separating Frontage Road from the highway, then another to get into the northbound lane before making the sharp left turn onto the highway, all the time gaining speed. As she reached the ditch she breathed a sigh of relief to see the two officers emerging from it, covered in mud but unscathed.

She looked down the road and saw the troop carriers rushing toward them. How they would be able to help, she had no clue. The rig was huge, and had sliced through the two cop cars as if they hadn't been there. And unless they could get in front of him, she couldn't see what they could do to stop him. Shots would just be hitting the rear of the semi. They might take a few tires out, but that would only slow him down.

They need something bigger!

She wondered if the National Guard had tanks and reasoned they probably did, but doubted any were handy.

Her head whipped back toward the troop carriers as she heard something she couldn't quite make out. She pressed her hazmat suit against her ear in an attempt to hear just a little better. As she watched the troop carriers rapidly close the distance she saw something behind them, mostly blocked by the trucks.

What is that?

Then the sound became clear and suddenly two helicopters burst overtop of the troop carriers, rushing down the road at what seemed an impossible speed. Within seconds they whipped past her and after the semi, splitting to either side of the escaping vehicle then getting in front of it.

She could hear something being said over a loudspeaker, but couldn't make it out. It didn't seem to be persuasive as the rig continued to accelerate. They had to realize they were dealing with a panicked individual. There would be no reasoning with him.

Shots belched from the front of one of the choppers, tearing up the pavement in front of the truck, and again, no affect. The same chopper lowered itself in the middle of the road, boldly initiating a game of chicken that she immediately knew wouldn't turn out well. She began to step toward the action, but stopped, realizing it was too far away and there was nothing she could do. The rig continued to accelerate directly toward the helicopter.

Move!

But they didn't, instead simply hanging there in midair, daring the driver to hit them.

"Move!" she screamed.

Suddenly the chopper broke to the right, its cannon opening fire at the same time, but it was too late. The top of the semi caught the tail rotor, the sound of shredding metal as the blade fought back was soon overwhelmed

228

with the tearing and creaking of metal as the rotor was snapped off, sending the chopper spinning into the fields to the left of its slayer.

The chopper hit hard, tilting to its side, the main blades ripping into the field, then breaking off. It seemed like minutes, but it was only seconds, and in those precious seconds the two occupants of the chopper managed to jump out, sprinting in opposite directions as soon as the rotors stopped. She lost sight of one of them, but saw the second running directly toward her as an explosion rocked the entire area, a fireball ripping skyward, knocking the soldier to the ground as the shockwave overtook him.

As quickly as the explosion had expanded, it contracted again, and through the thick of the smoke she saw the semi continuing forward, the second chopper now well ahead of it, hovering to the side of the road.

Suddenly its cannons opened up, tearing apart the rig, then as if to compete with what had just happened to the chopper, its load of fuel was hit. She didn't know what hit her first. The heat from the massive fireball, the horrifying screech of hell opening in front of her, or the shockwave that knocked them all off their feet.

It didn't matter.

As she picked herself up she could see the rig had continued forward a short distance, then off the road and into the ditch. There was no way the driver had survived the explosion, even if the bullets hadn't already killed him. The chopper circled its kill then turned its attention to the wreck of the first chopper as a troop carrier arrived. She stood watching in shock as the occupants of the first chopper, apparently alive and uninjured, waved to their comrades.

Shouting all around her had her shift her focus to the activity at the truck stop. Troops were pouring out of the carriers, setting up road blocks and a perimeter, sealing in the occupants of the truck stop, and hopefully preventing any more of the horror of what she just witnessed.

CIA Headquarters, Langley, Virginia

"Tell us everything you know about Scott Fowler."

The question apparently came as a shock to Dr. Kapp, his eyebrows shooting up his forehead as his eyes opened wide. Morrison hadn't even given the man a chance to sit down, the question fired as soon as he walked through the door.

Leroux, already sitting, said nothing. Instead he simply acknowledged the man with a nod as Morrison pointed to a chair Sherrie had occupied the last time Leroux had been there.

He preferred the previous view.

"Fowler?" Kapp dropped into the seat with a wince. "I haven't heard that name in a while."

Leroux watched the man wince again as he crossed his legs. Leroux immediately thought arthritis or some sort of joint problem as Kapp was far his senior, but nowhere near old enough to be put out to pasture as some Leroux's age might think should happen.

Ugh. I do not *want to get old.*

"Tell us what you know," repeated Morrison.

"Well, I'll have all of our files sent to you immediately," said Kapp, quickly sending off a text message on his phone. He resumed speaking a few moments later. "Scott Fowler was Senior Vice President of Research and Development for about ten years until he abruptly left about two years ago. He was one of the founders of the company. One of the originals."

"Why'd he leave?"

Kapp shrugged his shoulders.

"Some would say greed."

"Greed?"

"He wasn't happy with the way things were going. The board had become more conservative in its approach. In the early days of the company they had been much more daring, taking risks that often paid off, but more often than not didn't. The hits though were huge, making every one of the early shareholders very rich. This made the board more risk averse, none wanting to endanger the fortunes they were sitting on by risking the stock price. They became more careful, drawing out every process, devoting little money to new projects until they could prove themselves, then the taps would be opened a little more, with yet more delays. He was not happy, so one day he announced his resignation from the board, walked out, and we never heard from him again."

Morrison's lips were pursed, his hands steepled in front of his face, his elbows on his desk as he processed the information. Leroux tried not to stare, his own mind racing. If Fowler had left in a huff, what did that mean? How could it possibly relate to their current situation?

A stray thought had his heart pumping in excitement.

What if Urban went to work for Fowler, and they had created their own company?

Leroux frowned to himself. The thought was stupid. They created a company that would then randomly release antivirals, soon to be *patented* antivirals, into the general population, then demand token amounts of ransom?

It was a stupid idea.

"How much is Fowler worth?" asked Morrison.

Good question! They were dealing with blackmailers. Perhaps the amounts, so far one, ten and a hundred million weren't token at all. Certainly the latest demand wasn't, and building up to the big numbers over time had been part of their plan all along.

"He holds almost ten percent of the company. With today's stock price, or at least before Wall Street collapsed this week, he would have been worth at least five billion."

There goes the blackmail for money theory.

"So he has no need of the money he's been demanding from you."

Kapp leaned forward.

"Fowler is behind this?" To say the man was shocked would be putting it mildly. Kapp shook his head. "I can't believe it. I won't believe it. The man was my friend. I knew him for over twenty years!"

"And when was the last time you heard from him?" asked Morrison.

Kapp's arms spread in front of him, his hands opened as his head bobbed.

"Two years. You're right, perhaps we were not as good friends as I thought." He sighed, almost muttering to himself. "Still, though, I just find it impossible to believe."

"We've traced the payments back to him. There's no doubt he is involved. Whether or not he's a willing participant, we don't know yet. We do know that it appears Dr. Urban is *not* a willing participant."

Kapp seemed to brighten at this bit of news.

"Thank God! I'd hate to think we had two maniacs at the company."

"So no one has heard from him?"

Kapp shook his head.

"Not that I know of. I will immediately ask, of course, but I have little hope you'll find him through us. I assume we have an address on file, of course, since he is a major shareholder and I'm certain would want to monitor the state of his holdings."

"Fine. Get us that information and make your inquiries. We need to find him fast."

Kapp rose, nodding to Morrison then Leroux, then left the office to return to the temporary quarters he had been provided with while quarantined in the complex.

Morrison looked at Leroux.

"Let's assume he gets us nothing. Focus that magnificent brain of yours on this and nothing else. Understood?"

Leroux flushed as he stood up, wondering if his boss knew everything he and Sherrie did.

"Yes, sir."

FBI Mobile HQ, New Orleans, Louisiana

"Please roll up your sleeve, sir."

Kane did as he was told, not bothering to question the man with the needle. Blood was quickly drawn, a label affixed, and the sample placed in a holder already containing at least a dozen other samples. Isabelle was next to be poked, she too not bothering to ask.

Kane found Special Agent Hewlett near the rear of the vehicle, leaning over a terminal.

"Hello Special Agent. Get a good sleep?"

Hewlett looked over her shoulder at him.

"About three hours, as expected."

"Anything important come up?" Kane asked as Isabelle joined him, rubbing her arm.

"The payments have been traced back to a former senior VP of BioDyne Pharma."

Kane let out a whistle.

"Interesting. What's his game? The blackmail amounts seem pretty small, at least the first two anyway."

"I pulled his file. This guy's worth billions. He holds about ten percent of BioDyne, so he's not hurting."

"So blackmail isn't his game then."

Isabelle shook her head. "So he's just a psycho?"

Hewlett shrugged her shoulders.

"Who knows? We're still trying to gather info on him, but it could take time."

"Is that why you called us here?"

Hewlett shook her head.

"Initial analysis on the bomb fragments came in," she said, shaking her head. "It's amazing what you can get done when you have *all* resources available to you." She picked up a file and flipped it open. "It was C4 as expected, shaped charge to take out whoever opened the freezer, minimizing any explosive power that might otherwise go to the apartment next door or above and below."

"A bomber with a conscience?" asked Isabelle.

Kane shook his head.

"No, a bomber with a job. His job was to kill Milner, then to kill whoever came looking for him. Not those who weren't involved."

"Agreed," said Hewlett.

"And the trigger?"

"We found some pieces. Basic mercury switch. Reliable, old school."

"No remote trigger?"

"Nope, just meant to go off when the lid was raised on the freezer."

"Can I see the trigger?"

Hewlett handed the file over and Kane flipped through, stopping at the blowups of the pieces of the trigger that had been found. His finger tapped his chin as he chewed his cheek for a moment.

"You know, this is an old Soviet design."

"That's what our guys said."

"Do we have footage yet of our killer?"

"We've narrowed it down to about a hundred. We restricted it to males, eighteen to sixty, who had visited no more than once after Milner entered the building for the last time."

Kane nodded slowly.

"It takes time to learn how to be a bomb maker. Narrow it to men at least twenty five years of age. And since we're dealing with a Soviet design, let's eliminate African Americans and Hispanics."

"What about Asians?" asked Isabelle as Hewlett motioned for one of the techs to modify the search parameters.

"No, east of the Urals there's an awful lot that look Chinese that are fiercely loyal to the old ways."

"Fifty-three," announced Hewlett. "That's a little better, assuming you're right to narrow it down."

"We're taking a bit of a risk with Hispanics since the Cubans were trained by the Soviets, and a little risk with African Americans," acknowledged Kane. "If we don't find anybody, you can broaden the search again." He pointed at the screen. "Now eliminate anybody with a domestic criminal record in the past ten years."

"Forty one," announced the tech manning the terminal. "But we don't have identities on most of the remaining ones, so it could be even lower."

Kane pointed at the screen.

"Focus all of your attention on these people. I'm willing to bet one of them is our bomber."

CIA Headquarters, Langley, Virginia

"You'll be happy to know all workers in your area have been found clear of the antiviral."

A cheer erupted from the workers, all standing in the halls or their cubicles, as the floor safety officer made the announcement. Even Leroux found himself joining in, albeit a bit timidly, shouting out in glee not his style. He was slowly coming out of his shell with Sherrie, but the rest of the world? It would have to wait. Leaving the nest would take time, but he had every confidence Sherrie would get him the socialization he needed to fully enjoy life.

"As each section is cleared, your access to adjacent areas will be opened. For now doors remained sealed to all sections. Security personnel are at every exit to remind you. Once an adjacent section is opened, security will be removed where appropriate. We expect the entire complex to be back to normal within the next eight hours. Quarantine measures will remain in effect for all external subjects. Those requiring access to the facility will need to enter into quarantine and await blood test results. Thank you for your cooperation."

There was some clapping, but Leroux was already in his seat, looking at trace results for the former BioDyne VP Scott Fowler. Beyond the one account, and a Post Office Box address provided by BioDyne, he seemed to be completely off the grid. But with billions at his disposal, he could easily have purchased a fake identity and be living anywhere in the world, including right here in Langley.

His phone vibrated on his hip, shocking him momentarily from his work. He looked at the display.

Black, D.

He answered, his heart picking up a few extra beats.

"Hello?"

"Hey, buddy, it's me."

Kane!

"How are you? You okay?"

"Yup, I'm fine. You?"

"We were just all cleared of the virus, so I guess so."

"And Sherrie?"

"She's in quarantine, but should know shortly."

"Fingers crossed, buddy. Listen, I need a favor if you've got the time."

"I'll try. Director Morrison's got me working on a high priority item. We're trying to track down a former BioDyne big wig. He's the money source."

"Yeah, I heard. Any luck?"

"No, this guy's gone off the grid by the looks of it."

"Well, this favor might help you out. Have you received a batch of files from the FBI here with about forty surveillance shots?"

Leroux opened up his Inbox and scrolled through, finding the data files in question.

"Yeah, I've got it here. What am I looking for?"

"One of these guys I'm pretty sure is former Spetsnaz. I need you to find out which one, then where he is. I'm willing to bet he's our bomber. Find him, and we might be that much closer to this BioDyne guy."

Leroux leaned back in his chair, his mind racing as he flipped quickly through the files. He'd be able to run them against databases, but knew that was already happening. Instead, he linked into the analysis feeds, spotted the one tracing foreign military databases, and brought up the already complete search.

"We've already found him."

"What? Why the hell haven't we been notified?"

"Not sure. The search just completed so the analyst might not even know yet, or is locked out of his office area while they decontaminate."

"Forget it. Send the results to my phone. What's the name?"

Leroux forwarded the file to Kane's phone, then read it himself.

"His name is Major Anton Koslov. Left Spetsnaz almost immediately after that Brass Monkey inci—" Leroux stopped himself. "Sorry, Kane, it's classified."

"Don't worry, I've read all about it. I have my sources."

Leroux could imagine the grin at the other end of the phone.

"I bet you do."

"So he was on the Russian side of that mission?"

"Yup."

"What about asking the American counterpart to Koslov's boss to make a call? Maybe a 'soldier-to-soldier' talk might be more effective."

Leroux shot out of his chair in excitement, printing off the file on Koslov. "He's actually here, right now! Sherrie went out on a mission with him and some of his team."

"Great. Let me know what you find out. And if you have any trouble convincing him, tell him I said to trust you."

"Do you know him?"

"I could tell you, but then…"

"Ha ha."

"Take care of yourself, buddy. We'll talk soon."

The call ended as Leroux pulled on the paper coming out of the printer, trying to speed things up, knowing it did anything but. The final page off, he rushed to the Director's office. The security guard opened the door to the executive section, waving him through.

"They were cleared as well," he said by way of explanation.

"Thanks!"

Leroux continued his run, reaching the Director's office slightly out of breath. Morrison's secretary looked up.

"Is he in?"

She nodded, picking up the phone.

"Mr. Leroux to see you, sir."

She hung up, waving him through.

"Thanks!"

Leroux nearly burst through the office door, but calmed himself, then opened the door and stepped through.

"What is it?"

"Sir, I know it wasn't part of my original assignment, but Dylan—I mean Special Agent Kane—called me and asked for a favor. We've identified a former Spetsnaz agent entering the building in New Orleans where the bombing took place."

"I heard they thought the trigger was of a former Soviet design."

"Well, with this guy being there"—Leroux handed the file over—"it pretty much confirms it."

"What are you doing to track this down?"

"I'm not, the analyst assigned to this is doing the usual traces, I'm sure. But I had an idea, or Kane did. I can't remember whose idea it was"—Morrison motioned for Leroux to get on with it—"but anyway, he served on the Russian team that was trying to recover the Brass Monkey missile a few years ago. He left shortly after according to his file. Kane was thinking that if the head of the Delta team that also worked that mission called the head of their mission, he might just be able to get something from him that our computers can't."

Morrison nodded.

"Do it."

"He's in quarantine, and I've been cleared."

Morrison scribbled a note on a piece of letterhead, signed it, then handed it to the still standing Leroux.

"Show this to the guard at the elevator. You'll be allowed down to the lobby and put into a hazmat suit. You can then travel freely. Now go!"

Leroux jumped slightly, then quickly left the room, his *Get out of Jail Free Card* gripped in his hand.

CDC Briefing area, New Orleans, Louisiana

"Mr. President, we have confirmed the source of the second outbreak was a hand dryer at a truck stop outside of New Orleans. From the description of the man given by the manager, we believe it was installed by the same man who installed the canister at the Superdome. It was installed in such a way that every time the hand dryer was activated, the canister was activated, allowing the antiviral to mix with the hot air and infect anyone using or in close proximity to the dryer."

The President's image on the monitor showed little if any emotion. He sat at the head of a large oval table in the Situation Room, and from different camera angles Katherine was seeing on their display at the temporary CDC briefing area she was in, there appeared to be at least a dozen people in the room with him.

"How many might have been infected?"

"We're estimating hundreds, perhaps low thousands. Tests of the canister are ongoing. We were fortunate in that there was still antiviral in the canister. BioDyne Pharma is testing the mechanism now to see how much is disbursed with each activation, how much the canister could contain, and still does contain. With that we should get a much better estimate, however it is irrelevant, Mr. President.

"Hundreds or thousands isn't important. We know that this strain was transmitted between two friends in the same car. Only one of them went inside. BioDyne is trying to identify what gene sequence is being targeted by this antiviral. However, if we assume it is still only transmittable from one person to the next if they have the same genetic pattern, then it must be very common. These men weren't related in any way. If the pattern targeted is that broad, we could be looking at a massive, deadly outbreak, far beyond what we've experienced in New Orleans so far."

"What are we talking about? Numbers."

"If he targeted men, fifty percent. Caucasian men, thirty-five percent, people with brown hair, sixty percent. We just don't know yet. There's an outside chance that these two just happen to have the same rare defect and it is less than one percent. BioDyne is working on it, but it could be weeks before they figure it out. Chances are we'll be able to narrow it down as the next sustained wave hits us. In fact, that's already happening."

"How bad?"

"We're still trying to sort through the tens of thousands who just have a flu. The symptoms at the outset are so similar that people are panicking and going to hospitals with a runny nose. We have hundreds now, however, spread from coast to coast, that seem to be exhibiting the same symptoms, but testing negative for any cold or flu. We believe these to be genuine cases of the new strain. The incubation period seems to be the same ten days, so the timing is right for these initial cases to be showing up.

"The problem, Mr. President, is these people will have possibly passed the antiviral on to hundreds of others in their daily lives during the past ten days, and those people to hundreds more. No matter what, we're looking at an exponentially growing outbreak. We just don't know to what degree of the population it will impact. It could be small again, or it could be very large."

For a brief moment she could have sworn she saw fear flash on the face of the most powerful man on Earth. It made her even more scared than she already was.

"What can we do?"

"We have to shut down all travel into and out of the country."

"That's already been done by the rest of the world. Europe grounded all flights, as have the Russians, Chinese, and everyone else. Canada closed the border last night and we're cooperating in reinforcing the entire border. The word is out in Mexico, so the number of illegals trying to get in has dropped to next to nothing. Will it be enough?"

"I doubt it. I've spoken to my colleagues at the World Health Organization and they are reporting cases showing up in Europe, Asia, Australia and other locations. They might get lucky, they might have more time to develop a cure as the majority of infected are here. We and BioDyne have already released all of our data to the WHO and it has already been disseminated to all who want it."

"Is there anything more we can do?"

"Let us keep doing our jobs. We need to determine who is being targeted, then try to figure out a way to kill it. As well, sir, we need to start thinking worst case scenario."

"What do you mean?"

"Survival of the species, sir. If it is all men that are being targeted, we need to start isolating men who are not sick. This has to start now, before it's too late."

There was a bonging sound from the speakers as someone else logged into the conversation. A black box flickered and became the image of the man from the CIA who had taken Katherine for a ride in his limousine.

"Leif Morrison here. Forgive me for being late, Mr. President. I have Dr. Hermann Kapp from BioDyne Pharma here with me. He has something you need to hear."

Quarantine Zone, CIA Headquarters, Langley, Virginia

Leroux felt painfully self-conscious, the hazmat suit he was wearing had him thinking all eyes were staring at him and judging him. *Check it!* As he walked through the halls toward the isolation unit the Delta Force team were being held in, he realized almost every second person was in a hazmat suit.

The world doesn't revolve around you, a-hole!

The thought he might be able to steal a minute and see Sherrie distracted him, and by the time he reached the isolation area he had forgotten his earlier nervousness, and had a smile on his face as he pictured the last time they were "together". A stirring had him quickly glance down to make sure a hazmat suit didn't accentuate the obvious.

Grandma in a bikini! Grandma in a two piece bikini!

Done.

He showed his ID to one of the security personnel guarding the entrance and he was let inside, only to find more personnel, all in hazmat suits, awaiting him. He was sprayed down to make certain he hadn't carried anything into the quarantine area, asked who he wanted to see, then let into a waiting area where he was allowed to take his head cover off. A few minutes later he was shown into a room, one side all window looking into an identical room, the rest all plain white walls with acoustic shielding.

He sat at the table and lone chair. A microphone sat in the middle of the table, along with a computer terminal. While waiting he logged in and found he had complete access to his data.

Movement had his head darting toward the window where he found who he assumed to be the leader of the Delta Force unit that had been involved in the Brass Monkey incident. Delta identities were even hidden from people with his clearance levels.

"Hello, sir—"

"Sergeant."

"Sorry, Sergeant, my name is Chris Leroux. I'm an analyst with the CIA."

"How can I help you, sir."

Leroux felt *very* uncomfortable with this turn of events. Having a man probably fifteen years his senior calling him 'sir' just didn't seem right. But then it was the military, and a sixty year old sergeant would still need to call a twenty-two year old Lieutenant fresh out of officer training school 'sir'.

"Sergeant, you of course are aware of the antiviral situation we are currently facing?"

"Of course."

"Are you aware that there is a second strain?"

"I've heard rumors."

"Well, there is, and this strain threatens to wipe out a significant portion of the population of this planet, perhaps all. We just don't know yet. What is clear is our containment efforts surrounding New Orleans were useless, as the more significant threat was being spread outside the city limits."

There was no response, except a slight downturn on the corners of his mouth.

"We managed to track down the source of the money funding this operation. We believe a man named Scott Fowler, a former VP at BioDyne Pharma, the company that originally developed the antiviral, is behind this. Unfortunately we have no idea where he is."

"I'm not sure how I can help you, sir."

"Well, we found the man—or rather the body of the man—who placed the canisters containing the antiviral. He was killed, stuffed in a freezer, then when the body was found, a booby trap went off, a bomb, killing a police officer and seriously wounding another. Analysis of the bomb fragments and trigger led one of our agents to postulate someone with former Soviet or Russian training might have been involved. That led to this man"—Leroux held up the photo of Major Anton Koslov—"being identified as having entered the building after our suspect, we assume to kill him then set the booby trap."

"What's his name?"

"Major Anton Koslov. Our information is he left Spetsnaz shortly after the Brass Monkey incident."

"I met him once at an exchange program a few years back. Nice guy, but intense. I could see him going private. The pride isn't there anymore." He paused a moment, as if looking into the past, then returned his attention to Leroux. "I still don't see how I can help you, sir."

"Well, a friend of mine had an idea."

"A friend."

"Well, he's an agent, actually, who's also a friend. He suggested I get you to call Major Anton Koslov's former commanding officer, a Lt. Colonel Kolya Chernov, and ask him to help us track Major Koslov down. A soldier-to-soldier call is the way I think he put it."

The sergeant laughed.

"Your friend I think overestimates the level of cooperation there is between the Russian and American militaries."

"My *friend* is Dylan Kane," said Leroux, gulping as he revealed the name of an agent.

The sergeant paused, his eyebrows shooting up for a moment as he too apparently realized the significance of what Leroux had just done.

"Really."

"Yes. I got the sense you knew each other, even though I never mentioned your name, since I don't have it."

The sergeant chuckled.

"No, I suppose you wouldn't, and I suppose he would." He leaned forward in his chair. "Mr. Leroux, if Dylan Kane thinks I should make this phone call, then I will."

FBI Mobile HQ, New Orleans, Louisiana

Dylan Kane sat on the running board that surrounded much of the FBI's Mobile Headquarters. He imagined they were for personnel to ride into or out of a situation on, the handgrips he spotted above seeming to confirm it. It had him thinking that the design was good only if you had control of the situation outside. If you were trapped inside, and tried to get away, your enemy would be able to hang on and ride with you.

This is America! Shit like that doesn't happen here.

Then he pictured G8 riots and realized things like that *do* happen here. Isabelle sat beside him, her legs outstretched, her face turned up to the faint warmth of the sun.

"If you tune out what you know, this would just be a normal, beautiful day. The kind of day that should be spent on a patio sipping beer."

Kane smiled at her then turned his own eyes skyward.

"That sounds like something we should do when this is all done."

She looked at him, but he kept his eyes on the sky.

"Do you think we're going to get out of this? I mean, stop this virus or whatever it is?"

Kane smiled, staring at the clouds as they were pushed through the sky by a steady but gentle breeze.

"My philosophy when I took this job was to treat life like I was already dead. As far as I'm concerned, I've lived about five years longer than I should have. If this is the end, then so be it. *But*, I like to think God has a plan for us that goes beyond allowing us to destroy ourselves with some damned virus cooked up in a lab."

"Perhaps. Or He's pissed that we were playing God, and that's His job. Have you read those briefing notes on the antiviral? It's amazing! They would be able to wipe out almost any type of virus in the entire world, especially now that this wacko has aerosolized it. They could just spray the cure for AIDS across Africa or Haiti. Just imagine the possibilities!"

"Yup. The problem is the virus they are wiping out is mankind."

"You're very cynical."

"It's my job."

"There's no way you're FBI. What are you? Military? CIA?"

Kane continued to look at the sky.

"If we don't get out of this, I'd like to say goodbye to my parents before the end."

He closed his eyes and tried to picture the last time he had seen his family all together, but couldn't, instead images of explosions and charred remains appeared, forcing him to give up and open his eyes again.

"Do you have any family?" he asked Isabelle. "I assume you're not married since I didn't have to spoon with your husband last night."

She chuckled.

"No, the job always seemed to get in the way of that. Cops, especially female cops, are chronically single. Men want to be the tough guy in a relationship, and most can't handle a strong woman who can quite often kick their ass, shoot them and arrest them."

"So it's just a series of meaningless hook ups then?" asked Kane with a wink.

He was rewarded with a none too soft punch to the shoulder.

"Watch it, mister, or you just might be sleeping at some fleabag hotel tonight."

"Hey, I never sleep with a woman I just met two nights in a row."

"Me neither."

Kane laughed out loud, tossing his head back.

"What the hell is that?"

He jumped to his feet and rushed away from the mobile HQ, pointing at the sky as Isabelle joined him.

"It looks like some sort of private airplane," she said. "What the hell does he think he's doing? Everything's supposed to be grounded."

"It's a Cessna 172. Some civie trying to make a break for it." Kane surveyed the sky then spotted what he was looking for and pointed. "Here they come."

Two F-22 Raptors screamed across the sky, chewing up the airspace in an amazingly short period of time, the Cessna seeming to be at a standstill. They buzzed the aircraft, most likely the flight leader ordering him to return to whatever strip he had taken off from, but the Cessna seemed undeterred.

It merely reduced altitude, probably with the intention of trying to fly between the buildings.

Ballsy. Stupid, but ballsy.

The amount of training it would take to escape and evade Raptors in a Cessna probably didn't exist.

Suddenly the door to the Mobile HQ burst open and Hewlett, along with several others rushed out, looking at the sky.

"What's the situation?" asked Kane.

"They've just been given the go ahead to shoot him down."

"Shit," muttered one of the FBI techs. "How far do we have to take this?"

"We're fighting to save the world," said Hewlett, not sounding that convinced.

"The world's already lost," said Isabelle. "If we're shooting down our own, it's already lost."

The two Raptors circled, coming in for an attack run, one in the lead, the second hanging back. As they circled, the Cessna made a last ditch effort to evade, banking sharply to the left, turning completely around, now heading back toward the Superdome.

But it was too late.

A missile dropped from the wing of the lead Raptor, streaking across the sky as its propellant lit, thrusting it at incredible speed toward the now retreating Cessna. The small plane banked hard, trying to evade the missile, but there was no hope.

The radar guided missile connected with the tail of the plane, sending it spiraling several times before it smacked into the ground, smoke pouring out the rear. Kane sprinted toward the aircraft, only a few hundred feet from where they were standing, as it ground to a halt, cutting a path in the pavement about fifty feet long.

He heard footfalls behind him as the Raptor's slowly circled overhead. As he approached the plane he heard children screaming for help and he froze, his mind flashing back to the most horrifying moment of his life, the one moment he had never been able to reconcile, to never compartmentalize and forget as part of the job.

The living nightmare that haunted him constantly.

He willed himself toward the plane, the smoke getting thicker, and yanked the door open. The pilot was dead, his head smashed against the control panel, his neck twisted unnaturally. Whom he assumed was the wife was moaning, blood flowing from her forehead. He pointed to the other side as the others arrived.

"Other side, get the woman!"

He pulled at the rear door, but it wouldn't budge. Two young boys sat in the back, no more than ten years old, screaming and crying. He tried to ignore their cries, to focus on the door, when flames burst from the fuselage in the rear.

"Dylan, get out of there! It's gonna blow!"

"We've got the woman!" yelled someone from the other side of the plane as he continued to pull on the door to no avail. The heat from the flames was becoming intense, the flames beginning to lick at him as he worked. He knew the plane could explode at any second, but he didn't care. He'd rather die today than let something like this happen again.

Last time he had no choice.

This time he did.

He pulled his gun out and fired at the window, splintering the safety glass. With his elbow he rammed it repeatedly until it fell out of the frame, then reached in for the first and older boy.

"Undo your belt!" ordered Kane.

The boy quickly flipped the clip holding the belt in place and sprung toward Kane.

"Help your brother first!"

The boy, oblivious it seemed to the flames now reaching the window, spun around and released his crying brother, then in a show of bravery Kane had seen in few men, shoved his brother toward the open window and into the arms of the stranger risking his own life to save them.

Kane pulled the little boy through the window, placing him on the ground as Isabelle urged him to run toward her. Kane turned back and pulled the older brother through the window, then carrying him under one arm, raced toward the other boy who was stumbling toward Isabelle.

"Run!" yelled Kane as he scooped the little boy under his other arm, rushing toward a group of dumpsters clustered nearby. Out of the corner of his eye he could see the other FBI personnel running, several carrying the incapacitated mother, when hell tore loose on Earth, a screeching roar from

254

behind him filling his ears, heat racing past him, sucking the air from his lungs as he dropped to the ground from the concussive force unleashed.

He hit hard, trying to protect the boys as much as he could, landing just past the dumpsters, but still in the path of the inferno rushing toward them. One of the boys was pulled from his arms, and he saw Isabelle huddling behind the bins. He grabbed the other boy tight and rolled them both as the flames roared past, his body getting toasted by the raging aviation fuel that quickly retreated back to its source as the initial blast consumed the fuel it needed to feed.

"On your feet!" ordered Kane, jumping to his, still holding the youngest boy. Isabelle grabbed the other kid and they rushed toward the Mobile HQ and safety as the other personnel picked themselves off the ground. As Kane came to rest at the side of the HQ with the others, he looked back. The plane was completely engulfed in flames, the body of the father they had been forced to leave behind now a barbecued mass he hoped the boys couldn't make out.

As he caught his breath, a loud noise above him, of something hitting the Mobile HQ, had him jumping to his feet. His head scanned the entire area, quickly settling on a group of people slowly approaching their position. The arm of one of those approaching whipped, sending something slamming into the side of the massive vehicle, then bouncing to the ground.

A rock.

"This is your fault!" yelled one of them as Kane pushed the small boy away from him and toward the rear where Isabelle took his hand and ferried him out of sight.

"Yeah, you people killed him!"

"Let us out of here! We're not sick!"

"You're killing us all!"

The shouts were becoming more angry, and more and more objects began to be thrown, most pried from the ground wherever the parking lot pavement showed fatigue.

"Let's get ready to move, people!" yelled Kane. The engine, idling to generate power, revved as someone put the vehicle into gear.

"Get them!" screamed someone, their voice filled with insane rage, sending the crowd into a mad rush of human flesh at the nearest target it could find. Kane ran around the rear of the vehicle to see Isabelle pushing the older kid inside, then jumping in herself as the other personnel scrambled in behind her. A glance over his shoulder and he knew they didn't have time.

He pulled his weapon and cranked off several rounds into pavement rather than the air, since bullets must come down somewhere. The crowd halted, then tentatively moved forward again.

"He can't get us all!" yelled someone, and the crowd surged forward again, confirming the man's point. There were dozens, and there was no way Kane could take them all out, nor did he intend to take even one of them out. These were innocent people, desperate people.

Scared people.

This could be happening anywhere, including his home town. It could be his family rushing someone like him in anger and fear, and he wouldn't want them shot unless it were completely necessary.

He fired a few more rounds, slowing them down, but the next volley did nothing.

They knew he wasn't trying to hit them.

The vehicle was rolling now as the last of the FBI personnel climbed aboard. Kane ran for the door. The door that closed behind the last man, the engine kicking it up a notch as the vehicle picked up speed.

Shit!

256

"Whatever happened to no man left behind?" he asked himself as he sprinted beside the vehicle, jumping on the running board and grabbing a hand hold. As the vehicle rushed toward the parking lot exit he heard pounding on the other side of the vehicle. He spotted footholds and shifted himself toward them, then quickly climbed to the roof.

Dozens of people were still chasing the vehicle, but they were quickly falling off in ones and twos, America's waistline saving the day, but several of those not spread out by takeout and high fructose corn syrup had managed to get on the very runners he had been wondering about earlier and were now pounding on the sides of the vehicle.

He flattened himself on the roof, spread eagle, then moved to the side, trying to keep his hand gripping something at all times. Fortunately there was a chrome rail that trimmed the entire top of the vehicle. He pushed himself to the other side, grabbing the railing just as the vehicle made a hard right, sending his body flinging over the side, much to the surprise of the civilians occupying it.

He grabbed the man he was staring at face to face by the shirt with his free hand and ripped him off the side of the vehicle, sending him tumbling to the pavement, as he twisted and planted a kick on another man's stomach, sending him doubled over in pain, his hands now gripping his stomach, then flailing in the air as he tipped toward the ground. Kane's feet found the running board, and he pulled his weapon on the final man who decided to jump before waiting to see whether or not Kane might actually shoot somebody this time.

The side cleared, he pulled himself to the roof, then slid to check the rear and found it clear as well. The vehicle was racing down the nearly empty streets now, the driver seeming to be in a panic as they were now clear of the danger. Kane dragged himself toward the front, the wind whipping at his body as it tried to pry him loose. He managed to reach the side with the door, then, slipping his right leg over the side, he pushed his head over the edge and spotted a handhold. He grabbed it with his right hand, then swung the rest of his body over the side, it flapping against the side with the wind for several seconds, causing the driver to speed up even more.

Another right turn had Kane firmly pressed against the side of the vehicle, the wind negated, and he managed to grab a second handhold on the side and get his feet on the running board. Stepping toward the door as quickly as he could, he reached out with his right hand as the driver began to pick up speed again, and knocked out a "shave and a haircut" as best he could, with the requisite "two bits" taps at the end.

Nothing.

He repeated it, then suddenly it felt as if the foot had been taken off the gas and the Mobile HQ began to slow rapidly. Before it came to a halt the door was pushed open slightly, Isabelle sticking her head out.

"Thank God!" she cried, pushing the door fully open, steps below it extending automatically. She reached out for Kane's hand who took it, then stepped onto the mini doorstep, grabbing the frame of the door opening with his left hand, finally stepping inside with a pull from Isabelle.

The door shut and the driver hit the gas.

"I'm so sorry, I didn't realize you hadn't gotten on!" cried Isabelle, hugging him.

"No worries. It gave me a chance to get rid of some hangers-on." He gave her a pat on the back and she suddenly released him, apparently realizing what she was doing. Kane turned to the driver. "You can take it easy now, they're long gone."

The man seemed visibly relieved and slowed to a regular speed.

"Where should we go?" he asked.

Kane looked for Special Agent Hewlett, who was still gripping hand rails, looking slightly pale.

"I'd suggest we go to the CDC setup at the LSU Hospital. There will be lots of security there, and we need these people to be looked at regardless," said Kane, motioning toward the plane crash survivors.

"Do it," ordered Hewlett.

Kane took a seat at one of the vacant terminals and pulled a Snickers bar from his pocket. Tearing it open, he broke off a piece and handed it to the smallest boy who immediately brightened, attacking the treat as if he had never eaten chocolate before. Another piece for the brother was devoured as well, leaving a small piece for Kane. He motioned to Isabelle, who waved it off.

"You have it; I think you've earned it."

Kane pursed his lips, his head bobbing in agreement.

"All in a day's work."

He popped the bite-sized piece in his mouth, savoring the peanut, nougat and chocolate concoction as he slowly chewed, drawing the experience out.

"If what you just did is a typical day's work, I don't want to know what an exciting day is."

Kane gave Isabelle a wink, then began to check his body for injuries, Isabelle seeming to be a little too eager to help him.

He smiled as he swallowed his bite.

Quarantine Zone, CIA Headquarters, Langley, Virginia

Command Sergeant Major Burt "BD" Dawson waited for the call to be connected, the red tape having been fairly slow to work its way through. It wasn't every day the American government called to talk to a Russian Special Forces unit.

"Lieutenant Colonel Chernov," he heard, the Russian accent thick, but Dawson knew the man spoke perfect English, it normal officer training in the former Soviet Union, and still in our so-called ally's army, to teach their men English for infiltration and interrogation purposes.

"Sir, is this line secure?"

There was a clicking sound and Dawson could see from the phone he was sitting at that the line had been secured from the other end, lines such as this used by the two countries to keep in contact when they didn't want any eavesdropping from third parties.

"It is now," came the reply in perfect English.

New England accent?

"I'm Sergeant White. I need to talk to you about one of your men."

"What do you need to know, Command Sergeant Major Dawson?"

Dawson chuckled.

"It's good to see your FSB is as effective as your KGB was."

"Perhaps too effective at times," said Chernov.

"Then down to business. You're aware of the situation we're facing here?"

"It would appear it is a situation we are all facing what with the failure of your President to contain the virus."

Dawson decided to give the Russian his jab.

260

"Our people have been tracking down every lead, and we have found that a former member of your team, a Major Anton Koslov, is involved. He murdered the suspect who planted the canisters of virus and then rigged a bomb to go off when the body was discovered."

There was a pause.

"Do you have proof of this?"

"We have video of him entering the apartment building of the suspect, and the trigger design is old Soviet style. Still used by your teams, I believe."

"If it is not broke…"

Dawson waited for a response, which seemed long in coming.

"I do not know where the Major is. I don't think I can help you."

"Sir, please wait. You know what we're facing here, and as you put it, what we're all facing. Finding your Major is critical. He could hold the key to finding the actual man behind this, who may have a cure, or at least be able to provide us with additional information that could speed up the process in finding a cure.

"Now, one soldier to another, I know if one of my men that used to be under my command were to be involved in something like this, I'd want to do everything I could to find him, and bring him in. I've read your file, sir. I know you're that type of commanding officer. You trained this man, you fought with this man at your side. I know you want to find out if what is being said about him now could be true."

Another pause. Dawson's heart was beating rapidly, knowing that he had either reached the man, or pissed him off. Either way, finding this Major Koslov would come down to the words about to come from Lieutenant Colonel Chernov's mouth.

"Da, you are right. I will call you when I know something."

"Thank you, sir, you have the number."

"Do svidaniya, Sergeant."

"Do svidaniya, sir."

The line went dead and Dawson sat quietly, calming his heart that was racing faster than it did on most missions. Then again, he had never been involved in anything that could end the world as he knew it.

The door on the other side of the glass flew open and the young CIA analyst Leroux burst in.

"Well?"

"He'll get back to us."

Leroux jumped up and down in his hazmat suit.

"I've gotta call Kane!"

"You do that. I'm gonna get some rack time. I have a funny feeling when the Colonel calls back, all hell's gonna break loose."

It better. Because if it doesn't, we're screwed.

Decontamination Zone, Interim LSU Public Hospital, New Orleans, Louisiana

"Mr. President, we have some good news."

It was Dr. Hermann Kapp from BioDyne who was speaking, and Katherine had to agree, it was good news. Great news. Fantastic news.

If it were true.

If it worked.

If! If! If!

"What is it, Doctor?"

"Well, when we first heard from Dr. Urban about the attack on the theatre in Los Angeles a year ago, we immediately began planning for a worst case scenario. We were able to design a compound that neutralizes the antiviral without killing the patient. It had already been under development from the beginning of the research just in case something went wrong and we needed to neutralize it in a patient, but once the attacks began, we realized we needed an aerosolized version as well.

"That research was completed over six months ago, but we had no way to test it. With the amount of antiviral recovered from the blood of the Superdome victims, we were able to quickly grow more, then contaminate an entire test facility. We then used our compound to decontaminate it. It worked. All antiviral on surfaces was neutralized within hours. Antiviral not accessible, such as inside closed compartments, etc., was not, however we have determined that the antiviral will die within twenty-four hours itself. As well, all of the animals we infected with the antiviral, from mice to primates, were cured by breathing in the aerosolized compound.

"Bottom line, Mr. President, is this: we have a way of stopping this. It's expensive, but it works, and we can go into production almost immediately. All we need to know is what genetic sequence is being targeted."

"And when will you know that?"

"With nothing to narrow it down, days, perhaps weeks, maybe longer."

"By then millions, or billions, could be dead," muttered one of the advisors over the live feed of the videoconference.

"We need to find Dr. Urban in order to target the compound properly, otherwise we're shooting proverbial blanks."

"We're doing everything—"

The President was cutoff when someone leaned into the camera view, whispering something in his ear.

"Ladies and gentlemen, we have a situation I need to deal with immediately. Continue what you're doing, and may God have mercy on us all."

His feed went immediately dead, the other camera views snapping off, leaving a grid of black. Katherine was about to stand up when a commotion started in the back of the room.

"You guys have to see this!"

"Put it on the big screen!"

The screen snapped to life with a CNN feed, the harsh red Breaking News bar across the top, with the text below indicating it was live footage from Charles de Gaulle Airport in Paris, France. A large jet was on a runway, its front landing gear collapsed, one engine smoking dark black.

And it was surrounded by dozens of armed troops.

"Turn it up!"

Suddenly the audio feed came in loud and clear, and Katherine forgot all of her problems as what was truly going on beyond her little bubble hit home.

"—the plane was ordered back to the United States, however the pilot indicated there was insufficient fuel. Company officials say they tried to find an alternate landing site, but were refused at every turn. Even countries with American Air Force Bases were refused by order of the local governments. The plane was left circling Paris for hours, until finally the pilot declared an emergency, and put the aircraft down. There are reports that the French tried to block the runway with vehicles, and that is what collapsed the landing gear when the plane hit a truck. The plane has been surrounded by ground troops, and no assistance has been provided by the French authorities to put out the now worsening fire in one of the engines.

"Our sources are indicating that airport authorities are under orders by the French government to not let anyone off the plane, nor to let anyone approach it. We'll switch now to our White House correspondent, Henry Powel. Henry, what's the latest?"

"Cooper, I've just been informed that the President left an important conference on the current antiviral outbreak to personally call the French President to try and resolve this situation. We're not certain if he's been able to reach him, however we hope to know more soon. There has been no official reaction yet from the White House, however this scene is being repeated around the world, with American flights being ordered back, or allowed to land so they can be refueled, then sent back with no one allowed to disembark. We—"

"Sorry to interrupt you, Henry, but something's happening…"

Katherine stopped listening, the feed itself absorbing all her senses. The engine was now fully engulfed in flames, and the one next to it appeared to be smoking now as well. The front door of the plane had just opened and one of the evacuation slides had inflated. A close up showed troops aiming their weapons, but not firing. A flight attendant jumped out and slid down the slide, stopping at the bottom as a second attendant followed. They took up positions on either side as passengers began to slide down the ramp, one after another, the flames growing on the other side of the plane.

A second door opened at the rear, and another slide deployed. More passengers began to slide down, and soon there were dozens running toward the troops, close ups showing the panicked women and children trying to distance themselves from the flaming aircraft.

Then the unthinkable happened.

At first she didn't know what had happened. It looked like a woman had tripped and fallen, then as if someone else had tripped trying to help her.

"Oh my God! They're shooting the passengers. Ladies and gentlemen, you may not be able to hear this, but our reports from the ground are that shots are being fired at the escaping passengers. At least one of the soldiers has opened fire on the escaping passengers!"

Katherine tried to block her ears with her hands, but she couldn't tear her eyes away from the horror she was witnessing. At least a dozen bodies were scattered along the runway. Passengers were now running away from the troops, some even trying to climb back up the slide they had just come down, while others still were evacuating the plane.

"It's not clear if the soldier is acting under orders, but the passengers are now running back toward the plane they just fled. Wait, something's happening now. The soldier who was firing has just been shot by his own troops. Ladies and gentlemen, from what we're seeing it's sheer chaos on the scene, we just don't know what is happening."

The camera began to zoom in on the bodies. Women, children, the odd man, lay on the ground, their bodies oozing blood onto the runway, some still alive, writhing in pain as they tried to drag themselves away from the soldiers.

Then there was a ripping sound caught on one of the audio feeds as the image flashed, the remaining jet fuel igniting, the entire plane erupting into a black and orange ball of rage, shrapnel bursting out in every direction, the flame and heat consuming everything within its path, the shrapnel the passengers' retaliation for the horror they had been put through, it tearing apart many of the surrounding troops.

Someone turned off the TV and Katherine removed her hands from her ears and looked about the room, her eyes a blur from the tears that now streaked her cheeks. She felt a pair of arms over her shoulders, and she realized it was Dr. Johnston. Turning her head in to rest on his chest, she let herself go, her sobs racking her body with heaves of remorse and frustration, as she cried not only for the passengers that had just died, but for the dozens who had died in this very hospital, and the millions or billions who would soon be dead.

Khamovniki District, Moscow, Russia

Lieutenant Colonel Chernov was careful not to touch the walls. He didn't even want to touch the floors. The place was a disgrace. An old Soviet era apartment block that like most things in Russia today had been left to rot and decay. It was disgusting. The rich got richer, and the average poor bastard, who was already *very* poor compared to Western standards, lived in squalor while million dollar condominiums were built on prime real estate.

And if you complained, you were liable to find yourself beaten to a pulp, or worse. There was no opposition in today's Russia. When the Communist party is your opposition, you know something is wrong. Democracy was a sham under Putin's leadership, more and more so with each election. Some people wondered why he even bothered having them, since it was impossible for him to lose. Koslov always said the reason was to let people learn to hate democracy. Putin's propaganda machine had the populace thinking their democracy was no worse, and perhaps better, than that in the West, constantly pointing to Florida in 2000.

"That could never happen in Russia!"

Yeah, because it would have already been 90% to 10%, so there would have been no point.

And instead, Russians were left with a decaying democracy, with money being wasted on weapons modernization and beating up gays, rather than fixing the economy, diversifying away from just oil, and employing people so they didn't spend their entire days floor licking pissed on vodka.

He knocked on the door of Major Koslov's parents.

He heard noises inside, footsteps approaching the door, then nothing.

He knocked again, and again nothing.

"This is Lieutenant Colonel Chernov. Open the door or I will kick it down."

Whispers, then the sound of locks being unbolted.

Chernov was finally greeted by a little old lady who was shaking, a forced smile on her face, motioning for him to come inside, an even older man attempting, and failing, to get out of a recliner, deeper in the apartment. Chernov stepped inside the small apartment, made smaller by the fact it was jammed with matching La-Z-Boy recliners sitting in front of a 58" Panasonic flat panel and a 7.1 surround system that Chernov had only seen once before in his life, and it wasn't in Russia.

A glance to his left showed a kitchen equipped with all the latest appliances, and glass faced cupboards proudly stocked. The floors were new hardwood, the walls freshly painted. The only evidence of the Soviet era was the entranceway, drab and unpainted, along with the curtains, still old and ratty lest new ones be spotted from outside.

"Please, have a seat," said the old lady.

"You are Major Anton Koslov's mother?"

She nodded.

"Yes, Colonel."

"It is urgent that I speak to him."

She looked at her husband, who shook his head, his gravelly, gruff voice suitable for singing Georgian folk songs.

"We have not heard from him since he left the military," he said.

"No word at all?"

"Nyet."

"No letters, no phone calls?"

"Nyet."

"Yet your pension seems to let you live extremely well," said Chernov, waving his arm at the room.

The old man looked at the window, focusing on the one thing that wasn't new.

"Can I get you anything, Colonel?" asked Mrs. Koslov, stepping toward the kitchen. "Tea, perhaps?"

"Yes, tea would be nice." He stepped into the line of sight of Mr. Koslov. "I have a feeling I'm going to be here a long time."

He sat on the edge of the living room table, staring directly at Mr. Koslov.

"I *will* have the truth, Mr. Koslov. Your son is involved in this virus thing, and may have access to a cure. Now you can tell me how to reach him, so I can get to him first, or leave it to the Americans, who are looking at total annihilation. Who do you think he has a better chance surviving with? Me, his old comrade and commanding officer, or a bunch of Americans hell-bent on revenge?"

The old man sighed and nodded, motioning to his wife.

"Give him what he wants."

Quarantine Zone, CIA Headquarters, Langley, Virginia

"BD!"

Dawson immediately awoke, the hand gently shaking his shoulder belonging to his best friend, Mike "Red" Belme. He swung his legs from the cot and onto the floor, stretching.

"What is it? Mission?"

"You've gotta call."

Dawson looked at his watch.

That was quick.

"Okay, thanks. I'll be back in a few. Better get the guys up, I have a feeling we're about to get into the thick of it."

"Will do."

Dawson headed for the interview room he had been in earlier, and a man in a hazmat suit handed him a file folder when he arrived.

"This just arrived for you, Sergeant."

"Thank you, sir."

Dawson sat at the table and picked up the phone as he flipped open the file.

"Sergeant White here."

"Sergeant Dawson, it is Lieutenant Colonel Chernov."

"Sir, thank you for getting back to me so soon."

"Did you get the data I sent?"

"I'm seeing it for the first time just now. It looks like you've found him."

"We got an address from his parents. They confirmed that is where he has been calling his home for the past two years. A satellite fly over just a few minutes ago shows people at the villa, one of whom appears to be Major Koslov."

"Thank you very much, sir."

"What do you intend to do?"

"Capture him, bring him in for interrogation."

"Not kill him?"

"He's our only lead to finding the men behind this. If we kill him, they get away."

"I want to be there."

"I can't sanction that, but if we happened to bump into a fellow soldier on the way, he'd be welcome to join us. But I doubt you'll be there on time."

"Likely not. Perhaps for the interrogation. I may be able to appeal to him as his former commander."

"If you can get to Washington with all the flights grounded, be my guest."

"I will find a way."

"Good luck."

"Good hunting, Sergeant."

Dawson hung up the phone and dialed the number he had been given for the Director's office.

"Director Morrison's office."

"This is Sergeant White, Delta Team Bravo. Let him know we've found our guy."

"I will tell him right away, Sergeant!"

The excitement in her voice echoed that in his heart.

Maybe there is hope!

Detective Laprise's Apartment, New Orleans, Louisiana

Dylan Kane stood with his hands pressed against the tile wall of Isabelle's bathroom, the rainhead equipped shower providing a steady stream of muscle relaxant as he tried to work the kinks of the past couple of days out. *Now, if Catalina and Jazmin were here, a massage would be just what I need.* A medic had patched up the few cuts he had suffered, but it was the bruises and overstretched muscles, tendons and ligaments that were the problem now. There was no permanent damage, and he could go into action right now, but it would literally be a pain.

And that was the spy business. It wasn't like the movies, where you were chasing or being chased constantly, with super cool toys where even your electric shaver could kill with cyanide laced blow darts or a nifty laser. It was hours, days or sometimes months of surveillance, tracking down clues just like a police detective, but with an arsenal of information and surveillance technology at your disposal that police didn't have, because as a spy, you didn't have to worry about someone's civil rights, only their human rights.

But occasionally there was action, usually conducted with surgical precision, quite often the target not even knowing you were ever there. And that's the part he lived for. He didn't mind months of surveillance, as long as in the end he got the bad guy or the target item that needed retrieval, or that piece of intel stored on a hard drive in the middle of a maximum security installation.

That was the life.

He heard the shower curtain scrape, and turned his head slightly to see Isabelle, naked, climbing in the shower with him.

"You were taking too long," she said, her voice full of bravado, the wavering of it revealing the actual truth. She was nervous. Scared even. He could tell she feared rejection. After all, he was quite a few years her junior, but the glimpse he caught of her climbing in told him she had *nothing* to be ashamed of. She clearly kept herself fit, and if this was what she wanted, who was he to say no. He had to admit he had been eyeballing her on several occasions, and Dylan, Jr. was already trying to take a peek.

"Uh huh," he said as he felt her hands begin to caress his shoulders, her fingers kneading his taught muscles with just enough strength to elicit a groan, but not enough to hurt. His head dropped to his chest as her fingers worked up either side of the back of his neck, then down again, her thumbs pressing into the center of his back, then rubbing hard outward, toward her fingers that gripped his sides.

It was heavenly.

Her hands slipped around to his front, sliding easily from the water up his rock hard abs to his chest, squeezing his pecs as she leaned against him, her breasts pressing into his back, her cheek on his shoulder blade, her breath hot against his back. Her arms wrapped completely around him, squeezing him into her as she turned her head and kissed between his shoulder blades, licking his skin with her soft tongue as he slowly turned around to face her.

He looked down at her, and she up at him, and she had a look that to him seemed a cross between lust and pleading, as if she feared his rejection even now.

He put that thought at ease as he leaned down and kissed her, wrapping his arms around her body and pulling her tight against him. She moaned, as did he, their tongues doing battle while he ground himself into her. Kane quickly found himself more aroused than he had been in a long time. This was a woman, a woman who knew what she wanted, and it was him, not some fantasy identity created at a third-world hotel where cheap love could be found at the drop of a hundred dollar bill from girls desperate to improve their lives, if only for a day.

This was real.

He pushed her away, turned off the shower then climbed out, scooping her into his arms as he carried her to the bed, gently lying her down on the sheets, all the while continuing to kiss her, and with his hands now free, explore her body, eliciting moans, groans and gasps as his talented hands and mouth gave her an experience he sensed she hadn't had in a long time.

She pushed him over onto his back, straddling him with a grin, dropping down and kissing him on the mouth, then moving south, slow, tantalizingly slow, agonizingly slow, inching toward what he hoped she planned, her eyes meeting his, the confidence of a woman restored, a woman reborn, as she was determined to be satisfied by him, and to satisfy him, taking a momentary refuge in each other from the chaos outside.

There were more important things to be doing, there were more significant places to be, but for this brief moment in time, they sought comfort in each other, not knowing if this could be the last time either of them would ever get to enjoy the company of the opposite sex.

And with one final giggle from her, and a groan from him, all the troubles of the world disappeared, lost to the paradise Kane now felt at the ministrations of this passionate New Orleans detective.

Quarantine Zone, CIA Headquarters, Langley, Virginia

Leroux sat on one side of the glass with Director Morrison. On the other side was the Delta Force sergeant, one of his men, and Sherrie. Leroux had been at his desk, sifting through search results that had provided essentially bupkiss. Where the former Spetsnaz Major and his presumed employer were remained a mystery.

Until Morrison pulled him from his office, nearly running for the elevators.

He hadn't seen the Director this excited before, then again, the stakes had never been this high before. The entire time he was on the phone with what sounded like the White House, pretty much on hold the entire time. The phone was still pressed to his ear as his free index finger was held in the air, everyone holding their breaths for the reply.

Or at least Leroux was holding his breath. He reached his limit and stifled a gasp, sucking in a lungful of air and blushing slightly as he saw Sherrie smiling at him. She knew him so well there was no way he could hide his excitement.

"Thank you, Mr. President."

The phone call was ended with a click and Morrison activated the mike.

"We're a go. Sergeant, get your men ready, requisition anything you think you'll need. I'm assigning Agent White to accompany you, along with a senior agent who will meet you on route. Get this bastard alive, bring him back here, and while in transit, you have my authority to question him in any way you see fit. Just make sure he stays alive."

"Yes, sir," replied the Sergeant. "Sir, Major Koslov's former commanding officer, Lieutenant Colonel Chernov, has requested he be allowed to interrogate the prisoner. He thought he may get more out of him than we could. I took the liberty of saying he could, should he be able to get himself here."

"That could be a challenge what with air travel pretty much being shut down."

"Agreed. But I've read his file. Expect him to be here, and if anything unusual is coming out of Russia, I'd suggest you let it through."

"I'll take that under advisement, Sergeant."

"Thank you, sir."

Morrison rose, as did everyone, then left the room. Leroux lingered at the glass as Sherrie approached, the two Delta Force men leaving in a hurry. Suddenly Leroux was overcome with a horrible sense of doom as he looked at the love of his life. A pit in his stomach almost overwhelmed him, his mouth filling with bile as he felt himself pale, as he had the intense certainty he would never see her again.

"Are you okay?" she asked.

"Oh, you know how I am," he said, managing to force a bit of a smile on his face. "I always get nervous before a mission."

She chuckled, placing her hands on the glass separating them.

"Don't worry, dear, I'll be okay. I'm going in with a Delta Force team. These guys are the best in the world, almost as good as me!" she said with a wink.

The confidence she portrayed had him feeling a little better, and he put his hand on the glass, covering hers.

"Take care of yourself."

"I will, as always."

She kissed the glass.

"I have to go, otherwise they'll leave without me."

Leroux shrugged as she headed for the door, thinking that may not be a bad thing.

"Bye baby!" she called, blowing him a kiss.

He caught it, but she had already turned, and his feeling of doom returned as his eyes filled with tears and he grabbed the edge of the table for support.

God, please take care of her!

Detective Laprise's Apartment, New Orleans, Louisiana

Isabelle couldn't remember the last time she had felt so totally satisfied. So totally a woman. She stared at the ceiling, staring into nothingness, wishing that the day would never end. It had been passionate, crazy, wild and tender. It had been everything.

Multiple times.

Oh God how many times!

She wished she had a girlfriend she could call and tell all about it, she was so excited. But she was forty, not a teenager, but right now, she felt like a teenager. She rolled onto him, her cheek on his chest, her hand stroking his stomach, her right leg flung across his nether regions as she closed her eyes and enjoyed the warmth of a man's body, something she hadn't felt in years.

She couldn't believe what she had done. It was so totally out of character for her. She wasn't a one night stand girl. To her sex was serious, important, to be shared by two people who cared for each other, not someone who had literally parachuted into her life that she barely knew.

Kane looked at his watch and she felt a pit in her stomach. He was bored.

"I guess we should get going," she said, beginning to push herself away.

"Why the rush?" he asked as he rolled on top of her, looking deeper into her eyes than any man she could remember.

"I just thought, well, it's getting late."

"I just got a message to report to the airport in two hours. They're sending a chopper to pick me up."

"When did you get that?"

Kane showed her his watch for a brief second.

"It's not just a watch."

She wrapped her arms around him, positioning herself for one last session of lovemaking with a man she was certain was a spy, a spy she would probably never see again after today.

And it broke her heart.

As if he could sense her feelings, what happened over the next half hour was exactly what she needed. It was love making at its best, slow, intense, lovers finding comfort in each other, no gymnastics or showing off, just the right kisses and caresses she needed at this moment, just the right memory she needed to end things with, and when it was done, she held him in her arms tightly, falling asleep relaxed and content.

She awoke to the sound of the shower, and she smiled as she remembered the last time it had been running and what had ensued. But she knew he had to leave, so her temptation to join him again would have to wait. She quickly straightened up the bedroom, gathering his clothes and setting out a new set for herself.

They exchanged kisses and places when he exited the shower, and when she came out, her stud had sandwiches ready for them.

"So why do you have to leave so quickly?"

"Mission," he replied, taking a bite of his sandwich. "They found the bomber, or at least they think they found him."

"And they need you?"

She immediately regretted the way she had said it, and his smile made her backpedal.

"I mean, of course they need you, I mean, you're very good at your job."

Thankfully he bailed her out.

"They need me because I've worked with all the parties involved, and can identify the guy on sight. Also, I'm one of the few agents in the region with my particular skillset, and they need someone who can operate out of country."

"Out of country? Where are you going?"

A thunderous sound that had been building for the past several seconds finally became too loud to ignore.

"What the hell is that?" she asked as she went to the window to look outside.

"That's my ride," said Kane, still at the table.

Isabelle gasped as she saw a military chopper settle down in the courtyard, several personnel in chemical warfare gear jumping out.

"I'll be going now."

Isabelle spun around as Kane stood up, wiping his face with a napkin and downing the last of his ice cold water. She followed him to the door and grabbed an ankle-length jacket as he picked up the backpack he had been toting around since he arrived by parachute.

He grabbed her by the waist, pulling her tight against him, and gave her the type of goodbye kiss she had only ever seen in the movies, a kiss that made her knees give out and her heart hammer so hard she could barely hear herself moan in pleasure.

He let her go and opened the door. She slipped on a pair of flats and followed him to the elevator then outside, the entire time saying nothing, just leaning on him, his arm around her shoulders. As they left the building, the pounding of the blades kept their conversation short as she held one side of her jacket up to block the dust from getting in their eyes.

"Take care of yourself," she said, one hand holding his cheek.

"I always do," he said with a smile, placing his hand over hers, pushing his cheek into her palm a little harder. "I had a wonderful time."

"So did I. I'm sorry if I pressured you into something, you know, you didn't want."

She looked down at the ground as her eyes filled with tears. A finger under her chin pulled her gaze back to his, a loving smile she hadn't seen for years looking down at her.

"I did nothing I didn't want to do. You're a remarkable lady." He kissed her gently, then pulled away. "I have to go."

He began to walk away when she realized he hadn't answered her question.

"Wait!" she yelled. He turned to face her, his arm raised to try and block the wind. "Where are you going?"

He wagged his finger at her.

"You know I can't tell you, but if you like cigars, I'll bring you back some."

She smiled and waved and he ran toward the helicopter, the soldiers helping him aboard. As the chopper lifted off, she could see him staring at her, a smile on his face as he never took his eyes off of her until the chopper banked away. She continued to watch it until it was no more than a pinpoint in the distance, finally turning around and heading inside.

And she knew two things from what he had said.

He was going to Cuba.

And he'd be back.

Eglin AFB, Florida

Kane spent the better part of the next two hours in isolation. His blood test taken earlier had come back clean, but because he had additional exposure, he had been tested again. But the time hadn't been wasted. He had been fully briefed and brought up to speed not only on the situation he was heading into, but the situation around the world.

He felt slightly sick to his stomach, especially after hearing about the hundreds killed aboard the plane as a result of the actions of a terrified young French soldier.

From what he now knew, he knew there were two antivirals on the loose, one that should burn itself out shortly, the other that could be far worse. Mankind was on the brink, and unless they could capture either the missing scientist Dr. Urban, or his partner or abductor, Scott Fowler, there might be no chance of recovery.

At this point the spread seemed fairly slow, but not contained. Cases were being reported all across the planet, with the vast majority in the United States, with Canada and Mexico pretty much tied for second. It made sense. The virus was following the trucking routes of the continent, and whatever the infected truckers had in common with the people they encountered, those people were then exposed, and possibly infected.

And with the spread being worldwide, they assumed it was something very common. But with the ten day incubation period, the patients were only now starting to get into numbers significant enough to detect patterns. Over the coming days and weeks they expected the cases to grow exponentially, with hospitals being overwhelmed worldwide within two weeks.

What was terrifying was that the only pattern they had been able to detect this time was so broad, so general, that if it weren't fine-tuned to a more specific genetic pattern, the world would never be the same in as little as a few weeks.

Because the only pattern that had been detected so far affected half the species.

All were men.

It was enough to scare the shit out of anybody, especially those with testicles. And apparently the President had a pair, because he had immediately taken action when he heard this. Governments around the world were now encouraging men to stay at home, and avoid contact with other men whenever possible. He had been told that the President was going to announce on television tonight that all men were to remain home unless they were deemed essential personnel, as well as the recall of all naval vessels from around the world. These would begin to be used as temporary shelters for those who weren't infected. Islands all along the coast were being evacuated, residents isolated and tested, and when cleared, allowed to return.

Massive quarantine areas for the uninfected were already being set up in athletic facilities and community centers around the country, with men undergoing a two-step quarantine process. Those without symptoms, and of low risk to previous exposure, were tested and ordered to remain at home, then when cleared, ordered to report to a second facility where they would be isolated for 24 hours while their second test was completed. They would then be allowed into the quarantine facility.

The hope was that enough men could be saved to repopulate the species should containment be lost.

It was a doomsday scenario they all prayed they were overreacting to, but with the evidence now in front of the scientific and political community, it was decided there was no time to waste waiting for confirmation. And with the President thankfully in his second term, he had decided he would fall on his sword as a laughing stock should it turn out to be nothing. But if the scientists' worst-case predictions came true, he may be the very savior of mankind.

Which just might go to his head.

Kane shook his own as he began to apply his camouflage face paint then gear up. He hadn't been to Cuba yet, his own area of expertise Asia and the Middle East, but his Spanish was pretty damned good by anyone's standards. The problem was he didn't blend, and cover stories of being in country as a business man didn't work in such a closed communist society—they were still too closely watched. Instead, most CIA agents in Cuba were either locals, ex-pats, or Latino Americans who could blend right in.

There was a knock on the door, then it opened before he could reply.

"Well, Special Agent, are you ready or what?"

"Good thing I'm decent. I coulda been in my birthday suit here," said Kane, grinning at his old friend Burt Dawson. Dawson had trained him years ago during his short stint in the Delta Force before being recruited into the CIA. Like almost everybody in his life, he hadn't kept in touch, but they'd had the good fortune to go on a couple of missions together recently and get reacquainted.

"Nothing I haven't seen before."

"Didn't know you had taken that close a look."

"Just checkin' to see where in the pecking order you fell in case there was ever a need to pull them out and measure while on a mission. You always want to put your best man forward."

"Yeah, well from what I saw of your team last time, something tells me Atlas has us all beat."

Dawson roared in laughter, and the massive form of Atlas poked his head in the room.

"I heard my name."

"Don't worry, we were just talking about your junk, nothing personal," said Kane.

Atlas nodded, his lips pursed.

"Then no harm done," he said in his impossibly deep voice.

He disappeared leaving Kane and Dawson chuckling.

"I assume my test came back clear?"

Dawson nodded. "Yup. So far we're all virus—rather antiviral—free. We're going in full NBC gear, so break out the bunny suit. You can leave the mask off until we're about to drop. If anyone is compromised they'll have to go into quarantine again when we return."

"Makes sense," said Kane as he checked his NBC warfare gear, then headed out the room with Dawson. "When do we leave?"

"Ten minutes if you're ready."

"I'm always ready."

"That's what I like to hear." Kane followed Dawson to the assembly area. Three Gen-3 Ghost Hawk "Jedi Ride" choppers awaited them, along with the rest of Delta Team Bravo, and a familiar face that was beaming at him.

"So we finally get to go on an official mission together!" he said as he approached Sherrie White, giving her a quick one armed hug. "How's our mutual friend?"

"Worried as usual, but otherwise great."

"And things are still going well between you two?"

Her smile grew even larger, the crinkles in the corner of the eyes and mouth betraying how genuinely she felt about his high school buddy.

"Glad to hear it. Now let's capture this sonofabitch so we can all get back to our friends and families."

"Sounds good to me," said Sherrie as they all turned to Dawson.

"Everyone take a knee," he said and they all dropped as one. Dawson handed out several photos. "The first is Major Anton Koslov. He's former Spetsnaz, so watch yourselves. He's very good. Assume he's better than you. The second is Scott Fowler, a former VP of BioDyne Pharma, and we assume the money behind these attacks. He apparently likes yoga and long walks on the beach." Chuckles. "The third is the scientist behind this, Dr. Victor Urban. We presume he's being coerced so should put up no resistance. Just try not to get poked by anything he might be holding."

Niner held up his hand, his mouth open, then he shook his head.

"Never mind. There's a lady present."

Sherrie looked over both shoulders.

"Where?"

More laughter, and Dawson shook his head at Niner.

"Niner, I've met your parents and they're good people. Are you sure you weren't adopted?"

Niner's face brightened. "You mean there's a chance I'm white!"

Atlas punched Niner in the shoulder, sending him tumbling onto his side in a fit of laughter. Dawson let it go for a few seconds, it always good to loosen up before a mission, and he was pleased that the two CIA agents were joining in with the fun. Bonding with your comrades-in-arms was the best way to know they had your back. Friends instinctively would die trying to save another friend, but they sometimes had to think about it to save a stranger.

"Now, Niner's questionable heritage aside, we need all three of these people alive. We're not expecting to find them all there, in fact I'm only expecting to find Major Koslov. The CIA thinks he can lead us to Fowler, who can lead us to Urban. We believe Fowler, and definitely Urban, know the exact genetic sequence that the antiviral is targeting. BioDyne needs that to come up with an antidote, and end this plague once and for all. If we can't find these people, it could be over for all of us, and there will be a lot of lonely women out there left to bury our corpses."

Everyone was solemn with the image that no doubt filled their minds. Kane's mind immediately pictured his mother at his father's funeral, of Isabelle at his, of Sherri at Chris'. He pushed the image away, instead focusing on the mission ahead that could end all of this.

"Now, you've all seen the layout of the compound we're going to. It was popular with the Soviets during the Cold War days, so expect it to have escape tunnels and the works. It's small, and appears from satellite overpasses to be lightly defended—perhaps a dozen men. We'll set up three sniper positions as discussed earlier, enter over the rear wall, and once the targets are secured, we'll eliminate the rest as the entry team leaves. We'll be picked up on the beach by our choppers, secondary rendezvous is four miles north where a sub will be waiting should the need arise. Any questions?" There was silence, everyone already knowing their job. "Good. One final thing. This is a CIA operation. Our friend who you've met before will be in command."

Kane gave the team a nod.

"Gentlemen."

Niner yawned. "From what I saw in Syria, he doesn't need us. Can I go back to my rack?"

"If you're not needed, maybe you'll learn something," said Dawson as he stood up, the rest following as the choppers powered up, drowning out a chorus of "oohs" and "burned!" catcalls.

"Good hunting!" shouted Dawson as he waved them toward the chopper. Kane followed Dawson to his chopper, Sherrie in tow. Only two choppers would be carrying personnel, the third would be on standby offshore should something go wrong. The intent was to slip in and out with the Cubans not even knowing they were there until they were long gone. There apparently had been some debate as to whether or not they should just ask the Cubans to arrest the occupants of the compound, but it was decided they would more likely kill everyone inside in a botched operation, and then all hope would be lost.

Kane strapped himself in, and double checked Sherrie's gear as the choppers lifted off, banking toward Cuban airspace.

And hopefully a cure.

Over Canadian Airspace

"Our escorts are back," announced the pilot over the internal channel. Lt. Colonel Chernov looked out the windows on either side of the Sukhoi T-50 trainer and saw two Canadian CF-18 Hornet's pull into position on each wing. So far everything had gone smoothly. A conversation with his commanding officer, along with several favors called in, and he was airborne on a stripped down fighter with extra fuel tanks, heading over the North Pole. They had refueled at the edge of Russian airspace while the Canadian and Russian governments coordinated the rest of the journey. And if they couldn't agree, it would be a short trip.

But the name of the game today was international cooperation. If there was a chance he could avert the crisis, he was welcome. An isolated landing in Iqaluit with their aircraft refueled and no human contact made, then they were off again, now headed for Washington, DC. They still hadn't heard from the Americans, but he was confident they'd agree. After all, this was their mess, and they were the most vulnerable. The risk of him introducing the virus was next to nil; if anything, he was the most at risk in this equation.

And his pilot.

"Did you ever think you'd see the day you were flying over the Canadian North, peacefully escorted?"

"Certainly not what I trained for, Comrade Colonel."

His pilot, Vlad Bodrov, was old school. He'd run the NATO borders in his MiG, turning back at the last second, spooking the air traffic and air defense controllers, the game constant for decades. A game a lot of Russia missed, the prestige of facing down the mighty West now gone.

290

But so was the expense.

Or at least it should have been. Putin seemed in a rush to roll the clocks back to the sixties, instead of ahead.

If they don't get Anton none of it will matter.

What disturbed Chernov the most in this situation was that it was a time to learn from each other, to cooperate, and to realize that everyone was sharing this blue ball and had no more right to it than the next man. But he knew, if history were to be heeded, that once this crisis was over, there would be rhetoric filling the halls of the United Nations, and within months, everything would be back to the way it was, old animosities and rivalries restored, cooperation a mere blip for the history books.

Or, if the antiviral had its way, it wouldn't matter, the population wiped out.

Sometimes he wondered if they should bother trying to stop it. Let it wipe out most of mankind, then we could start over, do it right, taking advantage of what we had learned from our past mistakes. And with a small population and modern technology, there'd be no need to fight over land or resources, there'd be plenty to go around, and the planet could heal itself of the scars of modern cities and mining.

It was a pipedream that he didn't even believe in, but he loved to think of such things and debate them in his head, or better yet, with a friend, the philosophical discussions that would result sometimes heated, but always stimulating.

Conversations he used to have with his good friend and comrade, Major Koslov.

He sighed as he gazed at the CF-18 out the cockpit window. He knew the interrogation could go one of two ways. Either his old friend cooperated, and gave the information they needed, or he'd be tortured until he did.

And if he was indeed involved in this crisis, then when it was all over, he deserved to die.

And he'd pull the trigger without hesitation, the major having dishonored his family, friends, unit and country.

All Chernov wanted to know was why the hell Koslov had participated in the first place?

Approaching the Cuban Coast

Kane looked out the side of the chopper as the coast in the distance rapidly began to fill their view. The Ghost Hawk's ridiculously quiet engines and propellers had them covering the ninety miles between the coast of Florida and Cuba in no time.

He watched Dawson activate his comm.

"Overseer, Bravo One. Status on coast line, over?"

"Bravo One, Overseer. You are cleared for insertion. Satellite shows no hostiles at the insertion point, over."

"Overseer, Bravo One. Roger that, insertion in sixty seconds, over and out."

"Let's go ladies, sixty seconds to the drop."

The doors were slid open and over the comm Kane could hear Dawson's second in command, Red, giving similar orders, though a lot less politely. The men checked each other's gear as the helicopters slowed and hovered about a hundred feet from the private beach. At this distance anyone in the compound shouldn't hear them, and if necessary, the choppers could abort and still be out of effective small arms range.

"Let's go!" yelled Dawson. Niner and Jimmy jumped out, followed by the rest of the team, then Sherrie jumped with a huge smile on her face.

She's loving this!

Dawson shoved him out then followed almost immediately, the moment his feet cleared the deck the chopper was already banking to hold off the coast for the evac order. Kane hit the water hard, holding his breath and his bagged weapon, his feet quickly finding the bottom, thankful the pilots had done their job right and placed them close enough to walk with their heads above water.

He pushed through the water and quickly made the shore, rushing forward to take cover near the tree line. Within less than three minutes the entire team of fourteen was assembled, their hazmat gear in place and comms activated so they could whisper rather than try to be heard through not only their own mask, but the others as well.

Kane looked at Red.

"Red, you take your team and set up three sniper positions to cover the compound as discussed. I want every inch of that thing covered. Once we're ready to leave, redeploy when we're clear to cover our egress, then meet us at the rendezvous point."

"Roger that." Red motioned to his team and the six of them broke from the group to get into position before the rest made their entry.

Kane turned back to the group. "Agent White, Niner and Jimmy, you're with me. We'll sweep left of the compound to the rear. BD, you take the right with the rest of the team. If you encounter the enemy, only eliminate them if necessary. We don't want anybody missing a radio check. If you do need to take them out, do it swift and silent, then get them out of sight. Understood?"

"Understood," said Dawson.

"Then let's go."

Kane rose from his knee, and broke left, entering the trees with Sherrie directly behind him, the two experienced operators behind her. Kane gently pushed aside the foliage blocking their way, careful to not snap any fallen branches and give away their position.

Someone behind him though snapped a branch, the nearness making him think it was Sherrie, her inexperience failing them. He raised his clenched fist, and everyone froze. He listened carefully, but could hear no one. He motioned for them to continue, and he took another tentative step forward, certain Sherrie wouldn't make the mistake twice.

They pushed forward, the foliage thickening, then suddenly thinning dramatically, it clear they were about to hit a path cut through the trees that led up to the compound. He motioned for everyone to stop, then carefully peered down both directions of the path, finding it clear. He rushed across at a crouch, disappearing into the foliage on the other side of the path, perhaps two yards wide. He checked again, then motioned for Sherrie to join him.

She darted across, pushing into the thick leaves, then turned to check what was happening.

Kane whispered.

"Watch the path. If it's clear, have them come across. Then follow me. I'm going ahead to make sure it's clear ahead."

"Okay."

Sherrie repositioned herself for a better view and Kane disappeared into the trees, carefully advancing, the compound less than a hundred yards ahead and to the right. He knew from the satellite photos that the trees had been cleared from the front of the compound and much of the left and right sides, but the rear, which had been cleared during the Soviet era, had been left to seed, the jungle quickly reclaiming much of what had been lost.

It was this complacency that he hoped they could capitalize on.

He just hoped that it was complacency, and not knowledge the rear was secure due to an array of landmines.

Sherrie leaned out and saw no one down the path that led toward the beach. A quick turn of the head and she saw it was clear in the direction of the compound. She raised her hand to motion the next Delta member across when she froze and stepped back into the cover of the leaves, the sound of boots on hard ground coming from her right.

Someone was coming from the compound, moving in the direction of the beach. She peered across at the other two, pointed at her eyes, then up the path. The one called Niner nodded, disappearing farther into the jungle as she did the same.

She could hear one set of boots on the ground, but a voice, talking as if to another. Her Spanish was perfect, but she couldn't make out what was being said.

Something moved over her boot and she looked down to see a large Cuban Boa slithering over her toe. She almost yelped out in shock, but instead was able to maintain control of her mouth, if not her heart.

The voice was closer now, and she heard something else.

Panting?

She looked through the leaves and saw it was a lone man walking a dog.

Some demon spawn of a dog that was all jaws and massive muscles rippling from end to end.

With a nose that was now upturned.

She had to act quickly or the beast from hell was going to find her. She looked down then grabbed the tail of the snake just before it disappeared. She yanked it toward her as she unsheathed her knife, burying it into the body of the snake as she pulled with the other hand, neatly slicing the now writhing creature in half. Her shoulders shivered as she watched the creature being gutted by her razor sharp Bowie knife.

It was disgusting.

She had never done anything like this, but it was the snake or her.

And she chose her.

The snake stopped moving, finally dead, and she pushed the body out in front of her, then shoved it even farther with the butt of her MP5K submachine gun. She quietly moved away from the snake, deeper into the leaves, until she could barely see the approaching guard and his companion.

"What is it, boy?" asked the guard, his Spanish pure rural Cuban, obviously a local hire rather than a true pro. From her vantage point she could see the dog straining on his leash, eager to get to whatever it was he was smelling. She just prayed it was now the snake and not her.

The guard trotted forward, helped along by the massive beast. She readied her knife. She knew she'd need to kill the dog first before it could start barking, and hopefully the two Delta guys could take care of the guard.

She'd rather be taking on the guard.

The animal was at the decoy now, sniffing at it, snarling, and shoving it with his nose.

"What have you got there, boy?"

It looked like the dog was nose deep in the guts of the creature, which Sherrie hoped would be enough to throw him off any scent she and the others might be giving off.

"Oh God, that's disgusting. Get away from that!"

The dog was pulled away with a yank of its chain. It snarled in protest, but a snap of the chain had it obeying its master, and as its head jerked up, Sherrie swore she made eye contact with it, its eyes and nostrils flaring for a moment as he prepared to charge her, then with another jerk of the chain, he was dragged away, his head turned toward her, but his protests ignored by the guard.

Sherrie's heart continued to pound in her chest. Two forms rushed from across the road toward her, one stepping in her diversion and muttering, "Eww!" as he approached her. It was Niner.

"Did you do that?" he whispered.

She nodded, remembering her tactical breathing and beginning to calm herself.

"Good thinking," said Jimmy. "Now let's find CIA boy."

Sherrie smiled at the moniker, then followed Niner as he led the way toward where she assumed Kane would be waiting. She grabbed a large leaf and folded it around her blade, wiping the knife clean before sheathing it.

Suddenly she heard something behind her.

Kane had taken up position on the left of the compound, along the cleared edge. Coded bird calls and he had pinpointed two sniper's nests with members of Red's team already in position. They seemed to have full coverage of the front and sides, and Kane assumed the rear as well with the third team that he couldn't see.

Leaves moved to his right. He dropped down and listened. It was approaching his position. It shouldn't be a friendly unless they were out of position. He listened carefully, but still couldn't hear the rest of his squad.

What's taking them so long?

He stepped deeper into the woods and shoved himself into the hollowed out body of a massive tree whose species was of no importance to him now. Moments later a guard inched by his position, gun at the ready, clearly looking for someone, probably him. Kane was about to step out from his hiding place when he heard something, as did his opponent. The man stepped back suddenly, placing his back against the very hollow Kane now occupied, meaning he had no way of getting at him unless he came out, giving the man the advantage.

Niner crept by the opening, followed by Jimmy then Sherrie, both inching forward nearly silently. If you weren't listening for them, there was no way you could distinguish them from the background noise of the jungle. This man had known to listen, and had probably known to because he had either heard or spotted Kane, or heard one of the sniper teams setting up.

Or heard your damned bird calls!

Kane cursed himself. This guy was a local. He probably knew the species of this area by heart, having grown up with them his entire life. And he'd know when one was being faked and used as a signaling method. He saw the barrel of the man's weapon appear in front of his hiding place as it was raised.

Kane pulled his knife, flipped it over to his left hand, then jabbed it around the lip of the trunk of the massive tree, blind. It connected and sunk deep, fortunately not glancing off bone, and as he twisted, he felt muscle and organ tissue tear apart under the pressure from his blade, and the barrel begin to lower.

The man moaned.

Niner spun around and leapt forward, his own knife burying itself in what Kane guessed would be the man's neck judging by the height he had attacked at. At the same time Jimmy disarmed the man before he could fire as Sherrie raised her weapon, covering their backs in case the man had a partner.

Kane felt the body pulled off his knife by the others and stepped slowly out from the tree. He gave the thumbs up to the others, wiped his knife on the body before Niner and Jimmy pulled it deeper into the trees, then continued their way to the rendezvous, encountering nobody except one of their sniper teams about a hundred feet farther on, and another fifty feet deeper in the cover.

He only knew they were there from the birdcalls of earlier. This time Kane simply gave a nod of acknowledgement and continued on. As the brush grew thicker near the back of the compound, Kane began to smile to himself slightly, their fears the satellite photos were being misinterpreted settled. There was plenty of cover to reach the rear wall which the satellite surveillance had indicated to be pretty much unguarded.

Apparently whoever's compound this was, wasn't too concerned with security. It was token and seemingly unprofessional. They clearly weren't expecting any company.

A hiss to his left had his head spinning, and in the encroaching darkness he saw Dawson and the rest of his team huddled nearby. Kane approached along with Sherrie as Niner and Jimmy redeployed to provide cover.

"What took you so long?" asked Dawson.

"We encountered an unfriendly. Had to take him out unfortunately," said Kane. "He didn't have any radio equipment on him though, but he might be expected back soon."

Dawson nodded.

"Rear wall has been clear since we got here."

Kane held his hand out, palm toward the wall.

"Care to do the honors?"

Dawson smiled.

"Don't mind if I do."

Dawson activated his comm. "Bravo Two, Bravo One. Report, over."

Red's whispered voice came in through the comm. We've got two on the number one wall at the one-two and one-four corners. Nobody else on the wall. You're clear for your approach, over."

"Roger that." Dawson rushed forward, quickly reaching the wall. "Report?"

"Still clear."

He pulled his grappling hook off his belt, dropped the coiled rope on the ground then tossed the hook. It flew out of sight then he heard a slight noise as the rubberized body prevented any clanging sound of the metal, the hooks digging into the other side of the wall. He yanked on the rope then began to climb as the rest of the team advanced.

Reaching the top, he glanced down to make sure nobody had ventured to the back of the compound without them knowing, then flipped over the wall and dropped to the ground. He quickly advanced along the rear number three wall toward the wall to his left, the number four wall, ducking when necessary to avoid windows in the rear of the villa they were about to enter. Reaching the end of the villa and encountering no one, he turned back to see the progress of his team.

It appeared Niner and Jimmy were already at the far end at the two-three corner, giving the thumbs up, and the last of them were now over the wall, the last man, Atlas, having unhooked the grappling hook and rope so it couldn't be discovered by someone later.

"Report."

"Four at the number one wall now, all near the entrance. Almost looks like they may be expecting someone."

That could be good or bad. Dawson decided he better ask a higher power.

"Overseer, Bravo One. Do we have anybody approaching the compound, over?"

"Bravo One, Overseer. We've got a single vehicle about ten minutes out. Appears to be four occupants, over."

"Roger that, over and out."

Kane joined him at his corner, taking a look around it for himself.

"What do you think?" asked Dawson.

"Ten minutes is plenty of time. Let's finish this, then wait and see who's arriving. Worst case it's more guards, so better to do this before they get here. Best case, it's all three of our targets in a Christmas hamper."

Dawson chuckled.

"Then let's do this."

Kane retreated to the rear door of the villa as Dawson motioned for Atlas to cover the corner he had just been holding. By the time Dawson had reached Kane's position, the young pro already had the lock picked and the door slightly open, a mirror poked through so he could make sure the room on the other side was clear.

"We're good," came the whisper over the mike.

Kane pushed the door open, quickly entering, his Glock with suppressor held high. Dawson followed, then Sherrie along with the rest of his men save Atlas and Niner who were holding the rear of the building so they weren't surprised from behind. It was a kitchen, brightly lit, but empty.

Which was when the first surprise happened.

Who spotted him first didn't matter. They probably all did as the swinging doors of the kitchen suddenly flew toward them. Kane rushed forward, extending his left hand toward the head of their unknown guest, clamping it over the man's mouth as Kane's brain processed the identity of the man.

Hispanic, not one of the targets.

He pulled the man inside the kitchen, his wails of protest muffled, then cut off as Dawson buried a knife in the man's side and twisted, shredding several important organs. The man's life quickly began to drain out of him as they pulled him back toward the exit and tossed him out the door, all executed so quickly little blood actually made it onto the terracotta tile.

Sherrie grabbed a towel from a hook and tossed it to Jimmy who dropped it on the floor and used his boot to clean up the blood well enough that anyone who might stumble upon the scene could be forgiven for thinking it was just a kitchen accident.

The towel tossed outside with the body, Kane pushed open the left side of the swinging door slightly, checking the hallway they found to the right.

Clear.

He checked the left and nodded to the rest of the team as he indicated with hand signals for half the team to go left while he and the other half went right. Kane pressed right, Sherrie on his heels, Jimmy covering their rear as Dawson and the rest went left. A door on their right, facing the rear of the house, was closed, a light under it, the hallway lit merely by ambient light from wall mounted lamps at either end.

Kane listened at the door, then removed his Taser from his belt. He tried the knob and found it unlocked. He looked at the others then turned the knob, pushing the door open. He ducked to his right, edging inside to clear the inside wall, then stepped into the room, swinging his weapon along with his entire upper body as he cleared the room, including the area behind the now open door.

It was empty.

But the flush of a toilet, then sounds at a sink had them all reposition around the one other door in the room. The bathroom door opened and a knockout of a woman stepped into the room, naked as the day she was born, her store boughts proudly on display.

Kane hit her with the Taser.

As soon as she stopped shaking, Sherrie and Jimmy dragged her to the bed then bound and gagged her. Kane tossed a sheet over the poor girl, probably a prostitute brought in from Havana, so she could preserve what remained of her dignity.

Gunshots from the other end of the villa had Kane racing for the door.

Dawson squeezed off another round as he advanced into the living area. Though their weapons were suppressed, they were still fairly loud, but their opponents were using fully automatic, unsilenced weapons. There was no hiding their presence now.

Which meant time was of the essence.

They had to clear the rest of the villa as quickly as possible before any possible hostages might be killed, or their target could escape through some hidden tunnel that a paranoid Soviet general had installed decades ago.

"We've been made. Eliminate the guards outside," came Kane's voice over the comm.

"Roger that," replied Red, and moments later Dawson heard the distinct sound of sniper rounds then silence, the job done.

Dawson eliminated another hostile after seeing his face, confirming the man wasn't Major Koslov. It had been someone coming out of a bathroom that had discovered his team and before they could silence him, he had yelled, attracting the attention of the half dozen men around the corner.

This would be a lot easier if we were just eliminating those with guns.

This time however not only did you have to make sure the person was armed and a threat before shooting, they had to make sure that threat wasn't the target they needed *alive*. The room quickly fell silent as the last enemy was eliminated.

"Everyone okay?" he asked.

A round of affirmatives set his mind to rest.

"Let's finish this."

Kane rushed through the door, took a quick glance toward where the gunfire was, and went in the opposite direction. Dawson's team could handle themselves, and the rest of this end hadn't been cleared. The last thing Dawson's team needed was three more guns with an unknown number of hostiles possibly coming from the rear.

They advanced to the next door and Kane stood to the side, then knocked.

A burst of gunfire tore apart the center of the door. Kane grabbed a flash-bang off his belt, pulled the pin, then punched his fist through the weakened door, dropping the grenade inside then backing away as he covered his ears.

The roar was deafening and was greeted by several screams from inside the room. Kane kicked open the door and pushed inside, shooting two guards as they tried to reach their weapons, a third merely sitting up in his cot, his hands up, this apparently a sleeping area for the peons.

"Check him then secure him," ordered Kane. Sherrie quickly patted the man down as Jimmy cuffed him with a zip tie. Kane turned to Sherrie. "Watch him."

Sherrie nodded, taking up position so she could not only watch their prisoner, but was out of sight of both the window and the door. Kane nodded in approval.

She's going to make a great agent.

They advanced to the final door in the hall, Kane noting the weapons fire had ceased at the other end of the house. He knocked.

Nothing.

He tried the door and it was locked.

Stepping in front, he kicked it open then fell back to the side, Jimmy advancing.

"Clear!" he heard Niner call as Atlas and Niner entered the hall from the kitchen, everyone outside dead. He motioned for Niner to join them as Kane entered the room, its size and grandeur indicating it was the master bedroom. A king sized canopy bed, hand carved furniture, Persian rugs, silk wall hangings, erotic paintings, soft lighting and dozens of pillows.

Niner entered the room and whistled as he made his way to the bed.

"It's a Soviet fuck chamber," said Niner as he pushed some pillows aside, making sure the bed actually was empty and there wasn't a bevy of honeys in hiding. He seemed disappointed.

"All clear this end," came Dawson's voice over the comm.

"Clear here as well. We have two prisoners we're going to interrogate."

"We have one. I'll bring him to you, then we'll set up for our arrivals."

"Roger that."

Kane stepped out into the hallway and saw Stucco and Casey hauling a wounded man toward them. Kane pointed to the master bedroom. "Put him in here. I don't want them talking."

Stucco and Casey complied, then ran back to the other end of the house.

"Overseer, Bravo One. ETA on our new arrivals, over?"

"Bravo One, Overseer. Three minutes out. Be advised satellite is now out of range of target, new bird ETA five minutes, over."

Kane stepped into the room, Niner and Jimmy standing on either side of them, their NBC hazmat suits looking menacing, the wounded man clearly scared. Kane turned to Niner. "Make sure the other doors with our prisoners are open, then every time I inflict pain, open our door. I want them to hear him so they can start thinking about what's going to happen to them."

Niner nodded and stepped out into the hallway, returning seconds later, closing the door to the master bedroom.

Kane knelt down, his masked face staring directly at the man.

"We're going to do this the easy way, okay?" he said in Spanish. "I'm going to ask you questions, you're going to answer them truthfully. Every time you lie to me, I'll hurt you, and I'll get the truth anyway. Understood?"

The man nodded, his eyes wide, his entire body trembling, his fear obvious.

"What's your name?"

"Carlos."

"Carlos. You're Cuban?"

"Yes."

"Who do you work for?"

The man said nothing, instead looking away.

"No answer is a lie, Carlos, so I *will* have to hurt you." Kane pressed his thumb against the gunshot wound in the man's shoulder as Niner opened the door behind him.

Carlos screamed out in pain, his face going pale, and Kane stopped, not wanting the man to pass out before they could get any intel from him. The man's breathing was rapid, but as soon as Kane stopped the torture, his color began to return and his panting slowed.

"I'm really sorry about that, but you must understand that your boss knows about the virus that is spreading throughout the world. You've heard about it, of course?"

"Yes," gasped the man.

"Good. Now, are you a religious man?"

The man nodded.

"So you believe in God?" Nod. "And Heaven?" Nod. "So when you stand in front of God, what do you want to tell him about this moment of your life? Do you want to tell him you did nothing, and let mankind die from a virus, or do you want to tell him you helped by giving me the information I needed, and helped save mankind?"

There was silence, but the man's eyes darted to the left for a split second, then returned to Kane's. As soon as Kane looked to where the man had glanced, then back at the man, his prisoner could no longer make eye contact.

Bingo!

"Is there something over there I need to see."

The man swallowed, but nothing was said.

Kane motioned to Jimmy.

"Take a look over there. Hidden door, panel, transporter pad."

Jimmy stepped over to the corner where Carlos had looked and started moving things aside. Kane watched Carlos' face as Jimmy continued to tear apart the corner.

Suddenly Carlos' pupils dilated slightly, just for a moment as he held his breath.

Kane turned, holding out his hand for Jimmy to stop.

"What did you just touch?"

Jimmy stopped. "I'm not sure. This chest here. I tossed that chair over there."

"The rug," said Niner.

"What?"

"You kicked the rug the chair was on top of."

Niner dropped to a knee and grabbed the corner of a small Persian rug sitting in front of a dresser. He yanked it aside and smiled.

"Well, what do we have here?"

It appeared for all intents and purposes to be a trap door.

Kane turned to Carlos.

"Is it wired?"

Carlos said nothing and Kane jabbed his thumb into the open wound. Carlos howled then Kane let go.

"Is. It. Wired?"

"I don't know!" cried Carlos, his eyes filled with tears, a few having escaped to burn red streaks down his cheeks.

"Was he here when we arrived?"

"Who?"

"Your boss!"

"Yes."

"Was he in this room?"

"Yes."

"Where does this lead?"

"I don't know."

"And what is your boss' name?"

"Mr. Fowler."

Kane stood up and stepped back.

"Scott Fowler was here?"

Carlos nodded emphatically the greater the distance Kane put between them.

"He just went to bed to get ready."

"Ready for what?"

"Two girls are coming from Havana for the night. Mr. Fowler picks one, we get the other."

Kane frowned.

"Sounds like lose lose for everyone except Mr. Fowler."

Carlos shrugged then winced as the forgotten wound made its presence known.

"We win too," he said with a smile, his yellowed teeth Kane was sure a welcome sight to any poor hooker relegated to satisfying the dozen other men in the house.

"So that's who's coming now? Two hookers?"

Carlos nodded.

"Who's with them?"

"Mr. Fowler's personal bodyguard."

"Who?"

"Mr. Koslov."

Dawson and his team set up on either side of the gate that led into the compound and waited. The news that their target was in the approaching vehicle was a bit of a pisser. It would have been a lot easier to ambush a car with two men and two hookers. But then they wouldn't have known Fowler was here. Kane and his CIA partner Agent White were in pursuit along with Niner and Jimmy, all who had gone down the rabbit hole in the bedroom. Catching Fowler was a higher priority than Koslov, but if Fowler got away, they might need Koslov to tell them where he went.

And Koslov was far more dangerous than Fowler, so the decision to leave a ten man team for Koslov and send only a four man team after Fowler was easy, one of the sniper pairs now inside with them.

The roar of an engine struggling up the lane cut through the jungle had them all momentarily tense up. Dawson shook his head from side to side, cracking his neck as he double-checked his weapon. The plan was simple, the question was whether the execution would be. And that all depended upon a very highly trained occupant of the approaching vehicle.

A burst of static then something was said in Spanish that Dawson couldn't make out. Stucco, who had impeccable Spanish held the radio to his mouth, lifting the mask so it wouldn't be muffled, replied.

"All clear, welcome back, sir."

Casey and Atlas pulled open the two sides of the gate, the solid wood construction keeping them hidden from the approaching vehicle. As the gate opened the headlights from the vehicle sliced through the darkness, highlighting the courtyard. A black SUV pulled through the gates, but the blacked out windows prevented them from seeing inside.

As soon as the vehicle was clear of the gate, Casey and Atlas shoved the doors hard, closing it behind the vehicle as Dawson and Stucco shot out the tires with a single bullet to each then the four rushed the vehicle, their weapons high, Stucco shouting for them to not resist or they would be shot.

Dawson grabbed the passenger side door and yanked on the handle. Locked. He raised the butt of his MP5K and hammered it hard into the side window as did the others. The windows shattered, revealing an empty passenger seat, the driver, terrified, his arms raised, and two screaming ladies of the night in the back seat.

"Where's Koslov?" yelled Stucco.

"He left! He left!" cried the driver.

Suddenly the entire complex erupted. Dawson spun toward the villa and saw a fireball racing skyward and outward toward them as the explosion continued to grow. He threw himself to the ground, rolling toward the back of the SUV as flames whipped around him.

Through the roar of the initial explosion he could hear secondary explosions getting progressively louder, in a pattern too orderly to be random. He looked toward the house and saw row after row of explosions extending the entire width of the compound advancing toward them.

"Get out through the gate! Get out through the gate!" he yelled as he jumped to his feet and yanked open the rear door. He pulled one of the girls from the backseat as Stucco did the same on the other side, then raced toward the gate as the self-destruct mechanism continued to roar toward them. Atlas yanked open one side of the gate as they barreled through, Dawson feeling the heat on his back, wondering if the half-naked woman over his shoulder was getting burnt to a crisp or not.

Clear of the compound, he continued to run, not sure how far the chains of explosives extended, but within seconds of running toward the trees the explosions stopped and he finally heard the shouts of Red over the comm.

"Are you guys okay? Respond! This is Bravo Two. Are you guys okay?"

Dawson placed the girl on the ground and turned to look at the now blazing compound, his chest heaving.

"Bravo Two, hold for sit rep, over."

He took a quick head count and noticed the driver wasn't with them, but through the now blasted open gate he could see the flaming SUV on its roof, the driver most likely still inside.

"Bravo Two, Bravo One. We're all okay, over. Rendezvous with us at the front of the compound, keep your eyes out for our primary target, he wasn't in the vehicle, over."

"Roger that."

"Overseer, Bravo One. Do you have eyes on our target? He left the vehicle before it entered the compound, over."

"Bravo One, Overseer. A new bird just came online. Your target is on foot, two hundred meters north of your position. He appears injured, over."

"Roger that, in pursuit. Oh, and once this op is over, send locals to this location to collect two young women who are stranded, over."

"Bravo One, Overseer, will do, over and out."

Stucco told the two women that they would be collected soon as Red and his men rounded the compound to join them.

"Jesus Christ, BD. What the hell happened?"

"Our target bailed from his vehicle. There must have been a code word or phrase and when he didn't hear it, he jumped. He's two hundred meters north, Overseer thinks he's injured."

"Then let's get the bastard."

"My thoughts exactly," said Dawson with a smile.

Dawson took point, rushing forward into the trees, not concerned with the noise he might be making. They had to cover the distance fast in the event Koslov had a vehicle or some other means of escape stashed away. He knew if this was his command, he'd have at least two escape routes set up, with vehicles and supplies.

And there was no way this bastard wasn't prepared.

His mind flashed to the three prisoners who had still been in the villa when it had blown, including the woman who was most likely innocent in all this, the rest most likely locals looking for a paycheck.

"Overseer, report."

"Fifty meters, continue on your current course."

"Roger that."

He continued to race forward, counting his paces in his head down from fifty, and at twenty he motioned for his men to spread out.

"Stationary, ten meters ahead," came the satellite analyst's voice over the comm.

Dawson continued forward, quietly this time, his weapon aimed low so if he were forced to shoot, he would just hit the man's legs.

"Remember, we need him alive," he said quietly, the comm doing its job of transmitting the reminder to the rest.

"I see him," said Atlas. "Five meters to my two o'clock."

Atlas was at Dawson's nine o'clock, which meant Koslov was only feet away from him. Dawson inched forward, pushing as quietly as he could through the leaves, but he knew he was making noise, and the stationary man, who would be expecting their arrival, would definitely be hearing their approach.

"Surround his position, I will approach."

He could hear his men execute the order as he stopped behind a large tree.

"Major Koslov, this is Sergeant White, United States Army. I'm here at the request of Lieutenant Colonel Chernov."

"So that's how you found me."

"Major, you are completely surrounded, and there is no hope of surviving a fire fight. We want you alive. We realize you aren't behind this,

313

you're just the trigger man. If you help us, I've been authorized to tell you that you will be granted immunity from prosecution."

There was a laugh, then a groan.

"Signed by the President himself, I have no doubt."

"As a matter of fact, yes. I have it with me if you want to see it."

"Really?"

Koslov was clearly surprised at this development, as much as Dawson had been when he had been handed the pardon before they left.

"Can I come out and show you?"

"Yes, but no tricks."

"No tricks, Major, you have my word as a soldier."

"Then come."

Dawson pulled the envelope from one of his pockets, holding it up in one hand as he slung his MP5K over his shoulder. He flicked his night vision glasses up then turned his flashlight on, aiming it at the ground so he didn't blind any of his men.

He stepped from around the tree and walked not even five feet before he found the major sitting against a tree, his left ankle clearly giving him problems.

"Broken or sprained?" asked Dawson.

"Sprained I think. Hurts too much to run." He sighed. "I'm tired of running."

Dawson handed him the envelope with the White House seal on the front.

"From the President."

Koslov opened it, read it quickly, then motioned to Dawson.

"Pen."

Dawson retrieved a pen, handing it to the injured Major.

Koslov signed, handing the pen back, then tucked the envelope and its contents into his shirt.

"What do you want to know?"

"Where is Scott Fowler?"

"Inside the villa," said Koslov with a smirk.

"He escaped through the tunnel in the master bedroom."

"Then your guess is as good as mine. I'm sure your satellites have picked him up."

"Yes, but where is he going?"

"Tell your navy and coast guard to be ready. He will be coming *very* fast."

"And what about Dr. Urban and his wife?"

Koslov grinned.

"You'll need Mr. Fowler for that. He's the man with all the answers."

Kane quickly climbed the rungs of the ladder at the end of the tunnel then pushed open a hatch slightly, looking to make sure they weren't about to be ambushed. Everything clear, he shoved it open all the way and climbed out, edging forward, his weapon raised, as he confirmed the immediate vicinity free of any enemies. Sherrie and the others exited the hole when Kane heard something in the distance.

An engine?

"Let's go!" he yelled, racing into the trees toward the sound of the motor that if he wasn't mistaken was for a boat. He burst through the trees and nearly found himself falling headlong over the edge of a cliff.

"Hold up!" he yelled, turning around and pushing forward with his arms outstretched to prevent the others from falling. He caught Sherrie just as she came through the trees, the two Delta members, covering the rear, stopping in time.

"Thanks," gasped Sherrie as she looked over the edge. "There's steps over here," she said, pointing to the left.

Kane stepped around her and ran down the steps, the others following. As he looked down into a cove he could see a sleek cigarette boat pulling away from a dock. Kane raised his weapon and fired at the front of the boat. The pilot looked back and Kane could see enough of the man's features in the moonlight to see it had to be Scott Fowler.

"That's Fowler!" shouted Kane to the others. "Don't fire, that boat's liable to be a powder keg."

He reached the dock and sprinted along it but the cigarette boat's engine was gunning now and it was out of the tiny cove and out of sight in seconds. Kane turned around and rushed toward a second boat tied to the dock, pointing.

"Get that thing going!" he ordered, Niner jumping in and beginning to hotwire the boat with instructions from a specialist over an isolated frequency. Jimmy and Sherrie removed the lines as Kane jumped in, Niner firing up the engine. Kane took the controls and pushed the throttle all the way forward, the engine chewing the water as the nose rose high in the air before the craft began to rapidly move forward. The prow dropped as they picked up speed and soon they were skimming along the water, bursting from the cove and banking in the same direction Kane had seen Fowler go.

"Overseer, Thunderbolt. We're in pursuit of Fowler. He's in some sort of cigarette boat near my location. Do you have him, over?"

"Thunderbolt, Overseer. Affirmative. Steer zero-four-zero degrees. Looks like he's heading for The Bahamas, over."

"Do we have any assets in the area that can stop him?"

"Affirmative. We have a carrier group returning to base, over."

"Have them put everything they've got into this but remind them we need him alive!"

316

"Copy that, relaying instructions now, over and out."

Kane leaned over the steering wheel, keeping below the windshield to reduce the spray from covering the plastic panel of his hazmat suit. As the cool night air from the ocean began to permeate his suit, he realized how damned hot he was.

Fighting in this shit is insane!

Outside of training, he had never had to wear this type of equipment before, his missions quite often involving jeans and a t-shirt, or light combat gear. He yanked at the clothes on his chest, pulling them away from his sweat soaked body.

"Is that him?" asked Sherrie, pointing in the distance.

Kane peered but couldn't make out anything, then suddenly he spotted something, bouncing above the waves, no lights visible, and distant enough to not make out any details.

"It has to be," said Kane, adjusting his course slightly. He looked at their speed, and with only about a hundred miles separating the two coasts, and their speed better than 50 knots, they were looking at less than two hours to get there. He glanced at the fuel gauge. Full.

These boats had definitely been prepared for a quick escape.

He glanced back and saw his three companions sitting low in the back, relaxing, their arms and legs spread as they tried to cool themselves off. Kane had to chuckle at the sight, modesty at this point lost on them all.

"Overseer, Thunderbolt. Where are those ships, over?"

"Standby Thunderbolt."

He leaned forward, willing the boat to go quicker, when he spotted something on the horizon. With the waves kicking up a bit, it was hard to tell what he was looking at, but whatever it was, it was getting big quick.

Could it be?

Suddenly the entire horizon seemed to light up as dozens of ships running perpendicular to his course turned on every light they had, search beams cutting through the water, helicopters and aircraft overhead turning on their search lights, aimed at the water below.

"We've got company!" yelled Kane, the others quickly joining him.

"Jesus, it's like the whole damned Navy is out there!" exclaimed Niner.

Kane continued to push the boat toward the fleet now in front of them, the beams cutting through the night sky in search of Fowler's boat.

"There it is!" yelled Sherrie, pointing straight ahead.

And indeed it was. A search light had spotted it, and with the call of the operator going out, all the beams immediately converged on the area, the cigarette boat soon bathed with so much light, Fowler would be quickly getting sunburnt if he didn't surrender. At least half a dozen choppers rushed toward the position, two of them settling just above the waves in the path of the boat.

Fowler jerked to the left, evading the choppers, but cutting his speed dramatically as Kane gently adjusted his course, the distance now rapidly closing.

The choppers repositioned themselves and Kane could now hear orders being issued over a PA system, floating over the waves, their engine drowning out the specifics.

Again the still well-lit boat swerved to the right, trying to evade capture. At this point smaller boats deployed from the large naval ships were in the water, racing toward the target.

There was no escaping, it was just a matter of time, but Kane refused to ease up on the throttle. He needed to get there to make sure there wasn't a firefight that may result in the death of a key witness.

"He's surrendering!" said Sherry. "Look!"

Kane watched as the cigarette boat came to a halt. They were close enough now to see a figure standing, hands raised, and finally Kane began to ease up slightly on the throttle.

"Overseer, Thunderbolt. Notify the flagship that we are approaching and are a friendly, over."

"Thunderbolt, Overseer. Already done. You are to report to the flagship where the prisoner will be held in quarantine, awaiting your arrival, over."

"Roger that, over and out."

Kane examined the signal flags around them, searching for the flagship when they were approached by two other vessels that pulled along either side of their boat.

"Special Agent Black?"

Kane nodded.

"Please, sir, if you'll come aboard, we'll take you to the USS George H. W. Bush."

Two men jumped aboard and Kane yielded the controls to them as his team climbed aboard the other vessel. Within seconds they were racing through the now well-lit waters, Kane stretched out in the back like the others, all still in their gear, when there was a tremendous roar to the starboard side. Kane's head spun as if it were on a swivel and cursed.

The cigarette boat was in flames, the other boats pulling away, some of them on fire as well, their crews bailing.

"Overseer, Thunderbolt! Do they have Fowler, over!"

"Thunderbolt, Overseer. Stand by, over."

There was a pause as they all waited to find out the fate of Fowler, perhaps their only lead to Dr. Urban and the truth.

"Thunderbolt, Overseer. Negative, he was still on the boat when it detonated, over."

Kane, now standing, kicked the gunwale, uttering a string of curses that would have a sailor blushing. He turned to the pilot.

"Get us aboard as fast as possible and tell them to have a helicopter prepped to take us to the mainland."

"Yes, sir!"

Kane sat down, all their hopes now resting on a crooked ex-Russian Special Forces Major.

Aboard the USS George H. W. Bush
Carrier Strike Group Two, Off the Florida Coast

Kane soaked his head in the shower, his mind still back on the ocean, wondering why Fowler had killed himself. It made no sense. With his money and resources, and with no qualms on how he used it, prison might be a temporary thing, assuming he even made it there. He had cards, high cards, that he could use to get himself a pardon. He knew the government was desperate. There was no way they wouldn't let him go if they could get Dr. Urban back.

Something didn't make sense.

He quickly rinsed himself off then entered the locker room, getting his cellphone from his locker. He dialed a familiar number.

"Leroux here."

"Hi buddy, it's me."

"Hey! How are you? Are you okay?"

Kane could hear the excitement and concern in his friend's voice. He vowed when this was over that he'd try to make some time to spend not only with his family, but with his friend. Probably his only real friend in the world.

Now that's depressing.

"I'm okay, and so is Sherrie. Listen, I want you to do something for me."

"What's that?"

"Gather all the footage you can get your hands on of the Fowler takedown, and look for anything unusual."

"Such as?"

"I don't know. Unusual. Transporter beams, mother ship beam-up, whatever. Something doesn't make sense. I just don't buy him killing himself."

"I'll get the tapes right away and let you know."

"Okay, thanks, buddy. Get back to me when you find something."

"Will do."

Kane tossed the phone back into his locker and began to dress, his mind slightly more at ease now that Leroux was on the case.

CIA Headquarters, Langley, Virginia

To say Leroux was exhausted would be an understatement. His eyes were drooping, and he was repeatedly yawning to the point where he was sure the walls of his divider were pulling toward him with each deep breath like a Disney cartoon.

He had been asleep when he received Kane's call. CIA Headquarters was in lockdown until all personnel were cleared, which should be any time now. Then it would be business as usual within, with all external visitors quarantined and communicated with through isolation booths.

External security had been increased dramatically with several National Guard units arriving a few hours ago to beef things up. Reports of several Federal buildings across the country being attacked by protestors had everyone on edge.

Didn't these people realize we're trying to help?

But it was anger and fear that motivated them. They wanted *in*. They wanted to be where it was safe, or at least where they thought they would be safe. The President's address to the nation earlier on live television had done little to calm things. He had condemned the events in Paris, but urged calm from everyone. He had ordered dusk to dawn curfews, and during the day only women would be allowed outside unless the men occupied essential positions.

The nation was effectively shut down.

The stock markets were closed the world over, the selloff so steep that it was agreed it was better to close them until the crisis was over, if it were ever over. Should things recover, the markets would reopen, take their hit, but at least the panic of the antiviral would be finished.

But now he had a job to do. It had been months since he had kicked his Red Bull habit, but he eyed the can he had grabbed from the vending machine, but hadn't yet opened.

It's for your country!

He popped the lid, yanking back on the tab, the slight hiss weak compared to a can of Diet Coke that he usually liked to enjoy now. He took a sip and the psychological effect took hold almost instantaneously, his brain signaling the rest of the body that energy would soon be flowing, so get ready.

He opened up the first video file that had arrived, and started going through it. There weren't many, only a couple of dozen files, each lasting less than ten minutes, many from too far away to get any details without enhancement. He had already filtered those out and sent them to the specialists with an order to hold until he knew if he needed them to look at them or not.

The first video showed a pretty standard takedown, albeit on a Naval scale that was probably unprecedented for one man. This particular angle missed the actual explosion, the camera man turning away for some reason just before it happened, then the video went dark as the crewman hit the water.

The next two videos didn't prove much better. But on the fourth he hit the jackpot.

Langley Field, Air Combat Command

Lieutenant Colonel Chernov didn't expect much of a welcome wagon when his plane touched down, especially since they were escorted in by four F-22 Raptors after a handoff from the Canadian CF-18's. They had almost been at the border when word finally arrived that they were allowed to enter US airspace and land at Langley Field.

And now they were surrounded, having been ordered to a remote corner of the tarmac. As he exited the aircraft, they were approached by several dozen armed men, all in NBC gear. It reminded him of chemical warfare training back home.

Unnerving, but not unusual.

He held up his credentials.

"I am Lieutenant Colonel Chernov of the Armed Forces of the Russian Federation. I believe you are expecting me."

One man stepped forward.

"Colonel Chernov. I am Captain Lewis, United States Air Force. I need both of you to come with us through decontamination, then we'll get you prepped for your trip to Langley."

"Langley?"

"Yes, sir. You'll be briefed along the way."

Decontamination Zone, Interim LSU Public Hospital, New Orleans, Louisiana

Katherine looked up as Dr. Corkery sat down beside her, his shoulders slumped, the bags under his eyes with bags of their own. He looked as exhausted as she felt, and as demoralized as she felt.

"I take it you've heard?" she asked.

He nodded.

"I think it's already too late," he said. "Last count I heard on CNN was over a hundred thousand men in the US alone are presenting, with that number expected to increase exponentially. They're talking half a million by tomorrow, ten million within a couple of days." He turned to Katherine, his eyes glassed over with tears. "We've lost!"

Katherine gave him a gentle smile, putting a hand on his shoulder and squeezing.

"It's not over until there's none left. We keep doing our job, we keep caring for the sick, we keep isolating those that aren't sick, we keep searching for a cure. That's our job as doctors. During the Black Death the doctors didn't give up. They kept battling the disease, and eventually they won. And during that battle they learned many valuable lessons, including lessons we use to this very day. They learned about quarantining the sick, about proper disposal of bodies, about proper hygiene practices. Over the coming centuries we perfected those practices, and we'll learn more this time. Almost half of Europe was wiped out in a couple of years, and they recovered, and so will we. It won't be easy, but we'll come back bigger and stronger than ever. Don't lose faith, Doctor. Mankind will survive."

"So you think it's over as well."

It wasn't the message she had wanted him to take from her statement, but he was right. She had lost hope. The quarantine they had in place was now merely to try and protect themselves. Carload upon carload of sick people were being brought to hospitals all over the city. The Superdome was being converted into a massive treatment center, and arrangements were already being made for mass cremations. Her heart broke as she thought of it, and she prayed every spare minute for a reprieve, but none came.

"If we haven't figured this out in the next few days, it's over. It will be too big to treat even if we have a cure." Her chin dropped onto her chest. "My father was just admitted to a hospital in Fargo. My mom doesn't think he's going to make it through the night."

Corkery put his arm over her shoulders and pulled her toward him.

"I'm so sorry," he whispered as her head fell on his shoulder, this near stranger opening the release valve on the emotions she had kept under tight control since she had heard the news.

She sobbed like she hadn't since she was a child, all hope, all will having long ago drained away.

Aboard the USS George H. W. Bush
Carrier Strike Group Two, Off the Florida Coast

Kane sat with the others in a quarantine room on the USS George H. W. Bush, but at least they were out of their bunny suits and had been able to shower. The ship hadn't been to port since the initial release of the antiviral, and none of its crew had been either. In fact the entire fleet had been steaming back to its home port, exercises in Korea over.

Niner was on a call with Dawson, and hung up the phone.

"Well?"

"They're about to start interrogating Koslov, but he's claiming only Fowler knows where the doctor is."

"Do they believe him?"

"No, but the information might not be very forthcoming."

"Meaning not quick." Kane shook his head then looked at Sherrie. "If we can't get that intel soon, your dating scene is going to become a little lopsided."

Sherrie forced a smile, and he knew she was thinking about Leroux.

"Those few of you that remain are going to be damned busy helping us women repopulate," she said, managing a comeback.

"Sign me up for some of that!" said Niner, who never seemed to be in a bad mood.

Sherrie glanced at him.

"They'll probably just use artificial insemination. Start exercising your wrists."

Jimmy belted Niner in the shoulder with a shout of "Owned!" as Niner looked at his hands, giving each a tender kiss that had the room roaring with laughter as the phone on the wall buzzed for attention.

Niner jumped and grabbed it, then turned to Kane.

"For you, Special Agent Black."

Kane rose and took the phone.

"Black here."

"Dylan, it's me!"

Kane immediately recognized Leroux's voice, and the excitement in it immediately began to excite him.

"What's got you so excited, Chris?"

"The tapes! I went through the tapes! You wouldn't believe what I found!"

"Okay, calm down. What did you find?"

"He didn't do it!"

"What do you mean?"

"He didn't blow up the boat!"

"Then who did?"

"It wasn't us. It just blew up, almost exactly twenty minutes after you said he left shore."

Kane's eyebrows slowly rose.

"As if it were on a timer."

"Exactly."

"But who the hell would rig their own escape boat to blow up after twenty minutes?"

And that's when Leroux dropped the bombshell on Kane.

Eglin AFB, Florida

Dawson was exhausted and pissed off. They had been interrogating Anton Koslov for over an hour now, and had gotten nowhere. He kept insisting only Fowler knew where the doctor was being held. Dawson didn't believe him, but Koslov kept insisting. Dawson wasn't sure what his game was, why he would keep up this pretense of not knowing anything, when he had a Presidential pardon against any prosecution. All he had to do was cooperate.

And he wasn't.

"So, now that Fowler's dead, what are you going to do?"

"What do you mean?"

"I mean, how will you get paid?"

"I was paid in advance."

"For how long?"

"What do you mean?"

"How long are you under contract?"

Koslov seemed to be caught off guard by the question.

"Actually, my contract is up at the end of the month."

"Kind of coincidental."

"What do you mean?"

"The world's going to end at the same time your contract does."

Koslov shrugged.

"So?"

"So, where are you going to spend all that money—I assume it's a lot of money?"

"Oh yeah."

"So where are you going to spend it if the world has gone to hell?"

"It won't all go to hell, and with the kind of money I was paid, I will be part of those that rule in the new world order."

Dawson harrumphed.

"From what I can see from the news, if anybody will be ruling this planet, it will be women, not men."

"Less competition."

"And a lot of anger directed at you since your face will be known to every survivor on the planet as the man who did this to them."

"Groupies."

Dawson had to admit the man had a flippant answer to everything, and it was tiring. The man wasn't scared at all. Was it because he figured he was safe on a military base that was quarantined? Or was it something else?

"You realize that we're putting you into an isolation ward with the victims of your disease if you don't cooperate. Your pardon will still be in effect. You'll be a free man, treated like any other infected citizen."

"I'm not infected."

"You will be once you're with them."

"Perhaps."

"So the antiviral is more specific than just men. It's men with some other trait?"

"I didn't say that. I honestly have no idea what he's targeted. I only know what the news tells me, and in Russia you learn not to trust the news."

"So you were given some sort of vaccine?"

"Vaccine? Never touch the stuff. Don't you know that scientific experts like Jenny McCarthy say they cause autism?" He smiled. "In Russia we get Oprah."

"You shouldn't take medical advice from Playmates. You just might get your kids killed, or your neighbors' kids killed."

"Don't have any kids. Hate my neighbors."

This is getting nowhere.

There was a knock at the door. Dawson opened it to find Kane standing there. He motioned Dawson to join him in the hall. Dawson looked at Koslov who was eyeballing Kane with what seemed to be amusement. *Don't let his age fool you.* Dawson walked from the room, closing the door behind him.

"What is it?"

Kane whispered something in his ear, and his jaw dropped.

Unbefuckinleivable!

Langley Field, Air Combat Command

Lieutenant Colonel Chernov dialed the number he had been provided with, refusing to accompany the soldiers to the awaiting vehicle, his finger held up defiantly in the air. After several rings the call was answered.

"This is Mr. White."

"Sergeant, this is Chernov. What the hell is going on?"

"What do you mean, sir?"

"I'm here and they're taking me to Langley. Where is Koslov?"

"He's here with us, in Florida."

"Then I need to be there, not in Virginia!"

"Agreed, sir. Put me on with the commanding officer there, then I'll make a phone call."

Chernov handed the phone to the Captain who was growing increasingly impatient if his pacing were any indication.

"This is Captain Lewis. Who is this?" – "Sergeant?" – "Listen, Sergeant, I have my orders, and this man is coming with me to Langley." – "I don't care how high you *think* your orders—" – "I see. The President. No, I guess it wouldn't hurt to wait ten minutes. Very well, Sergeant. You have ten minutes."

The Captain tossed the phone back to Chernov, who turned his back on the man and faced his pilot, Major Bodrov.

"We lost the Cold War to these people?"

Bodrov laughed.

Decontamination Zone, Interim LSU Public Hospital, New Orleans, Louisiana

"Are you okay?"

Katherine looked up to find Dr. Johnston rushing over. She patted Corkery on the chest and gave him a look of gratitude as he removed his arm from her shoulders.

"Thanks, I needed that."

"Any time, Doctor, my shoulder is always free of charge."

She chuckled, wiping her face dry with a kerchief from her pocket, then looked at the concerned face of Dr. Johnston.

"I'm okay, just having a moment."

"Nothing to be ashamed about. I've had several, but none with a young shoulder to cry on."

Corkery stood and patted his shoulder. "Come on, Doc, you know you want to."

Johnston laughed then sat down in the vacated seat. Corkery was about to walk away when Johnston held up his hand.

"You might want to hear this as well, Doctor."

"What is it?" asked Katherine, her emotions again compartmentalized.

"I've got some good news, if you can call it that."

"What?"

"Well, the CDC has confirmed that there hasn't been a single case of the BRCA1 variant of the antiviral outside of New Orleans that can't be traced directly back to the Saints game. It appears there have been no secondary infections."

"Thanks terrific news!" exclaimed Corkery. "Does that mean they're going to lift the quarantine?"

334

Johnston shook his head.

"No. The second variant seems to be concentrated here, which makes sense since the truck stop with the canister of antiviral was just outside of the city, and probably half the traffic was heading into the city, the rest heading around the country. This is still the epicenter of both outbreaks, so the quarantine stays in place."

"Seems rather pointless, considering its all across the world."

"I agree. I think it's now more optics than anything else. The President wants to be seen as doing something. Lifting a quarantine when so many people are sick would seem foolish to an uninformed public. I'm guessing that if we don't have a handle on this in a few days, he figures nothing will matter anyway. But if we do, he'll have only pissed off a few hundred thousand voters in New Orleans, rather than having appeared weak and overly compassionate to two hundred million voters."

"You're a cynical man, Dr. Johnston. I think you and I would get along just fine," said Corkery.

"If we make it out of this, we're all going for beers. Next person who cries, pays."

Katherine playfully slapped him on the back of his hand then stood up.

"That's enough 'me' time. I'm going to check on our patients."

Langley Field, Air Combat Command

"You have them?"

"Yes, comrade Colonel."

Lieutenant Colonel Chernov smiled. *Finally, something is going right.*

"Hold them until I get back to you. They aren't allowed to communicate with anyone."

"Understood, Colonel."

"I will contact you soon."

Chernov ended the call, stuffing the cellphone back in his pocket as a Humvee pulled up, a Major jumping out and running toward him.

"Colonel Chernov?"

"Yes."

"I'm terribly sorry for the confusion. If you'll come with me, we'll have you where you need to be in a jiffy."

A jiffy?

He decided not to ask.

"Very well."

The major turned to the captain and his men.

"Captain, you're dismissed."

The Captain snapped to attention with a crisp salute.

"Yes, sir!"

He turned and left with his men as they double-timed it back to wherever they had come from.

Chernov didn't care. He climbed in the Humvee and the major held up his hand when Chernov's pilot Bodrov tried to join them.

"My orders are for the Colonel only. You can remain here until the Colonel returns, or you can be refueled and begin your journey home. It's you choice, Major."

Bodrov turned to Chernov.

"Your orders, sir?"

"Return home. There's no reason for you to risk catching the virus."

Bodrov bowed slightly.

"Thank you, sir. It's been an honor."

He snapped to attention and saluted, Chernov returning the salute from the backseat of the Humvee.

"Do svidaniya, Major."

"Do svidaniya, Colonel. I trust that I will indeed see you again."

The Humvee began to roll and Chernov leaned back, his mind in Moscow, dreaming of the frigid Moskva River and skating in Gorky Park during his youth with his childhood sweetheart. He had married her, but she had died during childbirth, and the boy, his son, soon after.

It had been devastating, and he had sworn to never repeat it, instead marrying the Army and his country. He remembered the horror of watching his tiny child die and how long it had taken him to get over both their deaths.

And he knew if he couldn't get Koslov to talk, it was an experience that would be repeated billions of times over.

Eglin AFB, Florida

Dawson snapped his jaw shut, not sure how long it had sat there open in shock. The bomb Kane had just dropped changed everything, but at the same time, unless they got Koslov to talk, it changed nothing.

"Let's see how he reacts to this news," said Dawson, opening the door to the interrogation room. Entering, he sat down at the table across from their prisoner, Kane standing behind him, in the corner, saying nothing, simply staring at Koslov, his rippling arms crossed across his chest.

Dawson tapped a finger on the table and Koslov looked at him.

"Yes?"

"You lied to me, Anton."

"I did? I don't recall lying. What did I lie about?"

"Scott Fowler is alive."

Koslov chuckled, a smile spreading across his face.

"You finally figured it out, huh? You know, it was my idea."

"Why don't you run it by me?"

"I hired a decoy. Everything would be tracked back to the decoy, then if we were ever raided, we'd destroy the compound, and our Fowler double would escape. After twenty minutes into his hour long journey, the boat explodes, and everyone thinks he's dead."

"Did the double know that part?"

Koslov grinned.

"Nyet."

"So where is Fowler now?"

Koslov shrugged.

"You'd have to ask him."

Dawson jerked his thumb over his shoulder at Kane.

"Do you know who he is?"

Koslov shook his head.

"Never had the pleasure."

"He's CIA. Highly trained in interrogation techniques including torture. Due to the current situation, the President has lifted all rules. We're allowed to do anything we want, including torture you. To death if necessary." Dawson leaned forward. "If you don't answer my questions, you *will* answer his."

Koslov smiled slightly.

"I doubt it."

Dawson stood up.

"I warned you." He turned to Kane. "Your turn."

Kane walked over to Koslov, shooting him in both knees.

Eglin AFB, Florida

Chernov was escorted into a quarantine area and made to wait again, but at least this time the wait wasn't long. Within five minutes a sergeant appeared on the other side of the glass, his face grim, as grim as the pilot's who had flown him down here in a two-seater F/A-18F Super Hornet in record time. He imagined much of the country looked like this.

There wasn't much to smile about.

"Colonel Chernov?"

"Yes?"

"I'm Sergeant *White*."

Chernov smiled, understanding the need to maintain the man's cover.

"Nice to finally meet you, face-to-face, sort of," he replied, tapping on the glass.

"Sir, currently you are quarantined in an interim zone known to be virus free, but where the personnel are awaiting blood test results. We are in an area we can't guarantee is virus free, as we had to interrogate our prisoner, so volunteered to be potentially exposed. You may join us here in hazmat gear should you wish, or await blood test results, and interrogate the prisoner remotely."

"Sergeant, just let me in there. I don't give a damn about any virus."

Dawson's lips thinned as he nodded, apparently impressed with his Russian balls.

"Very well, sir."

Dawson left his room and moments later Chernov was escorted through several doors, sprayed down again then let through a final door where the sergeant greeted him with a slight bow.

"Colonel, if you'll follow me, I'll take you to where the prisoner is being held."

"Is he okay?"

"Define okay?"

"Alive?"

"Last time I saw him, yes. He won't be for long unless you can get some answers out of him. We've had our best try, but he just seems impervious to pain, and doesn't seem to care whether or not he dies." Dawson paused. "He's really rather remarkable."

"He is that," agreed Chernov as they approached a door. Dawson knocked, and a moment later a young man exited, blood on his clothes and knuckles. "Lieutenant Colonel Chernov, this is Mr. Black."

Chernov nodded.

"So, did you get anything out of him?" asked Chernov.

"Yes, but not what we wanted, nor will we. He's dying. He's got less than three months to live, and is hopped up on so many pain killers, he barely feels a thing. I shot him in both knees and he barely winced."

"You shot him? Mr. Black, that's a violation of the Geneva Convention!"

"Colonel, there is no Geneva Convention here. Geneva's dying like the rest of the world. Under Presidential order we have been authorized to use any and all means to get what we need in order to stop this virus," replied Mr. Black.

Chernov nodded.

"Fortunately for you, Russia agrees." He filled his chest with air, squaring his shoulders. "Let me speak to him."

Mr. Black opened the door.

"By all means, Colonel. Good luck."

Chernov entered the stark white room and nearly gasped. Blood was pooled on the floor beneath both knees, now bandaged up, and his former comrade's face was bloody and bruised. The so-called "Mr. Black" had certainly done a number on his old friend, but from as far as he could tell, there was no permanent damage except the knees. But if his friend only had a few months to live, then he wouldn't have much more use for them anyway.

"Colonel? What are you doing here?"

"Major. What the hell have you gotten yourself into?" asked Chernov as he sat down across from his friend.

"I messed up, sir."

"Clearly. And why didn't you tell me you were dying?"

Koslov looked away.

"I don't want people's sympathy."

"You won't get it from me. Not after what you've done."

Koslov looked back at Chernov.

"I deserved that. But if you think you're going to be able to appeal to my better nature to give you the information you need, you're wasting your time."

Chernov stretched his legs out and crossed his arms, getting comfortable.

"Anton, my old friend, I know you too well. You are dying, that I did not know, and it was the only piece of this puzzle that I was missing. Now that I have it, I know everything."

"Forgive me, Colonel, but you know nothing."

Chernov smiled.

"I visited your parents."

Koslov's eyes widened slightly and the muscles in his throat contracted for a split second as he swallowed, the micro-expressions written all over his face revealing all the truth Chernov needed.

Koslov recovered.

"And how are they?"

"Oh, they are living quite well. I especially like the television. I would get one myself if I could afford it."

Koslov scratched his wrist.

"My father won the lottery, offered me some of it, but I told him to spend it on themselves."

"That was very nice of you. Bullshit of course, but still, a very nice sentiment if it were true."

Koslov didn't reply, merely scratched his cheek, then winced slightly as he reset his broken nose. He didn't respond.

"Well, I know you care about your parents, that's obvious by how their tiny apartment is decked out. So, just to make sure they remain safe, I've had them picked up." Koslov's head darted up and he glared at Chernov for a brief instance. "Just to make sure nothing happens to them."

That did it.

Koslov leaned forward.

"Nothing better happen to them, or I'll kill you."

Chernov smiled, then pointed at Koslov's knees.

"You'll have to drag yourself on your bloody stumps in order to reach me." He leaned forward and wiped all friendliness off his face. "Let's cut the bullshit. The world is dying out there. If we can't stop it, your parents are probably going to die anyway. I don't care how much money you were trying to earn to secure their retirement, there will be nothing left to live for."

"That's not the plan."

So there's a plan!

"Why don't you tell me what the plan is?"

Koslov sighed.

"Fowler is going to release the information you need to stop the plague in three days."

"By then hundreds of millions could be infected, millions dead."

"That's the idea. It will motivate governments to act."

"To act on what?"

"Haven't you figured this out yet?"

"Consider me stupid, Anton. What the hell is going on? What is this all about?"

"Money!"

"What?"

"Money! Stock prices! The almighty dollar!"

"What?"

"Fowler has billions in BioDyne stock. He wants more. Billions aren't enough, not if you want true power. You need tens of billions. He strings BioDyne along with minor outbreaks, threatening a major one if they go to the authorities. They're terrified, so they don't go, paying his minor ransoms, and all along they are thinking it is a crazed former employee, Dr. Urban. It never occurs to them that it is one of their own behind this.

"His spies on the inside keep him informed of BioDyne's progress, and when they finally have developed an aerosolized compound that can neutralize the antiviral, he springs the major outbreak, piggybacked on a minor one, so they are distracted by the minor outbreak, which flares quicker, while the major outbreak spreads around the world. Only it's targeted much broader, so broad the governments will have no choice but to pay whatever price he asks for the cure.

"Only he doesn't need to ask. BioDyne, innocent in all of this, will offer up the cure, at cost plus the padding that any company will add, all they need is the final piece of the puzzle, which Fowler is releasing in three days. At that point the dead and dying will be in the many millions, and the antiviral will have spread around the world. BioDyne will sweep in and save the day, their stock price will go through the roof when the markets reopen, and Fowler will sell his stock at a massive profit over the coming months. He will be incredibly rich, cash rich, my parents will be taken care of for life, and I will die in a nice corner of the world on a beach somewhere without a care in the world.

"At least that's what was supposed to happen."

"What changed it?"

"You guys figured out it was Fowler. You were supposed to think it was Dr. Urban and Fowler would be kept clean in this entire affair."

"There's always a kink in every plan."

Koslov nodded, blowing air out of his mouth, puffing his lips out in the effort.

"Tell me about it."

"It's over, Anton. Give us the location of Fowler and Urban, and you can walk away from this. I promise you your parents will be taken care of, and you can go to that beach."

Koslov shook his head.

"I can't believe that. You know I lost faith in my country years ago. I don't believe they'll keep their word."

Chernov sat up in his chair, leaning toward Koslov.

"Listen my friend. If Moscow doesn't receive a call from me in the next thirty minutes that you are cooperating, they will kill your father, in front of your mother, in a most hideous way."

Koslov looked at Chernov, horror written all over his face.

"No. I don't believe it. They wouldn't!"

"They would, and they will. The world is desperate, my friend. They—I—will stop at nothing to end this. So what is it going to be? The life of your parents, or a payday for them that won't matter?"

Koslov dropped his head on the table, covering his eyes with his palms, his fingers squeezing his scalp. He threw his head up suddenly, dropping his arms.

"Pen. Paper. Before I change my mind."

Fisher Island, Miami, Florida
Outbreak Day #13

Dawson crouched behind the rear wall surrounding the waterfront estate in Miami. To say this place was spectacular would be to insult it. He had only seen places like this in the movies, and part of him had never thought they actually existed. The house, or mansion, was massive, well lit, heavily windowed, and therefore hard to approach without detection.

And standing inside, sipping a glass of wine while working on a laptop, was one Scott Fowler, former VP at BioDyne Pharma, and the most wanted man in the world right now.

Dawson turned to Kane.

"Your show, ready?"

"Not today. You take it. I have to go check on something."

And with that he disappeared around the corner, leaving Dawson a little surprised.

He shrugged his shoulders.

CIA. Always loners.

He activated his comm.

"Bravo Team, Bravo One. Prepare to go on my signal, over." He climbed up the few rungs of the combat ladder, standing at the top so he could simply flip over the wall rather than have to scale it. "Overseer, Bravo One. Proceed with operation, over."

"Bravo One, Overseer. Proceeding, over."

It took a moment, but suddenly the entire island was bathed in darkness.

He quickly cleared the wall and flipped over to the other side, the rest of the team following suit. As he sprinted for the house he could hear a backup generator starting up, and lights began to flicker back on just as he slammed into the wall beside the deck, only feet from a door leading into the kitchen.

"Bravo Team, Bravo One. Sound off if in position, over."

The entire team confirmed their objectives acquired.

"Niner here, I've got eyes on target, he's still in living area but he's on his feet. Looks like he's wondering what happened. He's approaching the window now."

"Charge in place?" asked Dawson.

"Affirmative."

"Blow it."

"Roger that."

There was a muffled sound to his right, accompanied by the shattering of glass as a shaped charge took out just the window, but not the target behind it. He rushed toward Niner's position and found him already through the window, chasing Fowler around the corner.

The man's fast!

Dawson ran after them and found Niner banging on a door moments later.

"What the hell happened?"

"It must be some sort of safe room. He went through and this damned door just shot up from the floor, damned near took my head off!"

"Blow it," ordered Dawson.

"Are you sure? We don't know what's on the other side, or how thick that damned thing is," replied Niner as he tapped on the metal. "I'm liable to kill him."

Dawson kicked the door, the substantial quality of it evident by the tone it replied with.

"Dammit."

348

"Okay, let's get some cutting equipment in here. The rest of you search the place, top to bottom, and secure the outside, I don't want him walking out of here through some secret exit."

It didn't take long for the cutting equipment to arrive from just down the street, this contingency planned for, and within minutes two Miami SWAT team members were cutting at the door.

"BD, I've got something down here!"

It was Red, and he sounded excited.

"Where are you?"

"Basement."

"On my way."

Dawson headed for the basement, the plans for the house memorized. At least the official plans filed with the city. *That safe room wasn't on them.* He rushed down the stairs and into the basement, but it wasn't just a basement. He had seen basements, in fact, he had seen some spectacularly finished basements. This however looked like any other level of the house.

Man, the rich really are in another world.

"Over here!" he heard Red's voice call. He followed it and found Red standing outside a door with Atlas. Dawson joined them and looked in to find Niner and Jimmy examining a woman who appeared to have been locked in the room, the door jamb splintered from where one of his men had kicked it open.

Dawson immediately recognized her.

"Mrs. Urban?"

She looked at him and nodded, her tear filled eyes accompanied by a look of relief at finally being rescued.

"My children?"

Dawson knelt in front of her.

"My name is Sergeant White. I'm with the United States military. Your children are safe and being taken care of by Canadian authorities."

"Oh thank God!" she cried, her shoulders slumping as her chest heaved as sobs of joy and relief overtook her.

"Do you know where your husband is?"

She nodded.

"He should be in the lab, at the end of the hall."

Dawson heard Atlas head down the hall.

"Locked door here, boss!"

"Check it for booby-traps, then open it."

"It should be safe, I go in there all the time."

"We'll just double check it to be sure," said Dawson, standing up. "Get her out of here, I don't trust this place won't turn out to be a repeat of Cuba."

Niner nodded, helping Melissa Urban to her feet. Standing, she immediately hugged Niner, then Jimmy and finally Dawson.

"Thank you," she managed between sobs. "Thank you so much."

Dawson smiled at her, then motioned for her to be taken outside to the waiting EMT vehicles where she could get proper medical attention.

"Door looks clear, BD," said Atlas as Dawson approached.

"Go ahead."

Atlas tried the handle, and the door proved to be unlocked. He pushed the door open as they all stood to the side.

Nothing.

The door swung open, revealing a stark white interior. It was clearly a medical facility, and as Dawson stepped inside, weapon raised, a glass wall directly ahead of them revealed a fantastically equipped lab if he ever saw one, and one lone man working inside, oblivious to the company he now had. He was in a hazmat suit with a self-contained breathing apparatus, and his back was now to them.

Dawson tapped on the glass with the barrel of his Glock.

The man turned around and nearly dropped the vial he was holding.

Dawson pressed the Talk button on an intercom located on the wall by the door into the isolation chamber.

"Doctor Urban I presume?"

Kane sat on the deck of the cigarette boat, his Glock in one hand, the other resting on the gunwale holding a pair of handcuffs, the waves gently rocking the craft from side to side. It was peaceful. Quiet, the private dock as isolated as one could get on the water in Miami. And with the entire island still bathed in darkness from the power shutdown, only those homes with backup generators spoiled the darkness. He had monitored the communications and knew that the mission hadn't gone as planned, Fowler too fast for them. It was a contingency he had planned on, and indeed had expected. And now Fowler was locked inside some sort of panic room.

Which Kane didn't buy for a second.

Panic rooms were meant for innocent people who needed to delay their potential attackers until the police arrived. Fowler was a mass murderer, who would plan far ahead of just waiting for police to arrive. He would have an escape plan, just like there was in Cuba for his double.

The sound of the rippling water was broken, the calm disturbed by something breaking the surface. Kane flicked the safety off his weapon, but remained seated. A hand clasped the metal rung that ran the entire perimeter of the boat, then another. A man's head appeared as he pulled himself into the boat, flopping onto the deck, gasping for breath.

Kane stood and aimed the gun at the man's chest.

"Nice to finally meet you, Mr. Fowler."

Fowler's eyes shot wide open and he rolled quickly to his feet, holding something too small to be a gun in his left hand.

"Don't move," he said as he edged his way toward the side of the boat.

"That's my line," said Kane, keeping a bead on the man's chest.

"Let me go, or Dr. Urban dies."

"Is that what you have there?" asked Kane, motioning to Fowler's hand with his chin. "A detonator of some kind?"

"Something like that. Just let me go, and Urban lives. Try to arrest me, and he dies."

"You know I can't let you go."

"Yes you can. The necessary information will be automatically emailed in three days. You'll have what you need for your cure."

"By then millions could have died."

"Not my problem."

"Why continue with this? You won't see any of the money. Your stocks will be seized before the markets open. There's no way you're going to see a penny of this."

Fowler shook his head, his expression almost one of pity.

"You're so naïve. You have no idea of how money works. When you *have* it, you're immune to the laws of man. Go ahead and seize my stock. It doesn't matter. I have identities created all around the world that will capitalize on this situation, providing me with far more than the pittance the stock in BioDyne was going to give me. And by the time you would figure out those identities, I'll be long gone with a new face, living a life people like you couldn't even imagine."

Kane smiled.

"It's pretty hard to spend money when you're dead."

Fowler shrugged his shoulders.

"And again I say you won't kill me, because you need me."

"Actually, I don't need you, I need Dr. Urban."

Kane squeezed the trigger.

"How do you open the door?" asked Dawson through the intercom.

Dr. Urban waved his hands.

"No! No! No! Don't touch it. He has to enter a code to let me out. Basically I'm locked in here twenty-four seven." He pointed to a cot in the corner of the lab. "I usually have to sleep here."

"What happens if we open the door?"

"Bad things."

Dawson was about to ask Urban to expand upon that when he heard a noise behind him.

"What the fuck?"

It was Niner who got in the first comment.

Kane entered the room, dragging a bloodied but breathing Scott Fowler along the floor. He tossed Fowler at his feet.

"Found something you were looking for."

Dawson shook his head.

"Do you shoot every prisoner you have?"

Kane shrugged.

"Only if they deserve it."

"Uh huh."

"He had a remote detonator for this place, I had to take him out, so I shot him in the shoulder. He'll live, and without a working arm, he wasn't able to operate the thumb necessary to fry the good doctor."

Dawson looked down at Fowler.

"Dr. Urban says you have a code to let him out of the lab."

Fowler nodded.

"What is it?"

"You really expect me to give it to you?"

"If you want to live through the night, yes."

Kane pointed his weapon at Fowler's chest.

"Now that we have the Doctor, we don't need you."

"I'll tell you everything you need to know!" cried the Doctor through the intercom. "Just get me out of here!"

"Fine!" shouted Fowler. "But I want immunity."

"Done," said Dawson. "Now open the door."

Fowler tried to stand, but was too weak. He pointed at the keypad with his good hand.

"Six-seven-four-one-eight, then press the green button."

Dawson stepped over to the pad. "Repeat the code."

"Six-seven-four-one-eight," repeated Fowler as Dawson entered each number as given. He pressed the green button.

A red light began to spin in the center of the lab and over the door, an alarm sounding. Urban shouted, rushing for the door, pounding on it as the recorded voice of a woman was heard over a PA system.

"Biological decontamination procedure commencing. Complete decontamination in ten, nine, eight…"

The countdown continued as Dawson stepped back.

"What the hell did you just do!" yelled Dawson as he stepped on Fowler's wounded shoulder.

"I just improved my negotiating position."

"How do I stop it?"

"You can't."

"Five…four…three…"

Dawson hit the button for the intercom.

"Doctor, what is the antiviral targeting?"

"Two…One…"

354

"It's targeting—"

"Commencing biological decontamination."

Flames shot from every direction as gas was pumped into the room and ignited, fueling a blaze that consumed anything alive or that had been alive. Urban's face pressed against the glass for several seconds as they watched in horror, his screams silent as the intercom was automatically shut off.

"Biological decontamination cleansing complete. Testing for biological organisms." There was a pause. "None detected."

Kane shook his head, grabbing a syringe off a nearby table and storming from the room. Dawson's boot continued to grind into Fowler's shoulder, his toe forcing the man's face toward the glass so he could see his handiwork.

The view suddenly cleared as the smoke was sucked out of the room and a gentle spray of water washed everything down, draining into the floor grates. Air blasted the lab dry as it was refilled with oxygen. The red lights stopped flashing, leaving a pristine lab, ready for the next scientist to move in.

"Biological decontamination complete. You may enter when ready."

Dawson motioned for Atlas to try the door.

Atlas approached and pulled on the handle. The door swung open and he stepped inside. He looked through the window to his right and shook his head.

"There's nothing left of the guy, BD."

Dawson's head dropped, his eyes closed as his heart filled with rage. *When this is over, Fowler dies.*

Kane filled the syringe he had taken with water, then waited several minutes in the hallway, trying to clear his mind of the horror he had just witnessed. He had seen men die in battle, bodies torn apart by explosives, but had never seen a body burnt alive by a machine with a sexy voice, doing its programmed job. That was a first. He had killed with weapons, he had killed with drones, but there had always been someone, somewhere, behind the controls.

He punched the wall then stormed back in the room.

"What's the genetic sequence the antiviral is targeting?"

"Fuck you. I want immunity before I tell you anything."

"We don't have that kind of time. People are dying."

"You've got all the time in the world, because I'm not saying a word until I have my pardon in writing, signed by the damned President himself."

"You'll get it, but we need that information now. We can't wait for the damned red tape."

"You'll have to."

Kane pulled the syringe from his pocket and dropped down beside Fowler.

"You want to play it that way, then fine." He plunged the syringe into the man's leg and pushed down on the plunger. He then yanked it out and tossed it down the hallway. "Now you're infected too, just like the rest of them."

Fowler's eyes shot wide open, and he paled as the blood drained from his face.

And Kane knew what he needed to know in that one instant.

CIA Headquarters, Langley, Virginia

Leif Morrison sat at a chair in the operations center, listening to the exchange over the comms. His eyes were closed, his hands were pulling at his thinning hair, and he wondered what the hell could go wrong next. He had already put out the request for the presidential pardon, and would probably have it inside of the hour, but like Kane said, time was of the essence.

"Overseer, Thunderbolt. It's men, over!"

"Thunderbolt, Overseer. Repeat your last transmission, over."

"It's men. The antiviral is targeting men!"

Morrison jumped up and rushed over to the station communicating with Kane, ripping the headset off the startled woman.

"This is Morrison. Can you confirm that?"

"Sir, I injected him with the antiviral and he got scared. Too scared. There's no way he'd have Dr. Urban create an antiviral that could affect him, unless he was going for something so big, it *had* to affect him. He's targeting *all* men. That's the only way to explain why he's terrified right now."

"So this is a guess?"

"Yes sir, let's call it a damned strong hunch."

"You better pray you're right."

"Already praying, sir."

"Good work, son. I'll pass the intel along."

Morrison turned to Dr. Kapp who was just ending a call from his cellphone.

"I've passed the information to our team. They already had a test compound prepared in the event it was just men. All we need now is to test it on humans."

Isolation Ward, Interim LSU Public Hospital, New Orleans, Louisiana

Katherine sat by Stanley's bedside, holding the man's limp hand. He had been given the injection several hours ago, but there had been no improvement. He was just too far gone. Only feet away Dr. Corkery was checking Richard's vitals manually, not willing to trust the monitors, looking for any sign of recovery, but so far there had been none.

Stanley's monitor flat lined, his chest falling one last time. Corkery rushed around the bed, calling for a crash cart when Katherine waved him off.

"Leave him be. He held on as long as he could. Let him rest in peace now."

"But the compound? It might work!"

"Not on him. The antiviral had destroyed too much of his system already." She turned to Richard. "Let's hope he shows some signs of improvement soon."

She shifted her chair to Richard's bedside, and waited, the entire ward now quiet, the women who had initially occupied it now all dead, the men now arriving all quite aware of what was being tested, all remaining as silent as they could as if any noise might cause the potential cure to fail.

Katherine's eyes blurred as they stared at the monitor, unblinking. The heart rate was steady but slow, the blood pressure low, too low. His breathing was labored, and there was no doubt he was in the final stages of the disease.

She closed her eyes.

"Look!"

She woke with a start, still sitting in the chair, her body leaning against the gurney, Corkery still standing on the other side, apparently having not budged.

She looked at the time on the monitor, realizing she had been asleep for at least an hour.

"What?" she asked, standing up, then she saw the answer.

Richard's heart rate was up ten points, his blood pressure up to 100 over 60, a little low but safe.

"I've taken a blood sample to see if we can get an antiviral count, see how much improvement there has been, but it looks very promising."

Katherine's head tipped upward, a silent prayer going through her head when she heard a moan. Katherine leaned over Richard as his eyes fluttered open, something that hadn't happened since hours before they began treatment.

"Don't try to talk, you've got breathing tubes in. Just nod or shake your head, okay?"

Richard nodded slowly.

"Are you feeling any better?"

He nodded.

"Would you like some water?"

He nodded.

Katherine took a wet sponge and placed it against Richard's lips, squeezing a few drops out to moisten his dry mouth. She placed the sponge to a nearby tray then looked at the monitors. His heart rate was now normal, his blood pressure normal.

Corkery leaned over so Richard could see him.

"Do feel well enough for me to remove the breathing tube?"

Richard nodded, a little more emphatically this time.

Corkery held his back up as Katherine loosened the tape holding the tubes in place.

"Just cough when I say so, and they'll be out in no time, okay?"

Another nod.

"Okay, ready? Now cough."

Richard coughed as Katherine pulled the tubes out in one swift motion, Richard then gasping for his own breath, his body taking over completely, the assistance of the machines now gone.

And he immediately seemed to appear stronger.

"Water!" he croaked, and Katherine gave him a glass, Richard managing to handle it on his own, his Adam's apple bobbing greedily as he sucked down the water. Katherine pulled it away from him.

"That's enough or you'll get sick."

Richard frowned, still eying the glass as it was put out of reach.

"What happened?" he asked. "Did you find a cure?"

Corkery nodded, smiling through his hazmat suit.

"It would appear so. You're the first person to be cured. At least we assume you're cured. We'll know for sure in a few hours."

"I feel fantastic, at least compared to before. I still feel weak, but a normal weakness, if you know what I mean. Like you're supposed to feel after a bad flu. Better, but like shit if you'll pardon my French."

"That's good. That's very good," said Katherine as she began to check his eyes, ears and throat, everything as expected.

"What about Stan?" Richard asked, pushing himself up so he could see to the next bed. "Why's the curtain closed?" he asked, his voice subdued, cracking.

"I'm sorry, Richard, but your friend didn't make it. He was just too far along. He tried as hard as he could, but the antiviral had just progressed too far for his body to recover. He died less than two hours ago."

Richard dropped back on the bed, his eyes filling with tears as he looked away in shame. Then his shoulders began to shake. Katherine pulled her hood off and peeled the gloves off her hands, taking Richard's hand in her now bare hands, squeezing gently, providing him with the first human touch he had felt since the ordeal began, her own tears rolling down her cheeks as the end might finally be near.

CDC Briefing area, New Orleans, Louisiana

"Mr. President, we have good news," began Katherine. "Of the two patients, one survived, and his blood has been cleared of the antiviral. He has been cured, Mr. President."

Katherine couldn't contain the excitement, and apparently neither could those listening in at the White House as cheers erupted from the other end, the CDC personnel and LSU hospital staff already having just finished their own hugging and kissing and cheering fest.

When things died down, the President asked the exact proper question.

"And the other man?"

"He was too far gone to save, Mr. President. We don't believe it is any indication of the effectiveness of the compound provided by BioDyne, simply the limitation of the human body."

"And how quickly can we begin to administer this compound?"

"Mr. President, Dr. Kapp here from BioDyne, perhaps I can speak to that." The monitor switched focus to the still remarkably kempt gentleman. "We took a risk that the compound would work, and began production before we had confirmation of the genetic sequence targeted. It was a risk that could have cost us millions, but it appears to have paid off. Due to this, the first vials of the compound are ready to ship already. Now that we have confirmation it works, we have already begun to license production facilities around the world to begin production. As they come online over the coming days, there should be enough injectable and aerosolized compound to treat the major centers within two weeks."

"Two weeks? Won't that mean potentially millions dead?"

"No, sir, only if the infection continues unchecked. Remember, once infected, it takes ten days for symptoms to show up, then about one day for the patient to succumb. We have tens of thousands of cases across the country right now. We will have enough serum to treat these people, we will just need to get it delivered."

"How can we help?"

"We've contracted FedEx, UPS and pretty much every major courier company to begin delivery to every major city in the country. They are already picking up the initial batches as we speak. We need you, Mr. President, to open the airports to these planes."

"Consider it done," said the President with a snap of his fingers, somebody running past the camera behind him. "Anything else?"

"The courier companies might need military escorts on the ground."

"Done."

"And we'll need the Air Force to begin spraying as soon as possible. This will essentially nip this in the bud after we have saved the initial waves of infected."

"And when can we declare ourselves free of this thing?"

"It could be years before it is completely wiped out, but continued spraying and then treatment of those who get sick should keep casualties to a minimum. But, Mr. President."

"Yes, Doctor?"

"Well, I hesitate to say this, but the cost will be substantial. Potentially in the hundreds of billions."

"Understood, Doctor. You'll get your money." The President stood up, the person controlling his camera refocusing. "This is excellent news ladies and gentlemen. I thank you for all your hard work and dedication. Now if you'll excuse me, I have a scared and tired nation to address."

"Thank you, Mr. President," said Katherine as she sank into her chair, the teleconference ended. She turned to Corkery and Johnston.

"So, who's buying the beer?"

Corkery shrugged.

"I don't know, who cried last?"

Katherine sighed.

"Fine, you win. I'm buying. And I plan on getting plenty drunk. And with how tired I am, that should be about one beer. Two tops."

Eglin AFB, Florida
Outbreak Day #15

Dylan Kane sipped his beer, the ice cold beverage a welcome respite, he having gone nonstop for days now. The Delta Team Bravo guys were scattered throughout the lounge, and Sherrie sat at the opposite end of the couch he occupied. Everyone was drinking, but it was quiet, the mood somber. Distribution of the vaccine or compound or whatever they were calling it had begun almost two days ago now, and patients were recovering all around the country, but thousands were too far gone for it to help.

In the end it was expected that tens of thousands will have died, but the world will have been saved. The man behind it, Scott Fowler, was placed unprotected in an infected isolation ward so he could see what he had done. Unfortunately he had become infected. The President had decided Fowler would be the last to receive the compound, meaning he was essentially dead.

And Kane had delighted in informing the mass murderer of this.

The door opened, and Lt. Colonel Chernov entered. The room stood to the superior rank, and Chernov waved them off. Kane and Dawson approached him.

"Gentlemen, I will take my leave of you now."

"Back to Russia?" asked Kane.

"Eventually. Your government has agreed to honor the Presidential amnesty, and I will take my comrade to some place hot where he can enjoy his final days."

Kane nodded, regretting slightly he had been forced to shoot the man in the knees, especially now that he knew the man was terminal, his last few months now to be spent in a wheelchair.

But he did help a mass murderer.

Kane's conscience was clear.

Handshakes were exchanged, then Sherrie joined them.

"I'm going to head back to Langley. There's someone there I need to hug."

Kane smiled.

"Say hi to Chris for me."

"I will," she said, giving Kane a hug, then a handshake to Dawson. "It was a pleasure working with you, Sergeant."

"Any time, Agent."

Sherrie turned to Kane.

"And what about you?"

"Oh, I've got some cigars to deliver."

"Cigars? Where the hell did you find time to buy cigars?"

"Buy them? I liberated them before the compound in Cuba decided to try and light them."

"And just who's getting these contraband cigars?"

Kane winked.

"I'll never tell."

Detective Laprise's Apartment, New Orleans, Louisiana

Isabelle shut the door and locked it, tossing her keys and purse on the kitchen counter and stepping out of her shoes. She peeled herself from her clothes as she stumbled toward the bedroom, exhausted, it having been all hands on deck since the outbreak had begun. Now with things calming down and the quarantine lifted, the city was starting to return to normal.

She looked forward to her first regular old murder tomorrow.

Naked save her bra and panties, she turned toward the bathroom when something caught her eye. She spun toward the bed and saw a brown, wooden box, polished to a brilliant sheen, with a red rose and a yellow piece of paper, folded, sitting on her pillow.

Her heart leapt as she jumped toward the bed, bouncing on it as she grabbed the note, unfolding it.

"Isabelle, I had a wonderful time. And as promised, these are on me. D."

Isabelle opened the box and laughed, a dozen Cuban cigars save one, sitting in the velvet lined interior. She snapped the box shut, then dared to call out his name.

"Dylan?"

But there was no answer. She rose and searched the apartment, but knew all along she wouldn't find him hiding, lying in wait to surprise her.

They weren't meant to be.

He was a spy, serving his country in God knows what hellhole, a man meant to be alone, attachments merely baggage that could be used against him, or worse, distract him in those moments when every split second counted.

Instead, for her, he was to remain a memory, a wonderful memory, of a man who didn't exist, who had never parachuted into a quarantined city with no thought of his own safety, who had saved the world and received no thanks for it.

And who would be remembered by her for the rest of her days.

THE END

ACKNOWLEDGEMENTS

As always many people were involved in one way or the other. I'd like to thank them in no particular order. The real Chris Leroux for spit balling this idea with me. The real Isabelle Laprise for her support through my career and finding those typos that all those eyes still missed! The real Fred Newton, the biggest Jag fan I know, who tried valiantly to change my opinion. In your honor, Fred, I let this one drive away successfully. The real Greg "Chief" Michael, who gently pressured me to finish this book, and swore up and down he'd never read a vampire book. I "gently" pressured him to read my book The Turned and though he's not a Twilighter now, he's at least become a fan of the Zander Varga series.

Others to thank include Leanne ??? for helping me navigate the streets of Washington, DC, Brent Richards and Ian Kennedy for their advice on some military technical terms and NBC gear, and of course thanks to my official researcher, my dad, who I now think longs for his old air force days where the workload was lighter.

And one last thing. I'm constantly asked when the next book is coming out. Visit my website at www.jrobertkennedy.com then sign up for the Insiders Club. You'll get emails about new book releases, new collections, sales, etc. Only an email or two a month tops, I promise!

Thanks again to my wife, daughter, parents and friends. And to you the readers, thank you! You've all made this possible.

ABOUT THE AUTHOR

J. Robert Kennedy is the author of eleven international best sellers, including the smash hit James Acton Thrillers series, the first installment of which, The Protocol, has been on the best sellers list since its release, including a three month run at number one. In addition to the other novels from this series, Brass Monkey, Broken Dove, The Templar's Relic (also a number one best seller), Flags of Sin and The Arab Fall, he has written the international best sellers Rogue Operator, Depraved Difference, Tick Tock, The Redeemer and The Turned. Robert spends his time in Ontario, Canada with his family.

Visit Robert's website at www.jrobertkennedy.com for the latest news and contact information.

The Protocol
A James Acton Thriller
Book #1

For two thousand years the Triarii have protected us, influencing history from the crusades to the discovery of America. Descendent from the Roman Empire, they pervade every level of society, and are now in a race with our own government to retrieve an ancient artifact thought to have been lost forever.

Caught in the middle is archaeology professor James Acton, relentlessly hunted by the elite Delta Force, under orders to stop at nothing to possess what he has found, and the Triarii, equally determined to prevent the discovery from falling into the wrong hands.

With his students and friends dying around him, Acton flees to find the one person who might be able to help him, but little does he know he may actually be racing directly into the hands of an organization he knows nothing about...

Brass Monkey

A James Acton Thriller

Book #2

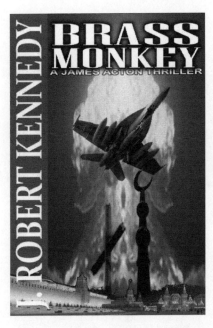

A nuclear missile, lost during the Cold War, is now in play--the most public spy swap in history, with a gorgeous agent the center of international attention, triggers the end-game of a corrupt Soviet Colonel's twenty five year plan. Pursued across the globe by the Russian authorities, including a brutal Spetsnaz unit, those involved will stop at nothing to deliver their weapon, and ensure their pay day, regardless of the terrifying consequences.

When Laura Palmer confronts a UNICEF group for trespassing on her Egyptian archaeological dig site, she unwittingly stumbles upon the ultimate weapons deal, and becomes entangled in an international conspiracy that sends her lover, archeology Professor James Acton, racing to Egypt with the most unlikely of allies, not only to rescue her, but to prevent the start of a holy war that could result in Islam and Christianity wiping each other out.

From the bestselling author of Depraved Difference and The Protocol comes Brass Monkey, a thriller international in scope, certain to offend some, and stimulate debate in others. Brass Monkey pulls no punches in confronting the conflict between two of the world's most powerful, and divergent, religions, and the terrifying possibilities the future may hold if left unchecked.

Broken Dove

A James Acton Thriller

Book #3

With the Triarii in control of the Roman Catholic Church, an organization founded by Saint Peter himself takes action, murdering one of the new Pope's operatives. Detective Chaney, called in by the Pope to investigate, disappears, and, to the horror of the Papal staff sent to inform His Holiness, they find him missing too, the only clue a secret chest, presented to each new pope on the eve of their election, since the beginning of the Church.

Interpol Agent Reading, determined to find his friend, calls Professors James Acton and Laura Palmer to Rome to examine the chest and its forbidden contents, but before they can arrive, they are intercepted by an organization older than the Church, demanding the professors retrieve an item stolen in ancient Judea in exchange for the lives of their friends.

All of your favorite characters from The Protocol return to solve the most infamous kidnapping in history, against the backdrop of a two thousand year old battle pitting ancient foes with diametrically opposed agendas.

From the internationally bestselling author of Depraved Difference and The Protocol comes Broken Dove, the third entry in the smash hit James Acton Thrillers series, where J. Robert Kennedy reveals a secret concealed by the Church for almost 1200 years, and a fascinating interpretation of what the real reason behind the denials might be.

The Templar's Relic
A James Acton Thriller
Book #4

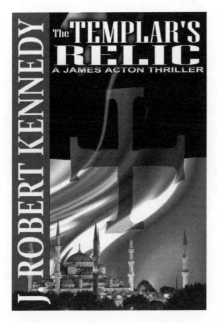

The Church Helped Destroy the Templars. Will a twist of fate let them get their revenge 700 years later?

The Vault must be sealed, but a construction accident leads to a miraculous discovery--an ancient tomb containing four Templar Knights, long forgotten, on the grounds of the Vatican. Not knowing who they can trust, the Vatican requests Professors James Acton and Laura Palmer examine the find, but what they discover, a precious Islamic relic, lost during the Crusades, triggers a set of events that shake the entire world, pitting the two greatest religions against each other.

Join Professors James Acton and Laura Palmer, INTERPOL Agent Hugh Reading, Scotland Yard DI Martin Chaney, and the Delta Force Bravo Team as they race against time to defuse a worldwide crisis that could quickly devolve into all-out war.

At risk is nothing less than the Vatican itself, and the rock upon which it was built.

From J. Robert Kennedy, the author of six international bestsellers including Depraved Difference and The Protocol, comes The Templar's Relic, the fourth entry in the smash hit James Acton Thrillers series, where once again Kennedy takes history and twists it to his own ends, resulting in a heart pounding thrill ride filled with action, suspense, humor and heartbreak.

Flags of Sin

A James Acton Thriller

Book #5

Archaeology Professor James Acton simply wants to get away from everything, and relax. A trip to China seems just the answer, and he and his fiancée, Professor Laura Palmer, are soon on a flight to Beijing.

But while boarding, they bump into an old friend, Delta Force Command Sergeant Major Burt Dawson, who surreptitiously delivers a message that they must meet the next day, for Dawson knows something they don't.

China is about to erupt into chaos.

Foreign tourists and diplomats are being targeted by unknown forces, and if they don't get out of China in time, they could be caught up in events no one had seen coming.

J. Robert Kennedy, the author of eight international best sellers, including the smash hit James Acton Thrillers, takes history once again and turns it on its head, sending his reluctant heroes James Acton and Laura Palmer into harm's way, to not only save themselves, but to try and save a country from a century old conspiracy it knew nothing about.

J. ROBERT KENNEDY

The Arab Fall

A James Acton Thriller

Book #6

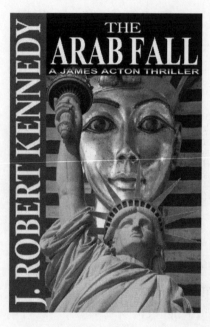

**THE GREATEST
ARCHEOLOGICAL DISCOVERY
SINCE KING TUT'S TOMB IS
ABOUT TO BE DESTROYED!**

The Arab Spring has happened and Egypt has yet to calm down, but with the dig site on the edge of the Nubian Desert, a thousand miles from the excitement, Professor Laura Palmer and her fiancé Professor James Acton return with a group of students, and two friends: Interpol Special Agent Hugh Reading, and Scotland Yard Detective Inspector Martin Chaney. It's work for the professors and their students, and a vacation for the two law enforcement officers, but as Reading quickly discovers, he and the desert don't mix, and Chaney is preoccupied with a message he has been asked to deliver to the professor by his masters in the Triarii.

But an accidental find by Chaney may lead to the greatest archaeological discovery since the tomb of King Tutankhamen, perhaps even greater. And when news of it spreads, it reaches the ears of a group hell-bent on the destruction of all idols and icons, their mere existence considered blasphemous to Islam.

As chaos hits the major cities of the world in a coordinated attack, unbeknownst to the professors, students and friends, they are about to be faced with one of the most difficult decisions of their lives.

Stay and protect the greatest archaeological find of our times, or save themselves and their students from harm, leaving the find to be destroyed by fanatics determined to wipe it from the history books.

From J. Robert Kennedy, the author of eleven international bestsellers including Rogue Operator and The Protocol, comes The Arab Fall, the sixth entry in the smash hit James Acton Thrillers series, where Kennedy once again takes events from history and today's headlines, and twists them into a heart pounding adventure filled with humor and heartbreak, as one of their own is left severely wounded, fighting for their life.

The Turned

Zander Varga, Vampire Detective

Book #1

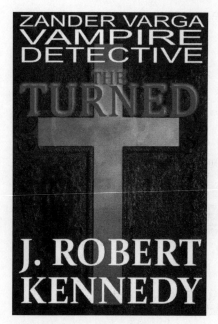

Zander has relived his wife's death at the hands of vampires every day for almost three hundred years, his perfect memory a curse of becoming one of The Turned—infecting him their final heinous act after her murder.

Nineteen year-old Sydney Winter knows Zander's secret, a secret preserved by the women in her family for four generations. But with her mother in a coma, she's thrust into the front lines, ahead of her time, to fight side-by-side with Zander.

And she wouldn't change a thing.

She loves the excitement, she loves the danger.

And she loves Zander.

But it's a love that will have to go unrequited, because Zander has only one thing on his mind. And it's been the same thing for over two hundred years.

Revenge.

But today, revenge will have to wait, because Zander Varga, Private Detective, has a new case. A woman's husband is missing. The police aren't interested. But Zander is. Something doesn't smell right, and he's determined to find out why.

CONTAINMENT FAILURE

From J. Robert Kennedy, the internationally bestselling author of The Protocol and Depraved Difference, comes his sixth novel, The Turned, a terrifying story that in true Kennedy fashion takes a completely new twist on the origin of vampires, tying it directly to a well-known moment in history. Told from the perspective of Zander Varga and his assistant, Sydney Winter, The Turned is loaded with action, humor, terror and a centuries long love that must eventually be let go.

Depraved Difference

A Detective Shakespeare Mystery

Book #1

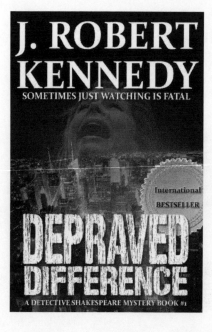

Would you help, would you run, or would you just watch?

When a young woman is brutally assaulted by two men on the subway, her cries for help fall on the deaf ears of onlookers too terrified to get involved, her misery ended with the crushing stomp of a steel-toed boot. A cellphone video of her vicious murder, callously released on the Internet, its popularity a testament to today's depraved society, serves as a trigger, pulled a year later, for a killer.

Emailed a video documenting the final moments of a woman's life, entertainment reporter Aynslee Kai, rather than ask why the killer chose her to tell the story, decides to capitalize on the opportunity to further her career. Assigned to the case is Hayden Eldridge, a detective left to learn the ropes by a disgraced partner, and as videos continue to follow victims, he discovers they were all witnesses to the vicious subway murder a year earlier, proving sometimes just watching is fatal.

From the author of The Protocol and Brass Monkey, Depraved Difference is a fast-paced murder suspense novel with enough laughs, heartbreak, terror and twists to keep you on the edge of your seat, then knock you flat on the floor with an ending so shocking, you'll read it again just to pick up the clues.

Tick Tock

A Detective Shakespeare Mystery

Book #2

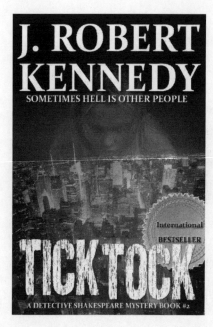

Crime Scene tech Frank Brata digs deep and finds the courage to ask his colleague, Sarah, out for coffee after work. Their good time turns into a nightmare when Frank wakes up the next morning covered in blood, with no recollection of what happened, and Sarah's body floating in the tub. Determined not to go to prison for a crime he's horrified he may have committed, he scrubs the crime scene clean, and, tormented by text messages from the real killer, begins a race against the clock to solve the murder before his own co-workers, his own friends, solve it first, and find him guilty.

Billionaire Richard Tate is the toast of the town, loved by everyone but his wife. His plans for a romantic weekend with his mistress ends in disaster, waking the next morning to find her murdered, floating in the tub. After fleeing in a panic, he returns to find the hotel room spotless, and no sign of the body. An envelope found at the scene contains not the expected blackmail note, but something far more sinister.

Two murders, with the same MO, targeting both the average working man, and the richest of society, sets a rejuvenated Detective Shakespeare, and his new reluctant partner, Amber Trace, after a murderer whose motivations are a mystery, and who appears to be aided by the very people they would least expect—their own.

Tick Tock, Book #2 in the internationally bestselling Detective Shakespeare Mysteries series, picks up right where Depraved Difference left off, and asks a simple question: What would you do? What would you do if you couldn't prove your innocence, but knew you weren't capable of murder? Would you hide the very evidence that might clear you, or would you turn yourself in and trust the system to work?

From the internationally bestselling author of The Protocol and Brass Monkey comes the highly anticipated sequel to the smash hit Depraved Difference, Tick Tock. Filled with heart pounding terror and suspense, along with a healthy dose of humor, Tick Tock's twists will keep you guessing right up to the terrifying end.

The Redeemer

A Detective Shakespeare Mystery

Book #3

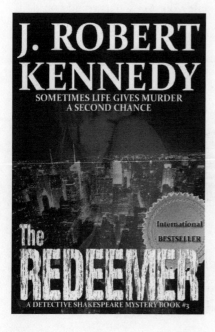

Sometimes Life Gives Murder a Second Chance

It was the case that destroyed Detective Charlie Shakespeare's career, beginning a downward spiral of self-loathing and self-destruction lasting half a decade. And today things are only going to get worse. The Widow Rapist is free on a technicality, and it is up to Detective Shakespeare and his partner Amber Trace to find the evidence, five years cold, to put him back in prison before he strikes again.

But Shakespeare and Trace aren't alone in their desire for justice. The Seven are the survivors, avowed to not let the memories of their loved ones be forgotten. And with the release of the Widow Rapist, they are determined to take justice into their own hands, restoring balance to a flawed system.

At stake is a second chance, a chance at redemption, a chance to salvage a career destroyed, a reputation tarnished, and a life diminished.

A chance brought to Detective Shakespeare whether he wants it or not.

A chance brought to him by The Redeemer.

From J. Robert Kennedy, the author of seven international bestsellers including Depraved Difference and The Protocol, comes the third entry in the acclaimed Detective Shakespeare Mysteries series, The Redeemer, a dark tale exploring the psyches of the serial killer, the victim, and the police, as they all try to achieve the same goals.

Balance. And redemption.

Rogue Operator

A Special Agent Dylan Kane Thriller

Book #1

TO SAVE THE COUNTRY HE LOVES, SPECIAL AGENT DYLAN KANE MIGHT HAVE TO BETRAY IT.

Three top secret research scientists are presumed dead in a boating accident, but the kidnapping of their families the same day raises questions the FBI and local police can't answer, leaving them waiting for a ransom demand that will never come.

Central Intelligence Agency Analyst Chris Leroux stumbles upon the story, and finds a phone conversation that was never supposed to happen. When he reports it to his boss, the National Clandestine Services Chief, he is uncharacteristically reprimanded for conducting an unauthorized investigation and told to leave it to the FBI.

But he can't let it go.

For he knows something the FBI doesn't.

One of the scientists is alive.

Chris makes a call to his childhood friend, CIA Special Agent Dylan Kane, leading to a race across the globe to stop a conspiracy reaching the highest levels of political and corporate America, that if not stopped, could lead to war with an enemy armed with a weapon far worse than anything in the American arsenal, with the potential to not only destroy the world, but consume it.

J. Robert Kennedy, the author of nine international best sellers, including the smash hit James Acton Thrillers, introduces Rogue Operator, the first installment of his newest series, The Special Agent Dylan Kane Thrillers, promising to bring all of the action and intrigue of the James Acton Thrillers with a hero who lives below the radar, waiting for his country to call when it most desperately needs him.

Containment Failure

A Special Agent Dylan Kane Thriller

Book #2

THE BLACK DEATH KILLED ALMOST HALF OF EUROPE'S POPULATION. THIS TIME IT WILL BE BILLIONS.

New Orleans has been quarantined, an unknown virus sweeping the city, killing one hundred percent of those infected. The Centers for Disease Control, desperate to find a cure, is approached by BioDyne Pharma who reveal a former employee has turned a cutting edge medical treatment capable of targeting specific genetic sequences into a weapon, and released it.

CIA Special Agent Dylan Kane has been given one guideline from his boss: consider yourself unleashed, leaving Kane and New Orleans Police Detective Isabelle Laprise battling to stay alive as an insidious disease and terrified mobs spread through the city while they desperately seek those behind the greatest crime ever perpetrated.

The stakes have never been higher as Kane battles to save not only his friends and the country he loves, but all of mankind.

In Containment Failure, eleven times internationally bestselling author J. Robert Kennedy delivers a terrifying tale of what could happen when science goes mad, with enough sorrow, heartbreak, laughs and passion to keep readers on the edge of their seats until the chilling conclusion.

13483769R00229

Printed in Great Britain
by Amazon.co.uk, Ltd.,
Marston Gate.